Better Off Read

Better Off Read

A BOOKMOBILE MYSTERY

Nora Page

CROOKED
LANE

NEW YORK

Published in the United States by Crooked Lane Books, an imprint of The Quick Brown Fox & Company LLC.

Crooked Lane Books and its logo are trademarks of The Quick Brown Fox & Company LLC.

Library of Congress Catalog-in-Publication data available upon request.

ISBN (paperback): 978-1-68331-992-4
ISBN (hardcover): 978-1-68331-643-5
ISBN (ePub): 978-1-68331-644-2
ISBN (ePDF): 978-1-68331-645-9

Cover illustration by Jesse Reisch
Book design by Jennifer Canzone

Printed in the United States.

www.crookedlanebooks.com

Crooked Lane Books
34 West 27th St., 10th Floor
New York, NY 10001

Paperback Edition: April 2019
Hardcover Edition: May 2018

10 9 8 7 6 5 4 3 2 1

To my grandmother, once a librarian,
always a lover of books.

Chapter One

In all her seventy-five years, Cleo Watkins had never harmed another human being. Not intentionally, and certainly not in anger. Cleo considered herself a proper, well-mannered Southern lady. She'd *never* harmed a book. Cleo was a librarian.

Now, however, Cleo considered the hardback in her purse. *Zen and the Art of School Bus Maintenance* had a fine, firm spine. It was compact, perfect for carrying along to appointments . . . and for winging at the man in the plaid purple shorts. Cleo steadied her stance in the overgrown lawn. She rolled her wrist and stretched her elbow. In a younger decade, she'd played South Georgia amateur softball. She bet she still had a good pitch left in her, and there'd be no missing Mayor Jebson "Jeb" Day and his smug, pink cheeks.

Catalpa Springs' new mayor stood a few yards away, too busy smirking to notice Cleo's ire. He plucked a dandelion, sun glaring off his prematurely thinning crown. Bermuda shorts revealed more pale leg than Cleo cared to see.

She smoothed her blouse and patted her soft white curls, half-expecting them to be as spiky as her emotions. She turned her mind and gaze to nicer things. The azaleas in the side garden were lovely this spring, flashy magentas against powdery pink crabapples. A cardinal flitted among the blooms. Cleo tried to follow the bird. However, her gaze kept catching on the horrible sight beyond: her beloved library, wounded.

Mayor Day straightened, beheading the dandelion with a flick of his thumb. "Yep," he said. "Like I was saying, Catalpa Springs has more important needs than a library. I can't authorize any repairs at present. You understand."

Cleo most definitely did *not* understand. She couldn't comprehend how this man—immature in years and character, not to mention lacking in manners and long pants—could be mayor of her charming town. She didn't want to understand his words.

"More important?" she said, her drawl lengthened with aghast. "The Catalpa Springs Library is an institution. A historic landmark. A community treasure." She waved toward the elegant folk Victorian structure, sorrowfully shrouded under blue tarps and wrapped in caution tape.

Several weeks ago a violent storm had brought down the great live oak that had stood beside the library for over a century. The trunk shattered the graceful curved porch. Branches pierced the roof, inviting in rain, hail, and an unhappy possum. The stately wood-paneled reading room suffered a soaking, as did many of its reference materials, including irreplaceable genealogies and local archives.

Cleo had wept at the damage. She could shed a tear now, but reminded herself again of important mercies. The oak had waited until after hours to give up its ghost. No patrons or employees had been present. The possum survived unharmed, as did the bulk of the collection. Only the roof needed fixing. And some soggy reference materials. And the porch and steps and entire east wing and staff room and possibly the electric and floors . . . and, most of all, their mayor's attitude.

Cleo stood to her full five foot three. "We *must* repair our library. Why, without a library, what are we?"

"Richer?" Mayor Day offered. "A town with a world-class fishing pier? My pier project will make money. It's a matter of priorities. I already have major investors." He nodded toward an SUV idling nearby. A bald man snoozed inside, air-conditioning fluttering his shirt collar.

"Vegas big," the mayor whispered, eyeing the slumbering man as if he were a prize bass on the line. "If we play our cards right, guess what? That's a hint, by the way. *Play our cards.*"

Cleo folded her arms and pursed her lips.

"A floating casino!" Jeb Day bounced in his rubber sandals with boyish glee. "Can you imagine?"

Cleo was trying hard not to imagine. During his mayoral campaign, Jeb Day promised to make the slow, meandering Tallgrass River, just outside town, a world-renowned sport-fishing destination. Little Catalpa Springs would be on TV, he said. There'd be fishing tournaments and reality shows and everyone reeling in cash and record-setting bass. Cleo thought it was all fish tales, getting larger with every retelling. Now they'd grown as big as a boat?

"We have the insurance," Cleo said, only to be cut off by the mayor. When he was done rudely likening the insurance policy to cow plops, she continued. "There's also the upcoming fundraiser, remember? The Ladies League Gala? The library will receive all proceeds from the silent auction. We already have some exceptional donated items." Cleo's firmness faltered. One donation was a tad too generous, a collection of first-edition Agatha Christies that might reel in thousands but snag her in romantic strings.

Mayor Day shrugged. "You ladies have all the little benefits and bake sales you like. Maybe you can buy a floorboard or two. But, seriously, why should the town put up the money? What would we get back from our investment?"

What would they get? A library! Entire worlds. Eras both long gone and not yet seen. Fantasies and facts. Knowledge and escape and inspiration. Solace. Cleo fought a renewed urge to hurl her guide to Zen and diesel engines. She reminded herself that religion in any form should not be used for violence. Besides, she needed the book. Her only remaining library was an aging school bus. Words on Wheels had a fickle transmission and was sounding wheezy lately. Calm spirit and mechanical skill would be necessary to keep the bookmobile rolling.

"Anyway," the mayor said, looking ready to leave, "I already met with some town council members." He named a riverside bar and several men, all wheeling and dealing and fishing types. Cleo pictured fat fingers, greasy from hushpuppies and fried catfish. She frowned, thinking of those same fingers messing with her library, touching her books.

"The way we figure," Jeb continued, "that tree did us a favor. Perfect timing too. Your other full-time librarian's likely to give notice, and that part-timer, Leanna, isn't a *real* librarian. Leanna's cute and young. She can get another job. Then there's you, Miss Cleo. You're surely getting set to retire. You're what, mid-seventies? That's a decade overdue. Get it? The overdue librarian? Ha!"

Cleo clenched her purse straps—better those than Mayor Day's throat.

He raised a placating palm. "Don't give me that stink eye. I'm not counting your years. That's wrong, right?"

It was all so wrong. "Why wasn't I contacted about your meeting?" Cleo demanded.

The mayor winked. "I heard you were out of state. A little romantic jaunt down to Florida? Good for you."

Cleo's cheeks flamed. This is what she got for agreeing to accompany Henry Lafayette on his old-book buying trip. The owner of The Gilded Page Antiquarian and Rare Books was the generous donator of the rare Agatha Christies. He was also a would-be suitor and sweeter than sugar on honey, although Cleo wasn't ready to let him know that. Ten years a widow, Cleo was settled in her singlehood. She enjoyed late nights reading. She lingered in bed on Sundays and let visiting grandkids make all the noise and messes they wanted to. Best of all, she did the driving. Oh, how she loved captaining that bookmobile and her daddy's vintage convertible.

A bee buzzed, snapping Cleo's thoughts back. "I was in Florida," she said, holding her chin high, "antiquing. Florida's not that far away, as you know."

Catalpa Springs perched just above the Florida line. Some Catalpa residents had Florida in their backyard and Georgia in the front, which Cleo thought must be unsettling. Florida was a lovely place, but not for Cleo. Their southern neighbor was for spring-breakers and sunbathers or—Cleo gave a little shudder—retirees. Cleo had tried retirement. Twice. It hadn't suited her then. It certainly wouldn't suit her now, especially with the library in danger.

"Antiquing?" The mayor raised suggestive air quotes. "Is that what you kids call it? All the more reason to retire. Just think—"

Cleo was thinking. Thinking that tossing her entire purse at the man's skull wouldn't make a dent in his sense or his manners. She turned to go. "Mayor Day, I will see you at the full town council and library board meeting next month and at the Ladies League Gala three Saturdays from now. Until then, I have a job to do. Words on Wheels is very busy."

The mayor shot her an alligator's grin. "Don't get too attached to that clunker of a bookmobile either. What with the budget and your last speeding ticket and . . . well, don't take offense . . ."

Cleo was already offended.

"I'm just saying," the mayor said. "We had to hide the car keys from my Granny Day when she got to a *certain* age and started getting pulled over and finding herself in Florida unexpectedly. It was for her own good."

For Mayor Jebson Day's own good, Cleo removed herself and her pitching arm from his presence. She stormed up the block and across Main Street, barely noticing the tidy brick buildings and bustling downtown. She dodged a bicyclist and waved distractedly to the bank president and a clutch of Ladies Leaguers, as recognizable as flamingos in their signature pink hats. She didn't stop until she reached Words on Wheels, sprawled across three parking spots by Fontaine Park, the heart of Catalpa Springs.

Rhett Butler, library cat, lounged on the bookmobile's hood, leisurely grooming his fluffy orange undercarriage.

"Come along, Rhett," Cleo called to the frowny-faced

Persian. "We have an urgent delivery." If Mayor Day could go fishing, so could she. Cleo was off to catch herself an ally.

* * *

Words on Wheels glowed in classic school-bus yellow, with a twist. Orange and red airbrushed flames fanned the front grill, tipped in icy blue. Over the windshield, *"READ!"* was spelled out in similar fiery colors, highlighted with stars. The name "Words on Wheels" sprawled in loopy cursive along each side. The bus was fun and flashy, and Cleo smiled every time she saw it. Here was another blessing, along with her grandson Sam.

Last year, the high school senior and some pals had repurposed the rusty bus into a mobile library as their Eagle Scout project. They swapped out most of the seats with handmade bookshelves, leaving the front and back rows for passengers and readers. They fitted rubbery jigsaw tiles on the floor and created a little kids' reading nook in the back. The boys didn't stop with carpentry. They also devised a program for providing mobile library services across Catalpa County.

Since the storm, Cleo had drafted Words on Wheels into full-time service. She made regular rounds, parking by Fontaine Park, schools, nursing homes, rural crossroads, and retirement communities. She even made home deliveries in special cases. Cleo thought of all the folks who depended on the bookmobile, how happy they were to see her pull up. How happy she was to hit the road.

"Mayor Day won't take away our bookmobile or our library," Cleo assured Rhett as they rounded the bus.

The Persian came to a claw-skidding stop, his tail puffed.

"I know—he is a rude man." Cleo was distracted, searching her purse for her keys. Then she looked up and realized what actually unnerved Rhett. Her young colleague Leanna stood by the bus, wearing a most unusual outfit.

"Why, Leanna," Cleo said, pushing back her bifocals and struggling for something nice to say, "don't you look . . . interesting."

Leanna wore black capri leggings, a matching T-shirt, sparkly silver flip-flops, and retro cat-eye glasses, all of which were normal and clear. It was Leanna's middle that was muddled. Lumpy fabric ringed Leanna from thighs to midriff, like a short stack of squished donuts. Leanna's expression was as droopy as her attire.

"Are you in a play?" Cleo asked encouragingly. This seemed improbable. Introverted Leanna dreaded public speaking and crowds, unless those crowds were quietly reading.

"I'm a biscuit," Leanna mumbled. She sank to a lumpy slump on a nearby park bench. "Can't you tell?"

Rhett approached warily, tail still puffed to double its usual size.

Leanna groaned. "I'm a monster. Hey, Rhett, sweet kitty, it's just me. Come here, you beautiful boy."

Rhett cocked his head, intrigued by the pretty lies. Truth be told, the oversized feline wasn't looking his best either. A recent tangle with burdocks had necessitated a shave, nobly—foolheartedly—performed by Cleo's hairdresser, Frank Kelly. Neither man nor cat had come out well, with poor Frank left googling *cat-scratch fever* and Rhett looking like a moth-chewed lion.

Rhett hopped on the bench and onto Leanna's fabric-padded lap, where he began kneading. Making biscuits, Cleo's mama would have said.

Cleo pointed that out. "See? Rhett knows you're a biscuit. But, uh . . . why?"

"Tammy Temps." Leanna said the name of her other part-time employer more bitterly than usual. "They assigned me to Biscuit Bobs. It's awful. I stand in the median out on Old Coopers Highway and wave. People whistle and honk and laugh." She dejectedly plucked at beige fabric.

Squinting, Cleo could discern layers, lopsided and heavy like the baked goods served up by the three Bobs who ran the diner/dive bar. "I'm sure folks are honking in support," she said.

"Right." Leanna sounded rightfully skeptical. "Stupid costume. I think I'm allergic to polyester, and I'm getting a rash and a sunburn and . . ." She took a deep breath and patted Rhett. "But it's a job, isn't it? I've gotta save up for college in the fall. Three years, and I'll be an official, bona fide librarian!"

Cleo heartily agreed. She opened the bus and climbed the steps. Leanna had years of foster care and troubles behind her, but there was always a place she felt at home: the Catalpa Springs Public Library. She worked as a shelving assistant and was a natural whiz at library technology, which she planned to study at college. Cleo dreamed of Leanna eventually taking the library helm, leaving Cleo free to hit the road in Words on Wheels. How could she tell Leanna that Mayor Jeb Day wanted to toss to the curb the library and all those it helped? She hoped Leanna wouldn't ask.

"How was your meeting?" Leanna stood, Rhett draped

over her shoulder, nuzzling her ear and purring loudly. "I hustled right over here on break to hear. Are the repairs a 'go'? Can we add in the wiring for the new computer station?"

"Come on inside, dear," Cleo said. Bad news was best told in the comforting presence of books.

Leanna put Rhett down and steadied herself on the New Reads shelf, listening with only the tiniest quiver of her lip.

"We'll fight it," Cleo said.

Leanna's quiver firmed. "Darned straight, we'll fight!" She stomped a flip-flop and refused to return to Biscuit Bobs for the lunch shift. "They can take this biscuit costume and fire me! We'll rally our allies! We'll . . ." Her battle cry was muffled in the struggle to extract herself from the fabric layers.

Cleo tried to dissuade Leanna, who needed her jobs. When she couldn't, Cleo said, "Then this counts as a work trip. We're delivering books to an important library supporter."

Leanna brightened. "Who? Where?"

"Krandall House. Interlibrary loans for Buford Krandall."

Leanna suddenly didn't look quite as eager.

"Mr. Krandall's the longest standing member of the library board," Cleo said, convincing herself as much as Leanna. "He has money and influence, although I know he can be a touch eccentric."

"He's weird," Leanna said bluntly. "You never know what he's up to, all those crazy do-it-yourself projects. Remember when he got into firecrackers and blew up that peach orchard? And those drones that chased people? He makes me nervous, like he can see through you and is picking out everything bad and taking notes."

Cleo pointed to a bag of books on the front seat. "That's

why I'm glad you're here. On the way, can you skim through his stack of interlibrary loans? I'll admit, I'm a bit worried about the subject matter."

Leanna buckled up. Rhett settled in his throne, a padded peach crate bolted to the floor beside Cleo. Cleo turned the key and waited until the engine sputtered to a steadier wheeze. She rolled down her window and adjusted her mirrors. Then Cleo Watkins put her bookmobile in gear and punched the gas. Tires squealed, Leanna whooped, and they were off, Cleo's white hair whipping in the wind.

Chapter Two

Potholes peppered the long dirt drive to Krandall House. Oaks crowded in, their limbs so low and grasping, Cleo felt like ducking. Mossy statues—many missing arms, heads, or angel wings—peered out from the tangled forest to either side. They bumped along slowly, the windows open since the bookmobile's air conditioner only managed to gasp cool breeze at high speed.

"Creepy," Leanna said in a hushed awe. "Those statues remind me of graves, and what's up with all the pinwheels up in the trees? They're usually happy and pretty. Here they seem menacing."

"Birds," Cleo guessed, taking her eye off the road for a second. Above, whirligigs spun in chaotic metallic blurs. "Movement is supposed to scare them off. Mr. Krandall has a touch of avian phobia."

Leanna muttered something that sounded like *"Of course he does."* "It's like a fairytale forest," she added. "Not the good kind—the kind where someone ends up in a cauldron. And these books! They're even scarier!"

"They are worrisome," Cleo agreed, internally chastising herself. One of her firmest beliefs was that librarians should never judge reading taste. *Still . . .*

"*Many Murders and How They Were Done,*" Leanna read out. "*Unsolved Murders of Georgia and the Florida Panhandle: Methods and Bonus Maps? Red Dirt Blood? A Southern Field Guide to Unsolved Crime?* What if Mr. Krandall's onto a do-it-yourself project of killing someone? Are we accomplices? Is the library?"

Cleo veered around a pothole and a direct answer. "All the books are by Priscilla Pawpaw, a local author. I'm to blame, I'm afraid. I recommended a gardening book to Mr. Krandall, and her guide to noxious and poisonous plants was beside it on the shelf. When he showed an interest, I encouraged him. I hoped he might tackle his vine problems. He found out she wrote other books. True crime."

Buford clearly hadn't been gardening, Cleo thought, as Krandall House came into blurry view. Kudzu raced up the walls of the moldering mansion. Poison ivy gripped the gate, and air-potato vine—Cleo's personal noxious-weed nemesis—dripped from decaying porch railings and once-stately columns.

Cleo turned off the bookmobile and told Rhett to stay. The cat needed no further encouragement. They opened the doors to a racket that sent Rhett hurtling to hide in the kids' nook.

"What *is* that?" Leanna asked, hands to her ears.

Metal clanged and grated. Deep thumps rumbled through the soles of Cleo's sandals.

Leanna inched backwards. "Maybe we should come back later. Later, as in never."

"He's a friend of the library," Cleo said. Buford Krandall was undeniably eccentric. But he did have influence around town and could, sometimes, be surprisingly rational and well-intentioned. "He loves books," Cleo bellowed over the din. "He's on the library board *and* town council, and as far as I know, he has no interest in fishing piers."

Leanna hoisted the bag of books. "Then we're at the right place."

Cleo followed, mentally reassuring herself. They were here for the library. And more . . . If Buford Krandall was up to something sinister, Cleo wanted to know what.

* * *

Ringing the front bell hadn't been an option in years. Vines locked the gate, and hollies blocked the verandah. Cleo and Leanna followed a flagstone path to the back, where they stopped short. A steel monster growled in place. Gears spun and locust-limb legs churned. A spiral fang jabbed the ground, spewing pale mud that trickled in slimy veins toward a nearby creek.

Cleo stepped back and into a bony touch that made her jump.

Buford Krandall had a ghost's complexion of chalky skin and eyes set in caverns shaded by a hogback nose. He wore a dark suit several sizes too large and likely dating from the era of his antique black parasol. Since a brush with a precancerous mole several years back, Buford had avoided the sun like Dracula with hypochondria. Library board meetings were held after dusk to accommodate him, and he was known for his lengthy walks at night. Night strolls were better for his health, he claimed. Better to pry into dirty laundry, others suspected.

"She's a stunner, isn't she?" he declared in his low, slow drawl.

"She?" Indignation restored Cleo's nerves. Why did men call their most terrible devices "she"? Gunboats and battleships. Bombs, bombers, and hurricanes. Cleo remembered when the National Weather Service finally began bestowing male names on storms. She and her best friend Mary-Rose had raised mint juleps to destructive equality. Recently, however, Cleo had read that more people perished during hurricanes with feminine names. Not because females of all sorts were inherently strong, but because folks underestimated forces with names like Mary-Rose or Cleo, Opal or Katrina.

Buford spun his parasol, sending wormy fringe flying. "Yes, ma'am. *She.* My gorgeous lady. My great-granddaddy made her. All this time, she's been waiting for me out in an outbuilding. Just look at her chew." He gazed fondly at the metal monster, his eyes gleaming.

"What's *it* chewing?" Leanna asked.

"Life's blood, dear girl. The cold, clear, pure blood of life."

Leanna put a protective hand over the library books, but not fast enough.

"Ah, my books," Buford said, whisking them away. "Just what I need. I'll tuck them on the back porch." He glided off ghostlike, leaving Cleo to wonder and Leanna to tiptoe toward the beast. By the time he returned, Cleo had one thing figured out.

"Water," Cleo said. "You're drilling a well, aren't you?"

Their host flashed sharp teeth. "I can't put anything past a librarian, can I? Yes, I'll soon be pumping up pure spring water."

Cleo didn't like to show off, but she spotted an obvious flaw. "Your water's all muddy, Mr. Krandall."

"Phase one," he said. "Drilling and agitating. See? It's already working." He pointed to the creek, winding through a brutally pruned cypress grove. "Go ahead, wave hello."

Wave? Cleo frowned at stubby stumps, wishing she'd never gotten Buford Krandall thinking about gardening.

"Ah, forgive me." He rummaged in deep pockets and extracted a small pair of binoculars. "Try these."

Cleo pressed the binoculars to her bifocals. She saw chartreuse needles and nubby cypress knees and . . . a pink sundress. A magenta cardigan. Freckles dotting high cheekbones and a face she'd known and loved since childhood: Mary-Rose Garland, Cleo's dearest friend and the unfortunate nearest neighbor to Krandall House. Mary-Rose's Pancake Mill was a local treasure, a historic sugar mill now engaged in other sweet enterprises, serving up pie and pancakes. The mill sat beside a large, round, spring-fed swimming hole, appropriately dubbed Pancake Spring.

"Mr. Krandall, what *are* you doing?" Cleo spun. "Your mud is flowing straight into the spring. You have to stop it."

"I shall. Phase two is pumping and bottling. I plan to take up every drop of water I can."

Buford was right. He couldn't trick a librarian. Cleo read widely, from mysteries to histories, to nonfiction, including local geology and ecology. "The aquifers and water tables are linked," she said, Leanna nodding vigorously at her side.

"Siphoning out water here will affect—" She stopped short. It would affect Mary-Rose and Pancake Spring, to Buford's malicious delight. Mary-Rose's relatives had acquired the mill from a spendthrift Krandall after the Civil War. Later Krandalls so resented the sale, they'd carried on a bitter feud with the "new" owners ever since.

"Yes, indeed," Buford said happily. "If Mary-Rose Garland wants spring water for her batter and bathers, she'll have to buy it in bottles. From me." He twirled the parasol, reminding Cleo of a deranged Mary Poppins.

Cleo took Leanna by the arm, consoling herself with the knowledge that wild Krandall schemes rarely succeeded. "We'll leave you to your projects," she said.

"I'll see you at the next library board meeting," he replied. "I hear there's trouble brewing. A fishing pier on the Tallgrass? A casino? Unseemly. Unnecessary. I don't approve."

With this, Cleo could agree. She remembered her library-saving purpose and told him about her upsetting meeting with the mayor.

Buford Krandall looked disturbingly pleased. "Ah, this is good, very good," he said. "Now I can go after our mayor with even more righteous gusto. We'll have a fine fight on our hands, Mrs. Watkins. I have ways to make Mayor Day come around, and I bet I can raise more money than your gala too. I have a plan we can take to the bank." Buford twirled the parasol. The fringe spun in confusion, much like Cleo's mind.

"I know," Buford said. "Let's give our effort a fishing name in the mayor's honor. 'The bait and hook'? 'Hook, line, and sunk'? Ooh, I have it: 'We'll be shooting fish in a barrel, and our boy mayor's a carp!'" His dark eyes glittered.

Cleo took a step back, pulling Leanna with her. "What are you planning?"

Buford waved a bony finger, miming chastisement. "Oh no, not yet, ladies. I am biding my time. Letting the gears turn. Assembling resources. Your lovely books should help immensely."

Cleo had to ask. "What is your interest in these books, Mr. Krandall? Are you writing a book yourself perhaps? Researching a mystery?"

"What a grand idea," Buford said. "When my venture is done, maybe so. I could connect the dots for those with less nimble minds. It is all linked, Mrs. Watkins, like those aquifers you speak of."

"Not good," Leanna said when they were back in Words on Wheels, bumping fast down the drive.

Not good, Cleo agreed. At the main road, she hesitated, but only for a moment. Cleo turned left, away from town, speeding around the bend to the Pancake Mill.

* * *

"I could kill him!" The words filled a lull in music and conversation. They rose to the tall open rafters of the mill house. They bounced from slow-spinning fans and the old wooden waterwheel and skidded off skillets sizzling with butter, batter, and blueberries.

Late-morning diners looked up from their pancakes.

Cleo, whose mind had drifted to Mayor Jeb Day, checked that she hadn't blurted out her thoughts. Her mouth, however, was safely full of bitter, unsweetened tea.

Across the table, Mary-Rose Garland sputtered like a berry

about to boil. Scarlet flared behind her freckles, and her hazel eyes snapped.

"Do you see what he's doing to my spring?" Mary-Rose slapped the table and the thankfully cold, built-in griddle.

Cleo saw. Muddy fingers gripped the waters. No swimmers made laps. No scuba divers hovered above the boil, the geologic spigot from which spring waters bubbled forth. A single couple walked the banks, slogging in thigh-high waders. Cleo recognized her gangly twenty-four-year-old grandson, Ollie. A recent college graduate, Ollie was presently engaged in what he called "gig" employment, and his father—Cleo's fretful eldest son, Fred—deemed unemployment. Ollie lived in the little cottage at the back of Cleo's garden. He helped with lawn mowing and sometimes paid rent. He was with a woman Cleo didn't recognize, in camouflage shorts and a matching tank top. They pointed and aimed binoculars in the direction of Krandall House.

Cleo turned her gaze to the only serene part of the scene, Leanna and Rhett. They sat at a picnic table, Leanna eating pie and soaking in some solitude, the cat eyeing the three resident peacocks with predatory interest.

"When did this start?" Cleo asked, meaning the drilling.

"When will it end?" Mary-Rose retorted. "Those Krandalls!" She dropped three sugar cubes in her already sweet tea. Cleo looked on with alarm and envy. Alarm because despite all the pancakes and pie Mary-Rose dealt in, she didn't have a sweet tooth. Envy because Cleo's new doctor considered Cleo's glucose levels high and had put her on a joy-crushing, low-sugar diet.

Mary-Rose gave her drink a violent stir. "The drilling

started last week. He doesn't care about bottling water. I swear, he's just doing this to mess with me. He says he'll siphon all the water away. I don't think it's possible, do you? Even if it's not, the mud and racket could put me out of business."

Cleo repeated her earlier hope: Krandall projects flopped. Eventually.

Her friend threw up her hands. "How long will that take? Months? Years? Krandalls are persistent."

"We could call someone," Cleo said. "The police or—"

"Oh, I've called," Mary-Rose said with a huff of frustration. "I called the police and might as well have talked to a fence post. I called City Hall next. As soon as Mayor Jeb heard the name Krandall, he hung up."

It all sounded fishy. Cleo told Mary-Rose about her earlier meeting with their young mayor.

Mary-Rose drained her tea to the sugary sludge. "Swapping our library for a pier? Appalling! Those scheming men. It's good-old-boy connections and corruption, like always and before and forever more. I am tired, Cleo. Sometimes I think I should give up and move down to Florida."

Cleo gasped. *Florida? Good gracious. Give up?* Mary-Rose was fiery, always ready to take on a good fight. She reached for her friend's hand. "Mary-Rose, I am so sorry."

Mary-Rose shrugged. "I know. You were only doing what's best for the library."

Cleo frowned. She didn't like Mary-Rose's tone, as bitter as unsweetened tea. "What do you mean?"

"*You*, that's what I mean. Meeting with that awful Krandall. Ollie and I both saw you. Are you giving that man special treatment because he's on the library board and battling the mayor? I know, 'if we can't beat 'em—' "

"No, no," Cleo said guiltily, for Mary-Rose was right. "I was thinking of the town. Catalpa Springs needs its library, and Buford can help. I didn't know anything about the drilling." But she did know about his books. Cleo held a librarian's vow of silence when it came to patrons' reading preferences. No one would hear from her, for example, that the Episcopalian priest's wife enjoyed steamy paranormal romances. However, no code took precedence over a friend's safety. Cleo reached across the table. "Mary-Rose, Buford hasn't threatened you, has he?"

Mary-Rose murmured something noncommittal. She craned her neck, looking over Cleo's shoulder toward the front door.

Cleo turned to see Ollie and his companion wiping their waders at the entry.

The woman clomped toward the restrooms in loud, squishy steps. Ollie kissed Cleo lightly on the cheek. "Hi, Gran," he said, his messy brunette locks falling over his face. Mary-Rose got a more serious greeting. "We got visuals. We reconned the northeast perimeter, like you suggested. We'll surveil the rest after dark."

"You didn't get made, did you?" Mary-Rose said.

They went on, sounding more like a tactical team than Cleo's friend and grandson.

"Ollie, dear," Cleo interjected. "You weren't trespassing, were you?"

He grinned wide. "I sure was!" He addressed Mary-Rose. "Now we wait for . . . you know what."

They nodded knowingly. "Need to know only," Mary-Rose said.

Cleo felt left out. "*I* can know," she protested.

But her friend was standing, pulling Ollie aside to the dim corner where the old wooden waterwheel peeked through high windows. Grumpy and defiant, Cleo sunk two sugar cubes in her remaining tea.

She couldn't very well chide her grandson for trespassing when she'd done so much herself. As kids, she and Mary-Rose had explored every corner of their town. They'd sneaked into abandoned buildings, scaled garden fences, and rowed up to private docks, making maps and journals of their discoveries. Cleo still occasionally engaged in a little offtrack information gathering. "Sleuthing," the *Catalpa Gazette* once grandly called her efforts, after Cleo had solved a rash of burglaries. The newspaper repeated the praise when Cleo quietly assisted in nabbing a murderous nurse's aide, and again when Cleo applied her research skills to a cold case. Cleo saw it as setting things straight, cataloging the truth, solving a puzzle. After all, librarians were good readers, not only of books but also of people and situations. Mary-Rose often joined in these endeavors. Why was her friend excluding her now? Was it because Cleo had met with Buford Krandall? Did Mary-Rose not trust her? That possibility hurt.

"We can all work together," Cleo said when Ollie and Mary-Rose returned along with the woman in waders.

Ollie, bright-eyed and flushing, introduced his companion as Whitney Greene. "She's—"

"Busy," Whitney snapped. "We have to go."

Cleo frowned at the young woman's abruptness. Whitney squished off, yelling for Ollie to follow.

Cleo reached out and squeezed her grandson's hand. "Ollie, dear, come for supper sometime soon. Bring your friend and tell me what's going on. I'll make your favorite chicken and biscuits."

He clamped both hands over hers. "I'd love to, Gran. When we're not so busy, okay? Nothing's going on. Nothing for you to worry about."

He kissed her cheek and hurried off.

Nothing to worry about? Cleo loved her grandson, but she didn't believe him one bit.

Chapter Three

Worrying was like a rocking chair. It kept your head moving but didn't get you anywhere. Cleo was sitting in a rocker as she thought this. She swayed faster.

"More tea? Scone?" Henry Lafayette sat in an identical chair, a tippy folding contraption of blue canvas and aluminum framing. A tiny tray table perched between them, piled high with goodies from the Spoonbread Bakery, the best (and only) bakeshop in downtown Catalpa Springs.

The bakery served up twists on Southern specialties. Cleo's favorite was the strawberry spoonbread. Sweet berries and cream topped the bakery's namesake, a cross between cornbread and a soufflé, so soft and airy it required scooping. However, in a sugar-ban pinch, a pimento-cheese scone would do. Cleo chose a golden pastry, surely fortified with unmentionable amounts of butter. She slathered on extra. It was a Saturday morning, after all, and she was keeping to her diet.

Words on Wheels stood behind them, parked at Cleo's now regular stop at Fontaine Park. A group of moms and toddlers filled the back nook, flipping through storybooks, reading aloud, and giggling. About a dozen patrons had already come and gone, all quizzing Cleo about when the main library would reopen. Cleo took a buttery bite of scone, thinking she should have told them all to storm the mayor's office, demanding their library back. Instead, she'd suggested letters and calls and support at the Ladies League Gala. What more could she do? *Something more than sitting around rocking and eating,* she thought.

"A gorgeous morning," Henry said, sounding as sunny as the day. He'd shown up soon after Cleo, bearing the picnic brunch, folding furniture, and flimsy excuse that he'd over-bought at the bakery.

Cleo agreed it was lovely. The park burst with blooms and their perfume. Happy laughter bubbled from the playground. Henry's aged pug, Mr. Chaucer, snored in the grass, his jowly gray wrinkles puddling, his tongue lolling. Rhett Butler hid nearby in a patch of ferns. The fronds wiggled, suggesting an impending feline game of pounce.

"You're distracted," Henry said, not a complaint, but an observation. "Any news from Mary-Rose?"

Cleo admitted she hadn't seen her friend since Wednesday at the Pancake Mill. "I think Mary-Rose is evading me. She finally called last night, but only after I left several messages, practically begging to hear from her. Then she claimed up and down that everything was *perfectly fine.*"

"Perfectly fine? That is disconcerting." A wry smile twitched under Henry's white beard, trimmed to a rectangular puff that curved around his chin and up to meet bushy tufts over prominent ears. Henry had well-hewn smile lines, round wire spectacles, and dapper if slightly rumpled good fashion.

Today he wore a light linen suit with a paisley pocket square, purple to match Mr. Chaucer's leash. He was on the short side of average height and somewhat padded around the middle, which Cleo certainly didn't mind since she was too.

Cleo smiled in return, appreciating his understanding. "I know," she said, forcing herself to slow her rocking. "It was such an obvious fib. Nothing's ever perfect with Mary-Rose, is it?"

It wasn't that her friend was a pessimist. Far from it. Mary-Rose was an aggressive optimist, always looking for ways to make things better for everyone. She plunged into causes, from saving tigers in the tropics to organizing food drives and preschool programs across rural Georgia. *Mary-Rose won't have to look far for problems to fix now,* Cleo thought grimly. She voiced the list jostling around her brain. "There's Pancake Spring, that awful drill, the library, the mayor, Buford Krandall . . . Then there's Ollie. That boy can't fool his grandmother. I know he's up to something, and I think he has a girlfriend too." Cleo took a breath and brushed a scone crumb from her blouse, blue to match the sunny skies.

Henry's smile lines crinkled. "Well now, a girlfriend seems nice. Is it your neighbor Deputy Gabby, like you've been hoping?" He poured icy tea from a sweating thermos, watching as Rhett launched his faux attack. The cat jumped high over the snoring pug before skittering back to his fern lair for a repeat performance.

Cleo thanked Henry for the tea, though she was feeling slightly awash. "No, I wish it were Gabby. This young woman wears camouflage. She's rather rude, and I don't think she's from here." Cleo frowned, wondering if that last part was true.

There was something familiar about Whitney Greene, something Cleo couldn't place, yet left her feeling unsettled.

Henry, who'd moved to Catalpa Springs from Atlanta about two years ago, chuckled. "An outsider, you think? Some of us can be all right." He sipped cold tea and arranged his pocket square to a perfect point. The point promptly wilted.

"It's not that," Cleo said quickly. She had friends and family from all over. Cleo rocked and mulled the possibility— ever so slight—that she might be biased by grandmotherly aspirations. She wanted only the best for her grandson. Like nice Gabby Honeywell, who was a lovely neighbor, a former beauty queen, clever and kind, and gainfully employed by the Catalpa Springs Police Department. Cleo knew Ollie fancied Gabby too. He blushed something silly every time he came within stammering distance of her.

Cleo turned the conversation to someone she knew she should worry about. "I wish Buford Krandall had told me more about his interest in those murder guides and plans for the mayor. If only he'd stop drilling too. I should have been more forceful with him on all accounts."

Henry stroked his beard, the signal of a good idea taking form. "We could visit him and ask again. Maybe he's ready to brag or move on to a new project. In any case, I've wanted to see Krandall House and its private library. Mr. Krandall has bought books from me. He's reputed to have an outstanding collection."

"I do have some books I could deliver," Cleo said. Seeing Henry brighten, she added disclaimers so as not to raise his hopes. "I have a few more bookmobile stops scheduled and couldn't go until this afternoon. You're probably busy."

"I'm completely free," Henry declared without hesitation.

"I've never been invited inside. It's a strange, disturbing place, and Buford Krandall can be odd and prickly."

"Buford, odd? Ha! There's an understatement." The female laugh that followed bordered on a cackle and was punctuated in a booming woof. Rhett bolted for the nearest tree. Mr. Chaucer struggled to his feet, dazed. Cleo turned to see Kat Krandall-Stykes digging in her boot heels by the bookmobile, arms straining to hold back a mastiff the size of a pony.

"Beast, sit!" Kat commanded. "Stay!" The dog did neither, stretching a prodigious snout to within inches of their picnic. Kat, tall and sinewy, had to grab onto a slender redbud tree for support. "Heel! Good boy." Beast continued to strain and pant. The sapling began to bend. Mr. Chaucer wobbled over to gape up at the giant dog with similar fawn coloring and a wrinkly black snout.

Cleo made introductions. When she got to explaining Kat to Henry, she hesitated. "Kat runs Paradise Landscaping. She's . . . uh . . . related to Buford Krandall by marriage."

"By separation, you mean," Kat said. "Buford and I have the longest running divorce proceedings in Catalpa County. I married that loon when I was twenty, served him papers at thirty, and I'll be rid of him—mark my word—by the time I turn fifty. I've got three months and five days to make it happen." She chuckled and told Beast to sit. Beast remained firmly standing. Hunched low on a tree limb, Rhett twitched his tail, eyes pinched into a deep frown.

"Oh, that's quite a record," said Henry politely. "Mrs. Watkins and I were considering visiting your eventual ex this afternoon."

Kat shook her head and the thick brunette braid reaching nearly to her waist. "Tell Buford I said 'bye, will ya? But seriously, why go out there? The driveway's a minefield of potholes, the landscaping's a hazard, and he's wackier by the day."

"I have books to deliver," Cleo said, giving their official reason before asking Kat if she knew about Buford's disagreements with the mayor and his secret and somewhat worrisome plans to raise library funds.

Kat was considering when a squirrel hopped past, sending Beast into a barking lunge. Mr. Chaucer sat back, eyes agog. "No," Kat said, voice and arms strained with the effort of holding her dog. "Spring's my busy landscaping season. I don't have time to keep up with Buford. He's always planning and plotting and after someone, though. Watch out for him. He likes the upper hand, and he's conniving. He tricked me into marrying him. But you'll see. I'll be rid of that crazy Krandall soon. Soon!" Her chortle ended in a yelp as Beast launched at the squirrel, dragging her along too. "Be careful!" she yelled over her shoulder.

Henry and Cleo watched them plow through the playground, kids parting before merrily chasing after them.

"So, when shall I meet you?" Henry asked.

Cleo thought of Kat's warnings and decided she was glad Henry would join her. "Three thirty," she said. "I'll pick you up."

* * *

Cleo, Rhett, and Words on Wheels swung by The Gilded Page later that afternoon. Mr. Chaucer snoozed on a satin pillow in the bay window. Henry stepped out and turned the door sign to "CLOSED," a technicality. Although rare-book collectors occasionally made the trip to Catalpa Springs, Henry did most of his business online. From what Cleo could tell, the shop was primarily for Henry's own enjoyment, a showcase of his treasures and handiwork. He and Mr. Chaucer lived upstairs. In the back, he had a book surgery, where he meticulously repaired sagging spines, cracked covers, and worn pages.

The former pharmacy he occupied had also gotten a makeover when he moved in. The wide plank floors gleamed again, as did the tin ceiling, hidden for decades behind acoustic tiles. The refurbished exterior reminded Cleo of Old World bookstores, like she might see in Paris or London, if she ever got to go. Henry had chosen a stately slate blue for the wood-paneled front and glossy ebony for the door. Gold paint highlighted trim and scrollwork and announced the store's name and vague hours: "The Gilded Page Antiquarian and Rare Books. Monday through Friday—when open. Weekends and holidays, nights, special occasions, and inclement weather—at whim."

The weather was threatening inclemency now. Henry carried an umbrella, along with a parcel neatly wrapped in brown paper and tied with string.

"Bait?" Cleo asked, nodding to the parcel.

"The best kind of fishing," Henry said. "Hooked by a book."

As she turned down the dirt drive to Krandall House, Cleo warned Henry about bumps ahead, thinking both of the lane and Buford himself. The weather had turned to roiling gray, and the oak tunnel was as dark as dusk. Overhead, the whirligigs raced. Cleo thought of nightmares in which one ran faster and faster, getting nowhere.

"Good gracious," Henry said. "This is not what I expected."

Cleo wondered if Catalpa Springs was as he expected. Henry said he'd chosen the small town for his "working retirement" because it was so pretty and calm, a friendly place. Cleo, however, knew that sometimes—thankfully rarely—her beloved hometown could be anything but peaceful and peaceable.

At the house, she parked, warned Henry of noxious vines, and led the way to the back.

"Mr. Krandall!" Cleo called. She headed to the back porch door while Henry drifted toward the mercifully resting drill. Cleo's knocks and calls got no reply.

"Perhaps he's out?" Henry said, rejoining her. "Taking a walk? It's cloudy, so he wouldn't have to fear the sun, though a storm's surely coming."

Cleo tilted an ear. "Listen, did you hear that? Was that a thump inside? If it's Buford, why isn't he answering?" A burst of wind made them shield their eyes. In the forest all around, the leaves rustled restlessly.

Henry called Buford's name, louder this time.

Amidst the murmuring breeze, Cleo heard what sounded like a door banging.

Henry heard it too. "Stay here," he said. He hurried down the path before Cleo could stop him. When he returned, breathing hard, he reported seeing no one. "The screen door to the verandah was swinging a bit, but it could have been the wind."

Or it could be trouble. "We should check on Mr. Krandall," Cleo said. "What if he's hurt?" She tested the door to the back porch. It opened with the squeak of rusty hinges, as did the entry to the kitchen beyond.

"What if it's a robber?" Henry asked. "Or Krandall

himself? I've heard he carries an antique pistol." But he followed Cleo inside, keeping close to her heels. They crossed a kitchen of yellowed linoleum and cabinets painted in faded sunflowers. In a large foyer muffled by carpets and tapestries, they stopped and called Buford's name. A winged chandelier hung high overhead. A grand staircase worthy of Scarlett O'Hara curved upward, and several doors opened to the verandah, darkened rooms, and a long hallway.

"Look, the library," Henry said in hushed awe. He stepped toward a dim, cavernous room lined in bookshelves and dark damask wallpaper. "Oh my heavens!" He gasped and rushed inside.

Books lay scattered across the floor. Spines were cruelly cracked and pages folded and crumpled as if viciously torn and tossed from their shelves. Henry bent to attend to the wounded.

Cleo slipped by him. The vast room felt claustrophobic, the air heavy with a musty scent of old pages and faint floral perfume. Vines blocked the light, swarming the windows as if searching for a way in. Cleo adjusted her bifocals and tried to make sense of the disorienting scene. Statues like those in the forest lurked in the corners. Bits of stone limbs and small heads served as bookends. She squinted toward a far dim corner. A rocking chair was swaying, so gently it might have been shoved by a draft or her imagination.

Never leave a rocker rocking, her grandmother used to say. *You'll be sick within the year.* Defiant young Cleo had left many a chair swinging, yet this one made her think her Grandma Watkins was right. She made her way across the room, careful to avoid books. A blanket lay on the floor in front of the chair, along with an upturned footstool. No, not a blanket, Cleo realized. Her heart jumped and adrenaline pricked her fingers. It was clothes. A loose dark suit. A pale hand.

"Buford? Mr. Krandall!" She rushed to the withered form. He lay on his stomach, limbs and books twisted about him. Cleo ignored the ache in her knees and knelt. Henry was soon beside her.

He started to turn Buford over. "CPR," he was saying. "Compression, airway, breathing—"

"Wait." Cleo placed shaky fingers on Buford's still neck.

"He's cold," she said. She steeled herself to lift his wrist. Chilly and stiff. But if Buford was so long gone, who or what had they heard?

Henry helped her up. Her knees felt unsure, for more reasons than arthritic stiffness. Had she imagined the movement, the noises? Leaves rustled outside, like armies of small running feet. A shutter banged. Though it was warm, Cleo shivered and let Henry put an arm around her and pull her close.

"We have to go," he said. "We have to call the police. Your phone, is it in the bookmobile?"

"Just a moment." Cleo prayed for Buford. No matter what troubles he had—and had caused others—she hoped his soul was at peace and his death peaceful. She doubted the latter. Her eyes fixed on the book open at his side. Priscilla Pawpaw's *A Guide to Getting Away with Murder*, Chapter Three: Bludgeoning.

Chapter Four

Cleo paced Words on Wheels, up and down the center aisle and back again, her sandals squishing on the rubbery tiles. As she went, she straightened books. In the cooking section, she paused, her thoughts turning to casseroles and logically on to death and funerals.

When folks passed on in Catalpa Springs, tactical teams of hospitality deployed, providing grieving survivors with enough food to last several lifetimes. There would be casseroles and salads. Sculptural molded aspics, whole hams, and platters of deviled eggs. Pies, cakes, cookies, and ambrosia fruit salad. Depending on the season and the deceased, Cleo gifted a nice peach cobbler or caramel cake or an easily freezable chicken divan (pronounced "divine" in her family).

She ran a hand over a cookbook compiled by the Ladies League. There'd be lots of good recipes inside, but who would be grieving? For that matter, who would do all the arrangements? There was the obituary to craft, so important and the first section of the *Catalpa Gazette* many Catalpa residents read, including Cleo. The funeral, a reception, tending the grave or scattering the ashes . . .

"The police sure are taking their time," Henry said. He tapped his watch, as if that would hurry them on, and attempted to stretch legs pinned under Rhett. A picture book lay open beside him on the back bench seat. He'd already flipped through the illustrations of a cartoon caterpillar. Like Cleo's pacing, the page-turning was for distraction.

Cleo felt bad for involving him. "They'll be here soon, I'm sure," she said. She wasn't actually sure, nor was the 911 operator with whom she'd spoken.

The woman on the other end had warned Cleo of a possible delay. Local police, firefighters, and EMTs were holding a "joint terrorism, conflagration, and mass hysteria simulation," the dispatcher reported in bored tones, each word squeezed between what sounded like loud and enthusiastic smacking of gum. Like any decent librarian, Cleo loathed gum. It was a vile substance, a destroyer of pages and marrer of desks.

Still, Cleo dutifully followed the dispatcher's instructions. She locked the doors of Words on Wheels, pulling down the sash windows for a necessary breeze. Wind flew through, ionically charged by the threatening storm. Cleo watched the restless clouds and shivering trees. The more she stared, the more vine-smothered stone figures she detected. She imagined them coming to life, clawing their way free, and trudging off into the forest. Or coming for the bus. Mama always said, Cleo had way too much imagination.

Cleo turned away, calming herself with the fuel of that imagination—a library stocked with good books.

"Henry," Cleo said, jolting him from another distracted flip through the picture book. "Did you happen to notice the rocking chair behind Buford? I could have sworn it was swaying ever so slightly."

Henry looked thoughtful. Instead of rubbing his chin, he scratched Rhett's. The Persian was practically smiling. Rhett adored male attention. "No," Henry said. "I'm sorry. I was blind to everything except those books on the floor. I should have paid more attention. It's my fault you had to discover that . . . him . . ."

"It's certainly not your fault," Cleo said, her guilt building. If only she'd rebuffed his chivalry and friendship. He could be at his bookstore, enjoying a nice read or a nap or some leftover scones. "But . . . I'm glad you're here," she admitted.

Henry flushed. "I did notice something. I'm not sure if it's relevant. That drilling machine, it looked broken."

"That drill's an oddball contraption," Cleo said. "I saw it operating the other day. 'Chewing,' Buford called it. It did seem alive, like something from Frankenstein. His great-granddaddy made it." She sifted her memory for the relative's name. *Aldridge,* she thought, thinking she'd check the genealogy references to be sure. Then she remembered that most were stashed or laid out to dry in unharmed parts of the library. Henry had taken in the soggiest volumes and was treating them in his bookshop.

A siren as faint as a mosquito caught Cleo's attention. She and Henry watched the oak tunnel light up in red and blue strobes. A police car bounced over the ruts.

"Thank goodness," Cleo said. "Before they get here, tell me, what about the machine?"

Henry hesitated, frowning in concentration. "It wasn't moving, as you say. But I'm interested in gears and how pieces fit together. I could see how it *could* move. That is, if someone hadn't wedged a pole through it."

"A pole? As in sabotage?" Cleo knew someone who'd love to see that machine slain. Its owner too. Her insides tightened. She'd called Mary-Rose right after speaking with the 911 operator. Her friend—Buford's neighbor and nemesis—didn't pick up.

"A monster impaled," Henry said. "Pierced straight through its cold, steel heart."

* * *

Deputy Gabby Honeywell looked like she'd rushed straight from the emergency training. She wore exercise shorts, a tank top, and combat boots, and jumped from the passenger seat of the patrol car before it came to a full stop.

Cleo was opening the front doors when Gabby jogged up. "Miss Cleo? Are you okay?"

Cleo, Henry, and Rhett stepped out, the cat stretching and yawning with feline nonchalance. Cleo assured her neighbor they were fine. "Buford Krandall is not." Cleo described what they'd seen and how they came to see it.

"A break-in?" Gabby said. Her partner, the portly Earl Tookey chuffed up. A candy bar balanced in his lips as he struggled to unzip a billowing hazmat suit. When Gabby said there was no immediate lifesaving to be done, Tookey prioritized the chocolate. "Whew," he said, after finishing the bar and stepping out of the crinkly suit. He wadded up the coveralls and lobbed them back toward the patrol car. The outfit underneath was similar to Gabby's, but far less flattering, though it would be hard for anyone to challenge a former Miss South Georgia on looks. Gabby had poise and long limbs and was Catalpa Springs Police Department's youngest deputy, as well as the only female and African American on the force.

Tookey, however, was a champ in his own right. He'd taken the regional BBQ title three years running. Cleo spotted telltale marks of Georgia mustard BBQ sauce speckling his T-shirt. A slight scent of wood smoke always followed him.

"Who'd rob that dump?" the barbequing sergeant asked, turning toward the house, plucking at his shirt. Tookey had the all-over soft pudge of an oversized toddler.

Henry answered. "Mr. Krandall had an outstanding book collection and private library. It's legendary in antiquarian and rare book circles. I recently sold him some exceptional pieces."

Tookey snorted. "Old books? Hardly worth breaking in for." He tromped off to "inspect the perimeter."

"I hope he knows that's poison ivy over on the fence," Cleo said.

Gabby yelled a warning, to which Tookey responded by waving her off and hiking up his socks.

"Good for Took to learn new things," Gabby said. She leaned to pet Rhett, who was twining and purring at her feet. "Hey, handsome neighbor boy," she lied to the choppy-furred feline. To Cleo and Henry, she said, "Tookey and I came out straight from an emergency exercise. The chief's on his way. We have orders to wait 'til he gets here."

A small parade of vehicles arrived a few minutes later. The

ambulance bumped in first, lights flashing, its siren choking off mid-wail. An SUV the size of an elephant lumbered in next, Chief Silas Culpepper behind its wheel. Cleo frowned. Mayor Jeb Day sat in the passenger seat.

The chief greeted them with a puffed chest and a hand on his holster. "This is how it's gonna go," he announced. "With a crime scene, the experts and emergency personnel go in first, and the police secure the scene and the evidence and . . ."

Silas Culpepper was a great explainer, and Cleo appreciated his interest in his field. Unfortunately, the chief often failed to recognize disinterest in his audience. As he droned on, Cleo's mind wandered to Buford, so pale. So cold and still. She shook her head sharply and refocused on Chief Culpepper's suspenders. She imagined the chief had an entire closet full of them, all hardworking. Today's, straining over his prominent belly, were red, with little blue lobsters clutching flags in their claws. Cleo wondered if the chief was one of *them*, a fisherman. He was chummy with the mayor . . .

Two EMTs jogged up with a stretcher and duffle bags. The chief interrupted his own exposition to bark, "Clear the way!"

Cleo scooped up Rhett, and she and Henry obligingly stepped aside and pointed to the back.

"It's too late for any medical help, I'm afraid," Cleo said, watching the men trot off. Rhett clawed his way to her shoulder, his favorite perch. He purred and nuzzled her ear.

"You'd know, wouldn't you?" Chief Culpepper said. "Why am I finding you at another crime scene, Mrs. Watkins? What kind of trouble did you get yourself into now?"

"Trouble for your library." The mayor sauntered up, his

smug smile more annoying than his Bermuda shorts and their remarkably awful print of orange plaid and pink flamingos. "Buford Krandall was your big library supporter, wasn't he? Your great, loony hope?"

"A man is dead," Cleo said in the chastising tone she leveled at gum chewers and loud cell-phone users in the library.

The impertinent mayor failed to notice. His cell phone beeped and he wandered off, poking at the tiny screen.

Henry bristled beside her.

Cleo patted her male friend—hardly a *boy*friend—on the arm. "Mr. Lafayette and I were delivering books."

"Books? That figures too," the chief said with exaggerated weariness. "What kind of books?"

With a wave of guilt, Cleo realized they'd abandoned their books on the back porch. She fought the urge to run back and retrieve them. They'd be safe with the police, she told herself. And better that the police discovered Buford Krandall's questionable reading taste on their own.

"I brought by some library books Mr. Krandall ordered through the interlibrary loan service," Cleo said. "I've been doing home deliveries since Mr. Krandall doesn't go out much during the day."

"A weird man," the chief mumbled, then glanced toward the house and looked appropriately chagrined.

"I brought a gift," Henry said. "A reproduction of an illustrated Tudor book of inventions."

An unexpected sadness struck Cleo. "How perfect. Mr. Krandall would have adored that." He might have gotten onto a new do-it-yourself kick, for better or worse. Cleo imagined a homemade trebuchet launching buckets of boiling oil at the Pancake Mill.

Henry was elaborating on the original book's age, illustrations, typography—

"Yeah, yeah," Culpepper said, pulling on his overtaxed suspenders, bored with details he wasn't personally providing. "Fascinating. You two stay here and talk all about it. We'll take your statements later." His eyes surveyed Gabby's bare legs. "Nice uniform, Honeywell. We should have emergency trainings more often. Now, when we get to the scene, Tookey and I'll go in first. You'll guard the door. It might not be a nice sight for a gal—whoops, I mean, a newbie—such as yourself." He waved to Jeb Day. "Mayor? You want to come with?"

Cleo admired Gabby's ability to maintain a pleasant, impassive expression. That mask had surely served her well in beauty pageants and the police force and being a pretty young woman in general.

"Crude man," Henry said as the chief's broad backside waddled out of sight. "We might as well wait in Words on Wheels." He swatted at a buzzing black fly. Cleo's mother said loopy flies meant a storm was coming. Her grandmother said the same of flicking cat tails. Cleo didn't need insects or Rhett to forecast this weather. Thunder grumbled to the west, and the clouds pressed low.

The brightly painted bookmobile did look tempting, but Cleo was tired of waiting. "How about we put Rhett safely inside Words on Wheels, then give it a minute or two and go check on Gabby? I bet she'd be awfully interested in the disabled drill."

Gabby wasn't waiting around either. They found her on the back porch, inspecting the kitchen door. "Was this broken when you went inside?" she asked, not turning to see who was approaching.

"Mr. Lafayette and I certainly didn't kick it in," Cleo gently joked.

Gabby didn't smile. "Look here." She pointed a gloved finger at a hinge. The surrounding wood was pale and recently splintered.

"Neither door was locked," Cleo said, serious now and ashamed of her previous levity. She must be in shock. "The kitchen door was already open a crack," she clarified. "I didn't look on the back side. I merely pulled it. I'm afraid I didn't wear gloves."

Gabby sat back on her heels. Her hair swung in a thick ponytail of shoulder-sweeping curls. She coiled a strand around her finger, staring wistfully toward the kitchen and the action beyond. "You couldn't know what you'd find. But you were pretty sure of murder when you called 911. Why?"

Cleo told her about the sounds from inside, the possible door banging, the moving chair, and the devastated library. Henry showed her the drill and the thick metal bar through it. They kept several yards back, so as not to disturb the chief's scene.

"A busted door, possible break-in, trashed library, vandalism . . . a deceased homeowner . . . ," Gabby repeated thoughtfully. "Then there are those books on the porch. Your library's books, Miss Cleo, both about getting away with murder. Was Krandall planning to kill someone?"

"Kill?" The chief approached, with Tookey at his heels and the mayor, on his phone, lagging behind. "That crackpot Krandall wanted to kill someone? Whoever it was, looks like they got to him first."

Chapter Five

"Murdered?" Mary-Rose repeated. Pleased pink bloomed beneath her freckles. "Dead? Gone? Passed beyond? Out of my hair?" She patted a loose bun where silver outnumbered her natural red.

Cleo was glad few were around to witness her friend's unseemly delight. The Pancake Mill opened from breakfast through lunch and was now closed for the day. Besides Cleo, Henry, and Mary-Rose, the only other occupant of the big, dim dining room was Mary-Rose's granddaughter, Zoe. The seven-year-old sat a few tables away, a book hiding her face, but not the riotous red curls that reminded Cleo of a young Mary-Rose. A soft clatter of dishwashing filtered through from the kitchen. Outside, the wind rippled Pancake Spring, and the resident peacocks fanned and fluffed their feathers.

Visitors loved snapping photos of the flamboyant birds framed against the historic mill and sparkling spring. Cleo knew the less lovely reason for their presence. Mary-Rose had gotten the flock to keep bird-fearing Buford Krandall off her property. It had worked. The peacock trio could be as territorial and threatening as a guard dog, particularly at night.

"I'll ask Juan to measure out extra batter," Mary-Rose was saying brightly. "We'll have a full house tomorrow. A give-thanks Sunday." She caught Cleo's stern look. "I am *not* applauding a death, Cleo Jane. But I will not pretend I am sad or sorry."

"Understandable," murmured Henry, who was enjoying pie and thus in restored good humor. Cleo eyed the slice with jealousy. It was peanut, a specialty of the Pancake Mill. Fluffy meringue topped creamy vanilla custard and a sweet whipped peanut base.

"Mary-Rose," Cleo said, forcing her eyes from the pie. "Be careful what you say. People may have heard about your feud with Buford Krandall and get the wrong idea."

"*May have?*" Mary-Rose grinned. "Of course everyone knows! I'll hardly be the only one celebrating. Half the town had troubles with that man peeping and prying into their business, and the other half worried about keeping on his good side. Speaking of peeping . . ." She jumped up and grabbed two pairs of binoculars from under the front counter. She was out the door before Cleo could protest, a jaunty spring in her step, Zoe skipping behind her.

"I'll just clean up my plate," Henry said.

Cleo swallowed her envy. She caught up with Mary-Rose on the boardwalk that zigzagged along the swampy border closest to Krandall House. Zoe leaned over the railing at the viewing platform, stirring polka-dot duckweed with a long stick, calling it "magic stew."

"Mary-Rose," Cleo said sharply. "Chief Culpepper might think you did it."

Mary-Rose snorted. "Did it? Please! I am an old woman, Cleo. We are old women. How would I kill a man in—what, his fifties? Although he was shriveled and likely vitamin D deficient, hiding from the sun as he did."

Cleo studied Mary-Rose. Her friend was a picture of robust health, and age was certainly no alibi for murder.

Mary-Rose adjusted her lacy, rose-hued cardigan, worn over a long, floral sundress. "I wouldn't have had time," she said primly. "I'm babysitting Zoe this week and next. Out of curiosity, though, how *did* he die?"

Cleo didn't know. Better Mary-Rose knew nothing too. "The coroner will determine that. Of course, you'll have an alibi for . . ." Cleo hesitated.

"Well? When?" Mary-Rose demanded, swinging to eye Cleo.

Cleo watched the swirling duckweed stew. A peacock called, an eerie laugh that echoed off the water and tall cypress. "The EMTs guessed early this morning or last night," Cleo said.

"Fine either way," Mary-Rose declared. "I was here all morning and home with Zoe and William last night. William's new knee is mending up nicely. We might go on a cruise when he's healed."

Mary-Rose's husband William had a new knee, an operation Cleo feared she might have to endure someday. She turned her binoculars back to Krandall House and zoomed in on Gabby. Her young neighbor appeared to be dusting the drill for prints. Chief Culpepper stood a few yards away, talking at

Mayor Day and Sergeant Tookey. Tookey munched another candy bar. The boy mayor poked at his phone.

Mary-Rose sniffed. "Look at those men, standing about. If they'd only acted when I called to complain. Well, I won't have to worry now."

Cleo *was* worried. "Mary-Rose, when did the drilling machine go silent?"

"Mmm? I don't know." Mary-Rose tugged her earlobe and shrugged.

Cleo frowned. Several decades ago, she, Mary-Rose, and a handful of other Catalpa ladies played a monthly poker game. Cleo wasn't a gambler and she'd never set foot in a floating casino—heavens, no! But she was good at poker, being good at reading people. Ida Gunny, for instance, sweated profusely when bluffing. Nancy O'Mallory would fold every time she sniffled. And Mary-Rose? Cleo's best friend had telling hands. When she was bluffing or lying, those hands flew straight to her pearls. On the rare days Mary-Rose wasn't wearing pearls, like today, she tugged her earlobe. Just like she was tugging it now . . .

Cleo knew the sign. She didn't know the reason. Raindrops spotted her glasses. Her vision was blurry, in more ways than one. "The storm's coming," she said. "Let's get inside."

Mary-Rose called to Zoe, and grandmother and grandchild swung hands all the way back to the mill.

* * *

Later, driving toward town in Words on Wheels, Cleo voiced her worries to Henry. "I think Mary-Rose knows something, at least about that drill."

47

"I know something too," Henry said. "I went to the kitchen for more pie."

A huff of indignation escaped Cleo's lips.

"To gather information," Henry said, rather righteously for a man who'd enjoyed *two* slices of pie. "A gentleman named Juan was cleaning up. He said that drill went silent late yesterday afternoon, when Mary-Rose drove out to Krandall House in a huff. Juan appeared to be unaware of Buford's death. I don't think he would have told me otherwise. He seems devoted to Mary-Rose."

So was Cleo. "I wonder what Mary-Rose did to make Buford stop drilling? *Said*, I mean." The bus rolled by pines, their needles drooping in the rain. Rumbles of thunder had Rhett cowering in his peach crate.

Henry said, "I don't know what was said, but Juan heard yelling. And a gunshot."

"What?" Cleo braked a little too hard around a curve.

"It's okay," Henry said quickly. "Buford wasn't shot."

Cleo was hardly comforted. A gunshot could still mean trouble. She thought of the chief's logic. What if Buford was planning to kill, but his would-be victim got to him first? "If the chief hears about this, he might say Mary-Rose struck out at Buford in fear for her life."

"He doesn't know yet," Henry said.

But everyone knew of Mary-Rose's feud with Buford Krandall. Cleo drove on under a din of spitting hail.

When she pulled up in front of The Gilded Page, Henry thanked her. "It was an, uh, interesting afternoon," he said, politely. Cleo waited until he'd gotten inside and the bookshop glowed with warm light. Then she punched the gas, eager for home.

* * *

When Cleo was little, it was Alice Tidwell, the doctor's wife, who delivered the news no one wanted to receive. If Alice appeared at one's door bearing a baked good, a death could be expected. At best, a dire disease with a poor prognosis. Cleo still remembered a sweltering summer day and Mama on the porch, wiping sudsy hands on her apron one moment, engulfed in Alice's prodigious bust the next. Auntie Violet had cancer. Alice Tidwell hadn't paid another visit until Grandma Watkins passed.

Cleo was easing Words on Wheels into her driveway, when her heart jumped. A figure stood on her porch, blurry through the rain-dotted screen. It was a woman, holding a tray. And another. And another still. Cleo's mind spun wildly to Alice Tidwell and a mass disaster. Then she noted the pink scarves and hats.

"Ladies Leaguers," she informed Rhett. She scooped up the rain-loathing Persian and hustled for the porch between thunder rumbles. A group hug enveloped them, led by Bitsy Givens, president of the Ladies League.

"You all shouldn't have come out in this weather. *I'm* fine," Cleo said.

"Nonsense." Bitsy waved a sparkly pink manicure. "You've had a shock. Besides, we had to do *something* for *someone*. It's not like Buford Krandall left behind a bunch of grieving relatives."

Cleo unlocked the door, and ladies streamed inside. Rhett led the way to the kitchen, surely expecting treats in return.

Bitsy hung back with Cleo. She slipped off her hat and adjusted strappy high heels. "We promise not to keep you up all night. We have some goodies to drop off for your honey Henry at The Gilded Page after this, and my Vernon's picking me up in a bit. He'll have Mama Givens in the car so I won't be able to dawdle. Mama's in a mood today. Rain makes her feet and her temper act up."

Bitsy's husband, Vernon, was president of the local bank. A big man in height, girth, and status, Vernon Givens was known for his pastel suits, generosity with home loans, and chummy, chatty demeanor. His mother, Maybelle, was the sour, shriveled opposite. Cleo had known Maybelle since childhood and watched her transform from schoolyard bully to senior-citizen tyrant. Maybelle did love her only son, a good trait. She also loved complaining about her ailments and making doctor appointments, with Bitsy as her chauffeur. Cleo dutifully inquired about Maybelle's health.

"Hardy as a mule," Bitsy said with a wink. "Let's go in and get a cookie. Jasmine Wagner brought homemade marshmallow moon pies, and they'll go fast."

Cleo decided watching her sugar was off the table for the night. She had suffered a shock. Besides, it was only polite to sample all the offerings, especially a moon pie.

Her kitchen overflowed with excited chatting, steaming casseroles, fruit salad, a pie, and Jasmine's famous graham cookies filled with marshmallow fluff and coated in chocolate. Rhett sat kingly at the table, enjoying kitty treats served up on a plastic plate.

"Thank you again," Cleo said to the ladies.

"Our pleasure," sang out a voice among the crowd. Laughter rose, a flask made the rounds, and clear liquid splashed in cups of orange juice and fizzy lemonade.

Cleo made up a plate and took a seat at the table between Rhett and Bitsy.

"A killer among us," Bitsy said, shaking her head. "It's awful. This sounds almost worse, but it's bad for the library, isn't it? Buford Krandall was our big supporter. I heard he was going after the mayor and gathering up major money somehow." She clicked her tongue in disapproval. "That mayor! Do you know he's out celebrating *in public*?"

Before Cleo could ask, a passing Leaguer provided the details. "Buying rounds of drinks at Biscuit Bobs. The merry widow Kat Krandall is out there too. We should stop by."

If anyone could justify merriment, Cleo thought, it was Kat, the long-divorcing spouse. But the mayor? How tacky. She tuned back in, hearing Bitsy evoke the mayor's name.

"Jeb Day's been honeying up to my Vernon, trying to get support for that fishing pier. He invited Vern on a boys' fishing weekend at the coast, dangling all sorts of temptations. Fishing pros, yachts, big money accounts for the bank . . ." Bitsy shrugged slender, tanned shoulders. "Vern likely won't go. My honey can't bear to hurt a bug, let alone string up a fish. He hasn't said no yet, though. Vernie does enjoy folks flirting with his money."

There'd been gossip when Bitsy wed Vernon Givens. Some folks said *she* was flirting with the bank president's fortunes. Bitsy was younger than Vernon—mid-thirties to his verging on fifty. She was also blindingly blond, a second wife, and a former employee. Cleo thought Bitsy had more than proved the gossips wrong. Bitsy worked hard, doing a lot of good around town. Then there was Maybelle. Maybelle occupied a wing of the Givens's home. To Cleo's thinking, any daughter-in-law who could tolerate that much sour and still come out smiling deserved every dime Vernon had.

"Don't you worry, Miss Cleo," Bitsy said. "We've got your back." She raised her voice, "Right, ladies? To the Gala!"

Cheers filled the room, and Cleo was regaled with details of fabulous auction items. The ladies eventually left in threes, one group heading to Henry's, the other planning to stop by Biscuit Bobs. Bitsy lingered, helping Cleo clean up and waiting for her ride.

A horn blared outside. "That'll be Mama Givens," Bitsy said with a little roll of her eyes. "You wouldn't believe how fast she is, reaching from the passenger seat to slap that horn. I joke she was an urban cabbie in a previous life. That gets her mad. She wants to be a queen, even in make-believe." Bitsy gave Cleo a long hug. "Oh, I almost forgot. I have a big, huge favor to ask you."

Cleo was already nodding yes. She'd do anything for the Gala, anything to save her library.

"Hummingbird cake," Bitsy said in a low voice. Vernon was hopping out of their SUV, jogging around to offer his mother an elbow. Maybelle swatted him off.

"Vernon's birthday's coming up," Bitsy said, speaking fast. "Hummingbird's his favorite cake. Mama Givens makes the very best, but she does hers by instinct, she says. She says I won't do it right. She's probably right. I'm not a baker. Or a cook . . ." The usually bubbly Bitsy looked deflated.

Cleo felt restored. Here was a problem she could solve, and immediately too. "If I recall, Maybelle *borrowed* my Mama's recipe." *More like swiped,* Cleo mentally amended, recalling the day Maybelle Givens invited herself into Cleo's kitchen and rifled through her recipe tin when Cleo's back was turned. Cleo—and Mama—would have given her the recipe if she'd just asked.

"Mama won the county fair cake contest many years running," Cleo told Bitsy, smiling with the memory. "She called it her 'hum with joy cake.'" Cleo ducked inside. She kept a folder with copies of her most requested recipes, the most popular being hummingbird cake. The tropical treat featured layers of pineapple and banana spice cake floating on great waves of cream cheese frosting.

Back on the porch, she slipped the paper to Bitsy. "Cleo, you're a lifesaver!" Bitsy said. She stashed the recipe in her purse as Maybelle stomped up the steps, Vernon hovering solicitously at her side.

"My corns are aching," Maybelle declared, making a beeline for the porch swing.

Vernon made up for his mother's lack of charm, politely inquiring about Cleo's health. He asked after Rhett and Henry and Words on Wheels and expressed sorrow for Buford Krandall.

"A good man," he said. "He was passionate. Committed."

"Crazy as a peach orchard boar," Maybelle said. "Let's get going." She kicked her feet, sending the porch swing precariously close to Cleo's sunroom window.

"We'll go, Mama," Bitsy said brightly. "You must be tired. You too, Vernon. You've had a long day."

"I have nothing to complain about, considering," Vernon said. He smoothed a cornflower blue tie over a peach button-down shirt. His trousers and loafers were creamy white.

"Yes, you do," Maybelle said. "You griped all the way here about that assistant of yours quitting and leaving a mess." She frowned at Cleo as if she were to blame. "He's going to have to hire a temp. You can't trust temps."

Cleo saw another chance to help. "I know just the person," she exclaimed. She described Leanna's temp gig as a walking biscuit advertisement. "Leanna's a lovely young lady. She's a fabulous library assistant, and she's already signed up with Tammy Temps. She's smart, efficient, great with computers—"

"You said she dresses like food and tramps about on the highway," Maybelle snapped. "Can't be that smart."

Bitsy looped her arm around her big husband's waist. "Vern, sugar, hire that girl. I know Miss Leanna from the library and Gala prep. She's a working whirlwind and cute as a button. I'll take care of it. I'll call Tammy Temps and set up the interview for first thing Monday morning." Bitsy got out her phone and made a note, verbally listing her schedule as she went. "Interview. Tammy Temps. Leanna . . . Oh, and Miss Cleo—I almost forgot! You said you wanted an unbiased estimate on the library repair costs? I've arranged for Vernon's favorite contractor to come by the library Monday morning too. Vern, hon, I'm sending you reminders right now. First the interview. Then the contractor."

"I go where you and the phone tell me," Vernon said with a chuckle.

"I'm telling you I need to get home!" Maybelle snapped.

When Maybelle got her way and the Givens drove off,

Cleo hurried to her phone. She'd already told Leanna about Buford Krandall's death. Now she wanted to report some good news and ask a favor of her own. Leanna was working at Biscuit Bobs tonight. Her young protégé had a librarian's gift for reading people. Cleo hoped she also had a knack for spying, specifically on a partying widow and a fishy mayor.

Chapter Six

Cleo stepped out into her garden early the next morning, soaking in warm dewy air and the symphony of birdsong. It was Sunday, a rest day for Words on Wheels, but still busy for Cleo. Friends and family were coming to lunch. The long-planned meal was casual but had taken loads of schedule juggling, especially for her twelve-year-old twin grandsons. Young people these days had busier schedules than adults.

Cleo mulled the menu as she inspected her heirloom climbing rose. Rhett pounced after a bug and found himself in damp grass. The Persian flicked his paws with each step. Then he froze, a foot raised, ears pointed at alert.

Cleo heard it too, a slight scuffling from the direction of Deputy Gabby Honeywell's patio. She walked to their shared chin-high fence and peeked over. Gabby was face down on the flagstone. Her elbows bent outward. Her legs spiraled up and around in impossible angles. If Cleo didn't know better, she might have called for emergency assistance.

Cleo, however, knew Gabby practiced yoga. The young

policewoman was also wearing Spandex, a clear tip-off of extreme exertion.

Gabby pushed up into a handstand. Cleo watched with awe and a little trepidation, remembering her cousin Dot's brush with yoga. It began in the library, like so many adventures and some misadventures. Dot borrowed a VCR tape featuring an attractive male yogi on a tropical beach. The man and setting were enticing, so much so that Dot fervently followed his every move. A few downward dogs and a corpse pose later, and Dot was nearly a corpse herself, prone in the ER with a viciously pulled back.

Rhett jumped to a fence post, announcing their presence with a loud meow.

"Hey, Rhett. Hi, Miss Cleo," Gabby said cheerfully, still in a perfect pose.

Cleo greeted her neighbor and waited for the invitation she hoped would come.

"Want to pop over?" Gabby swung her legs gracefully to the ground. "I meant to stop by and check on y'all last night, but I got in late."

Rhett and Cleo circled around the fence to Gabby's leafy back patio. Rhett ran to head-bump the again upside-down Gabby. The deputy laughed and lost her balance. "Rhett, you ruined a Pose Dedicated to the Sage Koundinya II."

"Goodness," Cleo said. "The name is as impressive as your balance."

Gabby grinned. "I signed up for a fancy yoga class over at the college in Claymore. They're big on long names." She patted Rhett, and he flopped in a blissful-cat pose. "Coffee? Tea? Cold drink?"

Cleo chose herbal tea, hot and peppermint. It was barely seven, but she'd been up for hours and had already had two coffees, double her usual single cup. Sleep had evaded her last night. She'd read—or told herself she was reading—until after midnight. She'd lain in the dark, woken frequently by worries and thoughts of Buford Krandall, and once by Ollie. Her grandson had returned to his backyard cottage at 1:36 a.m. Cleo had heard his laugh echo across the garden. There was other laughter too, accompanying a sharp female voice Cleo recognized as Whitney Greene's.

Cleo hadn't heard Gabby get in, but then Gabby was a quiet neighbor. She didn't slam screen doors like dear Oliver or broadcast her laughter, when she was laughing at all. Sometimes Cleo worried Gabby was too serious.

"Did you hear?" Gabby asked, bringing two steaming mugs to the patio. "The chief got a search warrant for the Pancake Mill and grounds, including the spring. Everyone's going out this morning. Everyone except me. I'm typing reports and following up on witnesses." She sighed, watching Rhett lazily swat at a butterfly while still lying down.

"A search warrant for the Pancake Mill? Why, that's simply absurd." Cleo kept her eyes on her mug, thinking it wasn't actually so outlandish. Did the chief know about Mary-Rose confronting Buford and the gunfire that followed? She surely hoped not.

"Just routine," Gabby said, which didn't sound bad until she continued. "Of course, everyone knows about the feud between Mary-Rose's family and Krandall's. Plus, witnesses overheard Mary-Rose at the Pancake Mill threatening to kill

Buford." Gabby gave Cleo an apologetic look. "I'm sorry. I know she's your friend."

"It's only a saying," Cleo protested. "'I could kill so and so.' It's awful, but not meant literally. I was there when she said it. She was upset and venting. She'd had a lot of sugar."

"Yeah," Gabby said. "I get that. But then another witness heard Buford Krandall say he was going to 'bury that Garland woman for good.' He could have been researching methods in those library books you took him. That gives her motive too, unfortunately. Self-defense." Gabby stretched languidly. Rhett did the same, exposing his choppy-shaved belly.

Cleo set down her mug, hiding the shake in her hand. "Do you know the cause of death?" she asked.

Gabby hesitated. She leaned back in her patio chair, watching a hummingbird sip at her feeder. The little bird hovered, wings a blur. "I might as well say," she said, as the hummingbird zipped off with a buzz. "Everyone will know soon enough. Mr. Krandall was dealt a fatal blow to the cranium by a blunt object. We're still looking for the weapon. We checked all those weird bookends in his library and statues by the house, but no joy. No blood, I mean."

Cleo shuddered.

Gabby continued. "What's really weird is that book we found under him, open right to his cause of death. Did you worry, lending him those books like that? Who reads that kind of stuff?"

Cleo gave Gabby an abbreviated version of her librarians-never-judge speech.

"Well, I can see that in your profession," Gabby said,

twisting a curl around her finger. "But police have to judge, and fast if there's a killer running around."

Cleo prayed they wouldn't jump to judge Mary-Rose. "Any other brushes with death around town lately?" she asked.

"Do you mean, did Buford try to murder someone else and miss? Not that I know of, but it's a good angle to keep in mind. The chief says, the solution is usually simpler. It's someone close. A spouse or relative . . . or neighbor." Gabby smiled over her tea mug. "I'm lucky to have such nice neighbors."

Cleo returned the compliment and added a lunch invitation. "It'll be friends and family. My cousin Dot and son Fred—Ollie's father—and his wife and kids. Leanna. Ollie too, hopefully, and Mary-Rose . . ." Cleo's guest list trailed off in uncertainty.

"I'm sure Mary-Rose'll be fine and eager to come to lunch," Gabby said kindly. "She's not supposed to touch anything during the search, anyway." Gabby got up to pat Rhett. "I'd be over in a heartbeat too, but I doubt I can get away. The chief is pushing for evidence, the murder weapon, an arrest, any progress. 'Critical first days,' as he says." She smiled grimly, ruffling Rhett's fur. "My first big murder case. It's not as glamorous as it looks on TV, is it Rhett?"

"No," Cleo said sympathetically, since Rhett was busy purring. "I don't suppose so." She and Rhett had to let Gabby get to work, but before leaving, she could suggest a more productive investigative direction. She described as much as she knew of Buford Krandall's boasts of saving the library and besting Mayor Jeb Day. She added, "Did you know that our mayor was celebrating at Biscuit Bobs yesterday? So was Buford's new widow, Kat. Like you said, the killer could be someone close. Money's a powerful motive too."

Gabby frowned in thought. "Buford and Kat Krandall were the oddest couple. I think they *liked* their divorce fight. I saw them in court once, having a grand time lobbing insults and legal threats. They went out to lunch afterward. I don't know if either truly wanted the divorce to end."

Cleo, feeling a twinge of tattletale guilt, reported on her recent chat with Kat. "Kat swore she'd be rid of Buford soon. By her fiftieth birthday, within three months."

Gabby took a note and promised to check into Kat.

"Then there's the mayor," Cleo said, feeling much better pointing Gabby toward Mayor Jebson Day. "Mayor Day was awfully happy about Buford's death. Buford was going to fight the mayor's pet fishing projects and gambling boat."

Gabby tapped her pencil on the metal patio table. "Our mayor could be holding the murder weapon while jaywalking in the buff, and the chief wouldn't let a lowly deputy like me confront him. I'll keep an eye out, though. You really have no idea how Mr. Krandall planned to save the library and get at Mayor Day's projects?"

Cleo shook her head dismally.

Gabby tapped some more. "Ooh . . . ," she said, pencil raised. "What if it was something with Mr. Krandall's spring-water scheme? That sure would put you in a devil's bargain, Miss Cleo. Save the library at the cost of your friend's business and Pancake Spring?"

Cleo shifted uncomfortably. Mary-Rose had already accused her of just that.

* * *

With lunch, Mary-Rose, and murder on her mind, Cleo strolled downtown a few hours later. Her cousin Dot, sixty-eight years young, ran Dot's Drop By at the center of downtown. The little shop offered grocery and deli items and single-serve ice creams scattered treasure-hunt fashion in a freezer chest. Jumbled shelves in the back stocked miscellanea from stockings to lightbulbs, to faded postcards.

This being Sunday, the Drop By would open briefly from about nine, when Dot got out of church, until eleven, when her devotions turned to supper. A blustery pastor once condemned Dot's Sunday hours as sacrilegious. Dot set him straight. Sitting through sermons sparked revelations, Dot contended, including those regarding missing ingredients.

As Cleo approached her cousin's store, she thought Dot was both charitable and a shrewd businesswoman. A small line had formed, waiting for Dot to unlock the doors. Cleo spotted Wanda Boxer in the queue. Cleo's gossipy neighbor to the north and the aunt of Mayor Day, Wanda could cast clouds over the sunniest of days. Cleo decided to avoid Wanda's gloom and stroll around Fontaine Park until Dot opened.

Sun filtered through long-limbed live oaks and their Spanish moss veils. The azaleas were as glorious as stained glass, translucent and glowing. Since her dear husband Richard's passing, Cleo had improvised her Sundays. Sometimes she went to the early-bird service, when the organ player was at her most energetic and uninhibited. Other times, she found divinity in nature or her garden, or inspiration in a good book.

Cleo walked slowly, savoring the beauty of the day and her

hometown. Until she turned a corner. Mayor Day balanced on a ladder propped against a lamppost outside City Hall. Gold plaid shorts rode high up his pale legs. He was stringing something to the lamppost. Cleo discerned nylon fabric, green and speckled and shaped like a fish. The bald man from Las Vegas she'd seen snoozing the other day had his hand on the ladder. He wore a dark suit, too woolly for the weather. His skin was tight and speckled with moles, reminding Cleo of a potato.

"Ah, Mrs. Watkins," the mayor said, beaming down from three rungs up. He flapped the fish flag. "What do you think? Looks just like a real bass, eh? These babies are top-quality windsocks. No other town has these!"

No other town would want them, Cleo thought. The fabric fish was terribly realistic, its mouth a gaping circle hooked on a metal lure and string. In the mayor's enthusiasm, the ladder tilted. Potato man yanked it back, sending the ladder and mayor swinging. Behind them stood a large box filled with similar flags.

"Why are you hanging bass on our lamps?" Cleo demanded. "The fishing pier isn't approved yet."

Jeb Day grinned. "Nothing wrong with a little advance publicity. Isn't that what you and those Ladies Leaguers are doing? Only difference is, I have loads of investor support."

"The library has community support," Cleo retorted, standing tall.

"Money speaks louder than books," the mayor countered. "Speaking of which, I've been looking at the budgets, and the library fund is downright paltry, down to nothing. I don't know if you could keep going even without that tree damage—am I right, Jimmy?"

The man, whom Cleo now knew as Jimmy, offered nothing, no words nor movement of his spud-like features.

Cleo summoned her Sunday-best manners. "I don't believe we've had the pleasure of meeting, sir." She held out a hand to Jimmy.

He let go of the ladder.

"Hold on tight, will you, Jim?" the mayor said shakily.

Jimmy ignored him and engulfed Cleo's hand in a clammy grip. "Jimmy Teeks," he said, his voice raspy yet surprisingly high. "Consultant."

"Cleo Watkins, librarian. What do you consult upon, Mr. Teeks?"

"Call him Jimmy," the mayor suggested.

Jimmy Teeks re-gripped the ladder and gave it a little shake. "Entertainment enterprises. Arrangements. Organizing. Enforcement."

Somehow Jimmy made even activities Cleo adored—organizing and arrangements—sound a tad treacherous. "I could use help with arrangements," she said, "for fixing our town's library."

"That so?" Jimmy said. He reached in his jacket and pulled out a card, which proved as vague as he was. It gave only his name and the embossed word "Consultant."

"How do I get in touch with you?" Cleo flipped the card, imagining she could dislodge a phone number and clarification.

"You *know* people," Mayor Jeb offered from above. "This is out of your league, Miss Cleo. Jimmy's here to snag big money. He's like a wedding planner for gambling enterprises.

He's a pro. A real *family* man, if you get my drift." The mayor winked and snickered.

Cleo recalled a popular book from Words on Wheels' self-help shelf: *Disarming the Disrespectful*. Smile, the book recommended. Appear calm and disinterested. Think happy thoughts. Jimmy Teeks certainly had his disinterested moves down. The bald man was yawning. Cleo turned her mind to her grandchildren, whom even in their most petulant toddler years had better manners than Jebson Day.

The mayor returned to his fish flag, which he tied up in a loopy bowknot. "There," he said proudly. "Look at that. Isn't she fine?"

Cleo changed the subject, hoping to catch him off guard. "Mayor Day, you were out at Biscuit Bobs yesterday, having quite a celebration, I heard. What was the occasion?"

A flash of *mind your own business* was quickly replaced by a sharky smile. "It was Jimmy's birthday. We threw him a surprise party. Right, Jim?"

Jimmy's spud features hardened. "Still waiting for my cake," he said.

The mayor descended the ladder rungs shakily. "On to the next lamppost!"

Jimmy Teeks stood back, hands deep in his pants pockets, letting the mayor haul his own ladder and flags. Cleo walked on, pondering the presence of the mysterious consultant. *Entertainment enterprises. A pro, a* family *man. Casinos . . . Las Vegas . . .* She crossed Fontaine Park at a rambling diagonal. When she came to the namesake fountain, she noticed a familiar pug sniff-inspecting a sweet gum tree. She called a hello. Henry waved. Mr. Chaucer wiggled and woofed.

After cheery chitchat about the weather, Cleo veered to a less pleasant topic. "I think our mayor may have hired a mobster." She informed Henry about the Vegas "consultant."

Since Henry was such a good listener, she continued on, telling him about the search of the Pancake Mill. Henry nodded and murmured as they strolled slowly back toward Dot's.

"My," Henry said, when they were in front of the Drop By, "small-town life is more dangerous than I expected. Murder, potential mobsters, slain drilling machines." He adjusted his straw Panama hat, reminding Cleo of a shorter, more rumpled Hemingway.

They peered inside Dot's big storefront windows. Cleo's cousin stood at the cash register, looking resplendent in her Sunday-best apron, a full-length affair of lacy ruffles and a bold peach print. Dot was adamant about aprons, which she wore for work, cooking, eating—even walking and driving. She had an extensive collection.

"Ah, Sunday supper supplies," Henry said, eyeing the line of customers. "My mother used to make the most wonderful tomato pies."

Cleo detected wistfulness. Henry had lost his parents a few years back and, tragically, his wife several decades ago. Their children and grandchildren lived far away, overseas and in Alaska, which might as well be the moon. Cleo thought of how fortunate she was. She should invite Henry to join them for lunch. Her palms went suddenly sweaty. *How silly,* she chided herself. They were mature adults, not teenagers.

"I'm debating between ham and fried chicken," Cleo said. She forged on, explaining the guest list. "Will you join us? If you're not busy . . ." Cleo realized, in all her years she'd never actually asked a man out. She rationalized that she wasn't *really* asking Henry on anything resembling a date. It was a group lunch.

"I'd be imposing," Henry said, gazing at his feet.

"No, no. It's casual," Cleo insisted. "Leanna will come and hopefully Mary-Rose and Ollie. Cousin Dot and my eldest boy, Fred, and his family. I invited Gabby just this morning, but she's tied up with work."

A broad smile broke through Henry's beard. "I'd love to join you all. What can I bring? I make pretty good deviled eggs, if I do say so myself."

Mr. Chaucer sat on his haunches and whimpered up at Cleo, his curlicue tail wiggling.

"Deviled eggs sound perfect, and of course bring Mr. Chaucer too." She added, with a little prayer for good measure, "It'll be a relaxed meal."

Chapter Seven

Cleo's kitchen smelled divine. A ham warmed in the oven, basted in brown sugar, mustard, and Coca Cola. Cornbread cooled on the counter, a big pot of green beans simmered on the stove, and potato salad chilled in the fridge. The dining table was set and dressed with a peony-print tablecloth and flowers from the garden.

Most of her guests would arrive in an hour or so. Cleo stepped out to sweep her front porch, mentally ticking off the confirmed visitors and their accompaniments. Dot with her famous mac and cheese. Henry with deviled eggs and Mr. Chaucer. Leanna with cheesy grits and hopefully no disreputable Biscuit Bobs baked goods. Fred and Angela—Ollie's stepmom—and their twelve-year-old twins, Leon and Theo. Angela would probably bring something healthy, a salad or fruit. Mary-Rose, thank goodness, was still coming and early too, bringing pies, granddaughter Zoe, and news. Her husband William was staying home to rest his bionic knee. The peacocks would patrol the police at Pancake Spring.

"It'll be a full house, Rhett," Cleo warned her cat. "Kids, a dog . . . you might not even get a chair at the table."

Rhett enjoyed staring down diners during meals. He threw back his tufted ears and scowled hard. To cheer him up, Cleo let the patchy Persian out to stalk geckos. He was meowing at the screen door, hounded by a squawking jay, when Mary-Rose arrived.

Cleo's friend managed a grim smile. Zoe streaked inside after Rhett, a book in one hand, a sorcerer's wand in the other. Rhett was about to be turned into a magical cat dragon. They bounded off in kid and feline delight. Rhett adored games of hide and seek, and ankle attack, and Zoe could hold her own.

"Coconut cream and key lime," Mary-Rose said, plunking a double-decker dessert carrier onto Cleo's kitchen table.

"Perfect, lovely, gorgeous." Cleo's mouth was already watering. She heard claws skid around the corner and kid feet and laughter race up the stairs. It wasn't clear who was chasing whom. Cleo pulled out two chairs. "Everything's ready. We have a half hour or so to rest. Tell me, how are you?"

Mary-Rose ignored the chair and resting. She paced. "I'm fine."

Cleo waited for a real answer.

Mary-Rose sighed. "I'm mad as a proverbial wet hen. That ridiculous Silas Culpepper has half the police in Georgia picking over my property. I was set to have such good business today too, what with the weather and, well . . ."

"And ghoulish gossips paying for pancakes with a view to a crime scene?" Cleo said, completing the sentence.

Mary-Rose sped up her walk and her words. "Folks are

already talking. They might as well do it while enjoying pancakes. This search is a waste of time."

Cleo got up to baste the ham. Mary-Rose was making her nervous, and not only because of her incessant circling. "I wonder if they'll find anything," Cleo mused, glasses steamed by the oven. Belatedly, she bit her tongue.

Mary-Rose stopped. *"If they'll find anything?* Good heavens, Cleo Jane. Over seven decades of friendship, and you think I might be a killer?" Mary-Rose's hands and voice shook, and she turned to stare out the French doors.

Cleo recalled other anxious times they'd weathered together. There was a winter long ago when Mary-Rose's then toddler son had a fever the doctors couldn't break. Poor Mary-Rose had been beyond worried and afraid, which came out as snappy and short-tempered. Maternal concern was understandable. Why was Mary-Rose so worked up now? Shock? Realization of a murder next door? Cleo refused to ponder less innocent possibilities. It was the stress, she told herself. Mary-Rose had been through a lot lately, between Buford's threats and her husband's surgery.

"Of course not," Cleo soothed, shoving the glistening ham back in the oven. "I only meant it's nerve-wracking, isn't it? You don't know what might be misinterpreted or found lying around. A blunt object covers a lot of ground."

Mary-Rose sighed and sunk into a chair. "Is that what they're looking for? I have loads of those. Fry pans. Mallets. Hammers. A baseball bat." She sighed. "I'm sorry I snapped at you, Cleo. I'm a tad on edge, if you couldn't tell."

Cleo poured Mary-Rose some restorative ice tea, the proper sweet kind.

Mary-Rose gulped half the glass. She put it down and traced lines in the condensation. "I wouldn't have minded whapping that annoying Krandall upside the head, but I didn't. You *do* believe me, don't you?"

"I do," Cleo said firmly and truthfully. "This search is good, if you think about it. Chief Culpepper can get a silly idea out of his head and move on. I'm sure the killer will be caught soon."

Mary-Rose scoffed. "Culpepper is methodical and clever, but I'll feel better when he finds another suspect to hound. You don't happen to know of any candidates, do you?"

Cleo detected another question behind Mary-Rose's words: *Was Cleo looking into suspects herself?* Cleo's skills in organization, research, and people-reading had proved useful for solving problems in the past. No, Cleo told herself firmly. She had a library to save. The police would do their job. She'd only asked Leanna to spy on the celebrations at Biscuit Bobs because Leanna was already there. Mary-Rose was innocent, and there were much better suspects. She informed her friend about the suspicious Biscuit Bobs celebration. "I told Gabby all about the happy mayor and widow. We'll soon know more," she said. "Leanna was there last night, keeping an eye and ear on the situation."

As if on cue, the doorbell chimed. Leanna stood on the porch, looking pretty in a retro polka-dot dress and matching oven mitts that gripped a deep casserole bowl. Before Cleo could quiz her, Fred and family pulled up. They all piled out of their car, converging with Henry and Mr. Chaucer.

Ideally, Cleo would have made introductions, but the buzzing oven timer pulled her back inside. She returned to the porch to find Fred frowning. She recognized the stubborn ruffled-feathers look her eldest got when refusing to comprehend. Dear Fred was like his father in so many ways. Fred liked routines and knowing everyone at the dinner table. He preferred things to stay the way they were, and he surely didn't think his widowed, senior-citizen mother might ever have a *male* friend.

Angela was covering for her husband's grumpiness with bright small talk. "So you're the owner of The Gilded Page, Mr. Lafayette? You've done lovely things with the shop's exterior. We'll have to stop in."

"An antique bookseller?" Fred enunciated the words slowly, as if the concept—and Henry's very presence—was incomprehensible. "So, you sell books to my mother's library? Is that why you're here, selling books?"

"No," Henry said. "I'm an, um . . . acquaintance."

Mr. Chaucer whimpered anxiously.

"He's a friend," Cleo said firmly. "Come in, everyone." The kids loped in first. Cleo gave the boys hugs, knowing any day they might hit the age of resistance. For Fred that period had lasted from ten until well into his twenties. Angela had done wonders for Fred, revitalizing his happiness after a traumatizing divorce at a young age and even loosening him up a tad. Cleo smiled at her daughter-in-law, thinking her an unlikely role model for loosening. Angela was a lawyer, briskly efficient and polished.

Cleo then properly greeted Henry, who was hanging back bashfully. "Your deviled eggs look angelic. And Mr. Chaucer, aren't you dapper?" The pug wore a silk bandana. The bit of fabric flair seemed to throw off Chaucer's already precarious balance. The old dog listed on his way down the hall to the kitchen.

Dot drove up next, and Angela sent Fred out to greet her. "Fred's a tad tense," Angela said in the few moments she and Cleo were alone in the foyer. "The washer started shooting water this morning, and the dog got skunked. It's an unfortunate combination."

Cleo expressed her sympathy. "And it's tax season," Cleo said. Her eldest boy was an accountant, following in his father's footsteps there too. Springtime filing deadlines hit Fred's nerves and back hard.

Angela sighed. "Indeed. Then add in all the sports the boys signed up for. Soccer, fencing, tennis, track. Honestly, it's exhausting. A nice low-key lunch will do us all good." She nudged Cleo and grinned. "Your *friend* Henry's a cutie. Don't worry—Fred'll come around."

* * *

Fred escorted his Auntie Dot straight from the door to the dining table. "Okay, it's noon. Food's ready. Where's Ollie?"

That Ollie was absent or late didn't surprise Cleo. "He wasn't sure if he could make it. We'll start. If he arrives late, he can fix a plate. I'll keep everything warm in the oven."

Cleo gave Fred the task of carving the ham, to distract him. Like his father before him, Fred couldn't stand mealtime tardiness and disruption. Dot plied the guests with aprons— Cleo owned dozens, thanks to Dot—and said grace. Everyone tucked in happily. Cleo gave thanks for family, friends, good food, and small talk that didn't involve murder.

Theo and Leon outlined their sports regime. Fred grudgingly grinned through a tale of the broken washer and stinky poodle combination. Henry impressed the kids with his knowledge of vintage comics. Leanna had everyone laughing about the woes of biscuit costumes and cheering for her interview at the bank. "Mrs. Givens is even going to help me dress the part," Leanna said with a nervous giggle. "She's going to lend me banker clothes."

Dot suggested Leanna add an apron to her outfit. "Money is filthy," the seasoned store owner said primly.

Ollie broke the jolly mood, strolling in as Fred was getting a second helping of ham and salty-sweet gravy.

"Where have you been?" Fred snapped.

"Sorry, Dad." Ollie swiped at a wavy lock that fell immediately back over his eyes. His jeans had muddy, frayed cuffs, and his T-shirt could have used a good bleaching. "Hi, Gran. Hi, everyone." He bounced on the soles of his sneakers, eagerly asking Cleo if it was okay to bring a guest. "Whitney," he whispered.

"Of course, how lovely," Cleo said politely.

"Whitney, this is everyone," Ollie said, waving in the scowling young woman. He ran through names and relations, ending with Rhett. ". . . and Rhett Butler, library cat. . . . One of us will have to steal his seat. Sorry, Rhett."

Whitney offered a bored "hi." Frizzy curls obscured her face but couldn't hide her surly expression. Cleo tried to think good thoughts. At least Whitney wasn't wearing waders or camo. She had on short jean shorts and a tank top, from which various bits and pieces of tattoos peeked out. Cleo thought she spotted a manatee with a knife, which begged questioning, but she wasn't about to ask. From mortifying past experience, Cleo knew guessing a tattoo incorrectly was as bad as misreading a little extra belly padding as pregnancy.

"Let's get you plates," Cleo said. In the kitchen, she directed the two twenty-somethings to the bountiful buffet. "Ham, cheesy grits, and mac and cheese in the oven. Green beans on the stove, and potato salad, fruit salad, and deviled eggs. There's cornbread too and pie for dessert."

"Awesome," Ollie said, beaming and blushing.

Oh dear, Cleo thought. Ollie seemed head over heels.

Ollie helped himself to big portions of everything. "Gran's the best cook," he said to Whitney, whose plate remained empty.

"Meat," she said with a curl of distaste to her lip.

Cleo's hostess smile faltered. "You're a vegetarian? Mac and cheese then? Grits?"

Whitney scowled down her prodigious beak of a nose. "Does the corn glop have exploited dairy products in it?"

"The grits?" Ollie interpreted nervously. "Yeah, they probably have some butter."

Cleo didn't bother mentioning the cheese, since Whitney was already wrinkling her nose over the green beans and muttering about hog fat. Cleo had no problem with vegetarians or vegans or those with allergies or special diets or who somehow didn't enjoy bacon in their beans. What she couldn't tolerate was rudeness.

"I guess you'll be having fruit salad then," Cleo said crisply. She returned to the table, where Fred sawed at his ham in a sullen silence. Mary-Rose was discussing peacocks with boisterous overenthusiasm. Zoe seemed to be lecturing Henry and the twins on the ways of dragons.

"So, Ollie finally has a girlfriend," Dot declared in a volume that cut over the dragons, peacocks, and silence, and surely carried to the kitchen.

Ollie and Whitney squished in at the end of the table, dislodging Rhett. Whitney picked resentfully at fruit and grudgingly gave spare answers to Dot's questions. Was she from Catalpa? No. Nearby? No. Was she here for work? Kinda. Was she enjoying Catalpa Springs? A shrug.

Cleo returned to the kitchen for more comforting mac and cheese. Henry followed, saying he was after grits and ham.

"I apologize," Cleo whispered. "I promised you a relaxing lunch."

Henry smiled and mock-whispered back. "These things can happen. I'm having a lovely time. I'll need a nap after all this wonderful food."

Cleo thought a nap might be good in any case. She was just sitting back down when the doorbell rang. Fred huffed. Ollie kept eating. Angela, nearest the window said, "It's a police car. A young woman. Your neighbor, Cleo?"

Mary-Rose dropped her fork. Ollie stopped shoveling grits.

"I did invite Gabby. Perhaps she found time after all." Cleo got up, along with Whitney, who was suddenly enthusiastic about fruit.

Gabby was in uniform, her cap in her hand and her face serious. "Come in!" Cleo said. "We're all in the dining room. Will you have some lunch? Dessert? We'll cut into Mary-Rose's wonderful pies soon." She felt oddly nervous in her own home.

Gabby stopped at the dining room threshold. No one was eating except Fred, who was determinedly chewing, making his father's point that meals should not be disturbed. Cleo realized how silly they must look, everyone decked out in aprons except the cat and dog, though Mr. Chaucer did have on a bandana. "We have an apron for you, Gabby," she joked. Gabby didn't smile back. She told Cleo she was sorry.

"Mrs. Garland?" Gabby said looking beyond Cleo. "Would you please come outside with me?"

Mary-Rose bristled. Red flared behind her freckles. "No. I am eating lunch with my friends. Whatever it is, it can wait."

"It can't." Gabby's expression breached no debate. "Ma'am, our divers found something in Pancake Spring. If you don't come willingly, I've been ordered to arrest you."

Sergeant Tookey appeared at her side. "What's taking so long? Oh . . ." The big baby-faced man rubbed his belly. His eyes lingered on plates and platters and glanced over guests, then snapped back to Zoe. Mary-Rose's granddaughter slouched in seven-year-old boredom, fiddling with what looked like a string of small beads. "What do you have there, sweetie?" Tookey asked, taking a step closer.

Mary-Rose's complexion went from fevered to ashen. "Leave her alone."

"Pearls," Zoe was already answering. She shot a scowl at Tookey. "It was supposed to be a surprise. Look, they're yours, Nana. Look, I found them where you dropped them." Zoe dug in her pockets and proudly produced more lumpy natural pearls.

"What a nice surprise," Tookey drawled with pointed sweetness. "We found some pearls too. In Krandall House. Where'd your granny drop these?"

"In the library at Mr. Creepy Crankpot's house after he shot at Nana." Zoe said.

"Who wants pie?" Cleo practically bellowed, clapping her hands.

But Zoe's words were out. Gabby produced an evidence bag. "It's okay," she told Zoe. "We'll just borrow these. They'll be safe. So will you. That man can't scare you or your grandmother again."

"I know," Zoe said, matter-of-factly. "Nana says he's gone away. She means he's dead."

"My lawyer will eat you for lunch for upsetting a child," Mary-Rose declared, waving a chastising finger in the direction of Tookey. Her chair scraped against the floor planks as she stood and tore off her apron. She sweetly asked Cleo to watch Zoe, before striding out so fast, Gabby and Tookey had to jog to catch up. The front door slammed.

"Who's her lawyer?" Angela asked, breaking the stunned silence around the table.

"Thurgood Byron, most likely," Cleo said. "He does all their business paperwork and—"

Angela was the next guest whipping off her apron and heading for the door with lawyerly urgency. "Bless his heart, but Thurgood Byron is not the man for a murder defense. I'll just go and see if she needs any extra help."

Ollie looked around wildly. "Whitney?" He dashed to the kitchen. The back door slammed seconds later.

Zoe slid under the table to sulk with Rhett. Fred threw down his napkin in frustration.

"Pie?" Cleo asked. Only Theo and Leon took her up on it.

Chapter Eight

When the dishes were cleared and the kitchen tidied and all the other guests were gone, Henry and Cleo took Zoe and the pets to Fontaine Park. They chose a shaded bench near the fountain the park was named after. Clear spring-fed waters pirouetted up and over three fluted tiers into a shimmering stone pool. A soft breeze kept the heat at bay. Zoe swung across the monkey bars at the nearby play area, Mr. Chaucer snoozed flat out on his back, and Rhett perched on a low-hanging oak limb. It should have been relaxing.

Cleo checked the time. Where was Angela? She stared beyond the dancing waters, eyeing the police station, willing her lawyer daughter-in-law to emerge with Mary-Rose in tow.

"Honestly, you don't have to wait," she told Henry again when the church bells announced another half hour had passed. She felt bad for entangling him in yet more troubles.

"I'm happy to," he said. He stretched out his legs. "It's a lovely day for the park. Angela and Mary-Rose will surely be out soon, and I have a feeling we'll learn something interesting."

Interesting wasn't necessarily good. Cleo noticed Rhett flattening his body to the branch. She understood why when a bark boomed over them. Beast, the mastiff, rounded the fountain, dragging Kat Krandall-Stykes behind him. The new widow looked far from merry. Her long braid hung limp, and her unheeded canine-obedience commands sounded half-hearted. Beast stopped at the fountain, seemingly aiming to lap up the entire pool. Mr. Chaucer belatedly awoke with a sneeze and wobbled over to watch in awe.

"Kat, I'm so sorry," Cleo said, noting the woman's bloodshot eyes. She wasn't sure if Kat was grieving or hungover or both.

Kat sniffled and, to Cleo's surprise, teared up.

Henry offered his pocket square.

"No thanks, that's way too nice," Kat said. She fished a crumpled paper towel from her overalls and swiped it across her reddened nose. "Why would she go and do that? Why kill him? He was mine."

Cleo and Henry exchanged a look. "She? Who, dear?" Cleo asked.

Beast, showing uncharacteristic sensitivity, came over to drool on Kat's boot. She rested a hand on his broad head. "The Garland woman. I heard she's been hauled in by the police. People are saying she killed my Buford. Why? They were just one-upping each other like he and I did. Like when she got those peacocks to scare him. That was a good move. He hated those birds. Said they sounded like alien wolves." A half smile twitched.

Cleo repeated her firm belief in Mary-Rose's innocence. "You said yourself how Buford liked digging into dirty laundry.

He got a lot of folks upset, not only Mary-Rose." It seemed a terrible thing to say of the recently deceased, but it was true.

"Yeah," Kat mumbled. "I know. Honestly, I hope it isn't the pancake lady. I like that place and her."

"We all do," Cleo said. "Now, let's think. Who else might have been upset with your husband?"

To Cleo's admiration, Henry produced a small notebook and pencil from his jacket pocket to record what turned into a lengthy list. There was the previous mayor, whom Buford also disliked with a passion. A dermatologist, sued for not removing Buford's then benign mole. A mailman, fired for refusing to deliver to Krandall House, which he swore to be demonically possessed. A florist, teachers, strangers, several grocery clerks, children, boaters, a falconer . . . "Buford shot at the falcon," Kat said. "You could put birds on the list too." She sniffed loudly and teared up afresh.

"You'll miss him," Cleo said, reading true sorrow in Kat.

"Yeah," Kat said, rubbing Beast's floppy ears. "I *will* miss him. You'll think it's weird, but I'll miss our divorce. It ended too soon. I was going to soak him for everything he had, so help me—"

Church bells rang across the park, covering Kat's lengthy outburst. She stuffed the sodden paper towel back into her overalls.

"Won't you get everything now anyway?" Henry asked gently. "You were still married."

Kat uttered a fresh string of curses. "I'll be lucky to get a dime. He always said he was making a will and leaving everything to anyone but me."

Cleo asked, but Kat claimed not to know where the will

81

might be or who would be the beneficiary. Kat flicked Beast's leash, as if activating a stagecoach pony. "We should go. No time for moping. I have a funeral and reception to plan. A proper send-off. The coroner says he can spring the body by next Sunday. Save the date!"

"Oh dear," said Henry—Cleo's sentiments exactly.

*　　*　　*

They sat for almost another hour. Cleo was drifting into a snooze, when Henry said, "Look, is that Mayor Day heading for the police station?"

Cleo blinked. She focused in on gaudy Bermuda shorts, a flash of pale male leg, and a fishing rod. That was their mayor all right. She asked Henry if he'd mind watching Zoe and Rhett.

Henry was happy to oblige. "Just don't get in any trouble. There are already too many people stuck inside that station today."

Cleo had no intention of getting stuck. She intended to get answers.

"Ah, Miss Cleo," Mayor Jeb Day said as she climbed the police station steps. He stood at the top, stalled by his ever-present phone and looking too pleased for Cleo's comfort. A fishing license dangled from a cord around his neck. "A big day for bluegill out on the river," he declared. "I hear our Chief Culpepper's landed an even bigger catch. Our killer. She's your pal, isn't she?"

"Mary-Rose is merely helping the police with inquiries," Cleo said crisply. "She is not a killer."

The young mayor smiled, more smug than sympathetic.

"I'm sorry. I'm sure it's upsetting when an *old* friend does something stupid like getting nabbed for murder. But everyone knows Mary-Rose Garland can get emotional. She was likely hysterical when it happened. A good lawyer could spin that as a psychotic breakdown. What this town needs now is to move on." He turned and headed into the building.

Cleo hustled after him, the foyer's arctic air-conditioning doing little to cool her temper. She forced sweetness into her tone. "You're right about moving on, Mayor. Now you can too. Mr. Krandall was pestering you, wasn't he? What was that all about again?"

Jeb Day spun so fast, his fishing license nearly bopped Cleo's nose. "Me and Buford Krandall? I hadn't spoken with that crackpot in ages."

Cleo held her ground. "It was something personal, wasn't it? I'll have to ask your Aunt Wanda." As a neighbor, Wanda Boxer could be nosy and disapproving and downright disturbing in her gardening. However, she knew every bit of town gossip, especially regarding City Hall, where she'd worked for decades. She also loved to talk about her nephew, the mayor.

"Aunt Wanda minds her own business," Jeb Day sputtered, as truthful as claiming snow on fire. "You'd do well to mind yours too, if you want to keep that bookmobile on the road." He stomped off, sneakers squeaking over shiny marble tiles.

Had she just been threatened in the police station? Cleo gaped as the mayor stormed by reception and pushed through a door marked "Employees Only."

Cleo followed the rules. Usually. She approached the reception desk. A woman sat behind it, chewing gum with loud enthusiasm. The receptionist blew a bubble, sucked it in, and said, "Welcome to the Catalpa Springs Police Department. How can we assist your safety today?"

Cleo recognized that bored tone. "I spoke with you the other day. You answered my 911 call reporting the trouble at Krandall House. You were *so* much help." She hadn't been, of course, but Cleo believed minor fibs were acceptable if complimentary and encouraging of better behavior. While the young woman chewed on that information, Cleo read her nametag: "Jayleen."

"Oh, yeah . . ." Jayleen said, stretching the words in slow realization, as if Catalpa Springs got so many murder calls they blurred together. "I was filling in that day. Reception's easier but dull as dirt. Anyway, like I was saying, how may the Catalpa Springs Police Department help—"

Cleo cut in, wondering how many times Jayleen would repeat the same line. "You can help me check on a friend. Two friends. Lawyer Angela Watkins and a *witness* giving a statement, Mrs. Mary-Rose Garland."

Jayleen blew a half-formed bubble. She sucked back the purple skin, frowning with mental effort. "The lawyer lady? Yeah, she's in there. She snapped at me. Told me to hurry up."

Hurrying up sounded like Angela. Cleo wished she dared demand the same. "And the other lady, Mrs. Garland? I assume she's still with her lawyers?"

"Gray-red hair, freckles, kind of strung out and excitable, like?"

It pained Cleo to agree to the description.

"Last I noticed, she was getting hauled off toward booking." Jayleen pointed toward the "Employees Only" door. She chewed vigorously, then followed with a gasp so loud Cleo worried she might be choking. "Hey, do you think *she's* the murder? Doesn't look the type, does she? You never can tell." Jayleen narrowed her eyes at Cleo, seemingly assessing criminal intentions.

"Booking," Cleo said firmly. "Does that mean she's under arrest?"

Jayleen had fallen back into boredom. "Probably. Locked up, key thrown away, and all that." The gum snapped and so did Cleo, who skirted Jayleen's desk and headed for booking.

"Hey!" Jayleen called, "Stop! You can't go in there. I'm calling the police."

Inside, Cleo did stop. Striding up the disorienting, glossy-tiled hallway was her daughter-in-law. Angela's sleek shoulder-length hair swung along with her shaking head.

"Ridiculous," Angela declared, as if finding Cleo was nothing to question. She caught Cleo's elbow and spun her around.

In the lobby, Jayleen was complaining loudly into her headset. "Wait," she said, pointing to Cleo and Angela. "Forget it. The old lady just came out. No, not the murdering old lady. The short one with fluffy white hair. She must have gotten confused. That snippy lawyer lady's helping her outside."

Cleo didn't have time to be offended. Angela marched them out the doors, where she stopped, leaned on the railing, and closed her eyes to the sun.

"I'm guessing it didn't go well?" Cleo said.

The usually unflappable Angela snorted. "In all my time as a lawyer, I've rarely encountered such infuriating behavior."

Cleo guessed immediately. "Mayor Day. He *is* most infuriating."

Her daughter-in-law shook her head, engrossed in searching her briefcase-like purse.

While Angela muttered about finding her cell phone, Cleo guessed again. "The chief? Silas Culpepper does drone on."

Angela had found her phone and was holding it to her ear. "Good guess. That man can be an explainer, but no, he was quite reasonable, considering."

"Thurgood Byron, then," Cleo said. *Really, who else was there?*

Angela apologized and tapped out a text message. "Sorry," she said, dropping the phone back in her purse. "Fred left me four texts and two voicemails. No, not Thurgood Byron. He's a dear, but bless his heart, he's gotten downright distracted. He would *not* stop talking about cases he's taken on at that gated community where he lives. What's it called? Happy Trails? Sounds morbid. Like when you tell kids their hamster went to live in the country."

"Mostly it's nice," said Cleo, who was suspicious of Happy Trails for other reasons. For one, its full name was Happy Trails *Retirement* Village. And for another, part of the property crept over the border into Florida. "Thurgood means well."

Angela smoothed her hair, sleek and immaculate even under stress. "Yes, we heard all about his good intentions. He's suing the Happy Trails homeowners association for a larger hot tub. He's also representing residents who want cocktails served at three thirty so they can be good and toasted by the four-thirty early-bird dining hour. He had a client facing down a murder charge—murder!—and he was complaining the gin and tonics didn't have enough oomph!" Angela pursed her lips. "Listen to me, meandering from the subject just like he was.

You asked who was infuriating?" Angela smiled apologetically. "Mary-Rose Garland."

"She can be stubborn," Cleo said, her heartbeat quickening.

"She's that. She let me stay as backup assistant to Thurgood. I completely respect that. I'd never, ever horn in on another lawyer's client. But then, against both Thurgood's and my advice, your friend confessed."

Cleo gripped the railing. It felt hot, burning into her hands, but she didn't let go. "Confessed? To what?"

"Sabotaging Buford Krandall's drilling machine. She was all clammed up, perfectly lovely behavior. Then Culpepper asked about her hobbies—book clubs, social clubs, activism. It's the kind of question police throw out to loosen up interviewees. Well, she loosened, all right! She opened her mouth and wouldn't shut it. She admitted to destroying Mr. Krandall's drill. She said they'd fought earlier in the day. A yelling match only, until he shot at her, aiming over her head at an empty bookshelf. After that, they got into a tussle and her pearls broke, like little Zoe said. Mary-Rose said she was so angry, she came back after dark and killed his drill. The police want to talk to Zoe as a key witness. They're trying to get her parents' permission. Where are they anyway? Mary-Rose did shush up again about them."

"Hiking in Europe," Cleo said, purposefully vague. Zoe's parents—Mary-Rose's son and daughter-in-law—were on a long-awaited and scrimped-for honeymoon in Spain. They'd fly home on the first plane, frantic, if they thought Mary-Rose or Zoe needed them. That wouldn't help anyone.

Cleo braced herself and asked, "Surely Mary-Rose didn't

confess to murder? And what did the police find in the spring that got them so suspicious?"

Angela had pulled keys from her purse, getting ready to go. "No, no murder confession, thank heavens! As for the spring, they found an arm."

Seeing Cleo's shock, Angela hurriedly clarified. "A stone arm. Marble. Probably from one of those statues at Krandall House. It wasn't too far into the spring. Someone could've easily chucked it in from the boardwalk."

Cleo groaned. She looked out to the park, where Zoe and Henry were swinging. Two sets of feet sailed skyward, soaring over a bobble-head pug. An orange tail twitched from a branch. "The chief will say that Mary-Rose was angry and scared," Cleo said dismally. "If she lashed out at the machine, she might strike a man." Especially *that* man.

"Exactly what Culpepper's saying," Angela said. "He had his suspenders in a twist, claiming Mary-Rose should be held for murder. It's a bluff. They'll let her out on the minor trespassing charges until there's firmer evidence. The bigger trouble is that the investigation will focus on her now. She does have an obvious motive, and she admitted to getting in a fight with the victim and vandalizing his property. If it turned really bad, a good lawyer could argue self-defense. Krandall did shoot at her." Angela squared her shoulders. "Don't worry, Cleo. I'll help her all I can. All she'll let me."

So would Cleo, and she wouldn't give Mary-Rose a choice in the matter.

Chapter Nine

When Ollie was little, he often went missing. Not seriously, but enough to give his mother fits. Miki—Cleo's first and forever daughter-in-law, whatever her flaws—might turn to the refrigerator, and in that moment, toddler Ollie would barrel toward the nearest escape hatch. In kindergarten, he'd strayed so frequently, his teacher had suggested an ankle monitor. His parents settled for a bell, until it became clear that bells attract bullies.

By elementary school, Ollie was wandering like a romantic poet. He'd follow pretty streams or lanes, forgetting the time. He'd pick wildflower bouquets. "I just wanted a few more," he'd explain, handing his frazzled mother fistfuls of flowers. "I wanted to see around the bend."

Cleo's dear, punctual husband, Richard, tried to step in. He taught Ollie to use a compass and read maps and navigate by the sun and stars. He gave Ollie watches for Christmas and birthdays. Ollie not only lost track of time, he also lost timepieces. Richard eventually gave up, once privately confessing to Cleo, "The boy might have something loose in the head."

Ollie was just fine, Cleo thought, walking to his backyard cottage the next morning. He was smart and generous and appreciated beauty and nature. He just hadn't found his calling yet, his direction. Cleo approached his door, newly painted periwinkle blue, a pretty contrast to the yellow cottage with crisp white trim. It was past nine on a Monday. Most folks would be up by now. Cleo feared it was still early for her grandson. She gave the horseshoe knocker several hardy whacks.

While she waited, Cleo did some gardening. She tugged at a dandelion and deadheaded geraniums in the flower boxes. She put her nose to her favorite shrub, the sweet olive. The unremarkable little flowers emitted perfume so intoxicating as to be nearly overpowering. Cleo was blissfully sniffing when her eyes fell on something much less appealing. An air-potato vine hovered over her back fence, an escapee from the old citrus grove returning to wild behind her property. Cleo's eyes narrowed. *Hate* was a word Cleo was loath to use, except when it came to air potatoes. The vine was like armed kudzu, its spuds dropping and sprouting like alien spawn. *Spawn* was another word Cleo avoided. It seemed unsavory, but then so was air potato.

She knocked again, with a vigor instilled by the vile vine and questions needing answers. She was about to give up and retrieve her longest garden clippers, when a muffled "Coming" came from the cottage.

Ollie, tousle haired and sleepy eyed, opened the door a crack. "Gran?" He wore cotton pajama bottoms and a rumpled T-shirt.

"Good, you're awake," Cleo said brightly. She stepped

inside and blinked into the dark interior. She couldn't say she loved what Ollie had done with the place. Papers covered the sofa, along with a massive rucksack and various items of camouflage clothing. Banana peels, an apple core, and a wilted salad in a plastic container littered the coffee table. *Better than junk food and beer bottles,* Cleo supposed. The snake plant by the door was yellowed and wrinkly, and those were hard to kill. Cleo couldn't stand to see houseplants suffer. She headed to the kitchen for water and realized it was already running in the shower down the hall.

"Oh," she said. "You have a guest?"

Ollie likely blushed, though it was impossible to tell with the heavy drapes drawn. Cleo tugged them open, gave the plant a drink, and by the time she turned, Ollie was clearing armfuls of papers and clothes from the sofa. He stuffed most of them under the coffee table, a young man's version of tidying.

"Please don't bother cleaning," Cleo said—another polite fib. "I just need to ask you something."

Ollie went the few steps to the kitchen, where he ran water over dirty pans and filled the coffee pot. Down the hall, a female voice yelled about "freezing" shower water. Ollie loped off to soothe his sputtering houseguest.

By conventions of mannerly visiting, Cleo knew she should excuse herself and leave. She disregarded decorum and settled herself on the sofa. Ollie returned and crashed about with dishes.

"Whitney needed a place to stay," he said, back still turned.

"That's nice of you," Cleo said. "I'll enjoy getting to know her better."

Ollie poured coffee, sloshing some onto the counter. He apologized for running off from yesterday's lunch. "Whitney remembered . . . no, *we* remembered we had . . . uh . . . something urgent," he stammered.

The sweet boy is a terrible liar, Cleo thought, watching him bump around his tiny kitchen.

"Whitney loved lunch," Ollie continued in a most blatant untruth. He brought Cleo a mug and perched on the coffee table, shoving aside some mess.

"This is lovely coffee," Cleo said, which was true and made Ollie smile. The shower shut off with a clanking of pipes. Cleo wanted to talk to Ollie before Whitney brought her disapproving presence. She dove right in.

"Ollie, what have you and your girlfriend been doing out at Pancake Spring?" A paper crumpled in the sofa cushions at Cleo's side. She pulled it out and then another, all trifolded flyers.

Ollie's cheeks blazed hotter. "She's not my *girlfriend*, Gran," he said.

Cleo shifted uncomfortably, recalling her own similar protests regarding Henry. "Then what have you and your *friend* been doing? When I saw you at the Pancake Mill the other day, you and Mary-Rose were awfully evasive. The situation is serious now, Oliver. Murder. The police will find out, whatever it is. Tell me, is it something to do with your environmental interests? Your volunteering?"

"That's it," Ollie said. He piled a stack of magazines over loose papers, making his coffee-table clutter taller. "We're helping Mary-Rose with spring stuff. We're, uh, getting rid of freshwater invasive weeds."

Her grandson was an innocent lamb if he believed invasive weeds could be *gotten rid of.* Cleo wondered if Ollie had spoken to Mary-Rose, if he knew of her absurd confession. A confession blurted, Angela said, when the police asked Mary-Rose about her hobbies, activities, and *activism.* Cleo suspected there was more to the goings-on at Pancake Spring than pulling weeds.

She smoothed the papers retrieved from the sofa cushions and was about to add them to the coffee table piles, when text caught her eye. *S.O.S. Save Our Springs. Radical action for the preservation of Pancake Spring.*

She unfolded a page. Ollie reached for the rest. "Sorry for the mess," he said, his voice strained. "Here, I'll take that and throw it out."

Cleo kept the flyer firmly in hand. " 'Save our springs,' " she read. She added a smile, hoping to put her grandson at ease. "Catchy. So this is what you're doing? Are you taking radical action against invasive hyacinth? Alligator weed? I could help. You know my campaign against air-potato vine knows no bounds."

He grinned, but the smile faded with the arrival of Whitney. She stomped down the short hall, decked out in baggy camo pants and a black tank top. She shot Ollie a dark look.

Cleo raised her coffee cup in greeting. "Good morning. I hope I didn't stop by too early." Her nicety wasn't returned.

"I was up," Whitney said. She went to the kitchen, where she finished off the coffee pot and banged it back into the machine unrinsed. Cleo studied her, her gaze bordering on a stare as she tried to place the young woman. She got nothing except that unsettled feeling again, like déjà vu.

"Where did you say you're from again, Whitney?" Cleo asked pleasantly. Whitney hadn't actually said when questioned by cousin Dot yesterday at lunch.

"Not here."

"And your relations?" Cleo persisted, as Dot too had tried.

"Nowhere. My dad moved a lot," Whitney snapped, eyes flashing a stop-bugging-me warning.

"She's with S.O.S.," Ollie offered. "Head of the southeast division, but she's gone all over the country saving water, right, Whit?"

Whitney's glare could have chilled a sizzling griddle.

"S.O.S. is an environmental group, devoted to clean water," Ollie continued.

"How nice," Cleo said, in her best grandmotherly tones. She pushed herself up from the couch, tucking the S.O.S. flyer in her pocket of her light cotton slacks. "Ollie, would you mind walking me back to the house? My knees . . . must be the weather." Cleo rubbed her knees for emphasis. They did ache a little in the mornings.

Whitney sighed and reminded Ollie of the time. "We need to get a move on, like, now."

"Okay," Ollie said, sounding torn.

Cleo felt bad, making him choose. She was about to cave and tell him she was fine.

"I'll just be a minute," Ollie said. "I'll walk Gran home and be ready to go as soon as I change, okay?"

Cleo turned to say goodbye to Whitney at the door. The girl was gone. Noises of slamming doors and drawers came from down the hall.

94

"I've disturbed your morning and your guest," Cleo said once outside.

Ollie assured her that she hadn't. "Whitney's amazing," he gushed as they made their way to the main house. "She's kind of shy about all she does and where she's from. She's not from anyplace in particular. She's moved all over—California, Washington, Idaho. She was in Connecticut a couple years and then went down to Florida last year to protect some other springs and manatees. When she learned about the drilling threatening Pancake Spring, she shot up here, ready to help."

"She found out about the drilling so quickly?" Cleo asked. "How?"

Ollie's grip on her elbow tightened. "I think Mary-Rose found S.O.S. online and contacted them. Whitney came up to do reconnaissance. She was going to bring in S.O.S. reinforcements, but the spring looks okay now. The machine is gone and so is Krandall."

Cleo worried about Ollie and his happy-go-lucky tone. They'd reached Cleo's porch. Rhett lay on the porch swing, gently swaying. The movement reminded Cleo of Buford Krandall's rocker.

She took her grandson's hand in both of hers. "Ollie," she said, "have you spoken with Mary-Rose or Angela since yesterday?"

His headshake confirmed her suspicion. "I tried calling Mary-Rose last night, but she didn't answer. I've kinda been avoiding Dad and Angela."

Cleo looked up at Ollie, who was taller than her by many

inches and backlit by the sun. "Mary-Rose was arrested and only got out last night. The police think they found the murder weapon in Pancake Spring."

"What?" Ollie said, swiping at his hair. "*In* the spring? Like the spring is a trash bin? Nature's dumpster?"

It was the shock, Cleo told herself. Shock victims often talked gibberish. "Oliver, this is serious. Mary-Rose confessed to destruction of property. She said *she* vandalized Mr. Krandall's drilling machine. You don't know anything about that, do you?"

"She confessed?" Ollie's eyes widened. "But she, we—"

A silhouette appeared behind Ollie. Shorter, ringed in frizzy hair, and bristling. "No, he doesn't know anything about that."

Cleo gave Whitney credit. The camouflage pants worked well. She'd come around the house without Cleo noticing her and stood, fists on hips, frowning intensely at Ollie.

"No, I—we—don't know anything about that," Ollie said. He scuffed dusty sandals, his head down and hair covering his eyes. His tone became defiant. "Whoever destroyed that machine did everyone and the spring and wildlife a favor. That's probably why Mary-Rose said what she said. The police will figure out that she couldn't have done it. Mary-Rose is strong—like you, Gran—but she couldn't lug that heavy steel bar out there, let alone jamb it through those cogs."

Cleo gasped. "Oliver, how do you know—"

Her query was cut off. "Ollie, come on," Whitney snapped, her tone glacial. "We've got to go. Business."

They left, Ollie loping alongside Whitney's stomping stride. Cleo waited until she heard the cottage door slam and lock. She heard another sound too. Gabby Honeywell looked over their shared fence. The deputy held a dandelion, but she didn't try to pretend she was gardening.

Gabby gave voice to Cleo's question and more. "How did he know how much that bar weighed? How'd he know about the cog? What's S.O.S.?"

Chapter Ten

Cleo didn't often give thanks for Wanda Boxer as a neighbor. Wanda was a meddler, a gossip, and an all-around difficult person, not unlike her nephew, Mayor Day. Now, however, Cleo could have hugged Wanda for interrupting Gabby's questioning. Wanda, stout and stormy, with a helmet of yellow-gold, spray-stiffened hair, stomped across Cleo's herb garden. She brought with her an air of Monday morning righteousness and the invigorating scent of crushed thyme and rosemary.

"That bus is an eyesore!" Wanda declared. She pointed to Words on Wheels, sitting sunnily in Cleo's driveway, mostly under the cover of trees and always beautiful. "We have rules. Rules about RVs and trailers and boats, and buses with flame graffiti on them should be included in those rules."

"So we do have rules." Cleo smiled brightly, knowing she hadn't broken any. She politely offered Wanda coffee.

"I have acid reflux," Wanda snapped. "You know that, Cleo. What are you trying to do, give me heartburn before work?"

Wanda worked in Human Resources at City Hall. Cleo thought the job an unlikely fit, given that Wanda didn't show any liking of humans.

Gabby narrowed her eyes, looking toward the pretty little cottage in Cleo's backyard. The periwinkle door and the curtains were again shut tight.

How *did* Ollie know about the machine? Cleo wanted to find out, preferably before Gabby and her colleagues did. "I'd better move my bookmobile," she said with false cheer. "I'm off to work too. I'm meeting a contractor at the library. Busy, busy." She made motions to leave, though she did feel sorry leaving Gabby with Wanda.

There would be complaints, many of which Cleo had already heard. The UPS man drove too fast and honked his horn too aggressively. The couple up the street turned on a questionable number of lights. Wanda was sure they were marijuana growers. Then there was the high-pitched keening that Wanda kept hearing, yet no one else seemed able to detect. Cleo thought it might be Wanda's own head about to explode, but she kept that theory to herself.

"I'll need to talk with you later," Gabby said to Cleo.

Cleo would never evade Gabby, who was just doing her job. "Of course. Until then, you have the perfect person to speak to right here. Wanda knows *everything* that goes on in City Hall. Absolutely everything."

Wanda couldn't help agreeing. "I do. No one knows more about City Hall happenings than me."

"She's your gal!" Cleo said encouragingly. "Wanda, tell Gabby all about that Las Vegas gambling consultant your nephew hired. Jimmy Teeks. Did I hear a rumor that Mr. Teeks has *mob* connections?" It wasn't a lie. There was such a wild rumor. Cleo had started it by speculating to Henry. Even if he kept it to himself, it was still a valid rumor. She spelled Jimmy's name for Gabby, speaking loudly over Wanda's sputtering protests.

Gabby was making a note.

Cleo took a breath, in preparation for dusting off her poker bluffing skills. "And then there are Mayor Day's troubles with Buford Krandall. Didn't those two meet several times? Three? Four?"

"There was only one meeting with that awful Krandall," snapped Wanda, who loved to correct. "No more! After that, the security guard was ordered to keep Krandall out. Just because City Hall is a public building doesn't mean you have to let everyone in."

"Is that so?" Gabby had her pen poised for more notes. Cleo waved goodbye, hurrying to her house to collect her purse, cat, and the keys to Words on Wheels.

* * *

Cleo pulled the bookmobile over just a few blocks away, parking in front of the Catalpa Springs Public Library. She sat a moment, admiring the lush, though overgrown, garden and remembering Mondays past. How she loved her first step inside, when the foyer was still dark, and the air smelled of books, ink on paper, and fresh promise. Not today. The front door was blocked by hazard tape. The blue tarp slapped at the roof, as if mocking her.

Rhett meowed and pawed the door to be let out. "You wait a moment, Rhett," Cleo said. She rattled a container of tuna treats, and he bounded back up the steps. While he was purring and crunching, Cleo slipped his harness around his shoulders. The library was still a hazard. That's why they were here, to get an honest estimate from the Givens's contractor.

At the click of the harness, Rhett stiffened and promptly collapsed onto his side.

"Come now," Cleo said to the dramatic Persian. Rhett continued to play stricken. His legs and tail stuck out straight. His belly heaved, and his face pinched deeper into a resentful, sour frown. Bits of uneaten kibble lay at his whiskers. Rhett detested his harness and made sure those feelings were well known.

Cleo opened the doors to temptations of birds, green grass, and geckos. If Rhett didn't budge, she'd scoop him up and carry him. Rhett's tail twitched and nothing more. Cleo was bending to lift her cat when she sensed they weren't alone. She looked up to see Bitsy Givens in a flowery sundress.

"My goodness, look at you," Bitsy drawled in faux horror to Rhett.

"What's wrong with that cat?" Maybelle Givens appeared behind Bitsy like a cranky shrunken shadow in a black tracksuit. "*Is* it a cat? What happened to its fur? Looks like it has termites."

Cleo scooped Rhett up protectively. "He's fine," she said, grimacing as Rhett employed his claws to heft himself up so his chest balanced on her shoulder.

"I'm not fine," Maybelle declared. "My corns are the size of peanuts, and I'm getting dragged out to a destruction site."

Cleo hugged her Rhett closer, disturbed not only by Maybelle's foot imagery but the sight beyond. Leanna teetered toward them, hobbled in tippy heels, a look of distressed determination on her young face.

Bitsy had the opposite reaction. "Isn't Leanna looking darling? I dolled her up for her interview earlier this morning, and it worked. She got the job!" Bitsy clapped. Leanna wobbled faster, ankles turning such that Cleo cringed.

Leanna, a year-round devotee of flip-flops, wore spiky heels and a tight-fitting suit coat and skirt combination that looked more uncomfortable than her biscuit costume. Her honey hair hung in bouncy curls, and mascara obscured her eyes.

"Congratulations, Leanna," Cleo said, happy for the job if not her unwieldy attire. "When do you start?"

"Tomorrow." Leanna grabbed the bus and gripped onto the handrail as if for dear life. Once stabilized, she brightened. "I'm so excited. It's perfect. I can't thank Mr. and Mrs. Givens enough. It's part-time, so I can keep up my shelving duties for Words on Wheels, and no more biscuit suits!"

"You are such a doll!" Bitsy patted Leanna on the shoulder, compromising her shaky balance. "Vernon should never have hired that former assistant of his. She was lazy and unorganized. His files are a mess."

"She was cute," Maybelle muttered. "Hot, actually."

Bitsy's beaming momentarily flickered. "You're cute, Mama Givens. Let's get you resting in the car so I can take Cleo over to the library. Vern's already inside with our contractor, DeWayne Patterson. DeWayne will give you a good, honest estimate on your repairs."

"I don't want to rest," Maybelle said, as pouty as Rhett.

"I want a book." Her mouth kept moving after the final word. Cleo smelled the cinnamon heat of gum.

"I want my library fines forgiven too," Maybelle said, dark eyes gleaming. "You don't have a real, working library. I shouldn't have to pay."

Rhett's claws needled Cleo's shoulder. Cleo took it as a warning. "Okay, we can forgive your fines," Cleo said out of gratitude for Vernon's and Bitsy's generosity toward the library and Leanna. "But no more folding down pages to mark your place, Maybelle, or I'll have to ban you for good. And absolutely no gum allowed on the bookmobile."

Maybelle snorted. "You can't ban me or my gum. My son's bank president. He's helping you out and hired your friend here who can't walk right."

"I'll practice," Leanna said in a small voice.

Bitsy intervened. "I'll show her the ways of heels, Mama. It's all a matter of believing you can, like anything."

Cleo reached into her purse and handed Maybelle a Catalpa Springs Library bookmark and a tissue, the latter intended for the gum.

Maybelle defiantly decorated the bookmark in a gummy pink glob and folded the paper in half. "There," she said, handing back the destroyed bookmark. "Let's see what you're hauling around in this old thing." She made for the bus.

"Do you need a hand, Mama Givens?" Bitsy hustled to her mother-in-law's side. Cleo held out a hand too, but Maybelle swatted them both away. "What are you implying, Cleo? I'm no invalid. I'm only five years older than you, and look at you, out working still. You have to work, I suppose. It's sad."

Cleo wasn't sad. She loved her job, and she was downright

thrilled to put Rhett down and let him tug her toward the library.

* * *

"Skunks," DeWayne Patterson announced as Cleo and Rhett made their way up the makeshift plywood ramp at the back of the library. A slender man in coveralls, boots, and a ball cap, DeWayne pointed at a gap between what used to be Cleo's cozy staffroom and the outdoors.

Rhett threw his ears back. Cleo sniffed and wrinkled her nose. Skunks were cute, and she enjoyed seeing them visit her backyard. They were, however, possibly a greater hazard to books than Maybelle Givens. *Possibly.*

"Must have wiggled right on in through this hole." DeWayne's voice was muffled, as he was on the floor, stuffing his head and shoulders into the same jagged opening. Cleo was glad she'd put Rhett on his harness. This is exactly the kind of situation she wanted her cat—and contractors—to avoid.

"They can get their heads tiny as mice," DeWayne said. He kept on talking, a rapid ramble about rodent head sizes big and small.

Cleo imagined a furry black-and-white family on the outer side, tails twitching with anticipation. "Maybe you shouldn't . . ." she started, but then decided DeWayne knew what he was doing.

"Yep," he declared when he reappeared. "That there's one of your problems." He appeared unskunked and unscathed except for dirt on his forehead and his cap sitting crooked. Cleo eyed the embroidered bass and hook on the front of the hat,

which looked newer than anything else on DeWayne. Fish—
specifically fancy, expensive fishing piers and a fish-crazed
mayor—were also her problems. She reminded herself that she
didn't begrudge all men who fished. Just one. Her thoughts
turned to Mayor Jeb Day and whether Gabby would take the
bait and investigate him.

In the background, DeWayne was listing the library's
many structural issues. She heard terms regarding plumbing,
plaster, and stucco and then the heartening phrase "not so
bad." As DeWayne spoke of the intricacies of wiring, she
let her mind wander to Ollie and Mary-Rose and that slain
drill.

"I think it might be a good idea," DeWayne was saying
now. "I heard you might have to shut otherwise."

Cleo snapped back to attention. DeWayne had pushed his
cap back and was scratching at his forehead, the only broad
part about the slender man.

"I'm sorry," Cleo said. "What's a good idea?"

"A loan from Mr. Givens's bank. He gave me a nice little
loan to redo my place and buy a new work truck, and the interest isn't so bad. He's a good man. You should go ask him. He's
around at the front, I think, or inside somewhere."

It sounded more fruitful than nosing after skunks. With
Rhett back on her shoulder, Cleo went in search of Vernon.
The library occupied the former residence of a town founder.
The staffroom, once a summer kitchen in the back of the
house, opened to a central hallway, short but grand, with tall
ceilings, dark wood wainscoting, and fine bookshelves that
used to display new acquisitions. Cleo ran a hand fondly over

the librarians' station, a U-shaped counter opening to both the hall and the main fiction room. How many enjoyable hours had she spent here? How many days, years, decades? From her station, she could see everyone coming and going and catch little glimpses into each of the four main rooms too.

She peeked into Fiction, which also housed the periodicals, newspapers, and comfy chairs for readers. The room had been mercifully spared from crushing and rain, but was currently stuffed with stacks of rescued reference materials and rolled-up oriental rugs from the hallway. Cleo walked slowly to the center of the hall, turning and taking in the rooms. Nonfiction occupied an airy space in the front, also serving as dry storage. Kids' and young adult books were tucked in a small former bedroom in the back.

Then there was the reading and reference room, a compact but stunning separate wing, with wood paneling, fine hand-hewn bookshelves, and antique touches dating to the late 1800s. It was a treasure and sadly the most damaged. Opaque plastic sheeting had been taped across the doorframe, and Cleo was almost glad she couldn't see inside. She breathed in heavily. The air no longer smelled fresh and bookish and full of promise. Mustiness pervaded, along with distressing whiffs of mold and skunk.

Setting down Rhett, she let him lead the way to Nonfiction. The cat headed for his favorite window seat, already occupied by Vernon Givens. The bank president wore pants the color of lime sherbet and a jacket of pale lemon. He was reading a book.

"Ah, Miss Cleo and Mr. Rhett Butler," he said, extending a hand to Cleo and following up with a scratch of Rhett's ears.

"You caught me having fun when everyone else is working. These books were in your returns box outside on the porch. I brought 'em in. Didn't want them to get misplaced or the borrowers to run up fines." He chuckled and patted the small stack. Cleo noted a few thin picture books, a romance, a mystery, and two more of greater interest. One was a guide to the limestone geology of Catalpa County. The other was Priscilla Pawpaw's *Killings in Cotton Country*. Both, if she recalled correctly, had been last checked out by Buford Krandall.

Vernon flipped through the geology book. "Who knew . . . we're sitting on a stone sponge."

The bank president shared his new knowledge of springs, sinkholes, and underwater caves. Cleo listened with interest and patience. As soon as he put the book down, she snatched it up and the true-crime book too. Cleo had told herself she didn't have the time or sufficient reason to get involved in Buford Krandall's death. However, now Mary-Rose was snagged in the official investigation, and Ollie might be caught up too. The police would look at the chain of events, details of actions, alibis, and physical evidence. Would they bother with books? Cleo gripped *Killings in Cotton Country* tightly. Buford Krandall had checked out Priscilla Pawpaw's true-crime books for a reason. Perhaps the books could tell her why . . . and why he had been killed.

"I'd better go check on Mama and then get back to the bank," Vernon was saying. He stood and dusted off his slacks. Rhett hopped down too, wandering to the end of his long lead.

Cleo thanked Vernon again for sending DeWayne and for coming by personally.

"I've missed the library," the banker said. "I wanted to see inside. It's pretty bad in the reading room, isn't it? But wood and roofs can be fixed. With money . . ."

He'd given Cleo a perfect opening for her question. "What about a loan for library repairs? Of course the town owns the building, so it would have to be worked out with the town council somehow. I suppose it's tricky."

Vernon flashed his banker's smile, chummy and sparkling. "You know, I do love to give out building and renovation loans," he said, buoying Cleo's hopes. "In fact, our mayor's already been asking about that."

"He has?" Cleo said. Was it possible that Mayor Day had come around? "That's wonderful."

But Vern was shaking his head now, and not in an encouraging way. "Good for the building, but not necessarily for you or library lovers. The mayor was thinking he might fix the building and renovate it back to a house. He says the town could rent it out to all those pro fishermen and sportscasters and big-time gamblers he imagines arriving."

When Cleo managed to speak, she gasped, "What?"

Vernon looked apologetic. "Mayor Day says this place could rent for a lot. He says historic buildings and library décor are popular with well-to-do types."

"Library *décor*?" Cleo sputtered. "A *library's* popular with *all* types!"

"Don't worry," Vernon said soothingly. "I didn't encourage him. You have Bitsy and her ladies on your side. Wait till Bitsy tells you her new idea. It could be a wild ride . . ." He grinned.

Cleo was up for any ideas, even wild ones. She went to

scoop up Rhett but found his harness lying empty. The big cat was an escape artist. Where had he gone? Cleo was afraid she knew when DeWayne's voice boomed from out back. "Skunk!"

The cry was followed by a familiar feline yowl.

Chapter Eleven

Five fluffy tails, black and white and curled aloft, bounced across the lawn like a feathered chorus line. One by one, they disappeared under a holly hedgerow. A puffy orange backside followed close behind.

"Rhett Butler!" Cleo cried. Her cat stopped just short of the shrubbery, halted not by Cleo, surely, but by the dense, spiky leaves. "No, no, you don't," Cleo fussed, hurrying after him, thinking of her son Fred's skunked pooch. Dunking a poodle in the bathtub was child's play compared to scrubbing an angry, clawed Persian. A darling but naughty grandniece once spritzed perfume all over Rhett, necessitating a shampoo and rinse. Cleo's hairdresser stepped in then too. He likely wouldn't make that mistake again, not with the wounds still healing from Rhett's recent grooming.

Cleo grabbed Rhett, who was wiggling his tail end, plotting a pounce. "You've gotten in enough trouble already," she said, expecting to be knocked off her feet by stink. Instead, Rhett's fur smelled of fresh grass, his breath of tuna treats as he nuzzled her chin. The skunk scent grew, however, with the approach of DeWayne.

"Ha! Missed me," DeWayne said, raising a fist in mock anger.

Cleo sniffed pointedly. "They may have gotten you a touch."

DeWayne sniffed his arms and nose-reachable chest of his coveralls. He scratched his head and sniffed again. "Nah, I think they only got a bit of my head. Your cat alerted me just in time. They were hiding under the sink. You're a hero, buddy." He reached to pat Rhett. Cleo managed to inch away before DeWayne could bestow skunk-scented gratitude. "There's some powerful soap in the staffroom," she said.

DeWayne went in search of suds, promising he didn't hold a grudge against the baby skunks. "They're just little bitty things and don't know any better," he said. "Besides, Mr. Givens wouldn't let me hurt 'em. He's had me live-trap mice and carry them out of the bank." The fix-it man headed for the library, whistling cheerfully.

Cleo and Rhett aimed for Words on Wheels, where Vernon was assisting his mother off the bus. Leanna and Bitsy were wrapping up Leanna's walking-in-heels lesson.

"You don't have any books I want to read," Maybelle complained. "Lousy collection."

"Not even a nice mystery, Mother?" Vernon suggested. "You like those."

"Read 'em all," Maybelle claimed. "Vernon, dear, I need to sit down. My feet hurt and my back's twinged from leaning over those little shelves. We have my foot and skin doctor appointments later this morning. Your present wife is likely to make me late."

Vernon escorted his mother to their vehicle, opening all the doors of the tank-sized SUV, fanning out the heat with the flaps of his jacket.

Bitsy maintained a smile, tight with tension lines at the ends of her lips.

"She's kinda mean to you," Leanna said. " 'Present wife'?"

Bitsy waved it off. "That's just her way. I love Mama Givens for loving Vern like she does. She's a sweetie under that gruff. I feel like she's my own mama."

Bitsy wasn't originally from Catalpa Springs, and Cleo didn't know any of her relations. *Bitsy's mother might be awful or an ax murderer,* Cleo thought. She'd have to be pretty terrible to make Maybelle Givens seem sweetly maternal. Cleo, of course, did not ask. She tactfully changed the subject, inquiring about Bitsy's new plan.

"Ooh! I had the best idea!" Bitsy said, clapping her hands. "What if you took some of us Ladies Leaguers out for a spin in the bookmobile? I want everyone on board with the library cause. Ladies Leaguers *love* trips, and some are seriously wealthy too, and potential donors. All you'd have to do is drive us around to your normal stops. You won't even know we're here. Well, you might hear some ruckus, but it's still okay, right?"

Vernon strolled past, chuckling. "Ever been on a party bus, Miss Cleo? Prepare yourself."

Bitsy was twisting her fingers, looking so earnest, Cleo couldn't have turned her down if she'd wanted to, which she didn't. Cleo enjoyed showing off Words on Wheels. "It's a wonderful idea."

Leanna was agreeing. "I know a reporter at the *Catalpa*

Gazette. Toby. I could call him, and maybe we'd get in the paper too—at least some photos."

Bitsy beamed. "I told Vernon, you're a go-getter, Leanna. Yes, you call and get your pretty faces in the paper! I'd better go. Mama Givens likes to get to her appointments an hour early so she can fuss about long waits."

"Thank you all again," Cleo said, a sentiment echoed enthusiastically by Leanna.

"We love the library," Bitsy said. "Mama Givens does too. Don't let her fool you. She took a book. It's in her purse. A romantic suspense, which is why she was being so sneaky. She doesn't like anyone to know her soft side. I wrote down the title and stuck it on your seat so you have a record."

Cleo narrowed her eyes at Maybelle. The older woman sat in the passenger seat of the Givens's SUV. The door was wide open, and her unnaturally ink-black hair ruffled from a side blast of air-conditioning.

Bitsy air-kissed Cleo and offered Leanna a ride home, which Leanna gratefully accepted. Cleo watched them both teeter away, feeling a tug of silly jealousy. Would banking dilute Leanna's love of libraries? Cleo assured herself that wouldn't happen. How could it? What could be better than a life with books?

A scratchy bark interrupted Cleo's thoughts. She turned to see Mr. Chaucer doing his wobbly pug best to pull Henry Lafayette her way. Mr. Chaucer sniffed the skunky air, snorted, and sneezed, knocking himself off balance.

"Bless you," Cleo said.

Henry wore a fine but slightly wrinkled spring linen suit in natural off-white. The silk handkerchief in his jacket pocket was grape purple, coordinated to Mr. Chaucer's leash. He stroked his beard. "I've been thinking," he said. "Why would Mary-Rose confess so readily, and to something she probably didn't do? Or, at least, didn't do alone?"

Cleo was afraid she knew the answer. She mulled it in her mind before saying it out loud. "Because she's covering up for someone."

"Exactly!" Henry said. "Not just anyone. Someone she loves."

Cleo feared she loved that possible someone too. She pictured Ollie hefting the heavy drill-slaying bar.

Henry tugged at his beard. "So . . . I was thinking we could go talk to Mary-Rose again. Chaucy and I are free this afternoon or tomorrow or—"

"How about right now?" Cleo asked. Part of her didn't want confirmation of Ollie's involvement. But, then, knowledge was always a powerful asset, and if this Monday was like others, she knew where Mary-Rose would be. Words on Wheels was scheduled to make a stop there. Cleo looked down at the panting pug. "Want to take a ride, Mr. Chaucer?"

At the word *ride*, Mr. Chaucer picked himself up and trundled toward the school bus. His owner looked just as pleased.

* * *

"Nice place," said Henry as they drove up to Happy Trails, its entryway flanked by stately palms and beds of brightly clashing flowers. A polished stone slab bore the retirement community's name, carved in looping script and underlined with the logo of a winding trail.

Cleo pulled up to the guardhouse, a little wooden structure

with bright white paint and a flashing tin roof. Cleo's favorite gate guard, Tamara, was holding down the fort. She waved to Cleo, and both women opened their windows.

"Thank goodness you're here!" Tamara said. "If I'm really quick, can I run in and swap out books?" She named the novel she'd just finished, number two in a saga of time travel and the Scottish Highlands. Cleo had to give bad news—book three was checked out, with holds a mile long.

"Well, shoot!" Tamara said. "Can I still pop in? I'm all out of reading, and there's not a lot to guard at this gate." She scowled and added, "Unfortunately."

Cleo wished *she* were fresh out of crime. She pulled Words on Wheels into the striped triangle of pavement between the entry and exit lanes and urged Tamara to take her time. Picking the right book shouldn't be rushed. Henry stepped out to let Mr. Chaucer inspect and sprinkle the palm trees. Rhett tagged along, pouncing at and missing a blue butterfly.

Tamara was in her thirties, a tall woman with generous curves and pretty braids, some of them tinted blue. She had a big imagination, and a penchant for action and adventure stories.

"You might like this," Cleo said, pointing to a selection from the sparse New Reads shelf. Most of her new acquisition requests were on hold, awaiting library repairs and fresh shelf space. She and Leanna refreshed and rotated the bookmobile with materials from the main library. Cleo had counted on building repairs starting soon. "Soon" might turn to "never." Should she cancel her orders? Cleo thought of all the wonderful new items on her list. Books Tamara would love. Books for kids and seniors and everyone in between. She sighed, facing the slim pickings on the New Reads shelf and the awful prospect of her town without a library.

Tamara read the back cover of the novel Cleo recommended. She flipped it over and examined the cover art. "Looks a little old-fashioned and young," she said. "I mean, it's a kid detective, right? Is this even for adults?"

Cleo assured her it was. "It's historical, a different time and place, like you enjoy. Why don't you give it a try? Let me know what you think. Get an extra backup book too in case you don't connect."

Cleo prided herself on matching books and people. She took the task seriously. She'd never recommend a book solely because it was the literary darling of the moment or a classic or the reading equivalent to healthy eating. She wanted patrons to read what they liked, be it for fun, enrichment, or fantasy. Even books about murder and true crime, though in Buford Krandall's case, she sure wished she knew why.

Tamara was still making skeptical sounds. Cleo refocused her thoughts back to books at hand. "I think you'd like the young heroine. She's clever and scientific, and no one sees her coming."

"I do like that," Tamara said. She was studying criminal investigation at the college in Claymore. Tamara chose another novel, a thriller promising action and bioterrorism and a hero named Stone. Stone had a SEAL Team Six pedigree and, if the cover art was anything to go by, fought his battles shirtless. "These'll keep me for a bit," Tamara said. "There's nothing going on otherwise."

"Enjoy the peace," Cleo said. "There's too much going on in my world."

"I heard. The old folks—I mean, our active-adult residents—can't stop talking about the murder and"—she lowered her voice to a whisper, looking over her shoulder—"Mary-Rose Garland."

Cleo cringed, thinking of her best friend as fodder for gossip. However, tongue wagging could provide useful information. In a tiny place like Catalpa Springs, folks saw and heard things, and listening was important, both for recommending good books and solving puzzles and problems. Cleo asked about Mary-Rose and was glad to hear that her friend had entered Happy Trails earlier that morning.

"At 8:36, precisely," Tamara said, after consulting a small pocket notepad. Mary-Rose had brought pie: a big slice of butterscotch for Tamara and a whole trunkful of fruit pies for her mother and the coffee room.

Tamara confirmed what Cleo suspected. "Those were bribing pies. Miss Mary made me promise not to tell her mother about a certain something no one's supposed to say."

Cleo said it. She hadn't gotten any pie, bribing or otherwise. "Her troubles with the law."

"Exactly. Of course, everyone except her mother knows. Even that wobbly dog likely knows."

"Yes," Cleo said dismally. "He knows." They watched Mr. Chaucer raise a leg in the vague direction of a palm. He teetered and toppled briefly. Henry looked tactfully away. Man, dog, and cat climbed back on the bus at Cleo's call to Rhett and rustling of his bag of tuna treats. Tamara greeted the pets with pats and beamed when Henry gave her a chivalrous little bow of greeting.

"Remember, no one's to say anything to Mary-Rose's

mama," Tamara said. "No need to get the old dear fretting. That lady already worries about the entire world and then some. When she comes by the gate, she worries about me sitting out here all alone. She always tells me to be careful not to get kidnapped or overheated or food poisoned from my sandwiches and heaven knows what else. She could get you mighty nervous if you thought too much about what she's saying."

Cleo well knew the many worries of Jo-Marie Calhoun, Mary-Rose's ninety-six-year-old mother. Sometimes she wondered if Mary-Rose's boldness was an opposite reaction. "What's the mood of the gossip?" she asked, hoping to get a feel of the situation they were driving into. "Are people leaning for or against Mary-Rose?"

Tamara tore her eyes from her new books. She shrugged. "Hard to tell. People love Mary-Rose. She brings everyone pie and is super nice. But I took a break over at the Social Hall earlier and overheard some people saying they don't blame her one bit. That Buford Krandall had it coming. That's their words, not mine. I only met the man once, and he was nice enough to me, even after I had to tackle him."

"Tackle him?" Cleo and Henry demanded in unison.

Tamara shrugged modestly. "He had it coming."

Chapter Twelve

"Tackle?" Cleo said again.

Mr. Chaucer groaned. Rhett, a pouncing pro, yawned.

"It was nothing," Tamara said, leaning back against the dashboard, inspecting nails done up in a sparkly red and white candy-cane manicure. "I mean, literally, it was actually nothing. I mistook him for a burglar. It was late. Dark, but a full moon. I was doing an overnight shift. They're the worst—nothing at all happens most of the time, just me and the frogs and crickets and my books and schoolwork. But there he was, a man, dressed all in black and carrying something that might have been a rifle."

Tamara's eyes twinkled. She waggled a finger and said, "He was sneaking. That's the truth. He was tiptoeing through that flowerbed over there—the one with the lantana and pink whatever flowers—and he was carrying a big backpack too. I gave him warning. I yelled for him to stop and approach the gate. Well, he took off running. Kind of running. More like skipping with a limp. I was able to catch up and get the jump

119

on him. I felt bad afterward, him being frail and rickety and falling face-first in a palmetto, but I *did* think he was an armed thief and/or sniper or, heck, a terrorist or spy or who knows what?" She patted her newly chosen SEAL Team thriller, as if confirming the very real possibility of foreign attack on Happy Trails Retirement Village.

"Understandable," Cleo said, supportively. "It sounds like you had to think and act quickly." She rather liked the idea of Buford getting a good tackling. Then she remembered the man was dead. How wicked of her. She turned her mind to important details. "Was he actually carrying a rifle?"

Tamara's face fell. "Nah. The long thing I took to be a sniper rifle was just an old cloth umbrella with fringe on it. He said he carried it in case the moonlight got too bright." Tamara didn't bother with euphemisms like eccentric. "Crazy," she said, head shaking. "I mean, the moonlight? You can't get a moonburn, can you?"

"When was this?" Henry asked. He'd been listening intently to the conversation.

Tamara held up a one-moment finger, ran to her guard-house, and returned with a calendar. "I keep a log of suspicious happenings," she said, flipping through filled pages that reinforced Cleo's leeriness of Happy Trails. Tamara pointed to a date several weeks back. Henry produced his small notepad and wrote down the information. They made a good team, Cleo thought. *Investigation* team, she clarified.

"The backpack?" Cleo prompted. "What was in it? Was he sneaking in or out?"

Tamara beamed. "This is just like my Criminal Justice 201 seminar. Us, hashing out the evidence and making case notes. Good question, Miss Cleo. He was sneaking out, not in. He went in earlier, another way. And don't think I didn't ask him what he was up to."

Cleo hadn't thought for a minute that Tamara would neglect to ask. She knew from their chats—and Tamara's voracious reading—that the young lady was inquisitive and sharp, with a good dose of rightful suspicion.

"Papers," Tamara said. "That's what was in the backpack. I made him open it, in case he was hauling off someone's silver and jewelry. He claimed he'd had a personal meeting with one of our active-adult residents. A famous author, he said. Priscilla Pawpaw. Well, I told him every one of our residents was famous in their own way, but I didn't know of anyone named Pawpaw. I'd have remembered. I like pawpaws, the fruit. Anyway, he had me call Priscilla Vinogradov—Miss V., we call her—and what do you know? She and Pawpaw are the same person." Tamara tapped her notes and nodded knowingly. "A name like that, it's hard to spell, let alone say. I see why she changed it for her books. What is it? German?"

"Russian," Henry murmured, still writing in his notebook. "Derived from the word for grape."

"Huh. Interesting . . ." Tamara said, taking notes herself. "She wears a lot of purple. Has purplish hair too . . . Wonder if that's a coincidence?"

Cleo gently veered the conversation back to Buford Krandall. "Did he say why he was visiting?" Cleo asked. Her heartbeat had quickened. Maybe she was right about Buford's reading list. He seemingly wasn't interested in just any old true crime, but something particular and known to Priscilla Pawpaw.

"He said he was a fan," Tamara said. "He went on and on

about her books. Said they were fascinating. Interesting. Educational. Do you have any in stock? Think I'd like them? Think they'd help with my studies?"

Cleo didn't need anyone else getting potentially dangerous tips. "They're all checked out currently," she said, making a mental note to collect the rest of Buford's library books. If the police didn't have them in evidence, she wanted to be next in line to read them.

"Must be really good, then," Tamara said, scribbling another note.

Or bad, Cleo thought, when the bus was moving again, rolling over speed bumps the size of hills. She also wanted to talk to Priscilla Vinogradov/Pawpaw about Buford Krandall's late-night visit. First, however, she needed to find out why Mary-Rose had confessed.

* * *

In the bright Social Hall of Happy Trails, pie plates lay scattered and empty but for a few crumbs and crusts. Henry was disappointed. Cleo, even more so. The Social Hall was mostly empty of people too. A single elderly gentleman snoozed in a recliner, a newspaper collapsed on his chest. In front of him, a widescreen TV displayed a flickering fireplace. The televised wood crackled and glowed while overhead an air conditioner exhaled icy breath. Mr. Chaucer ambled to the TV and settled down with a sigh, eyes aimed dreamily at the dancing flames.

With a cat-fancier's pride, Cleo thought Rhett wouldn't be so easily duped. The Persian had stayed back at the bus, sunning himself on the hood. Cleo knew he wouldn't go far.

Rhett loved a sunny snooze almost as much as the tuna treats he knew she kept in the bus.

"Where is everyone?" Henry asked.

Cleo glanced out picture windows facing Florida. She saw only a few golfers teeing up and a heron soaring by. *Perhaps everyone packed up and headed south,* she thought with a shiver only partially brought on by the overenthusiastic air-conditioning.

"Bingo," Henry said. He pointed to a whiteboard calendar. "Actual bingo. There's a game going on. Maybe that's where folks are." He leaned closer to read the handwritten marker text again. "Oh . . . oh dear . . . *strip* bingo? In the Red Room?"

Cleo didn't like the sound of that. She and Henry followed the directions from a handy floor map, though they wouldn't have needed it. Cheers and yelling announced the room long before they arrived at its closed door.

"Bingo!" A whoop went up, followed by a chant. "Strip, strip, strip."

Henry's mustache twitched over a devious grin. "You do know how to show a man a wild Monday morning," He cupped his palms to the little window in the door. "I don't know if you want to see this, Cleo," Henry continued. Mr. Chaucer whined anxiously, sniff-snorting at the door. "It's something . . . something I never imagined, that's for sure." He stepped back.

Men! Cleo punctuated this indignant thought with an audible huff. She pressed her glasses to the little door window. The room resembled a hotel ballroom, and Cleo could easily see how it got its name. The wallpaper was rich red with velvet floral embossing. The carpet matched, adding swirls of maroon and magenta. Cleo thought the décor was a health hazard, the patterns having the potential to induce vertigo or mental confusion.

"What is going on?" Cleo asked. Everyone seemed properly clothed. Cardigans were in place, blouses buttoned, and even feet were mostly covered.

Fabric sailed through the air to the "strip, strip, strip" chant, aimed at a woman raising her hands in victory. When the tossing settled, the bingo caller—none other than lawyer Thurgood Byron, dressed in a red velvet lounge jacket—read more letters until a hand flew up and the whoops and fabric onslaught began again. Cleo cocked her head. *What on earth?*

"Any ideas what's going on?" Henry asked.

"None," Cleo admitted, but she spotted someone who'd know the game and possibly much worse. Mary-Rose sat beside her mother, Jo-Marie, at a back table. Little Zoe was slumped to practically prone, a book the only thing holding her up. Jo-Marie seemed to be nimbly managing several bingo cards. Mary-Rose bounced a pen, one of her giveaway nervous tics.

"I'm going in," Cleo said.

Mr. Chaucer whimpered. Henry might have too.

"You stay here," she said. "I'll bring Mary-Rose out with me."

She made a ducking dash amidst another blizzard of fabric.

"Cleo Jane!" Jo-Marie said, happily. "You'll join us. I'm winning big." Her eyes darted about the room. "Competition's steep here." Jo-Marie, for all her worries, was intensely competitive. Cleo noted the pile of fabric in the basket of Jo-Marie's walker.

She complimented the winnings—whatever they might

mean—and asked if she could borrow Mary-Rose. "It's about . . . business."

Jo-Marie's sharp eyes shot up from her card. "Business? You mean pancakes? The library? What's this horrible rumor that you're closing the library? Why would you do that, Cleo?"

Nearby faces turned. A murmur rose. Soon half the back room was looking Cleo's way. Zoe had recovered her posture and was staring at Cleo too. Thurgood's number randomizer chose that moment to stall. A hush fell over the room, accusatory eyes finding their way to Cleo.

"The library is not closing," Cleo said. She never enjoyed public speaking, but suddenly she felt a swell of valor. She was among friends who loved the library as much as she did. "Write to the mayor. Call him. Show up at his door and let him know how much you value our library."

"Save the library!" a voice called from the front, soon joined by dozens of others. "Save Mary-Rose!" someone yelled, and that chant was picked up too.

"What?" Jo-Marie asked. "Mary-Rose? What's wrong with Mary-Rose?"

Thankfully, the randomizer recovered, and so did Thurgood Byron, who called out letters in quick succession. The bingo fans hunkered down. Mary-Rose, Cleo, and a delighted Zoe slipped out.

"Phew," Mary-Rose said, adjusting a hairpin in her off-kilter bun. "That was close." Inside, a strip chorus sounded again. Zoe joined in. Cleo glanced worriedly at the girl. Far be it for her to butt in on child-rearing decisions of others, but *strip* bingo? She ventured to ask what was going on.

"It's quilting bingo," Mary-Rose explained, as she, Henry, Mr. Chaucer, and Cleo moseyed back to the bookmobile at elderly pug pace. Zoe skipped far out front, joining a small line of two men and one nosy Persian cat outside the bus's doors. "The stripping refers to strips of quilting fabric. If you get bingo, everyone throws in a fabric piece. Big winners can make a whole lap quilt from their prizes. Mom doesn't quilt, but she likes the competition and pretty fabrics, and I want to keep her occupied. She doesn't know yet about, well, you know . . . I tried to convince the other residents to keep it quiet."

"We know," Cleo said, and explained that Tamara had already warned them.

"Tamara's so sweet," Mary-Rose said. "I should bring her a whole pie. And look at Thurgood, providing a bingo distraction right when I needed it. See? He's a good lawyer."

When neither Henry nor Cleo responded, Mary-Rose chattered on. "If Mom knew I was hauled in to the police, she'd be a wreck of nerves, but really, there's nothing to worry about. Nothing at all."

Cleo felt otherwise. She opened the bookmobile and let Zoe play head librarian.

"No gum," Zoe told the visitors. "No loud talking," she yelled. "No tearing pages or eating spaghetti. No cold drinks or milkshakes or ice-cream cones or dragons without leashes or . . ."

Cleo smiled. Zoe was a natural and promised to yell whenever someone wanted to check out. Rhett returned to sunning on the hood, sensing no one would be doling out tuna treats. Henry, Cleo, and Mary-Rose settled on a shady metal patio table in view of the bookmobile. Mr. Chaucer put his head down on Henry's feet and began to snore. Cleo considered her approach. Mary-Rose always faced problems head-on. She'd do the same.

"Speaking of secrets," Cleo said. "We know you're keeping one, Mary-Rose."

"I confessed to the police on record, Cleo. That's hardly keeping a secret."

"Yes, you confessed," Cleo persisted. "You said you stuck a heavy metal pole through that drilling machine. Where did you get the pole? Did you carry it all the way over through the woods? Stuff it in your car?"

Mary-Rose closed her lips tight, like she should have with the police.

Cleo continued on. "I don't think that's what happened at all. If you're lying, you'll only make the situation worse. The police will be looking only at you. A killer could get away while you end up in prison. What would that do to your grandmotherly reputation? Your business? What would your family think?"

Mary-Rose squared her shoulders. She was wearing her signature rosy colors, but her skin had a gray tinge under her freckles.

Cleo grasped her friend's hand. "Talk to me, Mary, please."

She was heartened when Mary-Rose squeezed back. "Oh, Cleo, you know I don't want killers running around Catalpa. This is only about that silly drill. I have Mr. Byron. He's a fine lawyer. Look, there he is now."

Thurgood Byron strolled down the walkway, a bottle blonde on one arm, a silver siren on the other.

Mary-Rose waved, and Thurgood managed to extract a

hand to wave back. His hair was an unnatural jet black, polished as shiny as his snakeskin loafers.

"Ah, my favorite criminal defendant," he declared when he got within a few yards. The ladies twittered obligingly and adoringly. Both looked on the young side of seventy, if not in their late sixties, and thus a good decade younger than Thurgood.

"Alleged criminal," Cleo grumbled, knowing this wasn't a helpful distinction.

Thurgood tipped his head and graciously repeated, "Alleged."

"My girlfriends," he said, introducing the pair. They waggled their fingers hello and drifted off, tempted by the bookmobile and its treasures. " 'Make hay while the sun shines,' as my daddy used to say," Thurgood declared, watching them with a sly grin. He then issued Mary-Rose some too-late advice to keep on keeping silent. "This too shall pass. I've got it under control. You're at the top of my docket."

"Before suing the caterer?" Cleo asked, testing the man's priorities.

Thurgood beamed. "The caterers settled. See? Success! Results! Cocktails will be served at three thirty with canapés and other suitable snacks, as demanded." He whistled on his way to the bookmobile, seeking a book of cocktail recipes and his lady friends.

"Success," Mary-Rose echoed, sitting straighter, chin raised defiantly. "The man gives good advice too. Make hay and enjoy the sunshine, Cleo." She winked in the direction of Henry. "One's never too old for love."

"But possibly too distracted for criminal defense," Cleo muttered.

Chapter Thirteen

Words on Wheels was attracting good business. Cleo left Henry and Mary-Rose to chat while she and Zoe helped patrons. When she returned to the table during a library lull, she took another stab at getting Mary-Rose to open up.

Her friend remained stubborn. "My spring. My problem," she said.

Cleo quizzed some more. How did Mary-Rose know where to impale the machine? Where had Buford Krandall been when she did it? Why hadn't he heard and come out shooting again?

"He was where he was," Mary-Rose snapped. "It doesn't matter how or where or when. There's no doubt that I *am* responsible. Stop fretting, Cleo. I swear, *you* take after my mother more than I do. I have a successful lawyer, and I will be just fine."

Successful if Mary-Rose needs a stiff gin and tonic and early canapés, Cleo thought. She exchanged a look with Henry and was gratified that he got her drift immediately.

"Mr. Chaucer demands his walk," Henry declared. The

Nora Page

pug lay on his back, fast asleep. "Walkies," Henry said loudly. He gently roused the dog. Mr. Chaucer rolled, groaned, and reluctantly stood.

"Walk?" Zoe bounded over from the bus. "Can I come? I can show you a secret. I know where there's a pond with snapping turtles, and there's a really big one we can pet if we sneak up behind it."

"Exactly what I wanted to do," Henry said, unconvincingly to Cleo's ears but thrilling to Zoe's. The little girl took off at a run. Rhett joined in.

"No turtle petting!" Mary-Rose called after them. "Her mother would have a fit if she knew what we've been up to. Rightfully so, for once. I had no idea Zoe followed me over to Krandall House."

Cleo suspected another young person had also followed Mary-Rose into Krandall trouble. "Ollie," Cleo said shortly. "I know you, Mary-Rose. You'd put others before your own safety. You confessed because you're trying to protect Ollie."

Color returned to Mary-Rose's face, an angry flush. "What? How do you know that? Ollie promised he'd keep quiet."

"I just know," Cleo said. Her suspicion was confirmed, but she felt worse for it.

Tense silence ensued as both Cleo and Mary-Ruse rummaged in their purses. Cleo produced her folding fan, snapped it open, and employed it with vigor. Mary-Rose brought out a water bottle and a folded sheet of paper. She handed the latter to Cleo. "Tap water," she said of the former. "I'll never drink bottled again."

Cleo agreed. "It would have a bitter taste." She took the

130

proffered paper and realized she'd already read it. "S.O.S. Save Our Springs. I know about this. I met Ollie's new friend, Whitney," Cleo said. "She's been staying at the cottage."

Mary-Rose groaned. "*New friend* . . . Darling Ollie. I think he's infatuated, and she's not. Poor girl—I feel bad for her too. I connected with S.O.S. I found them online, through some other environmental nonprofits I knew. They sounded perfect for my spring problems, so I emailed them, and Whitney got right back to me and raced straight up to assess the situation. I was so thrilled. Then Ollie got involved and now . . ."

And now they're all caught up in the ripples of murder. Cleo's stomach clenched as she forced herself to ask. "Did Ollie and Whitney have anything to do with Buford Krandall's death?"

Mary-Rose's silence hung heavy between them. After a few long moments, she spoke. "I don't know." Then she said, "No, of course they didn't. Only the drill. We had a plan to stop that awful thing for good. All of us. Me, Ollie, and Whitney. Ollie and Whitney were scoping out our attack the day you visited. They went out the night Buford died. I had to stay home because William's knee was acting up. I may not have been there, but I'm as much to blame as them, and I have a lot less to lose. They're young. They can't have a criminal record, even if it just ends up being trespassing. I already have a record for that. What's one more?" She smiled.

Cleo studied her sandals. When she and Mary-Rose were teenagers, they'd trespassed on Mr. Weber's property. He was a mean man, the kind who threatened kids and pets, and they were mistakenly sure he'd trapped Mary-Rose's cat. An off-duty deputy happened to be strolling by and spotted them crawling out his garage window. To this day, Cleo was certain that Mary-Rose ran slower so she'd be caught by the deputy and Cleo could get away. Cleo's strict father would have blown all his gaskets and then some. Mary-Rose's father was proud of her initiative. Her mother was worried, of course, but that wasn't unusual for Jo-Marie, whose forever mantra was that her three daughters would be the death of her. Then, like now, Mary-Rose claimed the misguided mission was her idea, and thus she should take the blame.

"That worked out," Mary-Rose said. "Miss Kitty came back, and with all those adorable kittens too. Things were better than ever."

Cleo didn't see baskets of kittens in Mary-Rose's future this time. She noticed that more bookmobile patrons were approaching and got up to help them.

Mary-Rose reached out and grabbed Cleo's hand. "This is my fault. I will not have Ollie get involved any more than he already has. He has a bright future. Cleo, you have to promise—and I mean truly swear—that you won't say anything about Ollie or Whitney or S.O.S. to the police, even your nice neighbor. That Buford Krandall was a thorn in all sorts of sides. If I take the blame for that silly machine, the police will have more time to concentrate on finding the killer, which isn't me, Ollie, or Whitney. If that gives the killer more time to make a mistake, that's fine too, right?"

"Or more time to kill again," Cleo pointed out darkly.

Mary-Rose pleaded and invoked their friendship, which hurt, but Cleo stood her ground. "I can't," Cleo said. "I can't because Gabby Honeywell already knows."

* * *

Henry returned with the pets, all looking overheated and a tad frazzled. Cleo was alone, simmering in the heat and her thoughts. Mary-Rose had rushed off, saying she must get her mother to a hair appointment and lunch.

Cleo noticed Henry was down one expedition member. "Where's Zoe?" she asked.

"Mary-Rose saw us on the way back and took Zoe along with her, promising ice cream. Sounds nice."

He eased himself down on a chair, extolling the cool shade.

Cleo told him about Mary-Rose's revised confession and the involvement of Ollie and Whitney. He shook his head. "As we expected. Zoe and I made a discovery too, although much more minor."

"A giant turtle?" Cleo asked.

"Better. We located the residence of Priscilla Pawpaw, aka Vinogradov. Zoe is very clever with directions and peeking in patio windows. She's clever around turtles too, thank goodness." He held up his ten fingers and admired their intactness. "We also learned that Miss Pawpaw appears to be home." He let Cleo take in this information.

"Is that so?" Cleo considered their next move. "I have a little bit more time here with the bookmobile. But after that, we could drive by Priscilla's place."

Henry agreed enthusiastically. "Perhaps she'll offer us a cold drink."

"And a clue."

* * *

Cleo knew Priscilla from the library. Unsurprisingly, the writer was a book lover and a good patron too. Priscilla had no fines that Cleo could recall, and kept her voice appropriately low in the reading room. Cleo approved of library quiet, although she feared it was becoming as outdated as rotary telephones and manners. She pictured the author. Priscilla was in her sixties and single, with wispy gray hair tinged a vague lavender. Aside from the purple, the true-crime author's most distinguishing trait was her jumpiness.

Knowing Pricilla's titles and topics, Cleo could understand. She'd be jumpy too if she spent her days immersed in tales of murder, crime, and all manners of unnatural death. Cleo eased Words on Wheels to a stop on Sweetgum Court. Pricilla's cottage had pale stucco and a door of goldenrod yellow, so glossy it appeared slippery.

"Let's be careful not to startle her," Cleo said as they made their way up the front steps. With choppy-furred Rhett at her heels, Mr. Chaucer having a sneezing fit, and Henry issuing repeated "bless yous" in the direction of his feet, they might be a startling set of visitors.

Her light knocking was met by a quivering "Yes?" issued through a crack in the chain-locked door. "If it's the petition regarding happy hour, I've already signed."

"We're here for less happy purposes." Cleo moved her face in front of the crack and reminded Priscilla where they'd met.

"Oh!" Priscilla said, eyes as round as Rhett's. "Yes, of course—you're the librarian. Sorry. I'm horrible with faces out of place. I remember your cat." Her eyes narrowed, aimed at Rhett. "What happened to his fur? Was he attacked?"

"Burdocks," Cleo said. "He had to be shaved by my hairdresser."

"How dreadful!" Priscilla sounded truly horrified. Cleo

imagined a new book idea taking form: cat-grooming disasters of southern Georgia and those who perpetrate them.

Cleo introduced Henry as the town's newest and only antiquarian bookseller. He tipped an imaginary hat, and they both apologized for the drop-in and the accompanying pets.

"We just had a few questions," Cleo said, "about Buford Krandall."

Priscilla fumbled with the lock. The door swung open, and it was Cleo's turn to be startled. "Buford? What a charming man!" Priscilla exclaimed. "Come in, all of you. I adore cats and little funny dogs and anyone who's a friend of Buford Krandall."

Charming? Buford? Cleo pondered the unusual description as Priscilla welcomed them in, still gushing that friends of Buford's were friends of hers. She seemed to float in a long lavender dress. A yellow scarf, draped loosely on her thin neck, was printed in the pattern of crime-scene tape. Cleo had seen the same pattern under Priscilla's logo on her books and business cards.

They settled on Priscilla's back patio, and ice tea was served. The pug and cat stretched out on shady tiles. Cleo, Henry, and their hostess sat in comfortable white wicker chairs around a matching coffee table with a glass top and lace coasters. The tea was syrupy sweet, as tea should be, and Priscilla gushed just as sweetly about Buford Krandall. According to her, he was intelligent, kind, and generous. A lovely gentleman.

"You were friends?" Cleo asked, both marveling and sad. She'd never heard anyone speak of Buford in such admiring terms.

"We are *professional* acquaintances," Priscilla said, cheeks reddening, back stiffening. "Mr. Krandall is a fan of my work. A huge fan. Rarely do I meet a reader who is so inquisitive and eager. He said he read every word of my books and the end-notes. Some readers complain, saying I include too many notes and parenthetical asides and details and diagrams and blood splatter patterns and whatnot. Not Mr. Krandall. He wanted to know more than space would allow in a printed book. He requested my notes. He even wanted my notes for my work in progress, *Fatal Florida*. I told him, he'd have to be a good fan and wait." She gave a laugh that might have qualified as a girl-ish giggle. Cleo had a bad feeling that was growing worse.

"He's going to attend my book signing at the Ladies League Spring Gala," Priscilla said. "I'll be signing *Murder and May-hem in Mississippi* and auctioning off a basket of books. The lucky winner also gets to take me out to lunch and pick my brain about murder. I bet I know who will win."

Cleo and Henry murmured how nice and other such polite affirmations. They shared a look of dread.

Henry—in what Cleo considered noble chivalry—took the lead. "Uh, Miss Pawpaw, Miss Vinogradov . . . Priscilla, ma'am, you do know that Buford is . . . I mean, have you seen the news?"

Priscilla's whole body jerked. "The news? No, I've been out of town. Florida, for spring break."

Cleo was shocked anew. Was quiet, jumpy Priscilla really saying she'd been enjoying a Daytona Beach keg-and-bikini party? Cleo was glad Henry was doing the talking, because she couldn't have uttered a sensible word.

Henry leaned down and patted Mr. Chaucer. The pug

sneezed. "Bless you," Henry murmured to Mr. Chaucer, but more so to Priscilla.

Cleo roused herself to assist. "Priscilla," she said, wishing she had a condolence casserole or pie to offer. "It seems you haven't heard. I'm afraid we have terrible news. Mr. Buford is gone. Deceased. Sadly. Unfortunately," she added after an awkward pause in which she wondered if Priscilla had understood.

"Unfortunately murdered," Henry clarified further. "We are so very sorry for your loss." He reached across the doilies, aiming to grasp Priscilla's hand.

"What?" Priscilla stood. The wicker chair tipped, and her voice wavered but was no longer quiet. "What? No!"

Mr. Chaucer jumped to his feet. Rhett, in feline defiance, pretended to sleep.

"I'm sorry," Cleo said. "It happened just a few—"

"I knew it," Priscilla interrupted. "I knew it when he asked for my notes. I never should have let him have them. I warned him. I told him and he didn't listen. I said it clear as day—as clear as the sky is right now: 'Don't try to solve murders! You'll get yourself killed!' "

Chapter Fourteen

On the drive back to town, Priscilla Pawpaw's words buzzed Cleo's brain like angry wasps. The anxious author had hustled them out her door, hoisting promotional crime-scene scarves on them as they went and locking the door chain as soon as they were out.

"Poking the truth is like jabbing a hornet nest," Priscilla had said, eyes bulging over the chain. "You know you'll get hurt. I told Buford. I told him."

Cleo had already poked, but in this case, it had drawn out information. Cleo was anxious to tell Gabby about Buford's visit to Happy Trails. His death might have no connection to his mucky spring-water business. Thus it might also have nothing to do with her friend and grandson.

"I feel awfully sorry for Priscilla," Henry said, sitting on the front bench seat with the cat and dog lying to either side. "Her biggest fan, gone."

Cleo felt bad for her too.

Henry continued. "We could bid on her auction offering at the Gala, win the prize of paying for lunch with her. Which reminds me, I have to round up some interested buyers in my Agatha Christies. Without Buford Krandall, I might have to bid against myself."

"I'll bid," Cleo said. "Cousin Dot is interested too. She loves Agatha Christie. She's always rereading her Poirots and Marples."

"Well," Henry said hesitantly, "these Christies are worth several thousand. There will be call-in bidders, I hope. I wouldn't want Dot to pay a lot for books meant for collecting more than reading."

All books were meant for reading, to Cleo's way of thinking. She rolled down her window farther and let the warm breeze fluff her hair and clear her mind. The landscape sped by, spindly palms and piney thickets, graceful oaks and manicured lawns. The most manicured was the Givens's home on the outskirts of town, just before the river. As they passed, a gardener was mowing precise diamonds in acres of grass. The modern Antebellum-style house was blindingly bright white, with columns ringing three sides. Cleo could picture Bitsy in another time, decked out in a hoop skirt, surveying the grounds and the river beyond. Another figure popped into Cleo's mental picture: Maybelle Givens in a dowager's dark dress, complaining about her feet.

Words on Wheels rumbled over the low bridge across the Tallgrass River, close enough to spot turtles sunning and a heron take flight. Near the turnoff to the public fishing pier and park, a bulldozer stood ominously in a gravel pull-off.

"What a shame to mess with such a pretty patch of riverfront," Henry said.

The old wooden pier was perfectly solid and functional,

set amidst shady oaks and mossy palms. The river rolled by peacefully.

Cleo said grimly, "Did you see the newspaper? There's an opinion piece by the mayor, saying how this area will 'develop.' He envisions mini-malls and parking lots, like over in Claymore and everywhere else."

"What about our downtown stores? Dot and her picnic supplies? The hardware store and bakery and florist? What happens to them in this plan?" Henry said.

The same thing that might happen to the library, Cleo thought. *Shuttering.* Her thoughts turned to her library troubles. She needed more allies, more funds, like Buford Krandall had promised. If only she knew what he was up to, she might help her library and the murder investigation.

As they neared town, Cleo spotted a banner fluttering overhead.

"What is that?" She squinted, trying to make out the words. Banners regularly announced big events in little Catalpa Springs. The Catalpa Flower Festival. Summer concerts by the "nearly world famous" town band. Pumpkins in the park in autumn and the lovely Catalpa Christmas fest. Was this banner announcing the Gala? Were those dancers on each end of the banner? How enterprising of Bitsy.

Cleo clung to that nice thought until the dancers turned into fish and too-clear lettering: "Catalpa Springs, Fishing Capital of the Universe." Cleo read each word out with appropriate aghast. *"Fishing capital of the universe"*?

"A bit much," Henry said dryly.

It was more than a bit much. Cleo stomped the gas in anger. Flashing lights appeared in her mirror. A siren chirped.

"Uh-oh," Henry said. Rhett purred loudly.

Cleo eased off the gas, hoping the police car would speed past. She couldn't afford a speeding ticket. *Another* speeding ticket. She pulled her bus into Speedy Auto Repair. She checked her hair, cleaned her glasses, and awaited the worst, hoping it wasn't the chief.

Gabby Honeywell tapped on the door. Cleo's law-enforcing neighbor had on her unreadable neutral expression, which could only mean one thing. Gabby was mad. Upset. Disappointed. Cleo's stomach pitched, until she saw Gabby's lip twitch, followed by a chastising finger.

"Cleo Watkins, you were driving like a bat out of Beelzebub's den, as my Granny Mimms would say." Gabby climbed the steps, greeted Henry and the pets, and smiled at Cleo. "What if you'd been flooring it like that out of town, and the sheriff's boys had pulled you over?"

"They have pulled me over," Cleo admitted. "They were very sweet and gave me a reduced ticket because I reminded one young man of his grandmother."

"Ha! Well you remind me of Granny Mimms. A demon on wheels. She clocked in at eighty on the very same birthday. You don't want to get a bad reputation like her, Miss Cleo."

Cleo didn't see a ticket pad. "I apologize. I was disturbed and distracted by that awful fish banner."

Gabby rolled her eyes. "I know! 'The universe'? Absurd. But I didn't pull you over *just* because of your speed. I spotted you and wanted to tell you something. It's about Ollie . . ."

Cleo clenched the wheel until her knuckles ached.

"Don't worry," Gabby was saying. "Ollie's fine. He's just over at the station answering some questions. I thought you should know. He's not under arrest, and his lawyer stepmom is with him. I'm really sorry, but I couldn't ignore what Ollie said this morning, how he knew details about that sabotaged drill."

Cleo knew how he had those details. *That silly, passionate boy!* She hoped Angela was making Ollie keep his mouth shut about his involvement. She'd keep quiet too, except to assure Gabby that she wasn't upset with her. "You were just doing your job," she said.

Gabby stooped to pet Rhett. "I'm still sorry. I feel rotten, like I was snooping on my favorite neighbor. We already had doubts about Mary-Rose's supposed confession, though, and Ollie knows his way around in the woods out by Krandall House. He grew up playing at the Pancake Mill, didn't he?"

"A lot of people know those woods," Cleo said. "Hunters, fishermen, hikers, me . . ."

The brothers who owned the repair shop, TJ and Joe, were headed their way. Gabby and Cleo waved, and the men raised their chins in unison. The brothers were both round and curly haired and given to wearing identical coveralls. Cleo was chagrined that she often couldn't tell them apart. One brother veered off to inspect the front of the bus. The other approached the door. He had "TJ" embroidered on his pocket, which meant nothing. The brothers, Cleo knew from past mix-ups, didn't bother to sort their uniforms.

"TJ, good morning," Gabby said, sounding confident in his name.

Cleo was impressed, but not surprised, when Gabby turned out to be right. TJ greeted Gabby and looked worriedly past to Cleo. "You all right, Mrs. Watkins? Bus okay? I tell you, that transmission, it's set to go on you any moment . . ."

Cleo put her hands to her ears. "I can't hear such negativity, TJ. The bookmobile is feeling just fine. I have a book I'm studying—*Zen and the Art of School Bus Maintenance*. All I need is regular oil changes and a calm spirit."

He snorted. "Right, Zen. I heard y'all meditating down the highway from a good half mile away. When's that library of yours gonna get fixed anyways?"

Cleo decided not to sugarcoat the situation. She told TJ about the mayor's library threats and fishing pier plans.

"Wait, you mean it's either the fishing *or* the library?" TJ said, sounding satisfyingly shocked. "What kind of choice is that? We already have a pier out at the park, and everyone local has their own secret fishing spot anyways. What's this new one supposed to do that's better?"

Henry answered with quiet sarcasm. "Ah, this pier would attract world-class sport fisherman. International, intergalactic fishermen, as the banner over there promises."

TJ snorted and muttered words inappropriate for a library—even one on wheels with a noisy engine. Cleo didn't chastise him. She understood his sentiments.

"Professional sport fishers?" TJ sputtered. "Rich outsiders with sponsors, swooping in to reel in all our fish? Wait till I tell Joe. He's gonna blow. Just like this bus."

"Exactly—tell Joe!" Cleo said, ignoring the dig at her bus. "The mayor's talking about a floating casino too. Imagine all the noise and disruption and pollution. All bad for fish. Warn all your friends, TJ."

"I sure as heck will," the mechanic promised. He glanced toward the back of the bus. "Hey, since you're here, can I look real quick? I need a new book. I like history and biography, something exciting."

Henry brightened. "I recently finished a wonderful account of the Lewis and Clark expedition. Unless someone else checked it out, it should be right back here." He led the way to the biography shelf.

With the men occupied, Gabby lowered her voice. "There's more, Cleo. Another reason the chief hauled in Ollie for questioning."

Cleo took a cue from Mr. Chaucer and groaned.

"It's his . . . uh . . . what do you call her? His houseguest? Colleague?" She nodded slyly toward the back of the bus. *"Friend?"*

"Whitney Greene, do you mean?" Cleo said, letting the "friend" innuendo slip straight past.

"Yes. What do you know about her?" Gabby wandered over to the first bookshelf, the New Reads. She looked through a cookbook, but Cleo could tell she was intently interested in the answer.

Cleo admitted she knew little. "She's not from here. Ollie told me she's moved around and works for an organization called Save Our Springs—S.O.S. She came up to help with the mud problem at Pancake Spring."

"I know a bit more," Gabby said, pausing in her cookbook perusal. "You should know too, since she's hanging around your place. She's not actually that much of an outsider. Her people are from Catalpa."

"Her people?" Cleo sorted through faces and family trees.

Whitney Greene . . . Cleo knew a Greenbriar family and some Greeleys.

Realization was beginning to take hold when Gabby snapped the cookbook shut and said, "She's a Krandall."

Cleo was glad she was sitting down. A Krandall. *A Krandall in her cottage?* A covert Krandall, cozying up to her grandson? "It was her hair," Cleo said, attempting to justify her unjustifiable observational failure. "It covered her face. She looked down a lot, and there was the camouflage attire." But now she saw hints. The prominent pointed nose. The eyes, small and inset. The penchant for stewing up trouble and stirring others into it. How had she not noticed?

"A Krandall?" TJ stepped up, holding a thick hardback. "Did I hear that right? There's a new Krandall in town? Thought we were fresh out of those, and good riddance."

Gabby leveled a serious gaze on TJ that had him standing straighter while simultaneously stepping back. She produced a folded flyer with a rather blurry photo of Whitney, face obscured by those frizzy curls.

Gabby handed TJ the paper. "If you see this woman, please call the Catalpa Springs Police immediately. She goes by the name of Whitney Greene."

TJ took the page, worry wrinkling his broad forehead. "Yes, ma'am. Is she dangerous?"

Everyone eyed Gabby expectantly.

"She's only wanted for questioning at this time," Gabby said. "In the *murder* investigation of Buford Krandall, as well as criminal trespass and destruction of property."

"Whoa," TJ said, clutching his book tight. "I gotcha. That girl could be a dangerous head-thumping killer. I'll put your flyer on our notice board. Joe and I will tell everyone to keep an eye out."

Cleo checked out TJ's book, and Henry accompanied the mechanic outside.

"*Is* Whitney dangerous?" Cleo asked, staring at a view of a raised yellow hood.

"Honestly? I don't know," Gabby said. She reached down to pet Rhett, who was back to fawning shamelessly at her ankles. "TJ's right—there's not a lot of Krandalls around. There's Buford's widow, but maybe Whitney as a niece would inherit something or hope to? But who knows, with an unpredictable guy like Buford. He could have made a will out to some cause. Like your library."

"I didn't kill him," Cleo said primly.

"I'm assuming that," Gabby said, poorly stifling a smile. "We need to talk to Whitney. I went to the station to run her license plate and information. By the time I got back to your place with Tookey, she was gone. Ollie won't say anything. Last I heard, he'd only give his name and rank as a springs defender. It's not helping the chief's opinion of him." She pursed her lips, her opinion clearly not high right now either.

"He's loyal," Cleo said, trying to explain Ollie's lovable features and flaws. "He becomes enamored."

"Uh-huh," Gabby said, sounding unconvinced and unimpressed. "So, did he know about Whitney's Krandall connection?"

Did he? Cleo replayed Ollie's eager introductions and descriptions of Whitney. "I think he would have said. He's not very good at keeping secrets. What's her exact relationship to Buford again?"

Gabby's pretty face squinched in thought. "Okay, so her father is Buford Krandall's estranged half-brother by their father's second wife. Whitney goes by the name of her mother's second husband." She threw up her palms. "Don't hold me to that. It's a very confusing family."

Krandalls were confusing. Cleo's thoughts swirled. She was careful about what she said out loud, so as not to get Ollie or Mary-Rose in more trouble. "Whitney came up here alone from Florida, Ollie told me. She supposedly rushed up to assess the situation at Pancake Spring before bringing in other S.O.S. members. What if she hurried up to Georgia by herself because she realized her uncle was involved? She might have been angry, embarrassed . . ."

"Greedy, opportunistic," Gabby added. "Say she *thinks* she could inherit and/or save the springs."

Poor Ollie. But Cleo saw a positive too. Now there was someone with much bigger murderous motives than Mary-Rose. Cleo added another possibility, telling Gabby about Buford's visit to Priscilla Pawpaw. "He borrowed a dozen or so notebooks from her, research notes. She thinks he was a super-fan of her books, but I suspect he was looking for something specific."

Gabby frowned. "Weird. I haven't seen notebooks in any evidence we collected. I'm supposed to go back out to Krandall House and find Buford's missing gun. I'll look for the notes when I'm there."

"What about Buford's library?" Cleo asked. "Someone tore it apart. There had to be a reason. To hurt something Buford loved? Looking for something?" She'd like to search the library herself.

Rhett flopped at Gabby's feet, and the deputy bravely ruffled his belly. "The chief thinks the books are a distraction."

"A distraction?" Cleo huffed. "I don't suppose he means books provide pleasant distractions from daily cares."

Gabby's snort was answer enough. "He still wants me to catalog all the books on the floor. See if there's any pattern. Like I'd know! It's more busywork."

"If that's the case," Cleo said, seeing an opening, "I'd like to retrieve the library books Mr. Krandall borrowed. Another patron has requested them." She gave thanks for Tamara, the Happy Trails gate defender, for expressing an interest in the books. "I could assist with your cataloging too. I am a professional librarian, and Henry is an expert in vintage books."

Gabby clearly saw through Cleo's intentions. She didn't shoot down the idea, though. "I'd have to ask the chief. If he sees it as a way to keep us out of his way, he might just say yes. I'll let you know." Her radio squawked, a garbled voice announcing a fender bender and a meeting at the chief's office. Gabby was adjusting her weapons belt, preparing to go. "Thanks for the tip about Priscilla Pawpaw and those notes," she said. "Drive safe. No more speeding, and call me if you spot Whitney Greene."

Cleo drove into town so slowly she got passed. Her mind, however, was racing. She spun through thoughts of Ollie and Whitney, Krandall House at night, the murky woods with its statues watching, the silenced drill, and a man lying dead.

Chapter Fifteen

Cleo dropped Henry and Mr. Chaucer off at The Gilded Page. Henry said he and the pug planned to have a nap, followed by a late lunch and a siesta. Perhaps a rare customer would come by, but hopefully not. Henry smiled warmly, "You do know how to make a Monday interesting, Cleo." He asked her to call with updates about Ollie and if she needed anything and urged her to be careful.

"Let me know when you make your next move," he added, his eyes bright with a twinkle and a wink.

"I only plan to read for now," Cleo said. "I'm going to spend all evening in with Priscilla Pawpaw's unsolved crimes. One of the books Buford checked out was dropped off in the library's returns box: *Killings in Cotton Country*."

"Doesn't sound particularly pleasant." Henry shuffled in his loafers. "Regarding, uh . . . pleasant things, when this is over, maybe we could have dinner? I'll cook, a repayment for your delicious Sunday lunch."

A lunch in which one guest was hauled off by the police,

another rushed to her aid, and two others rudely fled before dessert and cleaning up. Considering all that, Cleo thought she owed him a calmer meal. They could debate that later. "When this is over," she said.

"Soon, then," said Henry, an optimist.

As Cleo made her rounds in Words on Wheels later, she couldn't help thinking of Priscilla and her many unsolved crimes. What if this crime was never solved, the killer never caught? Without a culprit, suspicion would shadow Mary-Rose and Ollie. Their lives would never be the same. Worse, a murderer would lurk in pretty Catalpa Springs.

By the end of her day, Cleo's feet and head throbbed in dull aches. She'd had a busy afternoon, the frustrating kind, overfilled with lots to do, yet not enough getting done. The library remained unfixed and threatened. The bookmobile needed to be restocked and sorted, but Leanna wouldn't be in until tomorrow afternoon. Someone had sneaked gum on board and stuck the vile substance to the underside of a shelf. Maybelle? A child? Cleo decided to give children the benefit of the doubt.

But the underlying source of worry was Ollie. Cleo had called Fred at his office. Her eldest son was grumpy. He complained about the police jumping to conclusions and about Ollie wandering off toward silly whims instead of a sensible job. He even complained about Mary-Rose and indirectly chastised Cleo.

As if channeling his father, Fred asked Cleo to stay clear of her best friend. "Please, Mom. Look what trouble Mary-Rose has already caused. Oliver never would have gotten involved in this mess if it wasn't for *her*. We don't need any more trouble.

I told Angela too: stay away from Mary-Rose. Focus only on Ollie. Not that she listens to me either."

Cleo had called Angela next. She talked to her daughter-in-law's voicemail and later to Angela herself. Angela was much calmer than Fred. She said she had the "situation with Ollie" under control. "He won't be charged," she said briskly. "Surely. Most likely. Okay, probably. The police really don't have anything concrete on him. He's much better at keeping quiet than Mary-Rose."

Cleo didn't like that final "probably." Along her route, she parked the mobile library by the school and then downtown, within view of the wounded library. Several dozen patrons came by, many prodding her on the timing of repairs. Cleo gave what she hoped were rousing speeches supporting the library and instilling pro-fishing fears. She felt a little bit sullied, bad-mouthing fishing, but she justified her actions with the knowledge that the mayor—with his fish flags and banners and suspicious Vegas consultant—had started it.

Back home, Cleo pulled Words on Wheels as deep as she could down her driveway, almost bumping the garage, where she stashed Daddy's classic convertible. She hoped Wanda wasn't lurking in her garden next door, waiting to gossip and complain. Rhett hopped out of his crate and mewed chirpily.

"I'm glad to be back too," Cleo said. Even after the most tiring days, her spirits lifted whenever she returned to her house, a homey Victorian painted in sunny yellow, with white trim and a shiny metal roof. She admired the garden—more flowers, trees, and shrubs than grass. The jasmine was growing tall and glossy this year. A sphinx moth was sipping from flowers. In shape, coloring, and movement, the big moth disguised itself as a hummingbird. Cleo watched it hover and zip over a patch of blooms. Whitney had come in disguise too, calling herself an outsider with no ties to Catalpa.

Why bother with secrecy? Cleo wondered. Was the girl embarrassed by her eccentric uncle? Or was there a darker motive? Had she planned to kill Uncle Buford all along? Cleo rubbed at the tension thumping behind her temples. Rhett yelled meows at the porch door, wanting his dinner, but Cleo felt drawn down the garden path. She reached Ollie's little cottage. The periwinkle door was closed up tight. The drapes were drawn, and no one answered her knock. Angela had warned Cleo that once Ollie was done at the police station, Fred wanted his eldest son to stay at their place for the night. Whitney would be a fool—or awfully conniving and clever— to hide out where she'd last been seen, not to mention right next door to a police officer.

Cleo carefully felt under the right-hand flower box for the spare key. She opened the door, hoping the cottage was truly empty. A step inside assured her it was. The living room was dark and still and surprisingly tidier. The mess of papers was gone. So were the rucksack and the camouflage outfits. Cleo made her way to the bedroom. She found an unmade bed, but no evidence of a female visitor. No makeup—not that Whitney seemed the type to wear it. No female-sized shoes or toiletries and, most convincingly, no camo. It looked like Whitney was gone for good.

Cleo made sure Rhett was outside and then locked up. "A Krandall," she said again, still scandalized. She wondered if Mary-Rose knew. Mary-Rose was always good at faces. Cleo tried to call her friend. The phone rang and rang, the rings oddly echoing.

Rhett perked up his ears and tail and trotted back to the main house. Cleo followed the cat and the melodic rings. She found Mary-Rose coming up her front steps carrying a pie.

"Hang on, my phone's ringing," Mary-Rose said, thrusting the pie at Cleo.

"It's me." Cleo, now holding pie, was unwilling to risk tipping it to hang up.

Mary-Rose stopped the phones and took back the pie so Cleo could unlock the door. "I figured we needed this," she said.

Cleo eagerly agreed and ushered Mary-Rose into the kitchen.

Her friend plunked the pie down, then herself. "It's as low-sugar as my baker could do without artificial sweeteners. Raspberry curd with lots of meringue."

The meringue soared like snowy peaked mountains. Cleo worried she might drool.

Mary-Rose was saying she had more pie in a cooler in her car. "Chocolate pecan, Ollie's favorite. I have another for Angela, for her lawyering help. I know I drove her to fits." She shook her head. Her hair had come loose from its twist, and stands frizzed around her ears. Not even her rosy sundress brought color to her face. "Pie and apologies aren't enough. I heard. The police told me. I was consorting with a Krandall! I swear, Cleo, I had no idea. I never would have called S.O.S. if I'd known. I feel tricked and used and a big old fool, and now poor Ollie . . ."

"No, no," Cleo murmured soothingly, and busied herself filling the teapot and setting out cups and plates. Rhett upped his food demands. Cleo gave him an entire can of Fancy Tuna Feast to keep him happy and quiet.

"We don't know if Whitney did anything," Cleo pointed out. "Perhaps she did come up here to help with Pancake Spring. We can't judge all Krandalls based on Buford's bad-neighbor behavior. She could be completely innocent."

But in that case, why did she run away? Cleo told herself that pie would help her think. She sliced, admiring the glorious red raspberry and perfect fluffy topping.

"True," Mary-Rose said glumly. "Innocent until proven guilty, although try telling that to Chief Culpepper. What if Whitney is the killer? What if . . ." Mary-Rose jabbed her fork violently at the airy meringue. "What if she seduced Ollie into helping her?"

"No," Cleo said firmly. "Ollie would never get that far lost. He has a strong moral compass, if not a geographic one."

The teakettle whistled. Cleo laid out herbal tea packets and porcelain cups. How many hours had she and Mary-Rose sat in this kitchen? They always took the same seats. Cleo faced the stove, since she often had something cooking, baking, or boiling. Mary-Rose, the guest, got the view of the garden through the French doors. In the old days, Mary-Rose would visit in the afternoons and always leave by five. Any later and Richard, bless him, would fret about a delay in his five-thirty supper hour. Mary-Rose had sat right here with Cleo on the awful day Richard passed. They'd gotten through difficult times together. They'd get through this too.

Cleo put down her fork. "What happened when Buford shot at you?"

Mary-Rose fiddled with her cup. She dunked the peppermint tea bag and clinked the spoon. "It's all a mess and a half, isn't it? We were arguing and yelling, that's all. I was telling him to shut down that drill, and he was laughing at me, saying he'd get me for good this time. That's when he shot at me. Well, not *at* me. He aimed for one of his own shelves, nowhere near me. I still can't believe Zoe saw. How horrible! She must have taken our so-called 'secret' path through the woods." Mary-Rose moaned and held her head. "If Zoe's mom finds out, I'll never get to host grandmother weekends again."

"Let's hope we have it all resolved by the time her parents return," Cleo said. "When is that? In a week or a little more?"

Mary-Rose slumped deep into her chair, staring out to the garden. "A week and a half. I don't know how we'll figure out anything, Cleo. Whitney's disappeared, and who else is there? Other than me, of course. And Ollie, heaven forbid."

Cleo fortified herself with a sweet bite of pie before she answered. "Buford insinuated that he had something on Mayor Jeb Day, and the mayor had banned Buford from City Hall. Something was going on between those two." She took another bite and then described the mayor's consultant, Jimmy Teeks. "Henry and I wonder if he's a mobster."

"Oh, you and Henry?" Mary-Rose said with a twinkle in her tone.

Cleo forged on. "Then there's Kat Krandall-Stykes. I like her, so I hope she's innocent, but a spouse is an obvious suspect, especially one engaged in such a drawn-out divorce."

Mary-Rose shoved a piece of crust around her plate with her fork, looking hardly comforted by the pie or Cleo's list.

Cleo tried again. She'd been saving her biggest prospect for last. She filled Mary-Rose in on Priscilla Pawpaw, her books, and Buford's super-fan interest in Priscilla's research notes. "It could be my librarian's predisposition speaking," Cleo said. "But I think Buford's death connects to something in those books."

"Miss Pawpaw comes to the Pancake Mill," Mary-Rose said. "She always requests a table by an exit and won't put syrup on her pancakes. It's not even allowed on the table."

Cleo added the syrup information to her mental list, filing it under "suspicious."

Mary-Rose waggled her fork. "I remember when Priscilla Pawpaw gave a reading for the Happy Trails residents about two years back. She terrified everyone. Mom ordered new locks for her doors and didn't sleep for days. I bought one of Priscilla's books because I wanted to be supportive. The title's something like *Getting Away with Murder*."

"*A Guide to Getting Away with Murder*?" Cleo asked, quelling an image of the book by the same title lying crumpled beside Buford's body. The police had taken the book as evidence, and she'd be fine with them keeping it. Cleo wasn't superstitious, but that particular copy wouldn't be returning to her library shelves.

Mary-Rose shivered. "That's it. I didn't dare read it. Even her autograph was scary, in red ink and saying something like 'Lock yourself in with a good murder.' I have a scarf from her too. Looks like crime-scene tape. I kept it for Halloween. Where else would one wear that?"

Cleo had an idea, not about scarves, but about books. "I have her *Killings in Cotton Country*. It was left back at the library in the returns box, still checked out to Buford Krandall. What if we each read our respective Pawpaw books and then swap? We could look for anyone or any case we recognize. Someone from Catalpa Springs, a crime near here, a connection. Perhaps Buford recognized someone. What do you say? Want to make a new book group?"

Mary-Rose shivered. "Honestly? No. This sounds like a lousy book group. But I'll do it. I got us all into this."

"Together we'll all get out of it," Cleo said with more confidence than she felt.

Chapter Sixteen

Cleo faced a bright Wednesday morning with bleary eyes, a fuzzy head, and ears chafing at a mockingbird's cheerful trill. For two nights in a row, she'd stayed up late, reading. The night before, she'd spent with *Killings in Cotton Country*. Last night, she'd endured *A Guide to Getting Away with Murder*, swapped from her reluctant book-club partner, Mary-Rose. Each night Cleo read far past midnight, till hours when the frogs and crickets and night birds went silent and her old house awoke in creaks and groans.

Cleo added extra coffee to the percolator. She opened the refrigerator and stared, forgetting what she wanted. She eventually retrieved milk and realized what was happening. She had a hangover. A book hangover.

A library patron had told her the term, giving a name to a condition Cleo had known since childhood. Like the alcohol-induced variety, a book hangover came from overindulgence, from becoming so immersed in a world of words that one couldn't fully return to reality. Depending on the book, the hangover could render the reader dreamy or sorrowful, nostalgic or elated, or trapped in a distant land or time. Or—in the case of two straight nights of Priscilla Pawpaw—dazed, jumpy, and slightly queasy. Cleo opened the fridge again, retrieved the leftover raspberry meringue pie, and considered what she'd learned.

As promised by Priscilla Pawpaw's titles, Cleo knew a lot about murder. More than she ever wanted to know, and by methods she wished she could forget. She'd never look at snapping turtles the same again. Dear gracious. Or ironing boards or porta-potties . . . heavens! Now she knew why Priscilla avoided maple syrup, but she didn't want to think about it. She rubbed her forehead. The worst was, she'd only read two of the nine Priscilla Pawpaw books Buford Krandall checked out. She didn't yet have a clue to his interest. As of yesterday, when she and Mary-Rose had exchanged books, her friend didn't have any insight either.

Waiting for the coffee to burble, Cleo gazed across her backyard. The little cottage seemed lonely. Strangely, so did her house, where she rarely felt alone even when she was. Cleo sighed and poured kibbles into Rhett's food bowl.

"What was that Buford Krandall doing?" she murmured. She didn't expect her cat to answer, but she did expect him to be there. She looked around. No Rhett.

"Rhett?" She went to the staircase, leaned on the banister, and called upward. Was Rhett still in bed? He did enjoy wrinkling a freshly smoothed comforter. However, usually he'd hurtle downstairs when he heard Cleo in the kitchen.

No mews or thump or creaking floorboards indicated a large Persian overhead.

"Rhett Butler!" Cleo sang out. He had to be around

somewhere. He'd slept at the foot of her bed last night. In early morning, he'd chased a moth, stomping on her head in pursuit. Perhaps he was sunning on the porch. A cat door in the sunroom allowed Rhett access to the screened porch. Richard had installed it years ago for a previous cat, a lovely but pushy Siamese who demanded to be let in and out, in and out, driving Richard mad.

Cleo opened the front door, called her cat's name again. She was relieved to hear a chirpy merp in response. A furry face emerged, frowning over the edge of a cardboard box.

"Rhett, silly boy, what are you doing? Come get your breakfast." Cleo held the door. If a human was present to open doors for him, Rhett refused to stoop to his cat flap. Rhett yawned, showing his fangs. He hopped out of the cardboard box and languidly stretched. Like most cats, he couldn't resist boxes. Cat traps, Ollie called them.

"Come along, coffee and kibble are waiting," Cleo said. Rhett trotted to her, tail and head raised proudly. Cleo blinked. That box . . . it hadn't been there yesterday. It wasn't hers.

The box featured an image of Vidalia onions with the word "Sweet" printed below. It was empty of onions and most everything else, save a few papers. The pages were blue lined, their edges scruffy, as if torn from an old-fashioned school notebook. Anyone could have left the box. Cleo kept the screen door unlocked so visitors could reach the doorbell and the mailman could access the mail slot to her foyer.

Rhett head-bumped her shin, demanding his breakfast.

"Now, just wait," Cleo said. She didn't want to touch the papers. Rhett had already done enough possible damage by sitting on them. She gripped the box with her fingertips and carried it to a table that collected odds and ends and gardening bits. She read the top sheet. The handwriting was slanted and scrawled, the ink smudged, suggesting a leftie. The text described a house fire near Tampa and a family tragically lost. Foul play. Arson. Murder. Cleo remembered an arson account in *Killings in Cotton Country*. She bet the scribbler was Priscilla Pawpaw. Priscilla knew Cleo was interested in her research notes. Had the author left them for her? But Priscilla had also passionately warned Cleo not to get involved in solving crimes.

Cleo returned to the screen door and scanned her front garden. The only movement was a flash of red, a cardinal high in the magnolia. The air carried spring perfume and the soft sounds of violence, the chop, chop, chop of Wanda Boxer gardening. Cleo debated whether to go chat with her neighbor. It would surely be a distressing sight. Wanda employed a slash-and-hack approach to her property. She scalped her lawn, denuded the hedges, and ruthlessly beheaded flowers. Cleo thought that perhaps Wanda's nephew, Mayor Jebson Day, had inherited some of those genes, applying them to destroying nice things around town, instead of vegetation. However, Wanda also had sharp eyes and ears, and sometimes her gossip was even true. Ignoring Rhett's grumpy protests, Cleo stepped out.

"Hello, Wanda. Lovely morning, isn't it?" Cleo's bright greeting earned a scowl.

"Lubbers," Wanda said in reply. "They got my parsley and my begonias. Nothing lovely about lubbers."

There was always something folks could agree on, Cleo thought. With herself and Buford Krandall, it was their shared love of books and libraries. With Wanda, it was the reasonable and passionate dislike of lubbers. The massive grasshoppers were voracious and armored, as thick and long as fat fingers. Mama called them the devil's horses, an appropriate name, for lubbers could destroy an entire garden in the speed of a stampede. Cleo narrowed her eyes and scanned for signs of chewing. She listened for a lubber's devilish hiss.

"Staying home in your PJs today, are you?" Wanda asked, assessing Cleo's outfit. "Must be nice. That'll be a benefit of retirement, forced or not."

Cleo's eyes snapped from a gnawed leaf to Wanda's happily hostile face. "I am not retiring. I'm still the head librarian and—"

"Can you be head librarian of a bus?" Wanda asked. A stem of Cleo's climbing rose had recklessly strayed into Wanda's air space. Wanda aimed her clippers. Cleo looked away.

Wanda added sharp words to her clipping. "My nephew—Mayor Day, to you—says your whole library operation might have to be shuttered. No money. It's too bad, but he knows what he's doing. He has a master's in business administration."

"There will be no shuttering," Cleo said sharply, frustrated she'd willingly walked into Wanda's web.

Wanda turned her attention to her long-besieged privet. "Jeb has new and innovative plans. You're either in with the new or mired in the old, like that rattletrap bus of yours. Did you see our new town flags and banner? Fish capital of the world. Now that's something to be proud of."

"Capital of the universe," Cleo muttered, thinking she should have listened to her cat and gone inside for breakfast.

"See? Even you like the new motto. We have the best fishing in Georgia, that's for sure. Jeb came over to visit last night and told me all about it. Poor man's lonely, what with that wife of his off visiting her mother. *Again*." Wanda shook her head at her niece-in-law's daughterly devotions. "At least he has his projects to keep him busy. Jeb says there'll be fishing workshops and pros everywhere, more than you can shake a flounder at. I might take up fishing. I think I'd be good at it."

Wanda was tenacious and, judging by her gardening, had no qualms about killing living things. Cleo got to the point. "Wanda, did you happen to see anyone come by my place? Maybe early this morning or late last night?" She noted the hungry gossiper's glitter in Wanda's eyes. "Someone left a box on my porch. A gift," Cleo said quickly, hoping to dispel whatever lurid rumor Wanda might be spinning up. "I want to thank whoever left it."

Wanda looked unconvinced. She chopped at privet twigs, making Cleo wait. "Yes," she said slowly, stretching the word and Cleo's nerves. "Last night? I heard a visitor. It was late. The porch door squeaking woke me up. You need to get a man in to oil that hinge, Cleo. I considered calling the police, but what thanks did I get the last few times I called in crimes and nuisances? None—that's right. None. Remember the drone? And that police car . . . how many times have I complained about that?"

Wanda believed the presence of Gabby's police vehicle made the neighborhood look dangerous, thereby—and most illogically—attracting criminals. The other thorn in Wanda's side, the drone, was a toy owned by a man up the street. Any adult flying cameras in a little helicopter must be a peeping Tom, Wanda contended, a pervert set on spying through her second-story windows.

Cleo summoned the dregs of her pre-caffeinated patience. "Did you *see* the person who left the box?"

Wanda snapped along with her clippers. "No! What are you suggesting? That I'd be looking? Like some creep with a drone? No, I look away when you have that boyfriend of yours over. I don't take notice when your grandson's carrying on with a *wanted* woman." Wanda had raised her voice. A man walking by with a small dog shot them a worried look. "Your own grandson, Cleo, shacking up in your own backyard with a Krandall!"

The dog walker tugged his pooch away.

Wanda bellowed. "Shacking up with a potential killer! An eco-terrorist!"

"It's a historic cottage," Cleo retorted tartly. "There is no *shacking* involved."

Glowing with smug satisfaction, Wanda edged her clippers a smidge over their shared fence and gave Cleo's rose another snip.

Cleo gathered her robe and her temper and took her leave. " 'Bye then, Wanda. Thanks so much," she said with syrupy sweetness that a more perceptive neighbor would have pegged as extreme irritation. "Have a lovely day."

Mutters of lubbers followed her. Coffee and the mystery box called, but Cleo had another neighbor to visit first.

* * *

Gabby Honeywell didn't answer her door. Cleo lingered tactfully in case the deputy was in the shower. She peeked at the back patio to see if Gabby was twisted up with yoga. Rhett meowed, but no one answered. Cleo was heading home when Wanda yelled down the picket fence lines.

"She's out! Left this morning in that nuisance police car of hers. Speeding, always speeding, that one. A menace. I should call the police."

Irritated, Cleo waved cheerily and hustled inside. She fed Rhett a can of smelly Tuna and Mackerel Delight, one of his favorites. She treated herself to coffee, pie, and more of both, and she thought. She thought some more over the dishes. Then she called Gabby's cell phone. Her neighbor answered in a whisper.

"Cleo, hang on . . ."

Seconds passed and Gabby came back on in a low voice. "The chief is giving a briefing. I stepped out of the room but can't be gone long. Is everything okay?"

"Yes," Cleo said automatically. "No, not quite," she clarified, and quickly told Gabby about the box. "I think it contains some of Priscilla Pawpaw's notes. It can wait."

Gabby politely disagreed. "That could be important. Someone must have left it for you for a reason. There was no note with it? Nothing?"

A male voice rumbled in the background. "Something you want to share with the class, Deputy Honeywell? Secret notes?"

"Sorry, Chief," Gabby said, sounding admirably unflappable. "A tip has just come in. I'll follow up when we're done with our briefing."

"We're done," the chief said. "What's this big tip?"

"Cleo Watkins is calling, sir. She—"

Insults to Cleo's age and gender ensued. Cleo advised Rhett not to listen.

"What's Cleo Watkins meddling in now?" the chief said, when he'd settled down.

Gabby calmly reported the facts. "Someone dropped a box off on her porch overnight. It appears to contain notes by that true-crime author, Pawpaw, the one Mr. Krandall was so interested in. She's my neighbor. I was going to go over and—"

Again the chief interrupted. "You'll do what you were assigned, Honeywell, which you'd know if you hadn't skipped out in the hall to chat. You and Tookey are to search for—and find—that blasted Whitney Krandall woman. Whitney Greene, whatever she's calling herself. While you're at it, track down Buford Krandall's lawyer. We need his will, if there is one. Ask his widow again. She's sounding too happy, claiming he wrote her out. And don't forget the inventory of Krandall's library. I'll visit Mrs. Watkins myself. Tell her to expect me and not to touch that box."

"Yes, sir," Gabby said. Silence consumed the line for a bit, during which Cleo scratched Rhett behind his ears and he purred loudly. Gabby came back on with a long sigh. "Sorry. Did you hear all that? The chief's in a mood. It's this case. Hope I didn't throw you under the bus, so to speak."

A man in a mood was not Cleo's preferred start to a sunny morning, but she'd already withstood Wanda gardening. The chief could hardly be worse. She assured Gabby she'd be fine. "I'll be ready," she said. She would be. She'd don some fresh rubber gloves and snap a photo of every notebook page before Chief Culpepper arrived. Thank goodness for her children and grandchildren giving her a phone with a camera.

* * *

Silas Culpepper stomped inside, heady with cologne and bluster. He looped his thumbs through straining suspenders and surveyed the corners of Cleo's tidy foyer as if the mystery box's owner might be lurking behind the umbrella stand. He peeked among jackets on the coat rack and began to elaborate on the chain of evidence.

"Coffee?" Cleo asked.

He frowned at the disruption. "Sure. But as I was saying, the police should have received this evidence, not *you*."

"Oh yes," Cleo said agreeably.

The man *was* especially petulant and pugnacious in the morning. *Bless his wife's heart,* Cleo thought, but then Mrs. Culpepper got to scoot the chief out the door to work each day.

"I didn't ask for the box. It just appeared," Cleo said, leading him through to the kitchen. "Rhett found it."

"Who?" the chief said. "Who's Rhett? You have *another* boyfriend?"

Cleo focused on positive thoughts, like how wise she'd been to stash her lovely pie in the fridge. She'd felt petty doing it. Hiding pie was selfish, childish, even gluttonous, and not at all the act of a good hostess. Yet, now she felt justified. Silas Culpepper didn't deserve pie. He likely would have found something questionable about it anyway.

"Rhett Butler is my—" Cleo started to say. She stopped short, seeing where the naughty Persian was. Rhett was on the forbidden kitchen table and—worse—in the box, foot raised and enthusiastically cleaning his back leg.

Cleo regrouped. "Pie?" she asked brightly. "Coffee?" She pointed toward the fridge and coffee maker, both in the opposite direction of the table. "Help yourself. Pie's in the refrigerator." It was hardly polite to ask a guest to fetch his own food, but it worked.

While the chief poked about the fridge, Cleo scooped up Rhett. She plunked the Persian on a chair and, using a dishtowel in lieu of gloves, moved the box to the counter.

"Here are the notes," she said, putting out a plate and fork for the chief.

"Wait . . . Was that the box your cat was just sitting in? Was that flea-bitten cat washing his privates on my evidence?"

"What?" Cleo said, with feigned confusion, a deflection trick she'd learned from her grandchildren. "Rhett's been recently groomed. No fleas." The insult! She petted Rhett, who rightfully glowered at the chief.

Oblivious to Cleo's and Rhett's disapproving gazes, Silas Culpepper tucked into a hefty slice of pie. Cleo added flattery to the menu. "I am so very glad that *you* personally came to examine this box, Chief. I said to Deputy Honeywell, the chief will know exactly what to do, and she agreed. Such a smart young woman."

The chief puffed his chest and his overstretched suspenders, which today were gold with a measuring tape design. "Forensics. We'll look for fingerprints and any trace evidence. Handwriting analysis. DNA." He expounded on DNA analysis for the rest of his pie. Then he pushed his plate aside and snapped on latex gloves. "You did the right thing, calling us. Keep on doing the right thing, and stay out of my way. I understand, it looks bad for your grandson and friend, but if they're killers—"

"They're not," Cleo said firmly. She'd been about to inform the chief of a crust crumb on his nose. She let it go.

"If—I said *if*," the chief said, adjusting his suspenders. "But you should prepare yourself. You being a civilian and a lady of a mature age, you don't think the way we professionals do. We know the worst in people, what they're capable of."

Cleo smiled and let him go on explaining the ways of the world. Her smile faded as soon as the door shut behind him. Cleo was neither rosy-eyed nor sheltered. She knew what people were capable of. Heavens, she'd just spent two nights with the works of Priscilla Pawpaw. Cleo shook away the foggy remnants of her reading hangover. She had to focus. She had to be sharp. Do the right thing, Chief Culpepper said. Well, she'd keep on doing just that.

Chapter Seventeen

"Oh dear," Henry said. It was later that morning. He and Cleo stood on the curb, the wounded library to their right, Words on Wheels to their left, and Mr. Chaucer panting between them. It was only ten, but heat waves wiggled through humidity as thick as clouds. The air was heavy and still. Cleo's bus, however, was rocking.

Henry and Mr. Chaucer stared at Words on Wheels with wide-eyed worry. "My," Henry said.

"Yes," Cleo said, thinking she had been warned. Vernon Givens had asked if she'd ever been on a party bus. Well, now she'd be driving one. Words on Wheels was filled with jubilant and likely tipsy Ladies Leaguers. Pink hats fluttered like happy birds. Laughter rolled out the open windows, punctuated by an occasional "Whooo!"

"They'll settle down," Cleo said, hopefully. "I'm glad they're so excited." She was also happy she'd made Rhett stay home. Rhett didn't approve of rollicking.

Seven members of the Ladies League, led by Bitsy Givens, were squished aboard the bus, along with questionable accompaniments. Thermoses and flasks contained Bloody Marys and hot coffee. Baskets of buttery cheese straws made the rounds. Then there was Maybelle.

"Come on!" Maybelle yelled. She sat up front, within gripping distance of the driver and the door. "Quit your flirting, Cleo Watkins, and let's get rolling."

"Godspeed," Henry said gravely. Mr. Chaucer turned mournful eyes to Cleo and moaned.

Cleo climbed into her captain's seat and waved to Henry, who gave a jaunty salute. The engine protested, coughing, then wheezing, and finally roaring to a belch. The stop sign flew out, an occasional malfunction. Cleo wrenched it back in and revved the engine until the sputtering steadied. Her passengers cheered, and Cleo raised the handy microphone and made sure everyone was buckled up, drinks stowed.

"Our first stop is the . . ." Cleo paused. She'd planned to visit the elementary school, but young children probably shouldn't be exposed to rowdy philanthropists. She thought fast. "Happy Trails Retirement Village," she announced. The Happy Trailers approved of early cocktails and were always happy to see Words on Wheels.

"Woo-hoo, Florida!" someone yelled from the back of the bus.

"I don't want to go to Florida," Maybelle Givens grumbled.

Cleo smiled. Yes, there was always common ground. "We'll be sticking to the Georgia side," she assured Maybelle and herself.

Bitsy, decked out in a lacy pink confection of a sunhat, a matching sundress, and a sunny mood took a seat beside her mother-in-law. "Oh, Mama Givens, this is gonna be such fun.

I'm so glad you let me twist your arm into coming along. We're all honorary librarians for the morning. It's thrilling, Cleo! Just thrilling."

It was a delight to have such happy passengers and vociferous support. Cleo felt a surge of hope. She gave the bus a boost of gas. Her passengers whooped again, and they were off.

At the Happy Trails guardhouse, Cleo pulled up and introduced everyone to Tamara. Tamara showed off her latest reading, praised Cleo's literary advice, and got everyone cheering to the chant of "Save our library!" Cleo's thoughts flashed to Save Our Springs and the missing Whitney Greene. They rolled on to the Social Hall, where another rollicking group was steaming out, waving strips of colorful fabric.

"Strip bingo," Cleo intoned, tour-guide-like, into her microphone. Her intended explanation was cut off by cheering. When her passengers quieted down, Cleo continued. "Strip bingo awards strips of fabric to quilters. Words on Wheels has a selection of crafts books, including several on quilting. Happy Trails is also home to a *prolific* local author, Priscilla Pawpaw."

An idea sparked. "Would you all like to meet her?" Cleo asked, seeing a proverbial two-birds-with-one stone opportunity. She could entertain the Leaguers and ask Priscilla Pawpaw about the anonymous box of notes. Her guests enthusiastically agreed.

"Wonderful. I'll pop over and see if Miss Pawpaw can spare a moment," Cleo said. "Who would like to be the honorary librarian while I'm gone?"

Hands shot up. The basket of cheese straws was passed

around and thermoses opened. Cleo tactfully suggested that snacks should be enjoyed outside on the patio tables.

"I'll have to do it," Maybelle grumbled. "Cheese makes me bloaty. Tomato juice gives me heartburn."

"Lovely," Cleo said. "About volunteering, I mean. If anyone wants to borrow a book, just scan their library card on this handy little device, like at the market and—"

"I get it," Maybelle snapped.

"Mama always uses the self-checkout at the supermarket," Bitsy said. "No matter how many groceries she has."

"I'm no idiot," Maybelle said. "I don't want people touching my food."

"I'll be back in a jiffy," Cleo promised. Bitsy assured her it was their pleasure. Maybelle griped it was better than sitting around bored.

Who could be bored around books? Cleo decided Maybelle was just trying to get a rise out of her. Taking a shortcut across the Social Hall's lawn, Cleo arrived at Sweetgum Court slightly out of breath and dewy, Mama's euphemism for sweating buckets. She employed her folding fan and headed for the row of stucco cottages.

Cleo was stepping up to Priscilla's glossy goldenrod door when she realized she wasn't alone. Shrubbery shuddered. Heavy breathing and muttered cursing followed. Chief Silas Culpepper pushed through the leaves, a petal on his prodigious belly and a frown on his red face.

"Mrs. Watkins? What are you doing here?" His frown deepened.

Cleo attempted to look innocently befuddled. "Doing? I

have Words on Wheels parked at the Social Hall, with guests from the Ladies League. We're hoping Miss Pawpaw can pop over."

The chief snorted and brushed vegetation from his belly. "Yeah, right. Like I believe that's all you're up to. What did I tell you just this morning?"

Cleo sped up her fanning. "You said to keep to my own business. I am. I'm in the library business, and Priscilla Pawpaw is a prominent local author whom I'd like to invite to speak with patrons. What are you doing? Checking to see if she wrote those notebook pages and dropped them at my house? How clever." Cleo hoped flattery might prompt the chief to give up some information.

He didn't bite. "I'm doing police business, and neither of us will be doing business with Pawpaw. She's gone. Seems our local murder expert has flown the coop."

Cleo thought his assessment a bit extreme. Priscilla could simply be out running errands. Or maybe she was inside, hiding behind her computer screen, determined to write without interruption. It was presumptuous of the chief—and herself, Cleo acknowledged—to appear without warning, demanding the author's attention.

"I know what you're thinking," Chief Culpepper said.

Cleo turned her mind to strip bingo. He could never know she was thinking of that.

"You think she went out shopping, don't you?" the chief said. "Wrong. I just talked to her neighbor."

A round, wrinkled face poked over the hedge. Short white hair set off rich brown skin. Sharp eyes sparkled behind rhinestone-crusted spectacles.

Cleo waved and raised her voice. "Good morning, Miss Adelaide. Do you need any books?" Adelaide Cox was ninety-six, sharp as a tack, deaf as a stone, and unmovable as a mountain about wearing her hearing aids.

"What?" Adelaide said, frowning. "Boots?"

"Books!" Cleo bellowed.

"Crooks!" Adelaide countered, eyes landing suspiciously on the chief.

"She heard Miss Pawpaw leaving this morning," Chief Culpepper said. "Not just leaving to go out for some milk. Hightailing it out of town."

Cleo made a polite effort to hide her skepticism.

"She had her hearing aids in for the four-thirty news." Culpepper thumped a finger at his ear, miming for Adelaide to attend to her hearing. The elderly woman flipped him a rude gesture and disappeared back behind the hedge. "She did," he insisted. "She hears like a bat once she's got those in. There's nothing wrong with her eyes. She spotted me the second I arrived. She had binoculars on me."

"A good neighbor," Cleo said. "But sometimes even good neighbors can misread the situation." She thought of Wanda and her rude words about shacks and shacking and boyfriends.

The chief peered under Priscilla's small front stoop, as if the jumpy author might be hiding there. "Yeah," he said, rising and stretching his belly. "That may be so, but Adelaide here saw Pawpaw stuffing her car with suitcases. In a mighty big hurry too. As a professional investigator, I deduce that Pawpaw was running. Now, is she our killer? A witness? A collaborator?" He might have gone on with his professional speculations, but Adelaide popped up again.

The elderly woman was jabbing a device into her ear. "She sped off like a bat outta you know where," Adelaide said. The hearing aid emitted a high-pitched buzz. She reared back with a "*Whoa*."

Cleo considered the situation. The chief was right. Why would Priscilla leave town? Another trip was a possibility, but Priscilla had just returned from Daytona Beach. Surely she wouldn't rush off again anytime soon or at four in the morning.

"Priscilla warned my friend and me when we were visiting," Cleo said. "She told us not to try to solve murders. I think she may have been scared."

"Your friend?" Adelaide said. "Looked like a boyfriend to me. He's a cutie. I like a man with facial hair."

Cleo didn't bother to correct her. "Priscilla said she warned Buford Krandall too. I wonder if that's what he was doing," Cleo mused. "Trying to solve a crime?"

"That warning sure did Buford Krandall a lot of good," the chief grumbled. "See, Mrs. Watkins? A man is dead. Murdered. A woman is presumably on the run. That's why you civilian types should keep your big noses out of police investigations."

"Big nose!" Adelaide exclaimed. "That man with the big nose, like a beak. He got himself murdered. I saw him in the paper. He visited Priscilla."

"Yes, ma'am," the chief said patiently. "That would be Buford Krandall. He was a fan of your neighbor's books. They had a nice friendly visit. We heard all about it, but thank you for the reminder."

Adelaide scowled. "Friendly? No, sir, not that other time he visited. I *almost* took my ears out, those two got so loud, yelling and fussing." She tapped an ear, and the high-pitched whine resumed.

Cleo surveyed the setting. The cottages were slightly offset, but she could see windows aligning between them. Adelaide could have a good view of her neighbor's activities. "Priscilla gave me the impression she adored Buford Krandall," Cleo said.

Adelaide got a hearty chuckle out of that. "She liked him the first time he visited. Sweet tea. Smiles. Flirting. Second time, they had a big old fight. She looked fit to kill. She'd know how to do it too, wouldn't she? She has all sorts of murdering ideas, that girl. She could do it right." Adelaide nodded approvingly.

Cleo shivered. Had she and Henry called on a killer? Is that why Priscilla was so adamant in warning them off? Cleo thought about Buford's body sprawled across Priscilla's murder guide, pages turned to the chapter on bludgeoning. An artistic flourish? An author's revenge?

The chief rubbed his temples as if in pain. "Okay, let's get this straight. The second time you saw them meet, they fought. Do you know why, ma'am?"

Adelaide, however, was messing with her ears again. The chief had to repeat the question twice before she answered. "Me? How would I know? I can't hear through walls. Now when they got outside, I heard her yell, 'Leave it be.' She was screeching that she didn't care what he'd found out. It's those quiet types, I tell you. Once a wallflower sort flies off the handle, watch out." Adelaide ducked back behind the hedge, muttering about noise and commotion.

The chief was grumbling too. Cleo left him to it. She

mulled Priscilla's angry words, as recounted by Adelaide. *Let it be. She didn't care what he'd found out.* It reinforced her theory that Buford Krandall's reading list might provide a clue.

At the front walkway, she heard her name. Adelaide chugged toward her, swinging a cane that barely touched the ground.

"I do need a new book," the older woman declared, waggling the cane at Cleo. "I want something spicy, and I don't mean Cajun cooking."

"The bookmobile has lots of options," Cleo said. She suggested titles Adelaide might like. Adelaide countered with her criteria, many of which Cleo already knew. The list got more difficult to meet every time. *No tiny font. No long paragraphs in italics. None of that sans serif font. A good spine. Not too heavy, the book or the story. No heroines under thirty. No serial killers. Nothing sad involving animals.* "And I want my hunk tall and handsome and sweet talking and good to his mama," Adelaide was saying. "No foul mouths. No boys, either. I want my hunk over thirty too. And no kilts."

"I'm sure we have just what you're looking for," Cleo said, not at all certain. She considered the thriller Tamara had checked out. There were more books in that series, though she didn't know the shirtless hero's age or filial affections. "Words on Wheels is parked right over . . ." She stopped and stared.

"Where?" Adelaide demanded.

Cleo froze. She blinked and looked again. She might lose her keys, but she'd never lost an entire bus.

The parking lot was empty. No bus, no strip bingo players, no ladies in pink hats. A young man puttered nearby. He was in a golf cart, aiming a watering wand at the many hanging baskets. Cleo scanned in all directions. Then she heard a horn, blaring. She knew that horn. That was Words on Wheels! The sound was coming from the south.

Cleo hustled around the side of the Social Hall for a better view. Over a grassy berm and across a clipped fairway, pink hats bobbed like flamingos on the run. They were following a flash of bright yellow.

Cleo flagged down the golf cart. She hopped in, uninvited, with Adelaide squeezing beside her.

"Follow that bus!" Cleo cried.

"Floor it!" Adelaide crowed.

"Yes, ma'am." The driver took off with admirable speed. They bumped airborne across the rough, spun out in a sand hazard, and barreled through a foursome of elderly men. One raised a putter in protest.

Adelaide yelled "Fore! Playing through!" and waved her cane menacingly.

Cleo was yelling in her head. *Faster, faster . . .* Words on Wheels was in danger, and she couldn't afford to lose her only remaining library.

Chapter Eighteen

The horn had gone silent. Words on Wheels had stopped too, and not gently. The bus tilted forward, front wheels lodged in a ditch, nose smack against a leaning palm. Cleo gave thanks to the unfortunate tree. A few feet more and the bookmobile would have hurtled into a water hazard. Cleo thought she saw an alligator's nose poking up among the reeds and lilies. They'd definitely crossed into Florida.

"Dang," their golf-cart chauffeur said, stretching the word in horrified awe. On their bumpy cross-fairway ride, Cleo had learned his name was Marco, he was a certified horticultural-ist, and his folks lived in Claymore.

"Now that's some bad driving," Marco said. He parked the golf cart and bounded around the front to help Adelaide and Cleo out.

Bitsy descended the bus's steps. She was hatless. A spa-ghetti strap slipped off one shoulder, and she was hobbling on a broken high heel.

"Stop, thief!" Adelaide declared, jabbing her cane in Bitsy's direction.

Cleo told Adelaide she could lower her weapon. "It's okay," she said, though it clearly wasn't.

Bitsy's face was as pink as her dress. "Cleo, I'm *sooooo*, so sorry! I don't know what happened."

The other Ladies Leaguers were gathered inside. Laughter and chatter drifted out, suggesting no injuries, thank goodness. No human injuries, that is. Marco was inspecting the bookmobile, bravely wading into the ditch and peeking underneath.

Bitsy pressed her hands in prayer formation. "I was in the back, looking at cookbooks. Mama Givens was only trying to start the air-conditioning up. She said she needed to give it a boost, and we started going, but we couldn't stop it. It's like the brakes gave out. They were smooshy, and then nothing." Bitsy exhaled and lowered her voice to a whisper. "Mama may have punched the gas once or twice, but only because she was trying to get a pedal that worked."

Cleo reminded herself to be thankful and gracious. "She's okay? You're all right?" When Bitsy nodded yes to both, Cleo allowed herself to internally vent. *Maybelle! Punching pedals!* This is how drivers of a certain age and gender got bad reputations, sullying their competent, safe-driving peers.

Bitsy was struggling to remove her height-mismatched shoes. Cleo offered her a shoulder to lean on, telling herself to be generous in other ways too. Could the brakes actually have failed? The bus was having some health issues—as was natural with age—but the brakes had felt fine earlier, and mechanics had just recently checked under the hood. Cleo took a deep breath and went to get a closer look at the damage—and the unauthorized driver.

Five cooing Ladies Leaguers were helping Maybelle disentangle from the seatbelt. To Cleo's eyes, Maybelle appeared more pleased than injured. Sympathetic words were being said. "There, there. You poor, sweet thing." Then there were not-so-sympathetic words. "Imagine," Cleo heard a snapping voice say, "Cleo Watkins driving us around in this death trap!"

Cleo bristled. *Death trap!* Such rudeness. There was surely nothing wrong with her bus that its rogue driver hadn't caused.

Maybelle stood, appearing quite spritely. She spotted Cleo and pointed a witchy finger. "You! Your bus, this book-heavy death machine, tried to kill me!" Maybelle twisted her neck with the dexterity of an owl and declared she had whiplash. "I need a doctor. And my chiropractor. I stomped on those brakes. Nothing happened! My corns are aching from it. Bitsy, call the podiatrist and the massage therapist and a lawyer. I'm suing!"

The cooing ladies in pink parted, and Maybelle stomped off the bus, robust with anger.

Cleo dogged her heels. "So, Maybelle, you were trying to get the air-conditioning going? Why were you buckled up?"

"For safety," Maybelle muttered. "Looks like I was right too."

"You had to put the bus in gear. You meant to move," Cleo persisted.

The older woman stopped and thrust fists to her hips. "So what? It was hot. If we couldn't get good AC air, we needed a breeze. Anyway, I like to drive."

Cleo did too. She looked back at the sad sight. Marco was inside. He saw her and held up the keys. Wise man. She should have removed them when she left her precious bookmobile with Maybelle Givens.

Maybelle was reinforcing this thought. "*You* left us— me—in charge, Cleo. You said I was the honorary, temporary librarian. If I'm going to work, I want some perks. So I took the bus for a spin. So what? I didn't know it would try to kill me." She jutted her chin defiantly and then seemed to recall whiplash. "Ow," she said, a hand clutching her neck.

Cleo suspected she was just fine. However, Words on Wheels and the library cause might be in for a whole lot of pain. The Ladies Leaguers were huddling. Their heads shook, and they flashed accusatory glances Cleo's way. Bitsy was among them, making the prayerful pleading gesture again.

Cleo saw another golf cart approaching fast, soaring across the fairway. A scooter zipped down the cart path, its driver hunched as if to urge it on. Help arriving? Not for her. Cleo needed a tow truck and a mechanic. She went back to Marco's cart to retrieve her purse and cell phone. Adelaide sat snoozing, head back, lips softly sputtering. *Ah, to be so relaxed.* A horrible thought popped into Cleo's head, a thought that made her shiver. She wondered if she *should* retire.

"No," Cleo said, aloud and louder than necessary.

"Gnomes!" Adelaide blurted. She started, shifted, and fell back to sleep.

The scooter skidded to a stop, and a young man jumped off. He was about Ollie's age, sporting similarly messy hair and a fledgling beard, and wielding a camera and a name tag. Toby. The young reporter Leanna said she'd call and ask to cover the bookmobile tour.

"*Catalpa Gazette*," he announced. "Man, I was going to blow off this boring bookmobile tour, but this is good stuff!" He bounded off to take shots of the wounded bus and

Maybelle, holding her neck and being attended to by the driver of the other golf cart, Happy Trail's resident lawyer and accident chaser, Thurgood Byron.

A bee buzzed around Adelaide and she awoke again, cane swinging. "What'd I miss? What's going on?"

"Nothing good," Cleo said.

*　*　*

Further assistance and bad news arrived in spurts. Cleo waited in the shade, watching and dreading. The chief sped over, siren blaring. The mayor arrived with potato-faced Jimmy Teeks and a tall middle-aged woman in teenager attire. TJ and Joe, the mechanics, rolled in in their biggest tow rig. Thurgood Byron briefed the press, all eager one of him. Vernon Givens stormed up in his black SUV, with Leanna in the passenger seat. Adelaide had gotten a golf-cart ride back home, deeming the post-crash "boring."

Vernon rushed to his mother, who was honing her wounded routine with the help of Thurgood. Leanna came over to stand with Cleo. Bitsy joined them.

Leanna tugged anxiously at her tight navy pencil skirt. She was buttoned up in a cream silk blouse with a big bow down the front. "Is your mama-in-law going to be okay?" she asked Bitsy, tugging a finger under the tight neck of the blouse.

Bitsy was looking more herself, except for her bare feet. Her lipstick and hat were back in place, and her face was coated in a heavy layer of powder. "Mama's fine," she said, and Cleo detected a hint of bitterness. "Don't worry, Cleo. Mama's acting up so Vern and that lawyer will fuss over her and I'll have to haul her off to every back, neck, foot, and head specialist in the county. She loves her doctors." She pursed her perfect lips. "Listen to me, being all ugly. I'm shaken up. Truly, I think she's okay, and it was kind of her fault."

Cleo remained tactfully silent, letting Leanna ask how the bus took off on its own.

Bitsy threw up her palms. "Mama started it up and took it for a spin. She's . . ." She seemed to be struggling for a nice word.

"Eccentric?" Cleo supplied. "Incorrigible?"

Bitsy gave a wry smile. "Those. And stubborn as a mule." She glanced back at her mother-in-law and husband. "It's Vern I'm most worried about. He told me this morning that Mama Givens didn't want to go on this tour and to let her stay home. I bullied her to come along. For her own good, to get her away from the house and doctors' offices! I was wrong there. Messed up again." She kicked bare feet at the grass. Cleo considered taking her shoes off too. Toes in grass seemed nice and calming.

Bitsy kicked a dandelion puff, sending seeds soaring. "The Leaguers are going to be disappointed in me too. A couple of them never did think I'd make a good president."

"But they can't blame you," Cleo said. "None of this was your fault."

"I chose the library as our cause this year and came up with the bookmobile tour idea. Jasmine Wagner, our VP— she wanted to redecorate the jail and pump in aromatherapy. She says it's a depressing gray place and that serene surround-ings and essential oils would help criminals reform."

Cleo had visions of Mary-Rose and Ollie locked away in grim, non-aromatic cells. Perhaps Jasmine should have picked the cause. She tried to fan away such awful thoughts. "The library is a great cause. They were all behind it this morning. When it turns out that Maybelle pushed the wrong pedal, they'll understand. Everyone's had a shock."

Bitsy reached out and squeezed Cleo's hand. "You're right. Positive thoughts. Speaking of which, Leanna, you're looking pretty as a peach blossom. How's banking going?"

Leanna bubbled about the joys of filing and working for Mr. Givens. "His previous assistant didn't do anything! I mean, no offense, but the computer files are a mess. I have loads to do. It's great." She fussed with her skirt and shifted in her pointy patent shoes and then asked, worriedly, "Is Words on Wheels going to be okay?"

Cleo almost feared knowing. She'd have to face the gory repair costs sometime. Or convince Thurgood Byron to switch clients and sue Maybelle Givens. "Let's go see," she said.

* * *

TJ—at least, Cleo thought it was TJ—was under the bus. Joe had his head under the hood. The mechanics had towed Words on Wheels to firmer, flatter ground. A long, deep gash marred the driver's side. The front bumper was badly crumpled, and a wheel looked twisted, like a broken limb.

"Tell us the damage," Mayor Day said, stepping up with an alligator's smile. His female companion, tall and busty, squeezed into tight capris and a bejeweled, belly-revealing top, gave him a *behave* look.

"Hang on," TJ grunted from somewhere underneath the chassis.

Cleo leaned toward Bitsy. "Who is that woman with the mayor?" she whispered.

Bitsy gave a little snort. "Her? Our town's new public relations maven, Mimi Cantor." She examined her glossy peach nails and added, "The Catalpa cougar. Our mayor's her plaything, if you get my drift."

Leanna sucked in a breath. "No! The mayor? Fooling around? His whole campaign was about family and fishing."

"Aren't those always the ones," Bitsy said dryly.

Leanna continued to tsk while Cleo's mind moved to motive, at least for the mayor's delight in Buford's death. Had Buford found out about the family-man mayor's fling?

TJ scooted out from under the bookmobile. He brushed off his backside. Grass stains and mud remained. "Well," he said reluctantly.

Everyone except Jimmy Teeks drew closer in anticipation. The Vegas consultant hung back, hands in his gray suit pockets, small brown eyes assessing.

"Well?" Jeb Day demanded, impatient for a man who could wait hours for a bass to bite.

"Well?" Thurgood Bryon parroted. "Is my client correct in asserting that that bus was a rolling death machine?"

TJ shot a befuddled look at Joe. Then he turned to Cleo. "Ma'am, your brake lines broke."

"I knew it!" Maybelle crowed. Vernon threw a protective arm around his mother, who was cackling about faulty maintenance. "I could sue the town."

"Good idea!" Thurgood said heartily. "Emotional and physical injury. Post-traumatic shock."

"Sue the librarian," Mayor Day muttered. Mimi Cantor put a soothing hand on his arm. He fussily yanked away.

"No, no, wait." TJ raised oil-stained hands. "Will all y'all listen? The brake lines broke 'cause they were cut halfway through, just waiting to go. If you ask me, someone messed with them. It's a good thing Miss Maybelle here wasn't going highway speeds like, uh . . ."

"Like our speed-demon librarian?" Mayor Day said, ever callous.

TJ stood straighter, frowning. "Listen up! Someone was aiming for this bus to crash."

Cleo stepped back, chills creeping up her arms.

"Someone could have gotten hurt," TJ continued. "Real hurt."

Jimmy Teeks was suddenly at Cleo's side. "Someone like you," he said, his voice high and gravelly. "Better watch your back."

Chapter Nineteen

After a day and a half of watching her back and locking her front porch door and distracting herself with chores such as organizing closets and pantry shelves, Cleo was bored. If this is what retirement was like, she was reaffirmed she wanted none of it. She told her Cousin Dot as much at the Drop By's deli counter. "I haven't even been able to focus on a book!" Cleo added, desperately.

"This is different," said Dot, ever sensible, right down to the blunt pageboy hairstyle she'd sported since kindergarten. She scooped some potato salad with sweet pickles and mustard into a takeout container. "You might have someone trying to kill you. It's hard to relax or set priorities or read in such circumstances. If you were truly retired, you'd have a nice routine. You could come here every morning, get the newspaper, and walk home and read it."

"That would be nice," Cleo said, thinking it did sound perfectly pleasant, though dull as sticks. Besides, she had a gripe with the *Catalpa Gazette* for featuring such ghastly, personal pictures of wounded Words on Wheels.

She wanted her bookmobile fixed and back. She wanted the same for her library. She wanted action, purpose, work, resolution . . .

Dot asked if she wanted fried chicken.

"I suppose," Cleo said, morose.

Dot tightened her apron and gave her cousin a stern finger-wagging. "Now, Cleo Jane, you know what our mothers used to say: it'll all come out in the wash. Be patient."

Cleo didn't want to upset Dot. She certainly would never question her Mama and Auntie. However, she knew full well that things didn't always work out. Or wash out.

"You need something to take your mind off your troubles," Dot said. "I'll get you started. I'm giving you enough salad and chicken for a picnic luncheon for two or three. Invite Oliver or Leanna, or Fred and Angela . . . or a charming bookstore owner." Dot wouldn't take no for an answer.

Leanna was at her bank job. Ollie was spending his Friday and upcoming weekend at Pancake Spring, pulling invasive pondweeds as penance, and pining for the still-missing Whitney. Cleo's son and daughter-in-law would be working, as would Henry. "Henry has books to sell and fix," Cleo said, eyeing the daunting picnic being packed. "I've already bothered that man enough."

"I hardly think that's possible. He's besotted with you, in case you hadn't noticed." Dot added a half-dozen deviled eggs to Cleo's tower of takeout. "Enjoy!" she said in a trill that bordered on a command, and ducked in the back to check on a batch of biscuits.

Cleo went to collect Rhett, who was sitting in the sun in Dot's doorway. As part of Cleo's precautions, she'd put Rhett's harness on for the walk downtown. Rhett, realizing more leash walking was expected, flopped to his side on the wide-plank floor, his tail twitching resentfully.

"For heaven's sake," Cleo gently chided. "Rhett Butler, I can't carry you *and* all this food."

Rhett remained unmoved and unmoving.

"I'll have to get you a baby snuggie," Cleo threatened. "I'll carry you right on my front, and won't you feel awfully silly then?" Rhett scowled and twitched his tail harder. Cleo put down her bags, lifted the Persian to his feet, and watched him flop over again, limp as a furry rag doll.

She heard a chuckle. "Tough work being a cat."

Vernon Givens stood outside the doorway, looking springy in pastel peach and minty sage green. "Here, allow me," he said, stepping gingerly over Rhett and picking up Cleo's bags. "Are you headed home? I'll carry your groceries, and you can get the cat. I'm on my coffee break. Just don't tell the bank president I'm playing hooky."

"I don't want you to go out of your way," Cleo said, as manners dictated. She was glad when Vern insisted it would be his pleasure.

"Gives me more time out of the office. Your friend Leanna is a stickler for work and order. She'll wear me out." He smiled and held the door for Cleo and Rhett. Cleo lifted up Rhett, who revived to drape over her shoulder and purr happily in her ear.

"How is your mother?' Cleo asked.

A cloud fell over Vernon's sunny features. "Her neck still hurts. She's seeing a specialist this afternoon in Valdosta. Bitsy's taking her up."

"I'm sorry," Cleo said, intending a general *sorry* for Vernon's worries, Bitsy's chauffeuring burden, and Maybelle's neck, if it truly did ache. Cleo had called Bitsy yesterday and was assured Maybelle was fit as a fiddle and calming down about suing. More unsettling was Bitsy's other news, reluctantly relayed. The Ladies Leaguers were holding a special meeting on Sunday to "sort out" the Gala plans. Bitsy swore they weren't backing away from supporting the library, but her tone was so sugary sweet and bubbly that Cleo immediately became suspicious. She hugged Rhett a little closer.

"I don't blame you or the bookmobile," Vernon said. "I blame whoever messed with those brakes. I'm just thankful Mama wasn't hurt worse. She's frail, always has been."

Cleo bit her tongue. Maybelle Givens was as frail as old jerky and had been for as long as Cleo had known her.

"I hope you're okay too," Vernon was saying. "You must be shaken." He looked down at her worriedly. "I mean, no one would have guessed my mother was driving that bus. You're the main driver, and you have a reputation for, well, looking into things."

Cleo understood what Vernon was skirting around. Buford's killer might have sent her a warning or tried to permanently take her out of circulation. But why? All she had was a longer list of suspects than when she'd started. On the other hand, there was also someone who wanted to shut down her library program for good. Cleo thought of the mayor. Would he do something so awful, thinking it was a prank, not realizing the danger? She considered Jimmy Teeks, his cold potato face and warning to be careful.

"I hope you're taking a little time off," Vernon continued.

They reached a side-street intersection, devoid of cars. Vernon made sure they stopped fully and looked both ways twice.

Cleo smiled up at the big man, as fretful as her Fred. "I don't have a choice," she said. "I'm on a forced vacation with both of my libraries wrecked."

It was Vernon's turn to say he was sorry. "Sign up for the Ladies League. They'll keep you busy." He regaled Cleo with tales of Leaguers manufacturing thousands of pink crepe paper flowers on his kitchen table. "Ladies are in and out of the house all the time, planning, fussing, Bitsy running every which way. She wants everything perfect, and I understand that. I'll be glad when it's done."

Cleo would be too, hopefully with everyone having good fun and profits going to the library. They turned up Magnolia, her quiet lane, and Rhett wiggled to be let down. "Oh, now you can walk," she said. Rhett pranced before her. She offered to take the groceries from Vernon. "It's just a few houses away. You're so kind to help."

"I always escort a lady to her door. What a lovely street this is. It's always been one of my favorites. Uh-oh, trouble."

A police car passed, moving fast. A few yards beyond, it came to a tire-squealing halt. Gabby Honeywell backed up and rolled down her window.

"Cleo!" Gabby said. "Just the library expert I was coming to find." She greeted Vernon and inquired about Maybelle.

Vernon gave the Maybelle report again and added gravely, "At least Mama's not the easily scared type, but Bitsy and a lot of the bank customers, they're worried. We're all anxious for the police to put an end to this."

"Believe me, we want that too," Gabby said. "Cleo, I know it's nearly lunchtime, and it looks like you have plans—"

"No plans," Cleo interrupted eagerly.

Gabby said what Cleo hoped she would. "I'm going out to Krandall House and got permission to bring a book expert or two along to help with the library assessment."

Vernon chuckled. "Back to work after all, eh? Don't forget your groceries." He raised the paper bags and with them the tempting scent of Dot's chicken.

Gabby sniffed the air. "Is that Dot's Friday fried chicken? Cleo, you *do* have special plans! Do you have a date?"

Cleo scooped up Rhett again. "I do now," she said. "I'll drop Rhett off at home. You said an expert or two. Can Henry join us? We can take this food along. Dot insisted I go on a picnic."

Gabby said Henry was more than welcome, as was the picnic. "If Dot insists . . ." She chuckled.

Cleo offered Vernon some of the goodies, but he politely declined. "I'll extend my break and see if I can round up my own lunch date."

Cleo thanked him again for his help with her groceries and the library. "I'll tell Bitsy she's married a perfect gentleman." She hurried home, plied Rhett with placating treats, and called another gentleman, who was eager to join them.

* * *

Cleo had never picnicked at a crime scene before. It didn't seem entirely proper, but it was pleasant. That is, so long as she avoided eye contact with the statues lurking in the woods and didn't think about her last visit. Cleo, Gabby, and Henry dusted off some lawn chairs and a rusty table on Buford's patio. From where they sat, they could see the backside of Krandall House and the disabled drill and the overgrown forest all around. Cleo laid out the takeout cartons and the big box of chicken. She held the paper napkins down with a bottle of lemonade she'd brought from home.

"This is good actually," Gabby said, surveying the scene. "I couldn't get an overall feel for the place before. I was too concentrated on minutia. Here, you can get a bigger picture. Think of Buford, all alone out here, stewing about his neighbor and his health, collecting and stitching up everyone's bad secrets, messing with that machine." She helped herself to potato salad and a deviled egg and glanced warily at a whirligig swirling from a branch above.

Cleo selected a drumstick. Although eager to study the library, she was famished. A sense of purpose had restored her appetite, and the chicken was perfect picnic temperature. Not too hot, not too cold, and still crispy and juicy with a buttermilk tang. Dot made the best fried chicken.

Henry complimented the meal. In between bites, he said, "I've been thinking about Mr. Krandall's book collecting. In my dealings with him, he sought out some fine first editions and some unusual texts—obscure works by inventors and a bit of Machiavelli. Nothing too controversial."

Gabby raised an eyebrow at Machiavelli. "Wasn't he into manipulation?"

"Machiavelli or Buford Krandall?" Henry said with a twitch of his mustache. "I suppose it doesn't matter which. Both liked manipulation, deceit, gaining power." He raised a crispy chicken leg. "But Mr. Krandall hadn't ordered any Machiavelli in some time, or any books from me. It appears he was more interested in the library and Priscilla Pawpaw."

Cleo told Gabby about her and Mary-Rose's two-woman Priscilla Pawpaw book club. "I hope we'll find the rest of his library books today so Mary-Rose and I can read them too. I have no idea why Buford was so interested, but each book features various places and crimes. It may be that only one or some of the books are relevant. When I delivered his last set of books, he said something like how he hoped they'd be what he was looking for. To clear things up." Cleo wished she could remember the exact words. The drill had been pounding and her nerves jangly. She glared at the infernal device now, sitting silent and still. Had it started all these problems? Or had her library books?

Gabby, nibbling delicately on a wing, said, "If you find anything—anything—in those books or the library, I'll consider it. Don't laugh, but I had this fantasy we'd come out here and catch the culprit. Whitney Greene, making off with her uncle's treasure. Priscilla Pawpaw, armed and crazed, typing up her next true crime book. Case closed." She grinned. "Rookie fantasies, right? But a picnic is nice too." She was reaching for another deviled egg, when she froze. "Hear that?"

Cleo listened. She heard leaves rustling but felt no wind. The sound was coming closer. Something running, crashing through the woods. Henry stood. Cleo did too, her heart thumping. Gabby was already up, hand on her gun, jogging toward the house, around the side, and out of sight.

"Should we follow?" Henry asked.

Neither of them moved. "It could be a deer," Cleo said. "There are a lot of deer out here."

"A big one," Henry whispered.

A peacock called out from the direction of Pancake Spring. Its wavering cry was overlaid by another and then another, both human and female.

"Stop!" Gabby yelled. "No! Get off me!"

Henry grabbed a big stick. Cleo hoisted the lemonade bottle and flexed her pitching arm. She prayed that Gabby's wish would come true, that they were about to catch a killer, not become the next victims.

Chapter Twenty

Cleo swung the lemonade bottle behind her hip, preparing for an underhand launch. She could imagine the feel of the pitch, see the bottle flying true. Henry held his stick out straight like a jousting ram.

Gabby's voice came from a thicket of saw palmettos. The sharp leaves and toothed stalks rustled and shook. Cleo spotted the beige of Gabby's uniform. Gabby was down on the ground. Limbs, feet, and leaves moved in a blur.

"Gabby!" Cleo cried. "We're coming!"

Henry yelled, "We're armed!"

"Hold your fire!" The voice was female, but not Gabby's. It was followed by a woof and then Gabby, groaning and pleading. "Ugh, stop! Stop licking my face, you beast!"

Cleo put a hand on Henry's still-raised stick. They rounded the palm to find Gabby, smothered with a slobbering, wiggling mound of mastiff joy.

"Beast, bad dog! Good boy! Sit! Stay! Stop!" Kat Krandall-Stykes declared uselessly. She grabbed Beast's back half and tugged him a few inches away, enough for Gabby to crawl out.

Gabby wiped her face, scowling at the doggy drool and dirt, rubbing at scuffs and scrapes to her arms. She stepped back to stand by Cleo and Henry and said in a low voice, "Please tell me no one made a cell-phone video of that. The guys at work would never let me live it down."

"You're safe with us," Cleo said. If she had to guess, her phone might be in her purse back in the patrol car. Henry declared his phone was at the bookstore. "Where phones should reside."

"Sorry," Kat called out, holding onto Beast with one hand and a tree with the other. "Beast likes ladies. Nothing makes him happier than discovering a new gal."

Beast strained at the end of the leash, panting feverishly, drooling a river.

Gabby smoothed her uniform, and Cleo saw the wisdom in beige polyester. No wrinkles, same color as dirt.

"Ms. Stykes," Gabby said, regrouping, "you and your, er . . . dog . . . surprised us. What are you doing here?"

"*Mrs. Krandall*-Stykes," Kat corrected, raising her chin haughtily. She was wearing her usual landscaper's uniform of boots and overalls. "I could ask you all the same. I'm the grieving, bereaving widow, remember? I'm here to reclaim my rightful home and chase off intruders. I hoped to pick up some stuff for the funeral too. Are those good enough reasons? So, what are *you all* doing here?"

Gabby started to explain that they were inventorying the library. She stopped and frowned. "Why didn't we hear you drive in?"

Kat shrugged. "Parked at the road and walked in. I don't want to ruin my suspension on that pothole driveway."

Beast suddenly swung his head, his nose straining in the direction of the picnic.

"Our food," Henry whispered. He backed away and around the corner. Cleo excused herself and hurried to help him.

"Quick, let's stash this in the trunk," Henry said, stuffing plates and containers into bags. "Evidence of illicit picnicking," he said with a laugh.

Cleo laughed. "I feel like teenagers about to get caught doing something naughty."

They were just closing the trunk of Gabby's patrol car when the big mastiff pulled his mistress to the back patio.

"Funny," Kat said, eyes scanning. "He's acting like he smells something. Must be a bunny. Good boy, where's the bunny?" Beast dragged her to the patio table, circling it until he, Kat, and his leash were tangled.

Gabby, still wiping slobber from her limbs and face, mouthed, "Thank you" to Cleo and Henry. Out loud, she said, "Mrs. Krandall-Stykes, I'm sorry, but you shouldn't be here. To put it bluntly, you're a suspect."

"Me? Still?" She shook her head as if in disbelief. Her thick braid swayed at her hips. "Did you know, our fine state of Georgia is the only one to let spouses disinherit each other? I'm sure Buford took full advantage of that little perk. I am entitled to a year of so-called support, which I plan to spend in advance for a blowout funeral celebration." She smiled. "Cleo Watkins here has more motive than me."

"Me?" Cleo said, flustered by an unseemly hope that Buford had left a fortune to the library. "Buford was a fine . . . a fine friend of both myself and the library."

Kat scoffed. "Excuse me for saying so, but that's a lie. No

one thought Buford was a fine anything." She patted her dog, who was enthusiastically digging a hole. "Anyone who says so was either duped, afraid, wanting something, or a bigger suspect than me."

Cleo might have been offended if she hadn't agreed.

Gabby took a deep breath. "Okay. My consultants and I should get to work. Mrs. Krandall-Stykes, I'm afraid—"

"Too bad," Kat said with a shrug. "If you shoo me off, you'll miss out on all I know." She patted Beast's rump. He'd dug himself as deep as his shoulders. "We saw someone, didn't we boy? Two someones. But if you don't care, fine by me. Just remember, save the date, Sunday. Funeral bash at the Pancake Mill. Noon. Potluck. Cash bar. I'm trying to get a band too." Kat waved upward with a rueful smile. "What will I do without him? I'll need a new hobby. Dog training?" Beast continued to dig.

Cleo was wondering what to question first, the someones or the party plans.

"*Two* someones?" Gabby said, voicing the more important of Cleo's questions.

Kat raised her eyebrows provocatively. "Yep, I'll trade you. You let me peek inside the house and get a few funeral decorations, and I'll tell you all about it. It could turn your investigation right around, Deputy. You'd be a star."

The peacocks erupted in chorus. Cleo looked toward Pancake Spring, picturing the sparkling waters, flamboyant birds, and happy swimmers and pancake eaters. It was a perfect spot for a memorial, unless that memorial was for Buford Krandall. "You're having a gathering at the Pancake Mill? Buford despised that place," Cleo said.

"I know!" Kat looked happier than Cleo had seen her in days. "It gets even better when you think about it. A potluck and peacocks for that bird-fearing germaphobe. Bring chips and something double-dippable."

Kat left Beast tied to a tree, which he set about uprooting. The widow was taunting the heavens as Gabby unlocked the police-installed padlock on Buford Krandall's kitchen door.

Henry leaned close to Cleo. "She's a better suspect than you."

* * *

Gabby led the way through Krandall House, Kat close behind her, murmuring assessing sounds of "hmm" and "mmm." When they reached the library, Cleo's stomach pitched once again at the book devastation and the memory.

"Shoot," Kat said. "Now this is plain mean. He loved his library. Who'd do this?"

Gabby shot a sharp look at the party-planning widow. She handed out disposable gloves to all and issued instructions: Look only, at first. Then Gabby and the library experts would start an inventory of the books.

Cleo scanned the room, wondering where to start. The chill had gone, replaced with muggy freshness. Cleo saw why.

"A window's open," Cleo said, pointing across the room. It was more than open. It was broken, the screen torn and a corner of glass shattered, enough for a hand to slip in and unlock the frame.

"Stand clear," Gabby said, but Cleo had already seen the imprint of a muddy footprint. A boot had stepped rudely on a book, leaving a zigzag tread on an open page. "I'm sure this wasn't here before," Gabby said. "You all stay put. I'll check the rest of the house. Make sure no one else is inside."

They listened to her feet travel up the stairs and overhead. Henry inspected a book of poems. Kat hummed.

When Gabby returned, finding no one, she said to Kat. "Okay, what—who—did you see, and when?"

Kat negotiated to borrow two stone-head bookends for her funeral potluck. "I came out for a peek the other day. Beast was at the doggy spa, and I hiked down the drive, like today." She wandered to a window and looked out through the grime and vines. "Guess who I found, having a friendly little chat like she owned the place? The darling niece I never knew I had." She ran a finger over a dusty shelf. "She was out by that drill with some bald guy in a suit. They didn't notice me. Without Beast, I can be stealthier."

Outside, Beast howled.

"The bald man," Cleo said. "Did he have lots of moles, tight skin, small eyes?"

Kat nodded. "Yeah. And a really high voice, kind of raspy."

"Jimmy Teeks," Cleo said. "The mayor's Vegas consultant on the pier and casino projects."

Kat grumbled that it figured. "Whitney's a true Krandall, all right. She and your Jimmy guy were chatting about her selling this dump for its river access. The back end of the property extends to the Tallgrass, a nice deep spot. She said that if she got control of this dump, she could get that water pump going again too, for the right price. So much for Miss Eco-Warrior, selling out to bottled water and riverboat gambling. Typical." She brightened. "Hey, I could fight *her* in court. She could be my next project."

Kat and Beast left soon after, Kat happy with her new litigation prospects, Beast on the trail of a rabbit. Cleo, Henry, and Gabby turned their focus to the library.

"I'll go back to the station later and pick up a tech guy to document the broken window," Gabby said. "It could just be kids on a dare. Let's do what we came to do first. Stay clear of that side by the window. What's our book strategy?"

Cleo and Henry had agreed on a plan. "I'll look for a pattern in which books were taken from their shelves," Henry said.

Cleo had a librarian's trick up her sleeve. "I'll flip through pages and covers. You wouldn't believe what people leave in books. Money, love letters, lottery tickets, lists . . ."

"Confessions?" Gabby said. She grinned. "I can still hope. I'll search the other rooms while we're here. I'm looking for Mr. Krandall's gun, and I'll try to find your library books, Miss Cleo, and more of those Priscilla Pawpaw notes. The dozen or so pages left at your door don't sound like enough for a whole book."

They worked in silent concentration. After about an hour, Gabby clumped downstairs. "Nothing," she said. "No more Pawpaw notes that I could find anywhere. I do have the library books. They were all on the nightstand by his bed. Not the kind of bedtime reading I'd want."

"No," Cleo said, from unpleasant experience.

Gabby set the library books on a side table and sunk into an armchair. "Any luck here?"

Henry rubbed his beard in thought. "Many of the fallen books are mysteries, but then Mr. Krandall had a large mystery collection, so it's not surprising. I found some impressive items." He gestured to several neat stacks. "I took notes of titles as I stacked them. I couldn't leave them lying on the floor." He estimated their combined value in a high five-figure range. "A layperson thief wouldn't have realized how much they're worth."

"So expensive books aren't what our killer and/or burglar wanted," Gabby said.

Cleo was next to report. She too had made neat stacks of books containing something other than their pages. "I found quite a few newspaper clippings, most decades old." She selected a book as an example. "See, several in this book alone, left at different spots. Perhaps he was marking pages, but I couldn't see how the pages were remarkable."

They gathered around her book collections. Gabby took photos of each book, the pages where they were found, and the clippings. She read out some as she went. "Buford Krandall ran for mayor three times? Imagine! A drowning, a car wreck . . . he's always been into dark stuff, hasn't he? Local politics, a divorce case, another divorce." Gabby collected the clippings in a large evidence bag. "I guarantee the chief won't be impressed with old news clippings, but I'll look into some of these events. Do you want to read through these and the library books too?" Her smooth brow knitted. "It's a lot to ask, I know."

"We'd be delighted," Cleo said enthusiastically. "Mary-Rose can help."

Gabby's worry lines deepened. "She's still a suspect too."

"Anyone can enjoy library books," Cleo pointed out. "And they're not evidence, according to Chief Culpepper."

"Okay," Gabby said. "Let's take some over to the Pancake Mill. Then I'll drop y'all back in town."

Cleo was feeling quite good about the plan. She had a

purpose and something she was good at too. Reading. Henry, in the backseat, mused about the daily pie selection.

They got out and were welcomed by scents of pie and pancakes. The peacocks strutted, and the parking lot was packed. Cleo's sunny outlook, however, soon dimmed. Mary-Rose, Ollie, and little Zoe sat at the bench near the entry, tugging off muddy rubber boots. Gabby leaned, head cocked. "Interesting tread pattern," she said in a neutral tone that made Cleo's heart leap. The zigzag resembled the muddy print left on Buford's book. "Out for a walk?" Gabby asked.

"Our secret trail!" Zoe exclaimed.

Mary-Rose placed herself between her granddaughter and Gabby. "We were walking around the spring, pulling invasive weeds," she said. She eyed the books in Cleo's arms. "Oh, joy, more for our ways-of-murder book group? Cleo, you're going to make us look ghoulish."

"Have you seen Whitney Greene?" Gabby interjected.

"She's gone," Ollie said, his mussed hair obscuring his face, his attention seemingly on his boots.

"No, she's not." Gabby reported that Whitney had recently been seen next door. "Talking about selling Krandall land and water to Mayor Day and his cronies," Gabby said, her tone nonchalant, her eyes watching Ollie intently.

Ollie's head jerked up. Cleo expected the blazing blush in his cheeks, but not the angry curses that followed.

Chapter
Twenty-One

Aside from all the murder, it was an agreeable way to spend a Saturday afternoon. Cleo and Henry sat on her front porch in padded rockers, reading through a stack of Priscilla Pawpaw books. Hummingbirds dive-bombed the syrup feeder, and the ceiling fan swirled softly overhead. Cleo heard the random patter and clink of raindrops on her metal roof. She looked up, an automatic response, though the view overhead was always blue. Haint blue. Her Granny Bess claimed blue porch ceilings kept haints away, as well as wasps. Cleo hoped that was true. She had enough to worry about without malevolent spirits and stinging insects.

Thunder ripped and cracked the sky. Mr. Chaucer moaned. The pug was curled up on Rhett's cat bed, the big Persian draped over him. Lightning lit up the porch, and Cleo put down *Murder and Mayhem in Mississippi*, waiting for the next rumble and breathing in one of her favorite perfumes, new rain.

Henry flipped another page of *Killings in Cotton Country*. "It's horribly addictive reading," he said. "I can't find any connection to Buford's murder, though."

Cleo couldn't either. "I wish we could talk to Priscilla. Buford must have given her some hint about what he was looking for." Cleo remembered the box of notes left right here on her porch. They'd arrived the very morning Priscilla Pawpaw fled town. With Leanna's help, Cleo had printed out the photos she'd taken of each page. She'd already read through them several times, but it never hurt to reread or get a second opinion. She retrieved them from the kitchen and handed them to Henry, who read with interest.

"Mmm . . . Tampa, arson," he said, squinting at the loopy writing. "Tarpon Springs. That's a nice place. Ever been there? No? It's a quaint little town on the Gulf, settled by Greek sponge divers. They still dive for sponges. There's lovely Greek food."

Cleo prayed he wouldn't say they should visit.

"There's a chapter about an arson case near Tampa in the book I've been reading," Henry said. He put down the photos and reached for the book.

"It's in one of the other books too," Cleo realized. "They're all becoming a blur." She scanned the indexes of several books. "Here it is—*Sunshine State Crimes*."

Henry was looking through *Killings in Cotton Country*, the first Pawpaw book Cleo had read. They compared stories.

"Same crime," Henry said. "It doesn't seem like Priscilla to run out of fresh murder and mayhem." He flipped pages back and forth until Cleo asked what he was doing.

"A page is missing," he said. "From the arson chapter. I'm ashamed I didn't notice this before. It's been removed so cleanly, you'd only notice by the page numbers." He handed the book to Cleo.

She examined it, abashed she hadn't noticed either, but Henry was right. The missing page was easy to skip over. It had been cleanly sliced right at the binding.

"*Killings in Cotton Country* was in the library returns bin, along with another book Buford borrowed about local geology," Cleo said. She turned back to the *Sunshine State Crimes* and studied the text again. Five family members perished in a house fire, a mother and four children. The mother worked at a B&B in Tarpon Springs. "What was initially thought to be faulty wiring was later considered murder and arson by the controlling husband and father." Cleo sighed. "Terrible, just awful. What is wrong with some people? It was a long time ago. Twenty-five years or so? Look, my book has photos."

They bent their heads over pixilated pictures, one of a home reduced to its charred bones and another of a family on a picnic, the father a looming blur in the foreground.

Henry's book gave a similar introduction to the family, elaborating on the mother's dream of taking her children and leaving. There was the same photo of the scorched home, as well as details of the father's abusive offenses. Henry clicked his tongue. "Everyone claimed they had no idea he was a monster. I wonder what was on the missing page?"

The clouds let loose, and rain drummed the metal roof. Rhett scowled hard and snuggled closer to the whimpering pug.

Henry began methodically flipping page by page through another book. "We should check all of these. Do you have any other copies of *Killings in Cotton Country* in the library?"

Cleo knew without checking that the Catalpa Springs library carried a single copy of Priscilla's books, if at all. "I was lucky to get her earlier books through interlibrary loan," Cleo said. "Buford Krandall had all her works checked out."

Henry said he could order the book, but it would probably take some time to arrive, given the work's age and obscurity. "I'll check into it," he said. "We don't know if the page is important, do we? In any case, I'll donate it to the library so you can have a fresh copy."

Cleo thanked him. "I *am* curious," she said, trying not to get her hopes up that the page contained a clue. She watched the rain sheet down, thinking and listening as drops turned to a deluge rapping on metal and whooshing through the gutters. There was another sound too, shrieks and giggles and footsteps splashing up the walkway.

Cleo jumped up to hold the screen door for sopping Leanna and Bitsy. "You're drenched!" she said. "What are you doing out?"

Both women held impractical shoes. Their feet were bare and dresses plastered to their fronts. Leanna bent and shook out her hair. Bitsy arched her back and fluffed her dripping locks more elegantly. Makeup streamed down both faces. Henry went inside to fetch towels and tissues.

"We were walking from the bank," Leanna said, still winded and dripping. "We thought we could make it before the storm."

Bitsy fluffed and scrunched, attempting to turn straight, stringy hair bouncy again. "Ah, what a mess I must look," she said, accepting a tissue from Henry and swiping at her melted makeup.

"You both look lovely," Cleo said politely. "Fresh faced and dewy."

Bitsy laughed. "There's a nice way of saying 'drowned rat.'" Her smile wavered. "I feel like one too. I came to apologize—again—for Mama Givens. I talked to Vernon and we agreed, we'll pay for those bookmobile repairs. It was my fault. I shouldn't have let Mama get in the driver's seat. Vern's still upset I exposed Mama to that danger. The Ladies Leaguers are grumpy with me too." She took a deep breath and declared, "At least we're refreshed and dewy, Leanna."

Leanna was bent over, wrapping a towel around her hair. When she straightened, she said, "No one should be mad at you, Miss Bitsy. It's not your fault. Remember what you told me? Present the image you want to be." Leanna stood tall, her towel headdress tilting. "Like my banking clothes that Miss Bitsy lent me. I look banky, right?"

"You look very nice, dear," Cleo said, thinking Leanna looked uncomfortable and not herself in the clothes. Gone were Leanna's fun retro earrings and flouncy fifties skirts and comfortable flip-flops. Cleo never thought she'd cheer flip-flops. She chided herself for what was likely petty jealousy and offered seats, snacks, and beverages. Bitsy said she couldn't stay long. She and Leanna chose two wooden chairs so they wouldn't leave damp spots on cushions.

Bitsy's gaze drifted around the patio. She complimented Cleo's hanging baskets of petunias and the pretty blue of the ceiling. Then her eyes landed on the stack of books. "Goodness, what are y'all reading?" she asked. "These sound awful."

"They're Buford Krandall's," Leanna said. "From the library."

Bitsy picked up the top book on the stack, *Killings in Cotton*

Country. Henry had marked the missing page with a bookmark. Bitsy opened and flipped a few pages. "There's a page missing," she said.

"We should have had you here earlier," Henry said. "It took Cleo and myself an entire afternoon to find that."

Bitsy shrugged. "I only noticed because you had it marked. I'm lost when it comes to numbers. I sometimes think Vern married me so I'd stop messing up as a teller at his bank." She gave a self-deprecating chuckle and twined her fingers anxiously. "I had another reason for dropping by. Can I ask you all a big, big, big favor?" Her "you all" was aimed singularly at Cleo, who was already enthusiastically nodding.

"I need hummingbird help," Bitsy said.

Cleo looked to the red glass feeder, where a single bold little bird braved the storm.

"The cake," Bitsy clarified. "I read that hummingbird cake recipe you gave me over and over, and I'm sure I'm gonna mess up, and Mama Givens and Vern will be disappointed, and they're already worked up. It's Vern's birthday on Tuesday. The big five-five, but don't tell him I told you so. He likes to say he's as young as his current wife."

She laughed and added, to assuage Henry's shocked look, "He's kidding! It's our joke. He's stuck with me, and I'll always be younger."

Cleo enthusiastically agreed. "Absolutely. I'd love to. We'll make a little extra cake too, so you can taste it and make sure it's just right." She'd welcome a taste too. Cleo loved a good hummingbird, and it wouldn't defeat her low-sugar diet if Bitsy was taking most of the cake home.

Bitsy beamed, checked her watch, and said she had to run.

Before she did, she hugged them all in turn and Cleo twice, a towel between them to keep from getting damp. "Thank you, thank you, you're the sweetest!" She ran out, back in her heels, into a break in the storm.

"Poor Miss Bitsy." Leanna gave voice to their thoughts after Bitsy was out of sight. "She's so worried about doing stuff right and what people think and being perfect. It's gotta be stressful." Leanna produced a hairband from her pocket and tied her hair up in its usual messy bun. "Now, for some fun work! What's going on with these books?"

Cleo could have hugged her young protégé. She told Leanna what they'd been doing and how Henry found the missing page.

"A clue!" Leanna exclaimed when they showed her the book. She beamed at Henry. "You found a clue."

He ducked his head modestly. "Perhaps," he said. "But we don't know when the page was removed or by whom. It could have been years ago. Or been a printing mistake, though I don't think so. If you look closely, you can see the slice."

Leanna inspected the book. "Maybe Buford did it. I mean, he had the book checked out, and who else would bother? Anyone normal would make a copy or take a photo. I bet it was him."

"Or his killer," Cleo said.

* * *

Cleo convinced Leanna to stay for supper. She'd already easily persuaded Henry.

"But I'm interfering with your night together," Leanna whispered. They stood in Cleo's foyer beside the coat hooks that Cleo's husband Richard had installed when he and Cleo first moved in decades ago. Vernon Givens's "big" birthday of fifty-five seemed young indeed. From the kitchen came sounds of bowls clanging and snorty woofs. Henry was making a salad, and Mr. Chaucer had a surprising enthusiasm for lettuce snacks.

"It's not a 'night together' or a date," Cleo said. "Henry came over to help read all those books." It was all very proper and only polite to invite Henry to stay.

Leanna grinned wider. "I should leave you two to your murder books then."

Cleo resorted to mild begging. "Please, Leanna. I want you to stay. You're family here. Ollie's been staying at his dad's, but if he comes back to his cottage, we'll invite him too and Gabby as well, if she's ever out of work."

Leanna relented. "Okay, I'd love to join you all. I'll be your wingwoman."

Cleo returned to her kitchen, wondering what a wing-woman did exactly. Whatever it was, it was unnecessary, since she was not a date.

Later, Cleo thought it was a very good thing it wasn't a date. Her refrigerator revealed miscellaneous bits of left-overs and a dearth of staples. She managed a humble version of tomato pie, remembering Henry's fondness for it. Her mother would have deemed the ready-made piecrust she used a sin, but neither Leanna nor Henry seemed to care. She had some nice hothouse tomatoes from Dot's and lots of cheese—a constant among her bachelorette staples. Henry's salad was a perfect accompaniment, as was Leanna's sparkly punch of lemonade and tonic water and fresh peppermint from the garden. They kept the dinner conversation to lighter topics than murder.

Leanna spoke enthusiastically about organizing Vernon Givens's mess of files, so much better than tromping along the highway dressed as a biscuit. Henry had gotten in a new shipment of old books. He raved in his quiet manner about a lovely illuminated manuscript, so fine he was stashing it in his climate-controlled safe. He had a few repairs to make, a touch-up of gold leaf, a dab or two of paint and glue. He already had an interested buyer from overseas.

Cleo struggled to come up with something positive to share. She settled on her peach tree. Peach prospects looked good so far, better than last year's peach disaster of a too-warm spring and late killing frost. They listed their favorite peach dishes: peach pies, peach crisp, peach cobblers, dumplings, and dump cakes, and the many peaches Cleo and her mother used to preserve.

"I still put up some jars most years," Cleo said. "I have a few left from the year before last. We could have some for dessert." Her mother would have definite thoughts on serving—no, on *revealing* that one was serving—two-year-old peaches to guests. Mama's thoughts wouldn't be good ones, but the peaches would still be fine and sweet.

"Delightful," Henry said. "Can I help you?"

Cleo thanked him but said she could manage. She kept extra supplies and jarred goodies in a pantry at the back of the house. She wished she had a basement, but those were hard to come by in Catalpa Springs.

Cleo selected a jar. As she was turning out the lights, she

glanced out the row of paned windows that lined the little porch. They looked onto her back garden and the gone-to-wild orchard beyond her fence. She remembered that she hadn't gone after that potato vine. It was probably creeping toward the fence right now. Cleo glared toward the grove, half-expecting to see tubers inching toward her house.

To her shock, she did see movement. A figure was crawling in a back window of Ollie's cottage. A boot carelessly stomped the flower bed beneath. The person's back was turned. Cleo took in the bare legs and camouflage shorts, the lean torso and pouf of frizzy curls. Whitney! Cleo dithered for a moment—should she run to the phone and call Gabby or confront the so-called spring saver? In another moment, she'd decided. A jar of peaches in hand, pitching arm again twitching, she quietly opened her back door.

Chapter
Twenty-Two

Cleo wore sunglasses the next day, big ones, along with her broadest, floppiest brimmed sunhat. The glasses were appropriately dark. The hat was butter yellow, good for shading her eyes, inappropriate for a Sunday post-funeral reception. Fortunately, the entire affair at the Pancake Mill was inappropriate. Judging by the raucous live music and laughter, it was gleefully so.

Cleo stood just off the path to Pancake Spring, eyes not on the festivities, but on the packed parking lot beyond a leafy screen of palms, ferns, and flowers.

Henry had insisted on chauffeuring, driving absurdly safely and slowly. To bide her time in the passenger seat, Cleo had pictured how they could have arrived, zipping along the curvy road in her daddy's 1967 Ford Galaxie, the top down. Henry was also taking a long time to park. Cleo held a picnic basket heavy with a peach cobbler. She shifted the handle between hands and marveled at the crowd. Heavens, half the town was here, and then some. Most wouldn't be friends or bereaved. They'd have come for the spectacle, the event. They wanted gossip, a potluck, and a party. Kat Krandall-Stykes had placed a half-page ad in the *Catalpa Gazette*, inviting all, offering up free music, dancing, and open-mic eulogizing, as well as cash bars for both drinks and pie.

Among the crowd, Cleo spotted beloved faces coming her way. Her eldest son, Fred, was accompanied by Angela, Ollie, Leon, and Theo. The twins jogged by carrying inner tubes, giving Cleo jog-by greetings. Angela and Ollie hung back to speak with a friend.

Fred didn't take long to notice her face. "Mom! Is that a bruise? Why do you have a Band-Aid on your chin? What happened? What did you do?" His tone was more accusatory than sympathetic.

Cleo bristled. What did *she* do? Well! She'd attempted to apprehend a murder suspect by inviting said suspect in for dessert. When that failed, she'd tried to physically stop Whitney Greene from escaping over the back fence. In return, she'd gotten scuffed by a boot (likely accidental) and rudely pelted with air potatoes (absolutely intentional). Cleo thought it best not to tell Fred any of this. Her son would only worry and fuss. Plus, they were at a reception. Funeral receptions were like weddings. One should never upstage the bride or the deceased.

"It's nothing," Cleo said, shifting her picnic basket to her other hand.

Angela came their way, carrying a casserole dish on a cookie tray. Ollie dragged behind, shoulders sagging in a wrinkled dress shirt worn over dark jeans. He blanched when he saw Cleo.

"Gran?" he said, when he got within cheek-kissing distance

of Cleo. "Are you okay?" He turned to his stepmom. "See? See, I was right, wasn't I? I should have been home to help Gran."

Angela gave a little shrug and nodded toward Fred, the paternal worrier, who'd insisted that Ollie return to the safety of his childhood bedroom.

"I am fine," Cleo insisted. "A little shiner. I was hoping no one would notice." Only once previously in her life had she ever had a black eye. Back in her softball days, she'd been struck by—but still caught—a wicked fly ball. But this, from an air potato! The indignity! She supposed she should give Whitney some credit. The girl did have a firm throw and could scale a fence as quick as a fox.

"Did something, someone . . . ?" Ollie asked, shuffling anxiously.

Cleo couldn't say much in front of fretful Fred. Thankfully, Angela had not only a lawyer's efficiency but good intuition. "Fred, will you go set down this squash casserole? It's getting heavy to hold. Take your mother's basket too."

Fred scowled and peered in close to Cleo's face. She firmed her posture. "Fred, dear, take the casserole from your wife. It's hot. Mine's a peach cobbler. Just tuck the basket under the desserts table."

Fred would not be diverted from his fussing. "Was it him, your *friend*?" Fred sputtered. "Is that why you're not saying? There's domestic violence among elderly couples too."

Cleo issued an indignant gasp, loud enough to attract the attention of the peahens, which raised their feathers in a rippling shimmer. She added a sharp *"No,"* since Fred seemed in a bullheaded mood. The birds warbled.

"Greetings," Henry's cheery voice cut in. He would surely

have tipped his fedora except he was holding a casserole, funeral potatoes, one of Cleo's favorite dishes, being that it was often more cheese than potatoes.

Fred greeted Henry with a glare.

"Sad day, of course," Henry said, clearly sensing the chill. "The weather seems too nice for a funeral." He turned to Cleo. "Sorry to keep you waiting. It's a traffic jam out there. I had to park halfway to the road. I feel like I'm back in Atlanta." He added a mumbled, "Except I never encountered so much crime there." He adjusted his grip on his Pyrex dish. "Don't worry— I'll fetch the car and pick you up when we leave."

Men! Cleo thought, feeling frustrated affection for all three gathered anxiously around her: Ollie for his puppy-dog obliviousness, Fred for his bullheaded worries, and Henry for bordering on being too chivalrous.

"I am fine," Cleo said, drawing out her drawl for emphasis. "Fred, I had a run-in with an air potato, if you must pry."

Fred gave an exasperated sigh. "Mom, how? That garden is getting to be too much anymore. Ollie, why aren't you helping your grandmother more?"

Ollie's tone reverted to a teenage whine. "*You* said I had to stay at your place."

"Casserole!" Angela cut in. "Cobbler! Fred, go put these dishes down for us. Get them on the right buffet tables, savory and sweet. We'll catch up in a minute."

They watched Fred trudge toward the already overladen tables. People were picnicking on the lawn. Many had brought blankets and chairs. The male peacock strutted amidst the swing dancers and, except for all the dark attire, it could have been a wedding or the Fourth of July.

Angela said. "Okay now, what happened to your eye? I sense I should know, as lawyer and legal backup to people who tell me nothing."

Cleo half-wished Ollie had gone with his dad. "Ollie, I caught Whitney sneaking into your cottage last night, through a window," Cleo admitted. She reached out and took Ollie's hand. "Whitney and I had a . . . a disagreement. She tossed an air potato, and it caught my eye. Did you know she was staying at your place?"

Ollie's furious face was enough of an answer. "No!" he sputtered. "I can't believe she winged a potato at you, Gran! She's been lying the whole time, hasn't she? She doesn't care about Pancake Spring or the environment or . . ."

Or him. Cleo squeezed her grandson's hand tighter.

Angela gave him a sturdy slap on the back. "Go get some food, Oliver. And take Mr. Lafayette's dish over to the tables."

Ollie looked grateful for the small task. He took Henry's hot pads and dish. Before he left, he said, "I'm sorry, Gran. I won't let Whitney get away with this! If I find her, I'll–I'll . . ."

"Oliver," his lawyer stepmom cautioned, but not before Gabby had come up beside them.

Ollie flushed, from his anger or the sight of Gabby, Cleo wasn't sure. The young deputy wore a sundress printed with ruby roses that highlighted her curves and cleavage. Her long hair was down in loose, springy curls.

Ollie gulped and hurried off to the buffet tables.

Cleo complimented Gabby's dress.

"I'm undercover," Gabby said.

"Oh." Cleo had to smile, for Gabby was hardly going to go unnoticed. "What are you watching for?"

"Killers returning to the scene of the crime?" Henry asked.

Gabby responded seriously. "Yeah, actually. Look at all these people. If I took down everyone laughing, dancing, and toasting, my suspect list would stretch halfway across Georgia. I mean, look at Mary-Rose—she's not doing herself any favors."

Cleo spotted Mary-Rose sparkling behind the cash pie table. They all went to visit.

"Ten dollars a slice?" Cleo asked, reading the chalkboard menu. "That's highway robbery, Mary-Rose."

Mary-Rose admitted she might have to lower her prices. "That darned dessert potluck table is filling up fast with hefty competition. The florist brought caramel cake, and one of those Ladies Leaguers made a Lane cake. I haven't had a good Lane in years. It's like a county fair dessert competition over there." She shook her head but quickly brightened. "But I'm selling my pies for a good cause. All proceeds go toward environmental restoration of Pancake Spring and the cypress grove sullied by Buford Krandall's hostile actions."

"That's what he would have wanted," intoned a somber voice. Widow and party organizer Kat couldn't keep up the sorrowful act for long. She burst into a cackle and raised a plastic flute of bubbly. "You're a real peach for hosting," she said to Mary-Rose, handing over a ten-dollar bill for a slice of coconut cream.

"It's what Buford would have wanted," Mary-Rose repeated, and they both laughed some more.

"This is the most disturbing funeral reception I've ever attended," Henry said, when he, Cleo, and Gabby were out of earshot of the pie table. "And we've only just gotten here."

Gabby was scanning the crowd. "Let's hope it's the most

informative too. Tell me if you hear anything particularly suspicious. I'm going to check out those camouflage wearers over there. Maybe some S.O.S. types finally decided to come up and look for their missing colleague?"

She headed toward a group of young people in grungy shorts and tees. Cleo half-expected to see Whitney's frizzy hair appear among them. "I can't believe she was living in my cottage and I didn't notice," Cleo said.

"You had no reason to check the place again," Henry said. "Ollie was at his dad's. It was quiet and dark. Besides, Gabby said Whitney was probably just bunking down for the night, not making house and home."

Still, Cleo thought, *I should have* sensed *something.* She prided herself on her senses, observational and intuitional. Lately, they'd failed her.

She waved to Leanna, who was over by the band with Bitsy, Maybelle, and Vernon Givens. For once, Maybelle's dour dress looked perfectly appropriate. Bitsy had confined her pink to a belt around a black dress. Leanna resembled a mini-Bitsy, except her belt was a silk scarf with a retro cat print on it.

Cleo heard Maybelle evoke "aching corns" and "whiplash." She touched Henry's arm and whispered, "Let's keep moving."

A few yards on, Mayor Day was jollying it up with his good-old-boy friends. Jimmy Teeks stood off to the side, looking straight at Cleo with no reaction. Cleo was relieved to spot her cousin Dot and some ladies from church. Dot wore a black apron and a disapproving expression.

"This isn't right," Dot said, smoothing her already smooth front. "What's gotten into Mary-Rose that she'd allow this kind of debauchery and on a Sunday?" The other women bobbed their heads, scandalized, but titillated too, Cleo suspected.

"Receptions and wakes are often festive affairs," Cleo said, feeling she should stick up for Mary-Rose, despite feeling a similar unease.

"Yes," Dot agreed. "But celebrating's appropriate when remembering a loved one and good times, knowing they're on to a better place."

A few of the ladies said, "Amen" and glanced nervously toward Krandall House. From where they stood, Cleo could see a bit of mossy white pillar through the chopped cypress trees.

One of the women turned away. "How Mary-Rose must have dreaded that man, lurking up there, always looking. It's no wonder . . ."

Cleo didn't like the insinuation. "Yes, it's no wonder Mary-Rose got those lovely peacocks. Mr. Krandall had a touch of ornithophobia, so he never came down here. Mary-Rose had the situation under control. Such an easy, peaceable solution. That's Mary-Rose's way."

A cheer and clapping arose over by the band.

Dot and her friends looked rightfully doubtful. "It hardly seems under control," Dot said. "A killer roving free. Missing persons. And Cleo, we heard you were attacked in your own backyard. Are you all right? Why didn't you call me right away? What is Catalpa Springs coming to?"

Cleo repeated she was fine. Henry suggested a stroll around the spring.

"It'll be quieter," he said after they were away. They walked to the far side of the natural swimming pool and rested on a swinging bench with a view of the mill and party. Beast snouted in the weeds a few yards away, and little Zoe was making her way toward them in a dizzying string of cartwheels.

"This is a good spot. We can see everyone and who they're interacting with," Cleo said. She'd come prepared for such a view. She extracted a small pair of birding binoculars from her purse. She didn't need them to see who was who across the spring, but she liked to read expressions.

"Whatcha looking for?" Zoe asked, skipping over, face flushed.

Cleo answered with what they *could* be doing. "We're watching for wildlife. Egrets, ibis, turtles."

"And wolves in sheep's clothing," Henry said.

Zoe plunked down between them, sending the bench swinging. "Ooh . . . I know where one of those is. Want to see?"

Chapter
Twenty-Three

Cleo and Henry exchanged a look over Zoe's red curls. Zoe might know something. Or she might be caught up in imagination, the realms of reading and fantasy. Zoe had spent her final year of preschool pretending she was a fire-breathing triceratops who danced ballet and commanded an army of alligators. Zoe's mom—Mary-Rose's tightly buttoned daughter-in-law—worried whether triceratops could be admitted to kindergarten. Fortunately, the public school and library were happy to encourage both dinosaurs and dancing. In other periods, Zoe claimed personal access to magical doorways to Narnia and Hogwarts and King Arthur's court and other far-away lands, like Antarctica, Mumbai, and San Francisco.

"Ah," Cleo said. "So you know of one, do you? What kind of wolf is this?"

"Secret kind," Zoe declared, kicking up purple sneakers with flashing lights in their soles.

Like secretive grandmother, like granddaughter, Cleo thought, ready to write the wolf off as a fantasy.

Cleo kicked up her feet too, enjoying the sway of the bench.

She checked the crowd across the water. Dot and her friends were tidying the buffet tables. Desiree, the waitress, was manning the pie table. Kat stood on a makeshift crate/podium, holding a microphone, her voice carrying. She requested "memories of Buford. Bad preferred. Good if you have 'em." Gabby hovered intently in a shady corner. Kat handed the microphone over to the florist, who launched into a nice story about how much Buford loved flowers. "Irises, especially. But do you know what he loved the most? Prying! Let me tell you about the time I caught him in the dumpster behind City Hall."

The tale carried on amidst cheers and laughter. Glasses were raised heavenward and more drinks poured. Vernon Givens, bless him, got up next and launched into a more proper eulogy, remembering Buford as a good man of "strong character."

"Strong bad character!" yelled a heckler, sounding an awful lot like Maybelle. More toasts were raised.

"So? Don't you want to see?" Zoe asked, vexed. "The wolf? He wears a sweater."

Henry and Cleo again conferred silently over Zoe's head.

"Of course," Henry said. "We'd love to see. As long as this wolf isn't too far away."

"It's close. No one else knows." Zoe hopped up, bouncing on her flashing shoes, anxious for Henry and Cleo to catch up. "I'll go ahead and see if the wolf wants visitors."

"What do you think it is?" Henry said, mustache twitching over a smile. "An odd-shaped tree? A dog?"

"Invisible?" Cleo guessed with a grin of her own. She wouldn't mind if Zoe's discovery was make-believe. It felt like a small adventure to go into the woods. Zoe was leading them toward the not-so-secret trail that ran behind Krandall House. Generations ago, the trail had been a gravel road, connected to the Tallgrass River and flat-bottomed barges laden with sugar cane for the mill. The last time Cleo had hiked the trail—more years ago than she wanted to count—vegetation had overgrown all but a thin sliver of chalky limestone gravel.

The forest was so dark that Cleo had to remove her sunglasses. Ducking under a web of vines, she recalled her grandmother's tales of ghosts and spirits, particularly those that lingered after a "bad death." Granny Bess didn't necessarily believe in ghosts, but that didn't stop her from telling a good tale or scaring her listeners. There were always signs in her grandmother's stories. Omens. Cleo looked up and spotted one. High in a tree, a lone buzzard stared down at them. A single buzzard was bad luck in Granny Bess's stories, unless it flapped its wings—then it was good luck. Cleo stopped and waited, feeling silly but needing to know which way the buzzard would say.

"Come on!" Zoe's voice called, breaking the spell. The warty-headed bird lifted its wings and soared. Cleo couldn't recall if soaring counted as flapping. She reminded herself she didn't believe in ghosts or prophesies by birds.

"We're right behind you," Henry said. He looked back to Cleo with concern. "Everything okay?"

"Just bird-watching," she said, truthfully.

When they caught up with Zoe, she waved her hands like a game show hostess. "Ta-da!"

What she was showing them was real, but not alive: a life-sized dog carved from stone and dressed in a faded, ragged sweater. Whirligigs on sticks were stuck all around, unmoving in the breezeless heat. It took Cleo a moment to get her bearings. She realized they were behind the Krandall family cemetery, with Buford's backyard, drill, and vine-smothered home beyond.

"I've never seen this before," Cleo said. "You did find a secret place."

Henry was rubbing his beard and looking as if a bad omen had crossed his path. "I think it's"—he lowered his voice and leaned toward Cleo—"a grave."

Cleo read the inscription on the stone pedestal. The date was about ten years back. "Buford used to have a massive shepherd dog," she recalled. The dog was a mix of some kind, with weird yellowish eyes and the watchful, feral face of a wolf.

"The wolf in wool clothes," Zoe declared.

"Good. Lovely. Great job," Henry said briskly. "We should get back to the reception now."

Cleo smiled sympathetically. She couldn't fault Henry for feeling unnerved when she'd gotten edgy about a common vulture. The place was eerie, but also touching. Buford had loved his pet. It was another thing she had in common with the man.

"Yes, let's get back," Cleo said. "Zoe, let's all of us promise we won't come out here again. It's not your grandparents' property."

"Whose is it?" Zoe demanded.

"Good question," Henry said. "Maybe someone back at the party will know. Come along." He started back down the trail toward the spring and mill.

"Are you scared?" Zoe asked, catching up with him.

"Just eager to get back to that dessert table," he said, his hearty joviality sounding strained. "How about we all get some of Miss Cleo's lovely peach cobbler or caramel cake?"

"Brownies," Zoe said. "Chocolate cake and ice cream and pie and spinach dip with baby carrots and pretzels and . . ." She ran ahead.

Henry turned to Cleo just before they reached the opening to the sunny gardens and sparkling waters of Pancake Spring. "That girl's too perceptive. I did feel spooked. I can't even say why now. It's a lovely day, a pretty forest, nothing to worry—"

His words were cut off by footsteps pounding down the trail. Cleo's mind turned to Beast and Kat. Were they out here again? No, Kat was just at the microphone. Cleo stumbled quickly off the path. Henry did too. The sound of panting preceded the runner.

Cleo realized with a start, it wasn't the dog. It wasn't a ghost either.

Ollie might have sprinted straight past them if Cleo hadn't called his name and reached out.

"Gran!" He came to a breathless stop, his eyes wide and wild. "Gran. I have to get help. Don't go to Krandall House. Get out of here!"

"Ollie, Ollie, *Ollie!*" Zoe came running back, delighted to see her favorite honorary big brother.

Ollie uttered an oath under his breath, scooped the little girl up, and ran, yelling for Cleo and Henry to follow.

*   *   *

"What's going on?" Gabby Honeywell had an eye for trouble. She sprinted toward them, hand on a small strappy purse Cleo suspected held a gun. Henry and Zoe stood back by the trail-head. Ollie was pacing and gasping for air. In between, he was talking gibberish.

"Dead!" he cried, ignoring Cleo's attempts to soothe him. "No, no, no. She can't be."

Cleo hurried to Zoe. "I have a very important job for you. Run back to the Pancake Mill and find your grandmother. Now, this is the most important part: you have to stay there with her, okay? Stay there."

The little girl was already running.

Gabby had taken Ollie by the shoulders. For a second Cleo thought she might slap him. The dear boy was still talking in garbled outbursts. "The scarf. Too tight! I loosened it. I tried!" His words dissolved into moans. "Dead," he said again, coldly clear this time. "Someone killed her."

"It's okay," Gabby said, her expression and voice admirably calm. "Ollie, take a breath. Who's dead?"

Cleo knew. In the ache in her hands and clench of her stomach, she knew before he said it. She and Henry had sensed something earlier, the bad feeling.

"Whitney," Ollie said, gulping back a sob. "By the drill. On the ground. I tried to help her. I tried CPR. I couldn't feel her breath or her heart. That awful scarf was choking her."

Gabby procured a cell phone from her purse and called for help, waving her other hand high as she did. "No, Tookey, look to the northeast of the spring. The *other* side. Yes. Find the chief, call the EMTs, get them here fast. I have Oliver Watkins here. He's saying he just found Whitney Greene. He says she's deceased."

Within minutes, Tookey and the chief were chugging their

way. So were most of the other guests. In the background, the band played on, a jaunty swing version of "Jailhouse Rock."

The chief ordered Gabby to hold back the gawkers. "You!" he said, pointing to Ollie. "You're coming with us. Lead the way." He turned to the crowd. "Any doctors in this party?"

Three men identifying themselves as a pediatrician, a podiatrist, and a chiropractor, respectively, stepped up. Angela pushed through the crowd, followed by a fretful Fred. She positioned herself defensively in front of Ollie.

"I'm his lawyer. He's not going anywhere without me." Her tone allowed no protest from the chief or from her husband. She firmly sent Fred to keep an eye on the twins, who were planning to go inner-tubing in the spring.

Cleo watched as, one by one, the police, doctors, Ollie, and Angela pushed through the leaves and disappeared. *Like a magic door,* Cleo thought, *but not to a nice place.*

Under Gabby's stern direction, the crowd headed back to the Pancake Mill, with Kat adding encouragement of free drinks. The party organizer sounded shaken.

A small, redheaded figure stayed behind. Zoe.

"Are Ollie and the police going after the wolf?" Zoe asked. "I think it's a good wolf. I don't think it means any harm."

"I think you said you'd wait at the Pancake Mill," Cleo said kindly, torn between concern for her honorary granddaughter and the grandson swallowed up by the forest.

Zoe frowned. "You said to find Nana and make her stay by staying with her, only I couldn't find her so I couldn't make her stay, and everyone was running over here, and I thought if—"

"You're right," Cleo said. "You did the right thing." Cleo

was worried about Mary-Rose too. Where was she? How had she missed the commotion? Cleo prayed that Mary-Rose hadn't gone for a walk in the woods like Ollie, both for her safety and for how it might look. If Whitney's death was another murder, Mary-Rose would be a prime suspect again. So would Ollie.

"Why's Ollie upset?" Zoe asked.

Cleo thought fast. "He's worried about a friend," Cleo said. "Listen, I am too. I have another important job for you. Mr. Lafayette here needs a piece of pie. Could you help him?" She caught Henry's eye and hoped he'd understand why she was sending him off.

"I certainly do," Henry said. "But which flavor? I'll need your help choosing. Maybe we should each have a piece. Or two."

Zoe brightened. "Okay. There's cherry and coconut and . . ." She skipped off, the list of flavors sailing along with her.

Henry lingered a moment. "I'll keep her safely inside and look for Mary-Rose too. But what are you planning?"

Cleo raised her voice for Gabby to hear. "I think I dropped my keys back on that trail. Silly me—I'll have to go back and look for them. Maybe Gabby will escort me."

"Oh," Henry said knowingly.

"Uh-huh," Gabby said, her tone more skeptical. She joined them. "Keys, eh? Let me guess, Miss Cleo. You conveniently lost them somewhere with a view of the presumed crime? You want to go have a look."

Cleo didn't *want* to look. She wanted to help, and she needed to know that Ollie was going to be okay. "We don't know if it's a crime yet," Cleo pointed out. "If we took a little stroll, maybe we'd both know more."

233

"About your keys, right?" Gabby said.

The band was playing, and the lyrics "You ain't nothin' but a hound dog" floated across the crowd, with Beast howling the refrain. The dancing, however, had dwindled. People clustered in groups, heads together. Cleo could practically feel the gossip and speculation vibrating in the air.

Gabby shot another glance toward the trees. "Okay, I'm curious too. But we can't get too close."

"If the chief spots us, you can say I sneaked in, and you were escorting me back," Cleo said. They made their way up the trail to Zoe's stone wolf. Cleo didn't need her binoculars to see Ollie and Angela, sitting on Buford's back steps, both staring at their feet.

"See anything?" Gabby whispered. "I mean, those keys?"

Cleo was almost relieved by what she couldn't see. Whitney. Careful of vines and graves, Cleo picked her way to the edge of the Krandall family cemetery. She gasped. Behind the drill, she could see feet and legs and a cluster of people huddled around them. The broad, bent-over backsides of Tookey and the Chief blocked much of the prone body. *That poor girl.* Whatever Whitney was wrapped up in, whatever she'd done, she didn't deserve this.

The chief straightened, stretching his back and suspenders, turning their way. Gabby ducked behind a grave. Cleo backed into a palmetto.

"Let's go," Gabby said. "This was a bad idea, Miss Cleo."

Gabby was right. They should leave. What had Cleo accomplished other than risking getting Gabby in trouble and feeling like an awful ghoul? Then Tookey moved, and Cleo saw yellow. Bright yellow. A scarf, and a familiar one at that. She raised her binoculars to be sure.

"Look at the scarf," she said, handing Gabby the binoculars. "Ollie said it was too tight. He loosened it. It's probably the murder weapon."

Cleo stepped back, tripping on what she thought was a root. Looking down, she realized she'd stepped on a gravestone, furry with moss. Her Granny Bess would have seen that as an omen too, definitely a bad one.

Gabby was still staring through the binoculars. "If that is the murder weapon and Ollie messed with it, it's not good for him."

Cleo focused on the scarf. "Will the chief and Tookey recognize that scarf? Do you?"

"Looks like caution tape," Gabby said. "Looks familiar—wait, is that . . . ?"

"It's Priscilla Pawpaw's signature scarf." Cleo said. "She gives them out to promote her books." Her books on murder. An idea took form. "Priscilla thought Buford was her biggest fan. What if she believed Whitney killed him? A revenge murder?"

Gabby groaned.

Cleo wanted to too. Chief Culpepper was striding toward Ollie, handcuffs swinging.

Chapter
Twenty-Four

Catalpa Springs was going about its Monday-morning business. Birds sang, church bells announced the time, and residents were heading to work, opening shops, sweeping off doorways, and dissecting murders.

The town looked the same, but Cleo sensed an edge. People were worried. So was she. Without her bookmobile or library to fill her schedule, Cleo had roused Rhett and headed to Dot's Drop By for company and supplies. Their walk took them by the library, where they both stopped short. The sad scene was only getting worse. The lawn needed an industrial mower or a herd of weed-hungry goats. The blue roof tarp was askew, and a rude graffiti scrawl marred the already ugly plywood over the reading room window. *Decay spreads quickly,* Cleo thought. She sniffed and caught the whiff of skunk in the air. She was glad Rhett had on his harness.

Rhett wasn't happy. He pouted up at her. When he caught her eye, he promptly fell to the sidewalk.

"I know," Cleo said. "It's not right, any of it."

Rhett's tail slapped the concrete.

"Except the harness. That's for your own safety," Cleo told her cat. Not only for skunks. Two murders in her pretty town. A killer still walking free, regardless of what Chief Culpepper contended. Her heart tightened, picturing the dismal jail and innocent Ollie inside it, charged with strangling Whitney Greene. Angela said not to worry, that he'd be out on bond by this afternoon. Angela was brisk and confident, but she couldn't quell Fred's fretting, and this time, she couldn't ease Cleo's mind either.

Cleo was going to keep walking, when she saw Jimmy Teeks marching down the sidewalk toward them. The Vegas consultant wore shorts and a vest of crinkly fabric and many pockets. Fishing attire, Cleo guessed, in which Jimmy looked as comfortable as Leanna in a biscuit costume. A canvas hat hid his bald top, but not his potato features. He held a fishing pole around its middle, as if throttling it.

"Come along, Rhett," Cleo said, her pulse quickening. Ever since Jimmy's "watch your back" comment at the bookmobile crash, she'd been extra leery of the man. Rightfully so, she thought. Gabby had run a background check on Mr. Teeks and found nothing, not even his name or variations of it. He was either a perfectly spotless citizen, Gabby suggested, or not who he said he was.

Rhett stretched and rolled and remained stubbornly prone on the sidewalk. His leash had a long extension. Wanting to avoid an awkward chat, Cleo left Rhett lounging and stepped into the library's garden, where she set about looking busy. She pulled a few weeds and kept her ears and eyes keen, waiting for

Jimmy to pass. His shoes scuffed at the sidewalk. Slap, scrape, slap, and then the footsteps stopped.

"Hey there, grumpy guy," he said in his high-pitched rasp.

Cleo straightened and looked in alarm at Jimmy standing over her cat. She resisted the urge to reel Rhett in via his lead. Instead, she went to join them, explaining Rhett's leash and harness aversion.

"No one likes to be held back, do they, furry man?" Jimmy rested his fishing pole on a nearby post box and crouched to pet Rhett. To Cleo's surprise and irritation, the cat stood to rub and fawn and make a drooling fool of himself. Cleo wondered if she'd misjudged her pet's ability to judge strangers.

"He's a gorgeous cat," Jimmy said, and Cleo's feelings began to shift. A man who liked cats couldn't be all that bad, could he?

Jimmy scratched Rhett under his chin. "I always wanted a fluffy cat. I found one once, when I was a kid. It was gray. Pretty. Blue eyes. Great fur. My dad wouldn't let me keep it. Said it was girly, too fluffy."

Indignation replaced Cleo's remaining wariness. "Why, that is simply ridiculous!" she exclaimed. "Awful!"

Small, dark potato eyes narrowed.

Cleo stepped back. She'd more than stuck a bad-manners foot in her mouth. She'd insulted a possible mobster's father.

Jimmy's eyes seemed to get harder and smaller. "Yeah," he said, after an uncomfortable beat. "You're right. It was wrong. Unnecessary. Cruel."

"We shouldn't keep you," Cleo said, giving Rhett's leash the gentlest of encouraging tugs.

Rhett, the traitor, flopped on Jimmy Teeks's unmoving

feet. "You don't have any books for sale in that library, do you?" Jimmy said. "I need a something to read."

She had to disappoint Jimmy, who took the news stoically.

"We used to sell donated books and use the profits for the library," she said. "But those books are all in storage now. I could use the few extra dollars they brought in and a lot more too." She scooped up Rhett, who wasn't going to leave his new pal by any other means.

Rhett scrambled up to his preferred spot on her shoulder. Jimmy reached over and scratched Rhett's head. "You're a good cat. Hope you get your library fixed soon."

"Tell your boss that," Cleo muttered.

Jimmy's potato eyes narrowed again. "Is the mayor giving you trouble?

Yes! Cleo wanted to yell. "It's all about money, isn't it?" she said, trying to keep her tone light. "Mayor Day says the library fund has run dry, but I just don't see how that can be true. We used to be fine. Enough for what we needed and a little saved up."

"Is that so?" Jimmy He resumed his choke hold on the fishing pole. Then he turned heel and strode back toward City Hall.

* * *

At the Drop By, Rhett hopped on the window ledge, where Dot displayed vintage canisters and tin signs and now a fluffy orange cat belly. Cleo was happy to find Angela at the deli counter. Her lawyer daughter-in-law was picking up sandwiches. Pimento cheese and tomato for herself, ham and Swiss with chow-chow pickle—hold the onions—for Ollie.

"He wanted onions," Angela said, "but we can't have his breath offending the judge if we have to approach the bench. Details matter."

Cleo approved. Details did matter. She inquired about the time of the bail hearing.

"Later this afternoon," Angela said. "I'll let you know. I'm going to visit Ollie now. There's not much for him to do or say, but I want him ready."

Dot plunked paper-wrapped parcels on the counter. "I put extra filling on your sandwiches and added some chips and brownies. Grab a couple cold drinks from the cooler."

When Dot saw a problem, she applied food to fix it. She offered Angela ice cream but then realized it would melt and get fingers and tables sticky, and they probably weren't allowed aprons in court. Dot stuffed a handful of napkins into Angela's bag.

"It will turn out fine," Cleo said. "Right, Angela?"

When Angela didn't answer right away, Dot made up a packet of chocolate chip cookies and trilled, "Of course. Oliver had no reason to hurt that young lady. He's a nice boy, and when he brought her to Sunday lunch at your house, Cleo, they seemed so happy. Well, Ollie seemed happy. She seemed . . ." Dot frowned and wiped her spotless counter, mumbling that one mustn't speak ill of the recently deceased.

Angela gathered the weighty lunch sack. "I'll tell you the truth. The prosecutor will claim Ollie was angry for getting dumped, for Whitney's betrayal of him and the spring. Those are big motives. Plus he found her body. He touched the murder weapon, the scarf. It looks like Whitney was killed during or just before that funeral party at the Pancake Mill, so he had opportunity."

"A lot of people were celebrating Buford Kandall's death," Cleo pointed out. "Anyone could have slipped away."

"I said it at the time," Dot said. "That event was off. It wasn't right. There was an air of menace."

A mother and preschooler came in, making a beeline for the ice-cream freezer. Cleo leaned closer to the counter and lowered her voice. "The murderer could easily have been among us yesterday. I've been thinking. What if Whitney was killed not because of personal betrayal or anger, but because of something she knew or saw?"

Angela hoisted her heavy lunch bags. "It's a good theory, but just that. Ollie did finally admit that Whitney went back on her own the night they stupidly sabotaged that drilling machine. She claimed she dropped something. She was gone a few minutes. It would have been helpful if he'd admitted this sooner."

Oh, Ollie! Cleo shared her daughter-in-law's loving frustration. A darker idea struck her. What if the killer thought Ollie saw something too? She caught Angela's eye and guessed she'd already considered that too.

The mom and child stepped up to the cash register with their ice-cream sandwiches. Dot managed a cheery face and gave them some on-the-house cookies.

Angela put an ice tea and Coke in her to-go bags and insisted on paying Dot for everything. While Dot was banging on the cash register, Angela said, "Your theory only helps if we have firm evidence and a better suspect than Ollie. I'd like to know more about that scarf. Was it hers or the killer's?"

Cleo tried to remember if she'd seen anyone wearing a Priscilla Pawpaw promotional scarf/murder weapon at the reception. She couldn't, but a scarf could easily be tucked in a purse or pocket. It would be nearly as easy for the killer to slip away and meet Whitney at Krandall House.

"So, who would have had these scarves?" Angela asked.

"Lots of people," Cleo said. "Me, Henry." *Mary-Rose.*

"Me," chimed in Dot. "Mine's still in my fabric chest. I was going to incorporate it into a Halloween apron, but I won't go near it now."

"Priscilla had loads of those scarves," Cleo said. Her mind turned, and an idea brewed. Priscilla likely also had loads of her own books, including a complete version of *Killings in Cotton Country*. Cleo wanted a look at the page that had been removed from the library copy. With the new murder and arrest, the police would have little time or incentive to track down a single page. But Cleo did, if she could get inside Priscilla's house. A plan took form, involving a touch of trespassing and a certain watchful neighbor.

"There is something at Priscilla's I could check into," Cleo said. She ordered a couple of oatmeal cookies—an expedition required supplies, and oatmeal counted as healthy. Then she collected Rhett and carried him to the door.

"Should I know what you're doing?" Angela asked as they lingered on the threshold.

"Probably not," Cleo said.

"I thought so," Angela said.

Cleo waited for a warning, a caution that she was too old or out of her league.

"Whatever it is, be careful," Angela said. "I don't need any more family clients."

* * *

Mary-Rose picked Cleo up outside her house. "Should we be doing this in daylight?" Mary-Rose asked. "It's awfully clear and bright."

"Yes," Cleo said, primly for a person hoping to break and enter. "Sunny is perfect. We need to be spotted." Cleo scooched down, however, as they drove past The Gilded Page. The "OPEN" sign hung on the door, and a light shone inside. Henry would have come along in an instant. Cleo had already gotten him into enough tricky situations recently. Besides, it was Monday, when Mary-Rose went to Happy Trails anyway to visit her mother.

Tamara greeted them at the guardhouse. "The girl-detective book you recommended is awesome," she said to Cleo. "Do you have any others by that author?"

"I can look in the main library." Cleo had to lean over Mary-Rose to see out the driver's window. This was another reason she preferred to sit behind the steering wheel. "Have you seen Miss Pawpaw?"

"Miss V.? Nope. Not since she went and disappeared. You want my theory? She's the killer! Why else would she run for the hills?" Tamara gestured in the vague direction of west and hills. "Off to see your mama, Mary-Rose?"

"Yes," Mary-Rose said woodenly. "We're off to see my mother." As they pulled away, she asked, "Did that sound too fake? Think she noticed?"

"Only a little," said Cleo, in answer to both questions. She directed the way to Sweetgum Court. "Now, park right out front. Perfect."

With Mary-Rose at her heels, Cleo marched to the bright yellow door of Priscilla Vinogradov, aka Pawpaw, and knocked loudly.

"This isn't how we used to go about our trespassing," Mary-Rose said. She grinned. "Ah, the good old days, when we never thought we'd get caught. I guess we're not worrying about that now either."

"I'm counting on getting caught," Cleo said.

She bellowed Priscilla's name. She rapped at the door. No sound came from within. Cleo headed around the side of the tidy patio home. She stopped to peer in Priscilla's windows, right across from watchful neighbor Adelaide Cox's house. She cupped her hands to the glass and called again. She was starting to get worried. Perhaps the elderly woman had her hearing aids out or was napping or—

A high-pitched tone sounded in the shrubbery to her left. Cleo smiled.

"Stop, burglar!" A wizened face appeared over the shrubbery and widened into a smile. "Why, it's the fighting librarian! That's quite a shiner you have." Adelaide chuckled. "And Mary-Rose! Now this *is* a surprise. What are you girls up to? Breaking in? Doing some spying?"

Cleo said, pleasantly, "Why, yes, we are, and we're hoping you can help us. I'm betting you have a spare key. Good neighbors do, and we're worried Priscilla could be in danger."

Adelaide ducked back down, and Cleo worried she'd misjudged. Gabby had an extra key to Cleo's house, but nosy Wanda Boxer most certainly did not. Fred—the dear innocent—once gave Wanda a key, contending that if Cleo became ill or fell in the tub, Wanda could help. Cleo had waited a polite few days before changing the locks while Wanda was at work. Neither Fred nor Wanda would be finding her in her tub. Perhaps Priscilla felt a similar leeriness.

A click-clack sound approached. "I don't have a key," Adelaide announced, swinging her cane in a wide, shin-threatening swath. "But I know where to find her spare. Why do you want in? We looking for something? A body? You're a magnet for those lately, Cleo Watkins."

Cleo felt a twinge of unease. Surely someone had checked inside Priscilla's cottage since she'd gone missing. Gabby or the chief, a friend, someone . . .

Mary-Rose groaned, "Oh no."

Cleo heard a soft squeak of metal. She recognized the sound of a walker, as Mary-Rose surely had too. Even before turning, she knew who was behind it: Mary-Rose's mother.

"Yep," Adelaide said merrily. "Jo-Marie and I were visiting, strategizing what to do with all her strip bingo winnings. She had time, you know, since her daughter cancelled on her."

"Mama," said Mary-Rose with nervous cheeriness. "Cleo and I were just—"

Jo-Marie cut her off with a shake of her finger. "I know what you're doing, young lady. You cancel my visit to make trouble with Cleo? Cleo, your eye! Mary-Rose, your reputation! If I've said it once, I've said it for forever. You girls and your exploits will be the death of me. The death!"

"There're worse ways to go," Adelaide said. "Come on. Let's see what murder lady next door is hiding."

Chapter
Twenty-Five

Adelaide proposed a game. "Go ahead, try and guess where Priscilla hides her key. Remember, that woman knows all about crimes. She knows about psychos and killers and prowlers who could break in and do heaven knows what."

Mary-Rose and her mother looked appropriately aghast.

Cleo played along. She liked a puzzle. Where would the key be? In a fake rock? Under the garden gnome? Buried in the fire-ant mound over by the fence? Cleo hoped it wasn't the ants, though that would be a good place. No one would look there. Fire ants were worse garden invaders than even air potatoes—unless the air potato was flying toward one's eye.

"It's clever, actually. So obvious you'd never guess." Adelaide chuckled. "She has a cleaning woman who lets herself in, that's how I know." She went to a grouping of patio chairs and a table under the awning. The metal table sported a faded floral tablecloth, some dusty plastic placemats, and an ashtray. Adelaide lifted the ashtray and there was the key.

Jo-Marie fussed. "She might as well have put it under the

mat or right in the lock itself. Anyone could guess that. Burglars, strangers, killers . . ."

"Neighbors," Adelaide added with a chuckle. "Librarians. Pancake makers." She inserted the key in the sliding glass door.

They all hesitated. Jo-Marie leaned on her walker and declared the situation wrong.

"Pah!" Adelaide said. "We'll water her plants, check her mail. She'd thank us, if she knew. Now, what are we looking for? Bodies? Weapons?"

"Books," Cleo said. She slid the door open with effort and stepped inside.

* * *

Thankfully, no alarms rang out, and there was no sign of a body, live or otherwise.

"Shoot," Adelaide declared. "This is kind of a letdown. Not even a plant to water."

The living room was cozy and tidy, as when Cleo had visited before. However, the atmosphere seemed different. A stuffy emptiness pervaded, the quiet broken only by Adelaide's cane swinging over the tile and an ice maker groaning and clunking.

"Sounds like a good ice maker. Energetic," Adelaide commented, opening the fridge and freezer doors and sticking her head in. She exhaled. "Ah . . . cool . . ." Then she turned to yell, "Jo-Marie, want a Coke? She's got stacks of cold drinks. She surely wouldn't miss one."

Mary-Rose's mother hovered outside on the back patio, righteously refusing to be part of "this, whatever *this* is."

247

"You're already trespassing, Mama," Mary-Rose said.

"Abetting too," Adelaide said. "You stay outside, though. Be our lookout. If you see anyone coming, give us a warning. A sound. Something subtle, like those peacocks your daughter keeps. *Ha-ha, ha-ha!*" Adelaide's birdcall could use some work and was definitely not subtle.

Mutters about daughters and peacocks and "death of me" resumed on the patio. Cleo promised to be quick.

The built-in bookshelves in the living room held knick-knacks. The coffee table was piled high with magazines on subjects of gardening, cooking, and crime. Cleo peeked in a bedroom. The bed was unmade, clothes strewn over it, and the closet a mess, as if a mini-tornado had struck, or Priscilla—as Adelaide claimed—had run off in a hurry.

"Over here!" Mary-Rose called from a small room off the kitchen.

Cleo stepped into a box room that lived up to its name. Cardboard and clear plastic containers stuffed with books, crime-scene scarves, and papers towered around a cluttered desk. Cleo disapproved. Books should be neatly stacked on shelves, dusted and organized, preferably by the ways of Dewey's decimals.

"What a mess," Mary-Rose said. "How does she find anything?"

"I'm looking for *Killings in Cotton Country*," Cleo said. "That's why we're here. The library's copy is missing a page. This is an emergency book-borrowing situation."

They opened boxes and read out titles whose subjects ranged from murder and crime to noxious plants, to a surprising guide to spring bulbs.

"This is nice," Mary-Rose said, inspecting the bulb guide. "I wonder why Priscilla didn't stick to writing gardening books?"

"No fun in that," Adelaide said, fussing with her squealing hearing aid. It buzzed and she reared back.

"Got it!" Mary-Rose held up a familiar cover, a field of cotton, the fleecy puffs dripping lurid red blood.

Cleo couldn't wait. She took the book and was flipping to the missing page, when a wavering "*ha-ha, ha-ha*" came from the back.

"Peacock!" Adelaide cried.

Mary-Rose gasped. "That's Mama. That's the warning sign. Shh . . . someone's here."

They froze, listening to the rattle of keys and a scraping at the front door.

"Hurry," Mary-Rose whispered. "Let's go. Out the back."

Cleo clutched the book and made sure Mary-Rose and Adelaide were out before her. She muscled shut the stubborn door and quickly locked it and hid the key. With tiptoed steps and a squeaky walker, they made their way up the side pathway. They waited at the corner of the cottage until they heard the front door open and shut.

"Who is it?" Mary-Rose whispered.

"Shh . . ." her mother said. "We're going back to Adelaide's. Now."

But Adelaide was already back down the path, peeking in the window. She scuttled back. "It's her. It's Priscilla. Breaking in!"

Jo-Marie reminded her it was Priscilla's home. "We're the burglars," she said, hand fluttering dramatically to her chest. "Thieves."

"Let's all go pay her a visit," Cleo said over Jo-Marie's protests. "We'll ask her for a copy of the book. She'll surely sell us one. Then we can slip the 'borrowed' copy onto her bookshelf or her desk when she's not looking."

"What if she's the killer, and she figures out that we're onto her?" Adelaide countered. "What do we do then? Fight? Run?" She waggled her cane as if warming up for battle.

Mary-Rose amended Cleo's idea. "Mama, why don't you and Miss Adelaide go back and watch through Adelaide's window? That way you can call the police if you sense any trouble."

The two older women left, Adelaide grumbling about missing all the fun, Jo-Marie muttering that she already sensed trouble.

* * *

Priscilla peeked over her door chain with startled bunny-in-headlights eyes. Her odd purple hair frizzed out in tufts.

"You're back from vacation!" Cleo announced cheerfully, holding her elbow protectively over her purse and the book within. "Wonderful! Can we come in? We were over visiting with your neighbor Adelaide and saw you return."

"It's not a good time right now," Priscilla said, inching the door closed.

"No, it's not a good time!" Mary-Rose blurted with a slap to the door. "My neighbor has been murdered! Cleo's grandson is in jail, and another person was murdered during a funeral reception at my Pancake Mill. Strangled with your scarf! Let us in! Cleo has some questions." Mary-Rose was in high color. She stomped a foot and looked ready to kick the door in.

With shaky hands, Priscilla undid the lock. "My scarf?"

She wore a silk scarf, purple and draped artfully over a wildly printed lavender dress that hung to her ankles.

"One of your promotional scarves," Cleo specified. "The crime-scene kind."

Priscilla brightened. "Aren't those fun? Did I give you one? Do you need another? They're in my office."

"No!" Mary-Rose said. "We need answers and a book."

"A book? I just got in," Priscilla said. "You saw that. Let me freshen up. Have a seat. I'll be back in a wink. Help yourself to a cold drink if you like."

Cleo and Mary-Rose perched on the edge of the sofa. "She's twitchy," Mary-Rose said.

"She's always like that," Cleo whispered.

The ice machine clunked and groaned. Water ran in the back, and a toilet flushed. Cleo mentally prepared a list of questions. The book. The anonymous notes left on her porch. The cut brake lines of her bookmobile. Priscilla's fight with Buford. Whitney.

Cleo was deep in her lists when she registered a thumping that wasn't the ice maker. She looked across at Adelaide's house. Adelaide and Jo-Marie were slapping Adelaide's picture window, pointing in the direction of the street. Cleo sprang up and hurried to the door. Priscilla was already in her car. Tires squealed and rubber burned the pavement of Sweetgum Court, and the true-crime author was gone.

* * *

Cleo's purse felt heavy on her lap, not only because of the ill-gotten book inside, but also for what it contained. *Nothing,* she thought dismally, gazing out the passenger's window at a blur of green. It had all been a waste of time except to confirm Priscilla's flightiness. The page in question mostly contained photos. They were black and white and poorly focused and no one Cleo recognized, at least at first glance. A glimpse was all Cleo had gotten. Mary-Rose had been in a hurry to get going, and speeding cars were the one place Cleo couldn't even open a book for fear of motion sickness.

They were heading to town. Mary-Rose would then zip back to Happy Trails, having agreed to take her mother and Adelaide to a bingo game and shopping and an early-bird buffet in Claymore. Penance, Mary-Rose said.

When they reached downtown Catalpa Springs, Cleo asked to be let off by the park. She apologized again for getting Mary-Rose in trouble with her mother.

"This gives Mama something to chew on. Keeps her mind off her health. Keeps her young." Mary-Rose idled in a no-parking zone, blinkers clicking.

"You're a good daughter then," Cleo said. "Her mind will certainly be busy." She hugged Mary-Rose across the console and promised to call when she heard more about Ollie.

The day was sunny and hot, already feeling as steamy as summer. Cleo wasn't out for a stroll. She had a destination. When she got to The Gilded Page, however, the door sign read "CLOSED." Cleo's spirits dipped lower until she saw Henry and Mr. Chaucer coming down the sidewalk. Henry beamed. Mr. Chaucer woofed, tottering with the effort.

"Come in out of the heat," Henry said. They settled in his reading nook, a little area of armchairs upholstered in soft maroon velvet. The shop was cool and lit only by natural light, the view out the windows so bright it blurred. Cleo told Henry of her morning, hoping he wouldn't feel left out. "You didn't miss much," she said. "The book seems to be a letdown in terms of clues."

He rubbed his bearded chin, thoughtful. "It is interesting that Priscilla ran away from you. That's something. Did she seem scared or guilty?"

Cleo didn't know. "She always seems rather scared. I called Gabby on the way back to town. She and Sergeant Tookey will be keeping an eye out for Priscilla." She fished the book out of her purse. "I didn't get a chance to fully study it. Mary-Rose had to run. I thought you might like to see it too, since you discovered the missing page."

Henry was eager to look, but the doorbell interrupted. "Let me see who that is," Henry said.

Cleo sat back, soaking in the comforting company of books. Henry's shop was a candy store of bookish delights. The priciest, most valuable tomes resided in glass-paneled cabinets and air-conditioned cases, to be handled only with gloves. Other books were precious in their own ways. There were thick bibles with family trees drawn inside their covers, and cookbooks from Cleo's grandmother's generation and earlier, the marginalia and smudges revealing favorite recipes. Poetry, classics, art, fiction and fact, and words from centuries past all mingled in The Gilded Page. So did a small collection of vintage children's books and comics, like *Pogo*, featuring Cleo's favorite talking possum from the nearby Okefenokee Swamp. Cleo took a *Pogo* from the shelf, feeling the warmth of reuniting with old friends.

Mr. Chaucer roused himself from his red satin bed, yawned, and wandered to his water bowl behind the counter. Noisy lapping and snorting ensued, over which Cleo could hear Henry greeting Leanna.

Leanna was in her banking attire, taking mincing steps in pointy heels.

"I didn't recognize you at first," Henry was saying. "You look very professional."

"Like a banker?" Leanna asked with a beaming smile. She kicked off the shoes and exhaled with pleasure. "That's good. Miss Bitsy says that looking the part is half the battle. More than half. A lot."

"You're winning, then," Henry said. "Are you looking for a book? Or a certain librarian?"

Leanna said she'd seen Cleo coming this way. "My office window looks out over the park." She emphasized *office* proudly. "I'm done with work for the day and wondered if you'd heard anything? About Ollie or Words on Wheels or the Gala or library?"

Cleo reported waiting on all fronts. She explained her book-sleuthing expedition too and the disappointing result.

"I still want to see that page," Leanna said eagerly.

Cleo opened *Killings in Cotton Country*, with Leanna and Henry hovering at her shoulder.

"See?" Cleo said dismally. Page seventy-nine contained a few paragraphs of text and the same photo they'd seen in *Sunshine State Crimes*. The fated family on their picnic, blurry and smiling. Page eighty was filled with more photos. The husband and wife at their wedding. A small yearbook photo of one of the daughters, a pale girl with stringy hair and a tight smile. A skinny young man with long, would-be rock-star hair, bent over an electric guitar. As before, Cleo recognized no one. Neither did Henry and Leanna.

"It's good to rule out possibilities too," Henry said, the voice of optimism.

Cleo stared at the pages in frustration, willing something to materialize. Henry had taken the stack of Priscilla Pawpaw books to his shop to examine. She asked him to retrieve *Sunshine State Crimes* for comparison.

"Good idea." He read out the arson story again, summarizing and skimming. Suddenly Cleo didn't feel so down.

"Wait," she said, flipping back to page seventy-nine of her "borrowed" book. "There is something. *Cotton Country* was published a few years later and seems to have updated information. The father didn't kill his family and run off as was thought at first. His body was in the house too. Another family member was missing instead. Insurance investigators and the coroner figured it out later, after some mix-up."

Henry rubbed his beard in thought. "In the earlier book, Priscilla said first responders found all the children, teenagers and younger, in their beds. The mother was killed in the kitchen. Shot."

Cleo flipped to the photo page and they stared at the skeleton of the burned home. "It must have been difficult to identify the family members," she said quietly.

Hovering over Cleo's shoulder, Leanna summarized the update. "So, the father was found in a teenage daughter's bedroom in the basement. The teenage girl in the photo. She turned out to be the missing family member. Her boyfriend couldn't be found either. The boyfriend's the guy with the guitar and long hair. Liza and Clyde. Sounds like Bonnie and Clyde. Oh, but look. That terrible father had a gun at his side and the mother was shot. So he probably did it! He killed his family, set the fire, and shot himself. Awful!"

Cleo read and reread the words. The teenager daughter's name was Liza Blackwell. She was wanted for questioning. The boyfriend was Clyde Alvarez, a musician and construction worker with no fixed address.

"'Her disreputable and criminal boyfriend,'" Leanna said, quoting Priscilla's words. "'Weak-jawed, long-haired ne'er-do-well.' *Ne'er-do-well?* I've never seen that word written out before." Leanna snorted. "Seems kind of mean. Just because the guy didn't have a stable home or a good chin or haircut doesn't mean he was bad."

Cleo patted her young friend's hand. "Of course not, dear. Priscilla's writing is highly dramatic. Shock is her thing, in writing and perhaps in life too."

Cleo studied the pictures, hoping something else would leap out. The photos were muddy grays. The text didn't change. "I wonder what happened to those two missing young people?"

Henry produced a magnifying glass and they all stared at the grainy family photo. The unlucky mother looked thin to the point of malnourished, like her children. The father was a wiry little man. Cleo clicked her tongue. *Those poor children. That poor woman.*

"I wish we had a better photo of Liza and Clyde," Cleo said.

Leanna snapped her fingers. "Of course! We can search online. The police and sheriff's websites might have made wanted notices or missing persons alerts. Or the Florida Bureau of Investigation. School photos. Newspapers. Everyone has photos out there."

"This was a while back," Cleo pointed out. "Those teenagers would be—what? In their late thirties or early forties now? Back in the good old days, we didn't post our self-portraits on computers all the time for the world to see."

"Yeah," Leanna said. "That sounds nice to me. But it doesn't mean older things have stayed off the Web. A lot of newspaper archives are available, and school yearbooks and sports pages—all sorts of old, old stuff. We should do a library technology class about online archives."

Cleo shared a smile with Henry. Mr. Chaucer waddled over to them, looked up, and groaned.

"We're old, old stuff, Chaucy," Henry said with a chuckle. The pug sat back with a whimper. "Leanna, let me set you up on the computer in the back room."

Cleo settled back into a velvet armchair to wait. Henry joined her, flipping through the newspaper. It was quiet and cool, and Cleo felt herself drifting off into a nap that may have been a moment, minutes, or more.

"Miss Cleo," Leanna's voice was urgent. "Mr. Henry!"

Cleo's eyes popped open. Leanna stood in front of them, wringing her hands. "Come look and see, and tell me I'm wrong. It's a clearer image, but I have to be wrong."

In the back room, Cleo stared at the screen. She adjusted her glasses. She squinted and tried to imagine the person she knew with a younger face, different hair, and a vastly different life.

"Oh dear," Henry said. "I think I see it."

"No," Leanna said, stepping back. "No, I'm wrong."

A pain thumped behind Cleo's bruised eye. "I'm afraid you're not."

Chapter
Twenty-Six

Hummingbird cake was one of Cleo's favorites, her mother's specialty. Mama made it for birthdays, potlucks, and picnics. She once lugged a magnificent four-layer humming-bird on a summer beach trip, an infamous day when a loose dog stole their packed sandwiches and the sand blew in gales and stuck like gritty sprinkles to the cream cheese frosting. Mama carried on, as she did. She'd scraped off the sand and bundled Cleo, her sister Helen, and their grumpy father into the station wagon for the best picnic ever, sweet tea and cake.

Cleo got out her mother's original recipe card. Mama had written the instructions in her neat cursive, just the bare essentials. The ingredients. The oven temperature. The instructions: mix, divide, bake, cool, frost.

Leanna banged about in Cleo's walk-in pantry, repeating the ingredients. "Pineapple, got it. Sugar. Brown sugar. Flour. Oil. Pecans. Round cake pans. Cinnamon. Baking powder. Miss Cleo, have you ever thought of Dewey-decimalizing your pantry somehow?"

Cleo had to smile. Suggesting kitchen reorganization

might be considered sparring words by some Southern ladies, but Cleo adored Leanna's quest for order. "I alphabetized once," Cleo said, "but now I go by categories. Canned fruit and baking supplies should be on the middle shelves to your right."

An *ah-ha* signaled Leanna was on the right track.

"Are you sure we're doing the right thing?" Leanna asked, emerging with two types of canned pineapple in her hands.

Cleo selected the crushed variety and tried to sound as certain about their plan. "Yes. We're just chatting, and we have backup. Gabby's usually home by six or seven, and Henry will be sitting on the back porch right outside. We'll be fine." She wished Ollie were here. Her grandson was blessedly free from jail, out on a hefty bond, but dear fretful Fred had insisted Ollie stay at his place again. "Out of trouble's way," Fred said accusatorily, as if Cleo might be a cause of Ollie's troubles. She supposed her eldest son did have a point, considering her recent activities and what she was planning.

Cleo glanced out the back window and saw Henry reading, Mr. Chaucer sitting at his feet. She imagined borrowing Beast. Now there would be an attack dog, although she still wasn't entirely sure of the innocence of his owner.

"We owe our friend the benefit of the doubt," Cleo said. She checked the clock for the umpteenth time.

Leanna paced nervously. She'd changed back into her usual comfort clothes, knee-length leggings and a big baggy shirt. Her hair was braided and twisted into a bun, like her twisting hands. When the doorbell rang, Leanna jumped.

Cleo opened the door to a beaming Bitsy Givens.

"Y'all are beyond sweet to help me!" Bitsy said, giving Cleo air-kisses on each cheek. Her perfume and enthusiasm wafted over Cleo, and her prodigious purse bumped Cleo's hip. "Mama Givens is going to be shocked—shocked!—when I whip up the best hummingbird birthday cake in Catalpa County. Vern will be so surprised."

The Givens were in for a bigger shock than cake, Cleo feared, her head spinning from the situation and perfume. She stared at Bitsy. Were they right? That stringy-haired teenage girl in the photo could hardly compare to the polished, perfect socialite and philanthropist. Bitsy fluffed her hair.

"Let's get to it," Bitsy said. "I can't wait."

I can, Cleo thought. She led Bitsy to the kitchen, doubts swirling. Bitsy's polish and manner gave her pause, but it was her hair that had sparked recognition. When Bitsy and Leanna had arrived the other day in the rainstorm, Bitsy's hair was sopping and stringy. Right then, with her makeup running off and bedraggled, she resembled a mature version of Liza Black-well, missing teenager and possible murder suspect from Tarpon Springs, Florida. But how could Cleo ask? What if they were wrong? Cleo shivered. *What if they were right?*

"So, what's first?" Bitsy asked after hugging a stiff-backed Leanna. Only Rhett was relaxed, lounging on the kitchen table.

"Naughty boy," Cleo said. She scooped up the Persian and set him down on a chair. He scowled.

"He's a big doll baby," Bitsy said. "I love cats. I wish Vernon Junior wasn't allergic, or I'd get a pretty kitty like you, Rhett. You're a handsome lion in your summer haircut, aren't you?" Rhett kept frowning but gave away his true feelings by purring.

Cat people are nice people, Cleo thought, as she had with Jimmy Teeks. *They're kind and caring and likely fond of books and quiet reading too.* She knew she was trying to talk herself out of their plan. She handed Leanna a can opener for the pineapple and then began opening what she feared was a can of worms.

"Where did you grow up, Bitsy?" Cleo asked.

Leanna kept her head down, eyes on the recipe—anywhere but on their guest.

Bitsy waved a pink-manicured hand. "Here and there. Some in Florida, a bit in Georgia and Louisiana. Texas for a spell." She focused on tying an apron tight around her slender waist. "But there's no place like home. I consider Catalpa Springs my heart's hometown. It's where I met my sugar, Vernon, and where little Vern was born. How about you all? You're both lucky to be from here, aren't you?"

Cleo was lucky, she agreed. Leanna was from Catalpa Springs too, but not as fortunate in her upbringing.

"I moved around in a bunch of families," Leanna said, taking a deep breath. She shot Cleo a look suggesting she was steeling her resolve. "I often wished I'd had a nice family like yours, Miss Bitsy," Leanna continued, face growing tomato red.

"Oh, honey," Bitsy said, "I had a horrible family situation growing up. You are what you make of yourself. That's always been my motto. And look at you, Leanna, you did that too. You're gorgeous and smart, and Vern keeps saying what a gem you are at banking. I swear, the man wants to hire you full-time." She flashed a bright smile. "If I didn't know my Vern, I'd be worried, sending such a pretty young assistant to his office. Now, what does this say? Smashed ripe bananas?"

"Mashed," Cleo murmured. She peeled brown bananas, piled them in a bowl, and handed Bitsy the pastry cutter she used for such purposes. Bitsy mashed. Cleo thought of smashing and mashing and bludgeoning, and her heart rate quickened.

"Perfect," Cleo said when Bitsy was done. They mixed the dry and wet ingredients and poured the fruity batter into two round cake tins and a smaller tin for taste testing.

"Let's have some tea and chat," Cleo suggested. Leanna jumped up to fill the kettle and light the stove.

Bitsy took a seat next to Rhett. She stroked the cat and chatted about Vern's birthday gift to himself, a new golf club. "I couldn't have picked it out, no way. I told him, get yourself the perfect gift, and I'll wrap it up and call it a surprise. It's hard to wrap a putter, let me tell you!" She laughed, but her laugh stopped in a gulp. She stared at the stack of books on Cleo's side counter. *Killings in Cotton Country* sat atop a Betty Crocker. No one spoke.

"You were asking where I'm from," Bitsy said quietly. "You know, don't you? It's that awful book." Her voice was low and, for Cleo's taste, too coldly calm. Bitsy kept patting Rhett, who lapped up the attention.

There was no more delaying or dancing around the question. Cleo came straight out with it. "Bitsy, are you Liza Blackwell?"

Bitsy scooped Rhett onto her lap and hugged him close. Rhett's expression blended grumpiness and bliss. Cleo's forced herself to remain seated. Bitsy liked Rhett, she assured herself. He could safely suffer a cuddle. But what if Bitsy had harmed— killed—Buford Krandall and possibly Whitney too?

"I'm not Liza anymore," Bitsy said. "A long time ago I was. Figures I'd fall in love with a cute town peppered with true-crime nuts! I didn't think anyone would notice me. How many people even read that Pawpaw woman's books? And the photo is pretty bad resolution, isn't it? You can hardly see me." Her eyes glistened. A tear dropped on Rhett's head. The Persian detested water. He swiveled his furry face in frowning confusion.

"Sorry, Rhett," Bitsy said, wiping off his orange noggin. Her tears cut rivulets through her foundation, running dark with mascara.

"Miss Bitsy," Leanna said. "We're sorry to upset you!"

Cleo wasn't ready to issue apologies quite yet, but she got Bitsy a box of tissues. Rhett took the opportunity to jump from Bitsy's lap to the table. This time Cleo plucked the cat up and scooted him out the back door. She mouthed, "It's her" and "Okay" to Henry. He nodded, his cell phone clutched in one hand, a hiking stick with a sharp pointed tip in the other. His guard dog was snoring.

Bitsy dabbed at her eyes and blew her nose. "I'm the one who's sorry. Here I am carrying on, and it's only the truth." She gave a honking blow into the tissue and straightened her shoulders. "I'm not ashamed. I just wish you all—my friends— hadn't been the ones to figure it out."

Cleo's neck prickled. She positioned herself between Leanna and Bitsy, thinking she could shove Leanna out the back door to safety if necessary. "Didn't Buford Krandall figure it out first?" she asked. "How did he, anyway?"

Bitsy waved the crumpled tissue. "You know how Buford Krandall was. He had some kind of special gift, didn't he? Like some folks can do math in their heads or play concert piano.

He had an eye for faces and gathering up dirt. It wasn't just that book. He found a newspaper clipping showing a bigger photo of me. Old me. Is that what y'all found?"

Cleo explained how the missing page in Priscilla's book led them to look for more photos online.

"It was easy," said Leanna and then added, "Sorry."

Bitsy stood abruptly, her chair scraping and nearly tipping. "We know what has to happen, don't we? Shoot, but those cakes are coming out in a few minutes."

Cleo's kitchen seemed to darken, though the lights were on. "No one has to get hurt," Cleo said, forcing her voice to stay even, cursing herself. They should have waited for Gabby and hid the policewoman in the pantry . . . or let Gabby handle the questioning.

Bitsy cocked her head. "Hurt? You mean Vern? Oh, he'll be fine. He loves me! That's what I told that foolish Buford. Imagine, thinking he could blackmail me."

Cleo's thumping heart calmed a bit. "He wasn't blackmailing you?"

"You didn't kill him?" Leanna added hopefully. She blushed furiously. "Sorry! We kinda thought, you know . . ."

Bitsy groaned. "Of course, y'all did. Heavens, no! Buford tried to blackmail me. But to get blackmailed, you have to care. I didn't." She stomped a heel. "I did nothing wrong and didn't care who Buford told. It was my rattlesnake daddy who murdered my family. I'm not bearing his guilt. I got over that a long time ago. If it had helped, I would have told the police all about him, but what good would it do? My mother and sisters and brothers were gone, and for a while, everyone thought I was gone too. I had a chance to remake myself. I started over. I washed it off." She twined a finger around a curl, tugged it straight, and then let it go. The curl bounced back. "You are *not* what you're born to. Leanna, remember that. Upbringings like ours, they make us stronger."

Leanna frowned. "But weren't you worried what the Ladies Leaguers would think? Or Mr. Givens? Or, gosh, your mother-in-law?"

Bitsy managed a tight smile. "You know what? It'd be a relief. I know my family will support me, and I'll know who my true friends are." She shot earnest looks at Cleo and Leanna. Leanna was agreeing heartily.

Cleo had more decades than Leanna. She held back. "What did Buford say when you told him you didn't care?"

Bitsy scanned the room. "Is Rhett still outside? I wouldn't say this in front of him. Buford gave me that awful alligator grin of his and pretended like he didn't care either. Said, 'There's more than one way to skin a cat.' I told him I didn't care, I was better off than him in his moldering old mansion any day. Then I walked away and didn't give him another thought."

"Really?" Leanna said, sounding more impressed than skeptical.

Bitsy tugged at the curl again. "Okay, honestly? It bugged me, like upsetting stuff sticks and won't get out of your head, but I didn't kill him."

Cleo rinsed a mixing bowl. She tidied the counter, thinking. She could see Bitsy's scenario. She could imagine other scenarios too, involving a desperate Bitsy bopping Buford on the head and tearing apart his library, looking for more incriminating photos and clippings. That wasn't the Bitsy she knew, but she didn't really know Bitsy, did she? "You didn't hurt him?" Cleo asked, repeating Leanna's query, knowing the answer could easily be a lie.

"No!" Bitsy said, looking wounded. "No, no, I swear. I'll call up every Ladies Leaguer and Mama Givens right now if you want me to prove it. I'll even tell the cops what happened. We can go this moment."

Cleo mentally tallied the many reasons to disbelieve Bitsy. Bitsy wasn't who she'd said she was. She had a hidden past, ripe for malicious gossip. She was strong and capable and got stuff done. And what of the former crimes? The murder and arson? Priscilla Pawpaw had insinuated that the culprit was still in question, the case never officially closed.

On the other hand, Bitsy's actions in Catalpa Springs had been all about giving back. She helped people. She put up with Maybelle, for heaven's sake.

The oven timer buzzed, and everyone jumped.

"These have to cool," Cleo said, taking out the heavenly scented cakes. "You know Gabby Honeywell, the deputy? She lives right next door. Why don't we go see her?"

Bitsy reached for her purse. "Miss Georgia police? Perfect! I trust another woman to see me right. Are we going to invite your sweetie, Henry, in now, Cleo? He's been peeking in the window all night. I thought he was just anxious for cake."

Chapter Twenty-Seven

Everyone, including Rhett Butler and Mr. Chaucer, marched to Gabby's front door. Cleo raised a fist to knock. The door swung open, and she almost bopped her deputy neighbor on the nose.

Gabby jerked back, blinked, and offered a startled greeting.

"We have something important to report," Cleo said.

"I'm Liza Blackwell," Bitsy declared, head held high.

"Okay," Gabby said, expression and tone set to quizzical. "I'm sorry, Mrs. Givens, you're who? Is this an emergency? Otherwise, I have to run. There was a 911 called in for the mayor's house, and the chief wants everyone out there."

"Buford Krandall attempted to blackmail me regarding my previous identity," Bitsy said, speaking fast. "I'm telling you so no one can think I did him in. I have alibis and a clean conscience, and I've just baked a marvelous hummingbird cake."

Faint sounds of aggressive gardening floated down the picket fences. "Wanda," Gabby whispered and ushered them into her hallway. "Buford tried to blackmail you? And you said . . . ?"

Bitsy briefly recounted what happened. "You call the former sheriff down in Pinellas County, or better yet the insurance investigator. I'll give you his name. They'll tell you, my no-good murdering daddy set that fire and killed himself and everyone else. I wasn't there. I had no part in it. Will you need to arrest me?"

Gabby took a moment to consider. "Honestly, I don't know," she said. "We'll have to check up and contact Florida officials and get a statement from you."

The radio clipped to Gabby's chest chirped. The chief's voice squawked on, demanding to know her ETA. "That's estimated time of arrival, Deputy. *Arrival!* Get over here."

Gabby ignored him. "Come and see me tomorrow morning. Say, nine o'clock? Do not leave town."

Bitsy held up a hand. "I promise. I'm not going anywhere. Mama Givens has a chiropractor appointment tomorrow afternoon. She'd kill me if we missed it. Plus, Vern's birthday is tomorrow, and we'll be celebrating with homemade hummingbird cake."

Gabby jogged to her car. Cleo and company hurried back to her house before Wanda could catch up with them.

"I wonder what's happening at the mayor's?" Henry asked when they were back in the kitchen.

"Whatever it is, no one can say I had anything to do with that," Bitsy said. "I was with all y'all, baking up a storm. Think that cake's cool enough to decorate?"

Cleo turned the conversation to frosting, and everyone

taste-tested the sweet, buttery confection until they had the perfect consistency. They iced and sliced the little test cake and enjoyed some with herbal tea. Bitsy deemed it perfect.

"This will sweeten the blow for Vern," Bitsy said to Cleo on her way out. "I should have told him before—that's my only regret. I'll tell him tonight. I know he'll support me."

She sounded shaky. Cleo felt bad for Bitsy and angry with Buford, who wouldn't stop mucking with people's lives, even beyond the grave. "I can go to the police station with you," Cleo offered. "I can pick you up. I haven't driven my convertible in ages. It could do for a spin. We can leave the top up if you don't want to mess up your hair."

"I don't give two hoots about my hair," Bitsy said. "Let's be Thelma and Louise. Without the flying over cliffs and crashing and dying part, of course." Bitsy enveloped Cleo in a hug. "Thank you, Cleo. I'll repay the favor. I'll make sure the Ladies League doesn't give up on you and our library."

Leanna left soon after, promising to be extra careful on her way home.

Cleo and Henry watched her go. Henry reached for his coat. "You lock your doors too," he said. "Promise me, no more sleuthing tonight. I don't want to see anyone else getting hurt."

He kissed her hand, gallant and old-fashioned, and was off, his dog beside him. After he was gone, Cleo felt like Priscilla Pawpaw, nervously checking all the doors and downstairs windows too. In the living room, she stopped and listened, thinking she heard a noise outside. She listened harder but heard only Rhett's demands for his bedtime treat and crickets caroling in the garden. Under a bright moon, shadows stretched across the garden.

What if Bitsy was conning them? Bitsy, aka Liza, had been playing a part for years, and very successfully. The alternative was awful too. If not Bitsy, then who? An even better actor, no one would ever detect? Kat, the fed-up spouse? Priscilla? The author was an expert on murder and true-crime techniques, and her scarf had been used to kill Whitney. The mayor or his consultant, angry with Buford, but about what? Was Buford threatening to reveal the mayor's infidelity? Or was it something bigger, a threat to his pier and casino projects?

Cleo fed Rhett his treats. In her mind, she moved puzzle pieces that only got more jumbled. What if there were two killers? Whitney killing her uncle. Priscilla killing Whitney in revenge for her biggest fan. Cleo carefully kept Ollie and Mary-Rose out of the scenarios. She believed in their innocence wholeheartedly.

Cleo headed upstairs for bed, checking the front door once more as she passed. On the landing, she realized the frogs and crickets had gone silent. She peered out wavy old glass. A shadow moved in the garden, but when she blinked and refocused, it was gone.

* * *

The next morning, Cleo waved to Gabby from her front porch. Gabby was getting back from a jog or, judging by her sweating and panting, a sprint. Cleo and Rhett swayed gently on the porch swing, Cleo having a second cup of coffee, Rhett grooming his back leg. The young policewoman trotted up to stretch and chat.

"What happened last night with the mayor?" Cleo asked.

Gabby wiped a dewy, as in sweat-dripping, brow.

"False alarm," Gabby said with an exasperated sigh and eye roll.

"Oh?" Cleo prompted. She waited, gazing out at the garden. It was another sunny day, the heat already building to a steam.

Gabby looked about and lowered her voice. "Keep this between us, but the mayor's neighbors called nine-one-one and reported yelling at his home. I'm guessing it was a domestic dispute. By the time Tookey and I got there, Mrs. Day was conveniently "resting," as in shut up in her bedroom and refusing to come out. The chief and Mayor Day were saying the neighbors must have heard a fox or a drunk. Chief Culpepper and the mayor then enjoyed bourbon on the porch while Tookey and I got to tromp around in the dark—just in case, mind you—looking for drunk foxes and getting mosquito bites."

"Tookey got into more poison ivy. I'm starting to feel bad for him." She scratched her knee and a rash that looked worse than mosquito bites. "I did learn that the mayor is holding a press conference this morning, so you should be prepared for irritation too. He'll be talking up Catalpa Springs as the fishing capital of the galaxy and bragging about the murder arrest."

Cleo expressed her displeasure with a sniff. "Ollie is innocent. You know that."

Gabby gave a helpless shrug. "It's not up to me. The chief and attorneys decide."

And the mayor and the press and public opinion and a jury. Cleo tried to console herself with a belief in the jury system, but even there, her faith faltered.

Cleo forced her mind to problems she could fix. "I have some calamine lotion you could try on that rash. Aloe, vinegar, or honey can also work."

Gabby snorted. "Imagine the rude jokes from the guys at work if I showed up covered in honey. Vinegar always makes me think of Easter egg dyeing. I'll try that after I shower." She paused. "What do you think about Bitsy and her secret?"

Cleo agreed it looked bad. "I *think* she's telling truth. I want to believe her. Buford had dirt on other people too. They didn't all kill him."

Gabby agreed. "Of course, most folks aren't knocking on my door, offering up their secrets like Bitsy did. We've heard gossip about affairs Buford might have uncovered and folks he riled up, but nothing as serious as arson or murder."

Affairs. Cleo didn't like to spread gossip, but then, these were dire times. "You mentioned a possible domestic dispute. You know, our mayor is rumored to be having an affair with the town's new public relations maven."

Gabby was stretching, palms flat to the floor, a move Cleo could once do. "I've heard," Gabby said. "I could never ask Mayor Day. The chief would have a fit. Anyway, if I already know this bit of gossip, so does half the town, probably including the mayor's wife. What hold would Buford have over the mayor if everyone knows? Now, Bitsy, she had a deep secret."

Cleo realized she'd gotten the porch swing swaying fast. Rhett had his claws sunk into the cushions, ears back. She eased up. "Bitsy could be entirely innocent. Here and in Florida. Her father died of a gunshot from the gun found in his own hand. Her mother was shot with the same weapon. It makes terrible sense as a murder–suicide. Bitsy has her reputation to think of, but folks wouldn't hold her childhood against her. She's a good person who volunteers. She got Leanna a job and hasn't killed Maybelle, and she likes cats."

"Well, you make strong points regarding Maybelle and cats," Gabby said, grinning.

Cleo patted Rhett. "We discovered her past identity through Priscilla Pawpaw's books. Someone removed a page from a chapter that dealt with Bitsy—Liza Blackwell—and her family. There's no way to know who removed the page. It could have been chance, a library patron spilling coffee on the page and hoping to hide the evidence. Or Buford, keeping a record? Or maybe Bitsy herself? Bitsy would hardly admit to me if she harmed a library book. She's a great library supporter."

Gabby was balancing in a precarious pretzel stretch now, an ankle crossed over the opposite knee. "Yeah, 'cause book abuse is a crime not even a murdering arsonist would admit to," she joked grimly. "I haven't told the chief about Bitsy yet. I want to talk to her first and don't want him jumping to conclusions. He could go either way: yell at me for bothering a town bigwig's spouse or leap on the chance for a flashy arrest."

Cleo checked her watch. She told Gabby she was going to pick up Bitsy soon. "So she doesn't change her mind and she knows she has a friend. If she didn't harm anyone, she's taking a big risk."

Gabby came out of her twisty stretch. "I don't like you doing that alone. Tell you what, how about I tail you? Better yet, how about I put a wire in your car so I can listen in too? I'm on my own this morning. The chief and Tookey will be at the mayor's press conference at City Hall."

Cleo debated. It seemed a betrayal of friendship and trust. However, she had promised Henry she'd be careful, and there was no harm if Bitsy was innocent. She agreed. "It's a lovely day, and I'm putting the top down on the convertible. You might hear some wind."

"I'm fine with that. Just don't drive like Beelzebub's bat, so I can keep up with you, okay?"

"I'll try," Cleo promised, already anticipating the feel of the road flying under her wheels.

* * *

Cleo's father had kept his cherry-red Ford Galaxie locked up in the garage for years. About once a season, Daddy would take the car out for a spin. If Cleo was around, he always invited her. They'd put down the top and pretend they were flying.

Cleo rested her elbow on the doorframe, as Daddy always did. She took in the sights as well as the scents, from fresh baked treats at the Spoonbread Bakery to the liquid green of the Tallgrass River. Cleo would know the river's special scent anywhere. If she were ever forced to leave her hometown— heaven forbid—she'd want perfumes replicating the river and the jasmine from her garden.

Cleo slowed over the bridge, both to admire the view and let Gabby catch up. The Givens's home was just on the other side, set up on a small rise overlooking the river. Cleo marveled that Vernon didn't fish. All he'd have to do was stroll down the driveway and cast a line.

Cleo parked at the looping end of the long driveway. She started to unbuckle. Ollie might have beeped the horn, but Cleo thought it more polite to knock. Before she could get out, the grand double doors opened, and Bitsy trotted forth, mincing in towering heels and a business-like pink skirt and jacket.

"'Bye!" she yelled behind her.

The door slammed, and Bitsy jumped in the passenger seat. "Let's roll," she said. "I want to get this over with and get on to more important business. I got on the phone last night and talked three Leaguers down from ditching the library as our Gala cause. I argued it would be unseemly." She tied a pink silk scarf over her blond locks and donned dark glasses, resembling a forties film star. "I figured I had to make the most of my 'unseemly' argument while I could."

"You'll be fine," Cleo said. "Hopefully, the police can keep everything quiet." She took her time at the end of the drive-way, looking up and down the road. She didn't see Gabby anywhere.

Bitsy chattered on with nervous energy. "We have a lot of donations for the Gala auction. There's jewelry, spa dates, res-taurant gift certificates. You and your sweetie could bid on the spa and have yourselves a fine time."

Cleo let Bitsy have that happy joshing. "Or you and Vernon could," she countered. "How is he? Did you . . . uh . . . ?"

Bitsy snorted. "Did I tell him my deep, dark, unhappy past? Yes, I did it the best way possible, over cake and a shot of bourbon last night. He's fine. He was only upset that I didn't tell him sooner so he could support me. Vern's such a sugar bear."

"Of course," Cleo said. "I bet he loved your cake."

"*Our* cake," Bitsy said. "I confessed you helped me. No

more secrets! Vern and Vernie Jr. both loved it. Big Vern said it was the best he'd ever had. Mama Givens was spitting mad when she heard that." Bitsy laughed. "Vern's taking the morning off so he can take his mama to lunch, calm her down some."

Cleo savored the image of spitting Maybelle, outshined using the very recipe she'd swiped. She turned onto the bridge and back toward town. On the other side, she spotted Gabby's car, parked at the entrance to the perfectly fine and functional fishing pier. It was a good spot to wait. Gabby's unmarked vehicle looked like that of a park patron or fisherman out for a day on the river. Cleo glanced in her back mirrors, as she often did, following the rules of driving safety. A van was coming up fast behind her. Folks could be so impatient! Cleo liked speed, but she never, ever tailgated. So rude!

"What's going on?" Bitsy said, twisting to look behind them. "Oh my gosh, that jerk is right on our bumper. Let's speed up. I don't like bridges anyway."

The bridge spanned low over the slow water and was hardly scary. "He can pass when we get across," Cleo said. In other circumstances, she might have slowed down to teach the bully some patience. However, she pressed the gas harder for Bitsy's sake. A great jolt sent the car jerking forward, and not from the boost of the accelerator. They both gasped. Cleo's seatbelt bit into her collarbone and belly, and the car shuddered. Cleo stomped the gas. The van fell back. Was the driver feeling like a fool for texting or not paying attention? No, Cleo realized with terror. The van was surging again. "Hang on!" Cleo cried.

She leaned on the horn to alert Gabby. Just a few more yards and they'd be across. Several more after that and they'd pass Gabby, and the policewoman could activate her stick-on siren. Metal met metal again. Cleo's car spun, the back end swinging out, the front end skidding and slipping as if on oiled ice. Bitsy screamed as the car bumped off the road at the edge of the bridge, careening head-on into the marshy margin between land and river.

Bitsy yelled oaths and prayers until the moment the car smacked the tree and Cleo's head banged the steering wheel.

A dizzying pain shot through Cleo's skull and down her neck. In silly shock, she imagined hiring Thurgood Byron out from under Maybelle and her supposed whiplash. She pried her eyes open and tried to focus on the van. The vehicle was pulling up beside them, gravel crunching under tires. The windows were tinted so dark, she couldn't see in. The door opened a crack.

"Cleo!" Gabby sprinted up the road, a gun in one hand, her badge in the other. "Police! Keep back!"

Cleo looked toward her neighbor and then back at the van. She saw a hand in a black glove and a glint of metal. She stared, fixated, at the metal. It was small, round, a barrel. She fumbled, trying to start the motor again, to escape. The engine whirred and stalled.

"Police!" Gabby yelled again.

The van door slammed shut. Its engine revved, and the tires caught pavement, spitting pebbles. Gabby planted herself in the road, arms outstretched in a STOP gesture. The van wasn't stopping. It sped up, and Cleo put a hand over her eyes.

When she looked again, Gabby was on the side of the road, dusting herself off.

"Bitsy?" Cleo said, turning her attention to her passenger. "Bitsy!" Bitsy's long locks covered her face. Her chin hung to her chest. She wasn't moving.

Chapter
Twenty-Eight

Bitsy moaned and clutched her forehead, and Cleo exhaled heavily with relief. Gabby was beside them, calling for the ambulance and backup.

"No, sir," Gabby said coolly, when transferred to the chief. "No, it definitely was *not* the fault of Miss Cleo's *old lady* driving. I saw the incident. The van rammed her on purpose, on the bridge." Gabby bit her lip. "I'll write a report on why I was out here, sir."

To the EMTs, Gabby reported possible concussions.

"My head is just fine," Cleo protested. She'd have a goose egg to go with her bruised eye. How lovely she'd look for the Gala. If there still was a Gala. She held Bitsy's hand.

"Keep Bitsy still and seated," Gabby said. "Try to get her talking. Keep her awake." Gabby strode back up the road and out over the bridge, eyes to the pavement.

Cleo searched for a topic to rouse her passenger. Nothing too soothing or dull that might lull her to sleep. Something startling to wake her, but not overly upsetting. "Maybelle's corns!" Cleo blurted out. "Bitsy, how are your mama-in-law's feet today?"

"Huh? Her feet? Ugly." Bitsy held her head and made a pained sound. She took away her hand, looked at the blood smearing her palm, and shut her eyes. "Don't tell Mama Givens I said that."

"No, I won't. No napping, now." Cleo gently shook Bitsy's shoulder. She found some tissues in the glove compartment and pressed them to Bitsy's temple. The cut might need stitches, but thankfully it seemed superficial. "Speaking of Maybelle," Cleo continued brightly. "I remember when your mama-in-law accidentally flashed the entire school. Can you imagine?"

Bitsy blinked. She looked confused, which was understandable, given the bump on her head and the image of Maybelle's unmentionables.

Cleo went on brightly. "It was homecoming, and I distinctly remember her standing at a podium, lecturing us all about refraining from homecoming pranks and unseemly activities when *whoosh*, a great wind sent her dress flying up. Like Marilyn Monroe, yet not quite as alluring. The yearbook photographer snapped a picture."

Bitsy gave a look between a smile and a grimace. "I bet she cursed out that wind."

"Mad as an adder at everyone in sight," Cleo said. "That photographer didn't keep his film long. He was lucky to get away with his camera."

Bitsy chuckled and grabbed her head in pain. "Ow, laughing hurts. So does my knee. Skinned it."

Sirens grew louder. Cleo unbuckled herself. She pushed open her door, testing her knees before stepping out into ankle-deep water. She steadied herself on the hood and cringed at the sight of her car. The front tire was twisted against a cypress knee. The shining bumper was horribly crumpled, and the hood buckled. Another beloved vehicle wounded!

Cleo picked her way out of the reeds, water and mud oozing between her sandaled toes. The EMTs were jogging toward them. Bitsy was shakily undoing her driving scarf, unleashing her curls, and mumbling about needing a bucket of face powder.

Gabby rejoined them. "So what happened? I saw you coming over the bridge. Then that van was on your tail, out of nowhere. Road rage?"

Cleo didn't think so. "No one was coming when I pulled out. I looked closely because I was looking for you."

Gabby started to apologize, which Cleo wouldn't have any of. "We're lucky you were here. You saved us, and just in time too." She thought of the gloved hand, their helplessness. She didn't want to think what might have happened if Gabby hadn't been around. Who was the target? Herself? Bitsy?

"You saved us, Gabby!" Bitsy crowed, craning around the attentive EMTs. "Saved us by the skin of our teeth! Skin of our knees." She laughed shakily.

Cleo frowned. A thought rattled in her shaken head. It was interrupted by doubt and by Gabby.

"Did either of you see anything?" Gabby asked. "I couldn't make out the driver or a plate."

Bitsy was distracted by medical attention. "Ooh . . .

sweetie, watch where you're grabbing." She giggled. The EMTs were both male, young, and good looking. They eased Bitsy out of the car. She stood unsteadily, her arms draped over their shoulders.

Cleo hadn't seen the driver. "I was trying to stay on the road. Bitsy, honey, did you see him?"

"Mmm?" Bitsy said, wobbling with assistance toward the waiting ambulance. "Him? You think so? No . . ."

The EMTs got Bitsy situated and turned their attention to Cleo's knocked noggin. She accepted a bandage but declined further fussing.

"You should come with us, ma'am," the blond EMT said. "We can get you a head scan and observe you."

"You could stay for a hospital lunch," his dark-haired colleague added, as if that were an incentive. "Jell-O. Pudding. Turkey surprise."

Cleo declined politely but firmly. She walked to Gabby's car, where she sat in the driver's seat with the doors open, her feet kicking over pale gravel, her mind again remixing the puzzle pieces of suspects, this time with added words and faces. Her eyes glazed, blurring the green leaves and water until an image took shape, as unlikely and shocking as anything on Priscilla Pawpaw's pages.

"You sure you're okay?" Gabby asked, approaching. She had her hands on her hips and was frowning down at Cleo. "Forgive me for saying, but you looked spacey just now. You *could* have a concussion. You should get back to town. Let's call Henry or Leanna or your son or Ollie, although Ollie's on bail and should probably stay away from crime scenes."

Cleo did feel a little dizzy. She let Gabby call Henry and

heard her assuring and reassuring the silly, sweet man that Cleo was okay. She waited and watched as the chief arrived. Chief Culpepper seemed especially full of bluster this morning in his yellow smiley-face suspenders.

The mayor came next, followed by a van, white like the one that had attacked her, but distinctly different. This van was decorated in a satellite dish, the logo of a Valdosta TV station, and the claim "We Brake for Breaking News." Cleo remembered the mayor's press conference and his plan to crow about his pier and the murder suspect in custody. The reporters must have tagged along, in search of a more exciting scoop and a prettier river backdrop. She wondered what Chief Culpepper would say now. Surely he couldn't claim he'd solved the case. No one could ever think Oliver Watkins attacked his own grandmother. She leaned the seat back and let her thoughts roam.

* * *

Henry arrived at uncharacteristically high speed, his station wagon kicking up dust when he stopped. Even more unusual was his outfit. The typically dapper bookseller wore baggy striped pants, resembling pajama bottoms, and a rumpled linen shirt. "You look awful," he said, and then flushed and apologized.

"You don't look up to standards yourself," Cleo countered with a smile. "Where's your pocket square?"

"Left behind, along with proper pants and my dog. You do get an early start to trouble."

Cleo explained what had happened, leaving out the parts that might make her voice shake. Sergeant Tookey joined them. He was munching a hotdog with bacon and calling it breakfast. The sergeant leaned on the hood of Gabby's car, ankles crossed. On the bridge, a cameraman aimed a massive lens at Chief Culpepper and Mayor Day.

"Lucky break for the press," Tookey observed through a mouthful of bun. "The chief was right in the middle of his interview out in front of City Hall. He was just saying how we'd solved the crime spree, when we got this call saying someone tried to kill you. The reporter caught wind. Said it sounded more exciting and we should move the interviews out here."

"This destroys the chief's whole theory," Cleo pointed out. "No one would think a fine, upstanding, law-abiding grandson would run his grandmother off a bridge." She held her chin high and defiant.

Tookey popped the last bite of hotdog into chubby cheeks and chewed thoughtfully. "Isn't it supposed to be the person you least suspect?" He tapped his temple in a think-about-it gesture. "I'm just saying, that grandson of yours is hardly law-abiding, is he? He admitted to trespassing and socializing with eco-terrorists and destroying property."

Cleo swung her feet, kicking up gravel, a few pebbles of which landed on Tookey's shoes. She concentrated on the scene beyond. A young woman was powdering Mayor Day's nose. Chief Culpepper was adjusting his smiley-face suspenders. Cleo noticed that the camera had swung toward Gabby, bent to inspect Cleo's stricken convertible. "I'm glad Bitsy got to leave before all this," she said.

"Why?" Tookey asked, his baby-faced features sharpening.

Cleo touched her head, thinking the bump might have affected her good judgment. "Oh," she said, easily able to sound befuddled, "a proper Southern lady such as Bitsy Givens wouldn't want her photo taken with her hair and face a mess."

"I hear that," Tookey said. He scrubbed a napkin over his face. Cleo tactfully pointed to the red smudge on his nose. He dabbed, missed a spot, and scratched an angry red rash on his arm. "Don't you worry, Mrs. Watkins. We've got an all-points bulletin on that van. Everyone in Georgia and beyond will be looking for it. Don't worry about your car, either. I called TJ at Speedy Auto. He'll be out here ASAP. Hey, I think the mayor wants us in front of the camera, or probably just you."

On the bridge, Mayor Day was smiling their way and waving them over.

"Friendly today, isn't he?" Henry said with a hint of sarcasm.

"Cameras are on," Cleo said.

Henry stayed put to "hold down the car."

Tookey offered Cleo his elbow and gallantly escorted her over. He was promptly waved away by the mayor and chief.

"Here's our brave librarian now," Mayor Day said, eyes gleaming at the camera. "She's weathered many a storm, our Cleo Watkins, and is looking forward to a well-earned retirement."

The mayor looped an arm around Cleo's shoulders and patted her upper arm—hard.

"Can you tell us what happened, ma'am?" the female reporter said, pretty face wrinkling in concern. "How are you feeling?

Cleo took a moment to steady herself. She thought of Ollie. He needed help. She thought of Mary-Rose, who was always so bold. She stepped forward, removing herself from the mayor's sweaty grip. "I am fine, thank you so much. It's the Catalpa Springs library system I fear for. Our bookmobile needs repairs and so does our historic library building."

"Okay now, better rest your head," Mayor Day said. His arm was back on Cleo's shoulder, forcibly nudging her in the direction of off-camera.

Cleo held her ground. "Our mayor has been so supportive," she said, her drawl pouring out sugary sweet. "You all *must* come back in a few months, when he'll surely be cutting the ribbon on our repaired library." Cleo remembered Bitsy's tactic. If it's not real, pretend it is and make it so. She forged on. "This awful spate of crime will have ended too. The attack this morning on me and my passenger shows the investigation was mistakenly targeting an innocent young man."

She heard the mayor making hissing shush noises.

"Furthermore," Cleo said, raising her voice, "the incident also shows the real murderer is desperate and making errors, leaving a clear trail of evidence. A new arrest—the right one—will be made shortly. I can feel it."

Gabby was frowning as Cleo extracted herself from the reporters.

"I was totally with you when you outmaneuvered Day at his spin game," Gabby said. "But you do realize you taunted a killer about messing up? And a 'clear trail of evidence'? Were you bluffing? Or do you know something I should?"

Cleo knew nothing solid, and the more she thought, the

less certain she was. "I only meant to praise the talents of the Catalpa Springs police force."

"Uh-huh." Gabby sighed. She nodded toward Henry. "Let your knight in shining PJs take you home."

Cleo didn't argue. TJ and Joe were rumbling in with their tow rig, and she couldn't stomach seeing the full extent of her car's injuries.

Henry drove slowly until the turnoff to downtown, his shop, and Cleo's home. There, he sped up. They went barreling past at just above the speed limit.

"Where are we going?" Cleo asked. Weariness and aches were taking hold. She could use a long, hot shower and a longer nap.

"Pancakes and pie," Henry said.

Cleo's weariness lifted. "But aren't you wearing pajamas?"

"The kids do it all the time," Henry said, glancing her way and winking. "Why can't we?"

* * *

Mary-Rose and the three peacocks greeted them at the parking lot, all ruffling their feathers.

"Cleo, good heavens," Mary-Rose said. "I'm so glad you're okay. I was going to call, but you never answer that cell phone of yours."

"You heard?" Cleo said, and then again worried she might be concussed. Of course Mary-Rose had heard. The entire town would know by now. Even the peacocks seemed concerned. They cocked their iridescent heads, tiara feathers bobbing.

"You are pretty birds," Cleo said to them. "You aren't scary, are you?"

"They used to scare Buford away," Mary-Rose said with a wry smile. "A lot of good that did any of us." She held open the door to the Pancake Mill, shooing the curious birds so they wouldn't come in too. "We're busy today, but I held a table in reserve as soon as I heard, hoping you'd show up. Zoe's already there."

They entered to blatant gawking and light applause. Four pink-hatted ladies flocked to Cleo, who found herself in a swirl of air-kisses, perfume, and concern. They were led by Jasmine Wagner, VP of the Ladies League.

"You poor thing!" Jasmine said, tongue clicking. "How are you? How's Bitsy? What were y'all doing out together so early?"

Cleo decided she might as well keep talking up the reality she wanted. "Bitsy said how the Ladies League was still firmly behind the library benefit," Cleo said. "We were . . . uh . . ." Lying didn't come entirely natural to Cleo. She touched her bumped head, and the ladies clucked sympathetically while shooting each other sharp looks. "We were planning," Cleo said. "We were going to do some Gala organizing, and I picked Bitsy up."

High color rose under Jasmine's rouged cheeks. "Of course you were, and of course we're supportive. We'd only had some concern because, well . . ." She lowered her voice. "That bookmobile crash and your grandson getting arrested for murder and all. That could be bad for publicity, you know. We tend to favor good causes, like redecorating the jail."

"My grandson is innocent," Cleo said. "The real killer will be revealed soon. I've just said so in a TV interview." That wasn't a lie. She had said so.

"Is that so?" Mary-Rose asked skeptically when the ladies had gone.

Cleo managed a weak shrug. Her neck and shoulders ached, and that crazy idea and a jolting pain kept banging around in her head.

Mary-Rose asked waitress Desiree for pie, pancake batter, chocolate chips, and extra syrup and whipped cream.

"Blueberries!" Zoe added.

"Extra blueberries," her grandmother confirmed. "Healthy fruit, chocolate, and sugar. You're looking a might poorly, Cleo, as our grannies would say. But better than poor Bitsy Givens, in the hospital. How awful."

Cleo was glad Bitsy was in the hospital. It was her safety after she got out that had Cleo worried. Big pitchers of batter arrived. The tabletop griddle began to sizzle. Cleo helped herself to some chocolate chips and drifted in and out of the conversation.

Zoe drew her back in. "Look, Miss Cleo!" She pointed to a pancake spiral that filled the griddle. It was generously decorated with blueberries *and* chocolate chips. "Look what Mr. Henry and I made. Can you guess what it is?"

"A dragon?" Cleo said. She knew what her dear departed husband, Richard, would have deemed it: a disaster to flip. Oddly shaped and overly large pancakes were among Richard's greatest peeves.

Zoe giggled. "Kind of. It's a worm that likes books."

"Of course, a bookworm," Cleo said. "My favorite kind of worm."

Henry watched her with concern. She smiled, but when the others turned to the tricky three-spatula turnover of the batter bookworm, she let her mind drift again. She saw the van speeding. She felt the crash. She saw the door open and the hand in black leather. Did she see the driver? No, she'd seen a blur, a mask, the glove, the metal . . . and, she finally acknowledged with a shiver, the barrel of a gun.

Chapter
Twenty-Nine

C leo watched the news at five o'clock, tuning in to the station that had interviewed her, the "local" news out of not-so-local Valdosta. The Catalpa Springs story was teased with gruesome graphics, a knife dripping red over Fontaine Park. *There wasn't any knife,* Cleo thought with irritation. There was a van, a gun, faulty brake lines, a stone arm, and a crime-scene scarf. She fluffed a throw pillow, which Rhett promptly began kneading. The mayor wouldn't like the unpleasant graphic of their town either. On this, at least, she and Mayor Jeb Day could agree.

Commercials dragged on, followed by an unsurprising weather forecast: weather you could wear, hot and muggy with a chance of afternoon storms. After dull details regarding the Valdosta school board, Catalpa Springs was up.

"Listen closely, Rhett," Cleo said. Rhett purred louder. Cleo raised the volume. There was Chief Culpepper. He insisted the investigation was going well. "Beautifully, just fine. There is an art to investigation and—" A wise editor made a judicious chop of the chief's lecture. They cut back in, with him pushing out his suspenders and declaring, "We have made an arrest. A young, unemployed local man engaged in radical environmental action."

"Oh!" Cleo exclaimed in frustration. Rhett took no heed and continued working on the pillow.

"Oh dear," Cleo said next, for her face appeared on the screen. The camera resolution was too good. It picked up the sickly greenish bruise around her eye, the scrape from Whitney's boot, and the fresh red welt on her forehead. She looked like a boxer. A losing one! She assured herself that—as was always true—it wasn't looks, but words, that mattered. She listened to her speech about the killer. Gabby was right. Cleo had sounded a tad taunting. "The library," she said to Rhett. "Where's the part about the library getting fixed?"

A glittery smile took over the screen, as if the story had shifted to dental whitening. Mayor Jeb Day beamed at the camera. Cleo felt her blood pressure rise. The reporter must have interviewed him again after she left.

"Yes, our Miss Cleo is a living treasure," Jeb Day was saying. "Why, she might even be Georgia's oldest librarian. We'll surely be sorry to see her retire, but with this new accident and her advanced age, well, she's *overdue* for a well-earned rest." He grinned anew at his rude pun.

Cleo gripped a throw pillow.

The reporter put a dent in Jeb's fun. "We heard this wasn't an accident, but a hit and run, a would-be homicide. Can you comment on the Catalpa crime spree?"

Chief Culpepper popped into the image. "No comment on ongoing investigations other than to say that amateurs should stay clear. Let the experts do their work."

"So true," the mayor agreed smoothly. "Y'all come back when the chief has this wrapped up. And keep watching for our fine new fishing pier, where the bass will always be biting." He waved his hand like a game-show hostess toward the Tallgrass, flowing serenely beyond Cleo's crumpled car.

Cleo chucked the pillow at a nearby armchair. *Retirement! A living treasure! Overdue!*

Rhett groomed his backside, which Cleo read as an indictment of their impertinent young mayor. "Exactly," she muttered. Anger vented, Cleo slumped into the sofa, thinking the worst of the story must be over. The camera cut back to two anchors murmuring about awful business. "Is there any good news from Catalpa Springs?" the female reporter asked.

Her male colleague smiled. "Yes, indeed. As the mayor hinted, that tiny town is angling to become a world-class fishing destination. I hear you can bet on it!" He proceeded to extol the floating casino.

Cleo reached for another pillow.

* * *

The next morning, Cleo blearily jabbed on the coffeemaker and treated Rhett to a hefty helping of his favorite seafood dinner. She ate grim, sugar-free, fiber-tough cereal and drank a cup of coffee, then another. By the dregs of her second cup, her thoughts were back to the place they'd begun, where they'd been throughout her restless night.

"Should I ask her?" she asked Rhett.

He meowed loudly, demanding more food.

"You're right," Cleo said, deliberately misinterpreting. "I shouldn't, but what other way is there?"

The bank opened at nine. Cleo bided her time, visiting with Dot at her shop and walking around the park. At ten, she went to find Leanna, hoping her young friend would have time for a break. She found Leanna in her "office," a cubicle just off the lobby, stuffed with towers of loose papers.

"I'm making headway," Leanna said, pointing to a shorter stack. Out in the lobby the tellers laughed, and Cleo heard the unmistakable cackle of Kat Krandall-Stykes.

Cleo hesitated about revealing her purpose. "I was just walking by," she said, feeling she should walk straight back out. She had no business involving Leanna.

"You felt it, didn't you?" Leanna said with a big smile. "You sensed I had good news!"

Cleo dutifully asked. "I must have. What's the good news?"

"Mr. Givens wants to hire me full-time!" Leanna said. She cleared papers from an armchair by the window and gestured for Cleo to sit.

"That's wonderful," Cleo said to be polite, her urge to leave growing stronger. She surely couldn't ask now. But the killings . . . and Ollie.

Leanna lowered her voice to a whisper. "I don't know what to say, honestly. It's a big-time compliment, and I'd have more money for school, but no time to study. Banking's not as fun and fulfilling as my library work." She kept her voice low and leaned closer. "Why are you really here, Miss Cleo? Is something wrong?"

Cleo took a deep breath. "I was thinking about Buford Krandall and blackmail, and I was wondering how difficult it is to check a person's bank account." She paused. "Hypothetically, of course."

Leanna cut her off. "Who should I look up?" she asked, fingers poised over her keyboard.

Cleo immediately tried to talk Leanna out of her own plan. Once the words were actually said, it sounded illegal and dangerous, most of all for Leanna. Cleo chided herself. What had she been thinking? "No one. Honestly. I shouldn't have come. I was brainstorming, that's all."

"About who?" Leanna insisted. "Do you think you know the killer? I can check. I'm updating accounts to our new system. I'm in all sorts of accounts and screens all day long. Make me a list. If we can help Ollie and catch a killer, I'll take the risk. I want to!"

Cleo dithered. She stepped out the cubicle door, but then back in again. She wrote Leanna a list. Back home and waiting, she wondered if she'd made her list too long. She had one main suspect, possibly two, but she'd given Leanna five names. Cleo spent the rest of the day checking the time, cleaning her house, and reorganizing her pantry. Leanna said it would take her a while, as she had to fill in for tellers throughout the day.

By late afternoon, Cleo could stay cooped up no longer. She put on her walking sandals and tucked her phone in her purse. Rhett lined up to join her, looking too happy to burden with his harness. Cleo put on a sunhat, and she and Rhett strolled leafy streets. They ended up at the library.

The humidity heightened the skunky, damp scents inside. Cleo wished she had fans or air-conditioning, but the electric was shut off to the whole building. She opened the doors and windows to let in fresh air. She found a few books in the returns box and recorded their numbers and found their places on the shelves. It was nice to work, even if she felt like the captain mopping the floors of her sinking ship. Rhett snoozed on his favorite window seat.

Just before six, her phone rang.

"Miss Cleo?" Leanna's voice was between a whisper and a gasp.

"Leanna, are you all right?" A wave of worry and guilt crashed over Cleo. She never should have asked Leanna to check those accounts.

"I've got something!" Leanna said, words tumbling. "I'm sorry, but I so wanted you to be wrong about a name on that list, but now I think you're right, and it's all really wrong. I'm not making sense, am I? Are you at home? I'm just leaving the bank, walking your way."

"I'm at the library," Cleo said. She started to ask Leanna a question but then realized she was speaking into air. Leanna had hung up.

Cleo sat with Rhett, watching out the window. Leanna arrived at a speed walk, high-heels in her hand, her stockings springing runs.

Leanna thrust pages at Cleo. "Look, it's a separate account, set up before Buford Krandall was killed. Big deposits in cash, then big withdrawals, and then the murder and nothing. How'd you know?" She sat down heavily beside Rhett.

"We don't know yet," Cleo said. She stared at the page and the name on the account: Liza Blackwell. Liza, now Bitsy. It wasn't quite what Cleo expected. She mulled over the possibilities.

"It might not be what it seems," Cleo said. "We'll talk to Gabby. She can investigate from here. We can say you came across this account inadvertently as part of your work."

Gabby would know it was a lie.

"Goodbye, bank job," Leanna groaned. "Mr. Givens will know I was snooping. I actually had a legit reason to get into those other accounts, but not this one. I'll be lucky to be a dancing biscuit again. Oh no—do you think what I did is illegal? I'll have a record!"

Guilt pressed heavily on Cleo. She'd been selfish, thinking of ways to solve the problem, to save Ollie. She'd been thinking of Leanna's computer skills and cleverness, not the implications for her young friend's future.

Leanna shuddered. "But none of that matters if you're right."

A noise startled them both and made Rhett throw back his ears. Rapping at the front door and footsteps in the foyer. Leanna drew a sharp breath.

"Hello?" A voice like sour lemons came from the front. "Why's the door hanging open? Flies and mosquitoes could get in."

Maybelle could get in. Cleo wished she'd kept the library locked up tight.

Leanna exhaled. Cleo thought her relief might be premature. Of the two persons at the top of her suspect list, one was Maybelle Givens.

"Sorry, library's closed!" Cleo called out, but footsteps and thumps were already heading their way up the central hall.

Maybelle Givens brandished a cane with three prongs, the kind that allowed the stick to stand on its own. Cleo imagined the prongs morphing into points, a devil's fork. She met Maybelle's glare with a stern, steady look of her own.

"See this?" Maybelle brandished the cane. "I have to use it because my knee still hurts from that bus crash. You crashed

Bitsy too. Her knee's all scratched up. Thurgood Byron says we could sue."

"He would," Cleo muttered. She didn't want to take any more chances, especially with Leanna's safety. She nudged her young colleague. "Go find Gabby," she whispered. Leanna's eyes widened. "Go," Cleo said firmly. Then, as a cover said loudly, "Go to the staffroom and find those books we stored back there, Leanna."

Leanna turned and trotted off. Cleo tracked her progress by the slap of her feet down the hall.

Maybelle gave an appreciative snort. "Vern likes that girl," she said. "She's good with getting stuff done. Cuter too since Bitsy got after her. Could lose a few pounds or ten."

"Leanna is always lovely," Cleo said. "What can I help you with? Are you looking for a book?"

"I was looking for *you*," Maybelle said pointedly. "I saw the door open and thought I'd come give you a piece of my mind. You ruined my boy's birthday. You and your meddling friend Buford Krandall."

Cleo's heart quickened. Rhett flicked his tail. His ears were down, as horizontal as airplane wings.

"Vern's upset," Maybelle said. "He can't concentrate. He has important work, more important than shelving books." Maybelle scowled. "If you are working. It's a mess in here."

Cleo bit back a retort. "Is he upset about Bitsy? Where is she, by the way?"

Maybelle thumped her cane. "Bitsy! She's not even Bitsy. She's Liza something or other." A scowl sunk deep into Maybelle's perpetual frown.

"She's always been Bitsy to you," Cleo said, assessing

Maybelle. The elder Givens was in a fine fume. To hear her talk, Maybelle was a bundle of frailties and aches. Cleo thought Maybelle was stronger and heartier than she let on. It wouldn't take massive strength to hit Buford Krandall over the head. Guts, that's what was needed most. Determination. Anger. Maybelle had all of those. But could she strangle a young, fit woman like Whitney?

Cleo wanted to keep Maybelle chatting. "It's who Bitsy is now that matters. She did the right thing, telling you and Vernon and the police. She's a good person."

Maybelle snorted. "Good people don't live lies. They don't trick my boy. Poor Vernon, he does so much for everyone else, giving out loans and helping. There he was, thinking he'd found the perfect girl after such a disappointing first marriage. Do you know, that previous wife of his kicked me out of the house? Me! His mother!"

Cleo thought wife one sounded pretty sensible. With relief, she heard footsteps in the back. Leanna had been fast. It wasn't Leanna's voice she heard next, though. Cleo swung around, her heart thudding.

"Mama? Are you all right? Is she bothering you?" Vernon Givens wore a suit jacket of lemon-curd yellow and peachy pants, and he wasn't alone. Leanna stood at his side. Her eyes flashed white. She angled them sharply down, toward Vernon's gloved hand and the glint of metal pressed into her waist. *A gun!*

Cleo's head spun. This was all her fault. No, she corrected, it was Vernon Givens's fault. He'd been the name at the top of her list, and now she was sure he belonged there. The only question was whether the two main women in his lives knew. That and how she and Leanna could get away.

Maybelle greeted her son as if all was normal. "There you are, Vernie. You're working too hard again. Where's that Bitsy? I want to get home. She's going to make us late."

"She's in the car," Vernon said. "You won't have to worry about her bothering us again, Mama." His eyes narrowed at Cleo. "You won't bother us anymore either. It's a shame you had to involve Leanna. I had high hopes for her in banking—and more." He gripped Leanna tighter. With his other hand, he touched her hair. Leanna's knees shook.

Cleo remembered her phone, left on the window seat by Rhett. She inched that way. She was reaching for the phone when a cane smashed down on it, sending shattered pieces flying. Rhett flew too, off the bench and across the room, claws skidding down the hall.

Run, Rhett, run! Cleo thought, wishing she and Leanna could too.

Chapter Thirty

"See?" Maybelle said, waving a gnarled finger at Cleo. "Vernie's in a temper, and it's your fault."

Vernon Givens held his mother's cane in one hand, the gun still firmly in the other, wedged over Leanna's hip. He twirled the cane before setting it down.

"Nice how it stands up, isn't it?" Maybelle said. "Handy. It's new. Cost a mint. Thurgood says I can get it reimbursed if I win my lawsuit."

Cleo weighed her options. She and Leanna together probably couldn't overpower Vernon Givens. He was a big man and clearly mad in the mind as well as temper.

"I know what you did, Leanna," the bank president said, clucking his tongue disapprovingly. In an angry burst, he shoved Leanna at Cleo. They both grasped for each other. "You missed a page in the printer. Stupid. I told you how slow it is to print. You have to watch that it's done."

Cleo held Leanna's shaking hand. She considered her options. Her best and possibly only course of action seemed to be to lie. It had to be a good lie, her best bluff ever. "Well, it's good you found that page," she said. "We can give the full set to the police now, and Bitsy—Liza—will be convicted of murder. We're very, very sorry this happened to you, Mr. Givens. Maybelle, we're sorry for you too, aren't we, Leanna."

Leanna managed a jerky head bob.

Vernon's face was as colorful as his attire. Pink splotched his cheeks, and his blue eyes sparked.

Cleo knew she had to keep talking. "Yes, just awful. Of course the police told Leanna to check those accounts. You can put in a complaint with them. It's probably not even entirely legal, is it?"

Vern muttered no, it wasn't. He was looking slightly baffled, which was good.

"What's this about? What's she saying?" Maybelle demanded. "You think Bitsy—our Bitsy—had something to do with these crimes? Slander! We'll sue!"

"Bitsy was desperate to keep her past a secret," Cleo went on, mentally substituting Vernon's name for Bitsy's. "*She* thought it would bring down the Givens name." She tsked and nudged Leanna to do the same.

"What?" Maybelle squawked. "That's ridiculous. Look at all the extra mess she went and caused. Where is she?"

Cleo would like to know that too. They all looked to Vernon.

"You're right," he said. "Bitsy's ugly past would have looked very bad for me and Mama. I'm bank president. I have a reputation to uphold." Vernon grabbed the cane again and jabbed it toward Leanna and Cleo. "You're messing with me too. What else did you meddle in? Where are the rest of those printouts?"

303

Leanna said something incoherent ending with "desk."

"At the reading desk over there," Cleo said, pointing. "You'll see that Leanna printed Liza Blackwell's banking information, like the police asked. You can throw those out, but the police will just look again." She prayed her fib rang true—or at least gave Vernon pause.

He snatched up the papers. Maybelle sat on the window seat, grumbling that her feet hurt and she wanted to get home. "You work too much, Vernie," she said to her son, who was flipping through the printouts.

"How do you think I got to be bank president, Mama?" he snapped.

Maybelle looked more shocked than when he'd been swinging around her cane.

Vernon threw the papers down. "You're lying," he said. "You *didn't* tell the police. They wouldn't use a silly Tammy Temp to snoop at my files. You would, though, Mrs. Watkins. How'd you know? Or was it a guess?"

"There's more than one way to skin a cat," Cleo murmured.

Leanna sucked in air, and Cleo knew she understood. Buford had used that terrible phrase when Bitsy said she didn't care who he told about her past. More than one way to profit from the secret he'd discovered. More than one person to blackmail. Vernon cherished his reputation. There were other little clues along the way too, words Cleo wished she'd thought about more closely.

"Skin a cat," Vernon said with a sneer. "That's exactly what that crackpot Buford said. We can do this now or later. Either way, that lie you just tried to trick me with will come true.

Bitsy will be ruled the killer. Murder—suicide, just like her dear old daddy. Fitting, isn't it? Come on. Hurry up. Mama needs to get home and put up her feet."

Maybelle scowled at them, whipping her head from her son to Cleo and back. When she spoke, her tone was more leery than demanding. "What are you all talking about?"

Cleo felt a teensy bit bad for Maybelle. She didn't appear to know that her golden boy was a killer.

"Mama," Vernon said, his voice suddenly sugary, "why don't you go wait outside? These ladies and I have some unfinished business."

Leanna gulped audibly. Cleo could guess that unfinished business wasn't library or banking business. Her lying hadn't worked. She looked around. She could throw a book at him. She could signal Leanna and they could toss every book they could grab. Books shouldn't be thrown or harmed, but under the circumstances, Cleo would do it. But he had a gun . . . A morbid game of rock, paper, scissors played out in Cleo's head. Gun beats book, beats flesh and arms. Maybelle was gathering her purse and cane. On impulse, Cleo grabbed her, clutching the wiry older woman to her chest. Leanna leapt in to help. They managed to pin a thrashing, kicking Maybelle between them. She was as strong as a ticked-off mule.

"Maybelle!" Cleo cried. "Stop! Your son wants to kill us! You see that gun?"

Maybelle landed a firm back kick on Cleo's shin. "Slander!" she yelled. "Vernon, tell these crazy people they're wrong."

Vernon waggled the gun, not quite aiming at them, but not pointing away either.

"Bitsy said you don't like to harm anything or anyone,

Vernon," Cleo said, holding tight to Maybelle's bony body. "She says you don't even like to fish. Your contractor, DeWayne, said you don't let him kill mice—he has to live-trap them. You're a good man, Vernon. You don't want to hurt anyone."

"Of course he doesn't. You don't do that anymore, do you, Vernie?" Maybelle said. "Hurt animals and such?"

"Anymore?" Leanna whispered.

Cleo's pulse raced. She leaned into Maybelle, whispering harshly in her ear. "Your Vernon killed Buford. I bet he killed Whitney too, and Leanna and I will be next and Bitsy as well, if he hasn't already harmed her. Maybelle, you *have* to help us. For your family's sake. For Vernon's. This has to stop."

"Bitsy?" Maybelle said, suddenly indignant. "Why would he harm Bitsy? I know she's not really Bitsy, but she still runs me to my appointments. She's a fine daughter-in-law, like the daughter I never had."

"She's not *fine*, Mama," Vernon snapped. "You two, let go of Mama." He waved the gun.

Cleo and Leanna hung on tight. Beyond Vernon, Cleo could see through to the hallway and the open door to the staffroom. Her eye detected movement. Her nose caught a whiff. Cleo tried not to stare at the puffy plumes of black and white, all in a line, making their way across the hall. Behind them, a fluffy orange tail waggled, the sign of a Persian about to pounce. If Rhett launched, some little skunks would most likely run their way. A desperate idea formed. Cleo nudged Leanna, whispered, "Skunk—out the front." With Maybelle's grumbles covering Cleo's whispers, Cleo began a countdown. "Three . . . two . . ." She waited as Rhett's rump wiggled in attack anticipation.

"One!" She shoved Maybelle toward her son, counting on him catching her and dropping his gun in the process. Rhett pounced, skunks scattered, and a sulfurous stink filled the air, mixing with Vernon's curses. Cleo and Leanna raced to the hall, Leanna tugging Cleo along. Cleo hadn't thought about what they'd do once outside. She couldn't hope to outrun Vernon, but Leanna could. She remembered that night as a teenager, trespassing with Mary-Rose, about to get caught by the police. Mary-Rose, the faster runner, slowed and let Cleo get away. It was time to repay that good deed.

"Go!" she commanded Leanna, hearing footsteps pounding behind them, accompanied by more cursing and a crash and grunts. She anticipated Vernon's grasp or, worse, a bullet. "Run!"

Leanna was out the door, but she was still tugging Cleo along too. Cleo tripped on the step and faltered. "Leave me!" she cried. "Go get help!"

They were just down the steps when a hand did grip at Cleo's sleeve. She yelped, feeling herself fall and Leanna tipping with her. Unsteady arms caught her. She looked down to see a whimpering pug and up to see Henry, pulling her into his arms. Gabby stood beside him, gun in hand.

"Henry! Gabby!" Leanna cried. "Inside! It's—"

Gabby put up a shushing finger and gestured for them to get back. Gabby crept to the door. "Police!" she yelled. "Come out!"

After a tense few minutes, Vernon Givens staggered out. His elbow was twisted behind his back, wrenched there by Jimmy Teeks. Jimmy shoved the big banker, who fell to the floorboards in a pastel pile at Gabby's feet. Gabby had efficiently cuffed him and read him his rights by the time Chief Culpepper, Mayor Day, and eager cub reporter Toby from the *Catalpa Gazette* rushed up.

"The car!" Cleo cried, remembering Vernon's other possible victim. "Bitsy! I think she's inside!" The Givens's hulking SUV was parked out front. Cleo tried the doors and found all locked. Late afternoon sun bore down. The car would be boiling.

"I need a key," Cleo cried. "Maybelle!"

"Out of the way." Maybelle Givens pushed Cleo aside and raised her cane. She gave the front passenger's window a mighty smack. Glass fell in diamond chunks. They found Bitsy in the far back, limp on the floor. Her arms and legs were tied, and tape covered her mouth. Her face was pale. As gently as possible, Cleo tugged off the tape and fanned Bitsy.

Maybelle gasped, rounded, and stumped back to her handcuffed son. She gave him a slap and a tongue-lashing to end all. Cleo heard Gabby trying to restrain Maybelle and take away her cane. Henry and Cleo untied Bitsy while reporter Toby flitted among them, giddy at his biggest scoop ever.

The chief and newly arrived firemen pushed in to tend to Bitsy. Cleo went to check on Maybelle, now standing on her own in the overgrown lawn, looking withered and shaky. "I'm so sorry," Cleo said.

Maybelle snorted. Cleo waited for the gruff reply. Instead, tears rolled down the elder woman's cheeks, and she looked worriedly toward the SUV.

"Oh, Maybelle!" Cleo hugged Maybelle's bony frame. "Bitsy will be okay. I hear the ambulance now." Henry and Leanna joined them, along with Mr. Chaucer and a skunk-scented Rhett Butler. The pug sniffed at Rhett, drew back, and sneezed.

"You're a smelly hero, Rhett," Leanna said as they all stood in a loose circle around sniffling Maybelle. "You and the skunks."

"Rhett alerted us," Henry said. "Mr. Chaucer and I were out for a stroll when we saw Rhett in the next lot over. We thought it was odd that he'd be all alone. We came over and looked in the window, and"—he caught Cleo's eye—"I thought I'd lose you. I didn't know what to do. I saw Mr. Teeks driving by and flagged him down. Then I spotted Gabby and got her too."

"Good boy, Rhett," Cleo said, reaching to pat the Persian, who was looking mighty pleased for a cat who'd need a lot of bathing.

Maybelle frowned all around and pushed her way out of their circle. She sniffed mightily and declared, "That cat's fur is all choppy and messy. He reeks. Skunks and cats . . . that's no way to run a library, Cleo."

Cleo hid a smile, thinking Maybelle Givens would be okay.

Jimmy Teeks was stomping across the lawn. Cleo intercepted him. "I can't thank you enough, Mr. Teeks. I owe you all the books you ever want."

His expression didn't change, but his small eyes seemed to harden. "I'm not done yet," he said in that high, unnerving voice. "The mayor misjudged your library fund."

"Misjudged?" Cleo asked. She glanced over at the group of men. Jeb Day was looking ridiculous in polka-dotted plaid Bermuda shorts and a button-down dress shirt. He was shifting from foot to foot, nervously glancing their way.

"Mistaken. Misappropriated. It'll get it fixed. I've arranged it." Jimmy Teeks pointed a single stubby finger at the boy mayor, who dipped his head and slunk behind the bulk of Chief Culpepper. "I'll tell you why too," Jimmy said.

Cleo listened, fascinated, to Jimmy's story. When he was done, she gave the man a hug.

"What was that about?" Henry asked, when Jimmy Teeks left, blushing and stating he had "business to attend to." That business included jerking his head at the mayor, who followed behind him, looking scared.

Cleo relayed Jimmy's story as she and Henry gazed at the library. Cleo could once again picture the blue tarp gone, the New Reads shelf filled, and patrons streaming in, library lovers like Jimmy Teeks. Libraries and reading were his refuge, Jimmy told her, both as a kid from a bad home and as a young man doing a stint in prison. Jimmy had standards, a code. He'd never swindle a library, as he'd caught the mayor doing. Tipped off by Cleo, Jimmy had discovered Mayor Day was funneling library funds and other town monies to his pet projects and personal accounts.

"It's going to be all right," Cleo said, letting relief and marvel flood out. "Jimmy said he'd arrange it."

Henry reached over and tentatively reached for her hand. "I'm just glad you're all right."

Chapter
Thirty-One

Several days later, they all gathered at the Pancake Mill. The skies were as sunny as the mood. Ollie was back to furiously blushing in the presence of Gabby Honeywell, who was off duty for the day and still glowing from nabbing her first murder suspect. Mary-Rose's husband, William, was testing out his new bionic knee and getting walker and cane advice from Happy Trails residents, bused in by Tamara the gate guard. Cleo smiled, seeing Adelaide Cox and Mary-Rose's mother coaching William on walker maneuvers. Little Zoe and a friend lounged under a moss-veiled oak, engrossed in a reading competition. Pages flipped fast, eyes darting. The kids had already visited the guest of honor, Words on Wheels, newly fixed and polished.

Cleo couldn't stop looking at her beautiful bus. TJ and Joe had delivered the bookmobile just this morning. The mechanics had removed the dents, polished the bumpers, shined the wheels, and repainted the script in opalescent greens and golds that sparkled in the sun. The red and orange flames across the front were freshly tipped in icy blue. The bus looked like it was flying, even standing still.

"She's beautiful," Leanna said, and this time Cleo was delighted with the pronoun choice and with Leanna's plans. Leanna had quit her job at the bank. Vernon might not be there, but the upsetting associations were. Leanna had told Cleo how the bank president had been increasingly friendly and flirty. Cleo hated to think that he'd not only planned to murder Bitsy, his "current wife," but possibly try to seduce Leanna.

Leanna already had another gig lined up in addition to her bookmobile stocking and helping Cleo guide the library repairs. She'd be waitressing at the Pancake Mill, with a benefits package that included free pie.

"I'll have to jog around the spring between orders to work off all that pie," Leanna said, fork poised over a slice of chocolate pecan. They were enjoying a picnic potluck, Cleo's favorite kind of meal and with her favorite folks too—friends, family, and pets both furry and feathered.

Bitsy had filed for divorce and would be a whole lot quicker about it than Kat Krandall-Stykes. She wasn't leaving Catalpa Springs, though. Nor was she separating from Maybelle, for which the grumpy octogenarian seemed unusually grateful and almost maternal. Cleo had seen the two just the other day, heading off to the foot doctor and a Ladies League meeting. The Gala would go on.

Mary-Rose shooed a curious peacock away from the potato salad. Cleo's best friend was off the hook for sabotaging Buford Krandall's drilling machine. It looked like Ollie would be too, though the silly boy seemed almost disappointed, saying the sabotage would have given him "cred" among environmental activists.

Fred understandably disapproved of his son's sentiment, as did Angela. However, Angela used her lawyering skills to persuade Fred to let Ollie return to his cottage in Cleo's garden. Ollie needed to find his own way, Angela said. He needed to pay rent and get a real job, Fred grumbled. Cleo had a plan to make Fred happy and inspire Ollie to other endeavors: she would task the young man with air-potato control.

"How'd you guess it was Vernon Givens?" Mary-Rose asked, digging into a plate filled with salads: potato, macaroni, rice, broccoli and bacon, and sweet ambrosia. Cleo had gone light on the broccoli and heavy on the ambrosia. It was fruit and a salad, even if floating in waves of whipped cream.

Mary-Rose waved her fork, "I mean, the *bank president*? A man who wears pastel suits and was always so chatty and nice and doling out loans? Do you think he'll get a peach-striped prison uniform?"

Cleo shrugged modestly. "A bump on my head jostled the idea free." Her various bruises had dimmed to murky yellows. She hoped she could get through the summer with no further attacks by air potatoes or vehicles or anything else.

"No, I know you," Mary-Rose said. "There's more to it than a bump. Leanna said you *knew*."

"Cats," Leanna said. She was back in her vintage fifties attire, a red polka-dot sundress with matching flip-flops.

"Yes, cats. Something Bitsy said," Cleo explained. She lowered her voice, since Rhett was right behind them at the next picnic table, sunning on the bench, his paw hanging down and occasionally bopping Mr. Chaucer. She explained how the terrible skin-a-cat saying had gotten her thinking. "I might have forgotten all about it until the car crash, when Bitsy was talking about skinning her knee and us escaping by the skin of our teeth. It's such a trite saying, you don't think of its meaning. Buford meant it. He saw another way to use the information he had about Bitsy. He knew Vernon would care just as much, if not more. I think Buford might have been planning to use the blackmail money he got to help the library. He told me he had a plan, a solution we could 'take to the bank.' And Vernon did pay. He funneled money through an account he set up for Liza Blackwell, Bitsy's former name. Bitsy had no idea the account existed. It looks like Vernon was already planning to kill Buford and set up Bitsy to take the blame."

"The driver of the van that ran you off the road was Vernon Givens too, right?" Mary-Rose said, shaking her head. "Why? Where'd he get that van anyway?"

Cleo nodded. "Yes, that was Vernon. He'd have been delighted to get rid of Bitsy and me in one hit-and-run or fake carjacking. I think he tried before by cutting the brake lines in Words on Wheels. Or he was just hoping to scare me off. He never expected his mother to be on the bus that day, let alone driving. When he came after Bitsy and me on the bridge, he thought I was the only other person who knew Bitsy's past. In his twisted reasoning, he could be done with the whole thing if he got rid of us. The police found the van. Gabby said it belonged to a man Vernon gave a second mortgage to. The man couldn't repay the loan and owed him."

Cleo took a sip of lemonade, gathering her thoughts. "Vernon also tore apart Buford Krandall's library, looking for more incriminating clippings or photos. He cut the page from *Killings in Cotton Country* and returned the book to the library, thinking it would go unnoticed. That's what ended up tipping us off to Bitsy's secret past."

"Goes to show, you should never harm a library book," Leanna said.

They all raised glasses to that sentiment. "Or steal from a library," Cleo added.

Mayor Jeb Day, library swindler, was under investigation for fraud and misuse of public monies. Thankfully, the mayor had replaced the library funds and others. He had to. Jimmy Teeks, the enforcer, made sure of that before packing up and heading down to Florida on vacation. Cleo wasn't sure if she approved of Jimmy's destination or questionable ways, but she'd be forever grateful for his help, just as he was forever grateful for libraries.

"What did Buford Krandall have on Mayor Day, anyway?" Mary-Rose asked. She tossed bits of piecrust to the peacocks, who danced in delight.

Cleo admitted she didn't know for sure. "Gabby thinks Buford found out about the mayor's financial indiscretions, including some questionable loans he received from Vernon Givens. Buford was on the town council and library board and had access to accounts and statements. He might have noticed something and used it to go after both Vernon and the mayor." Cleo thought of her poker days, with Mary-Rose tugging on her pearls. "Or Buford might have been bluffing, working from intuition," she said, feeling a little sad for the man who'd tried to help her library, albeit illegally. "I suspected there was fishy business with the mayor's casino plans. Perhaps Buford thought the same and tricked the mayor into admitting something."

A woof reverberated over the spring waters. Kat Krandall-Stykes had two hands on a leash, but this time it was Beast digging in his paws behind her. The big mastiff was pining to play with the peacocks.

"Kat here gave me a clue too," Cleo said, as Kat inched Beast closer. "I wish I'd realized sooner."

"Me?" Kat said, out of breath from the dog-tugging effort. "Heel!" she commanded.

To Cleo's surprise, Beast sat, wagging his tail and panting earnestly at the peacocks, strutting and displaying their plumage a few yards away. "Kat, you said anyone with a kind word about Buford was lying or tricked or wanting something from him."

"Darned straight," Kat said, looking pleased. "I mean, he had a few good points—who doesn't? But it was doing Buford's true character a disservice if you discounted the bad."

Cleo agreed with her first point. "He loved libraries and books."

"And a good old drawn-out fight," Kat said.

Leanna snapped her fingers. "The day of the funeral reception, Mr. Givens got up and gave a long, gushy eulogy for Buford."

"There you have it," Kat declared. "I should have noticed."

Mary-Rose lobbed a piecrust over Beast, reaching the peacocks. "I was being horrible that day, saying such bad things about the departed." She smiled. "Good thing, or you might have suspected me, Cleo. You never did, did you?"

"No," Cleo said immediately. *Not really.* "I think, and

Gabby agrees, that Vernon made a point of giving that long-winded eulogy so folks would remember him being at the party. It was an alibi of sorts. He'd killed Whitney not long before. She'd been wearing the scarf he used to choke her, purchased at a yard sale along with some other supplies she got for hiding out in my cottage and likely Krandall House too. The woman who sold her the items remembered Whitney's hair and snappy attitude. Gabby said Vernon confessed to killing her, but claimed it was self-defense. Defense of his reputation. Whitney saw him inside Krandall House the night she and Ollie went to sabotage the machine. Remember how Ollie said Whitney went back on her own? She'd seen Vernon in the library and figured he was up to something. He said she tried to blackmail him, just like her uncle had. They arranged to meet the day she died. He was supposed to pay her, but instead he strangled her. She probably felt safe—or cocky—being so close to a big group of people. If he hadn't killed her then, he likely would have gotten her later. He had Buford Krandall's gun hidden in a vault in the bank."

Kat shook her head. "That's just plain mean. Poor girl, she seemed like a worthy adversary, a true Krandall through and through. A fighter, like Buford. We sure had some good battles over the years. You know the worst of it? He won." She raised a fist to the sky, grinning. Beast, sensing an opportunity, lunged, only to get scared off by three peacocks hissing. He turned snout and woofed at Rhett, who issued a hiss rivaling the birds'. With a mournful groan, the mastiff flumped on the ground next to the snoring Mr. Chaucer.

Henry ambled up, holding a plate of second helpings. "Who won?" he asked. "Cleo? The library?"

"Buford," Kat grumbled. "He left me that dump of a house! It'll take me years to clear those vines. I'll go broke buying weed killer, and I already got a rash. He did it to make me suffer."

Cleo couldn't hide her smile. Thurgood Byron had called her the other day. The Happy Trails lawyer was another man of poor filing habits and had forgotten where he put Buford's will. The eccentric Krandall had left his family home to Kat, with the condition that she wasn't allowed to sell the property and had to "maintain" it. He also left a hefty chunk of money and his library books to the Catalpa Springs Public Library. Cleo pictured the renovated reading room filled with new treasures.

Mary-Rose was eying Kat warily. "You're not starting up that drill and water bottling again, are you?"

"And make his restless spirit happy? Heck no. I'm thinking of getting the whole place designated as a bird refuge. Wouldn't he hate that? I'm taking down those creepy whirligigs and putting up feeders." She laughed. "A new project."

Later, Henry and Cleo strolled to fend off post-picnic drowsiness. They walked down the boardwalk, Rhett and Mr. Chaucer beside them. When they reached the viewing platform, they leaned on the railing, looking out toward Krandall House.

"All this because Buford Krandall happened to pick out a Priscilla Pawpaw book at the library," Henry said. "You never know where books will take you. I wonder how Priscilla's doing? Is she back?"

Cleo could fill him in. She explained how she'd run into the jumpy true-crime author at Dot's Drop By the other day.

Priscilla admitted to leaving the box of notes on Cleo's porch on her way out of town. She'd found them when packing her suitcase to flee. She was afraid that Buford had been murdered because he'd tried to solve an old crime, and thought she might be in danger too. While she didn't want Cleo to meet a similar fate, Priscilla was desperate for the killer to be caught and thought Cleo would be the best person to figure out Buford's interest in her books and notes.

The killings hadn't put Priscilla off crime, though. She had an idea for a new book, tentatively titled *Blood in the Catalpa Springs Waters*. Cleo had gently attempted to discourage her, both from the lurid title and from including Cleo in the story. Cleo had pointed out that the crime was already solved and thus not Priscilla's usual topic.

All the better, Priscilla had said. "I knew someday some fool would try to solve one of my cold cases. I yelled at Buford. I warned him. See what happened? Amateurs should *never* try to solve crimes. Why do you think I left town? Too dangerous."

Cleo wasn't sure she agreed about amateurs. She tried to explain that Buford Krandall had other interests in the Tarpon Springs arson and murder case. He hadn't wanted to solve the crime. His interest lay in blackmail. The author, however, refused to hear anything negative about her greatest fan.

Cleo and Henry lingered at the mill until the gathering wound down and the dishes were cleaned. When they were getting ready to leave, Henry cleared his throat. He rubbed his beard and scuffed his polished loafers in the gravel. "We, uh, said we might have dinner when all this is done. Dinner like a . . . well, . . . like a date?"

Cleo was aware of Ollie and his father coming down the

path behind her. Fred was a reminder of her dear departed husband. She'd always hold those memories close, and Fred too. A date didn't mean she was giving up her single self.

"Yes," she said. "I would adore that. Let's make it a date."

Henry beamed, and even Mr. Chaucer seemed to have a spring in his step as they left.

"A date?" Fred asked, frowning.

"Ooh . . . good job, Gran," Ollie said. "A boyfriend!"

"A *gentleman* friend," Cleo corrected. Cleo hugged her son and grandson. Then she and Rhett climbed into her beautiful bookmobile. She buckled up, lowered the windows, and adjusted the mirrors. She listened to the engine purr. Then, with her cat at her side and books in the back, Cleo Watkins punched the gas and let the wind whip through her hair all the way home.

Mama's Award-Winning Hummingbird Cake

Cake

3 c. all-purpose flour
1 c. granulated sugar
1 c. packed brown sugar (dark or light)
1 tsp. ground cinnamon
½ tsp. allspice
1 tsp. baking soda
¾ tsp. salt
3 large eggs, lightly beaten
¾ c. canola or other neutral oil
2 tsp. vanilla extract
1 (8 oz.) can crushed pineapple and its juices
2 c. mashed ripe banana (about 4 bananas)
1 c. chopped pecans, toasted, with extra for garnish
(optional, whole or chopped, candied pecans if you like)

- Preheat oven to 350°F. Coat two 9-inch round cake pans with cooking spray, and line the bottoms with parchment paper.
- Whisk the flour, baking soda, spices, and salt together in a large bowl.
- In another large bowl, whisk sugars, oil, eggs, mashed banana, pineapple, and vanilla.

- Pour wet ingredients into dry ingredients, and fold together until combined. Be careful not to overmix.
- Gently fold in the toasted pecans (saving aside some for garnish, if desired).
- Divide the batter between the pans.
- Bake until the cakes pull away from the edges of the pan, and a tester comes out clean, 35 to 40 minutes.
- Cool cakes in their pans on a wire rack for about 10 minutes. Then flip the cakes out and let cool completely on the rack before frosting (see recipe below).
- Frost the cake. Place one cake on a cake stand or plate. Spread on 1/3 of frosting. Top with the second cake. Top this cake with another 1/3 of the frosting, and spread evenly. Cover the entire cake with the rest of the frosting. Decorate with remaining pecans, if desired.
- For easiest slicing, refrigerate the cake at least 30 minutes before cutting. Enjoy!

Cream cheese frosting*

1 c. unsalted butter, at room temperature
16 oz. (2 boxes) cream cheese, cut into chunks
2 tsp. vanilla extract
½ tsp. salt
~5 c. powdered sugar

- Place butter and cream cheese in a large bowl, and mix on medium speed until smooth and creamy, about 3 minutes.

- Mix in vanilla and salt. Then gradually add the powdered sugar, until thick and spreadable.

***Note:** This recipe makes a lot of icing. If you like your cake less sweet, you can halve the recipe and still have enough for the upper and middle icing layers.

Acknowledgments

This is where words feel inadequate. To my family, especially my parents, in-laws, aunts, and grandmother, I have more gratitude than I can express for your support and encouragement. Thank you to friends near and far and to the wonderful writers of *Sisters in Crime*. I'm grateful for my beta readers, Jaime and Jane, who took the time to point me in better directions, and to Cynthia, the most encouraging of critique partners. Eric, thank you for your love, our travels, and enduring many a dinner conversation about mysteries and murder.

To Christina Hogrebe, agent *extraordinaire*, much gratitude for your insights and support and for finding this series such a wonderful home at Crooked Lane Books. To my amazing editors, Anne Brewer and Jenny Chen, thank you for believing in Cleo Watkins, senior sleuth, and for honing the manuscript into a book. Thanks to Jesse Reisch for the gorgeous cover illustration, Sarah Poppe for her publicity prowess, and Jill Pellarin for meticulous copyediting.

Most of all, heartfelt thanks to readers for joining Cleo on her bookmobile adventures.

Read an excerpt from

READ ON ARRIVAL

the next

A BOOKMOBILE MYSTERY

by NORA PAGE

available soon in hardcover from
Crooked Lane Books

CROOKED
LANE

NEW YORK

Chapter One

Cleo Watkins considered herself quite unflappable. After all, she had seventy-five and three-quarters years of living behind her. Most importantly, she was a librarian, the longest serving biblio-professional in Catalpa Springs, Georgia. Librarians saw a lot. They read even more. Librarians were a hard bunch to shock.

"Good gracious," Cleo said. She gripped her peach-colored cardigan tight and steadied herself against the doorframe of the vintage Airstream camper. Music boomed from outdoor speakers, blaring across the park and vibrating through Cleo's soles. Words written in morphing red, white, and pink light flashed across the tin-can ceiling.

Cleo's eyes caught a word: *"READ!"* Cleo was all for reading. *That's nice,* she reassured herself. She chased down more: *"INNOVATE! WORD! SPARK!"*

It was downright dizzying, as close as Cleo had ever

come to a disco and near enough by far. Except this wasn't a dance club. It was *supposed* to be a bookmobile. The vehicle's name pulsated across the ceiling: "BOOK IT!" Cleo tore her eyes downward and resumed her search. The shiny interior included laptops, a TV screen, and gaming consoles Cleo recognized from her grandkids' visits.

Where were the books?

Cleo drove a bookmobile, an entire school bus, fitted with shelves, named "Words on Wheels." Here, she saw no spines, smelled no scents of paper and ink. Cleo released the doorframe and stepped farther inside. *Ah, there was a book.* A beleaguered copy of *Gone with the Wind* propped up a window. Cleo turned away.

"Isn't this delightful!" exclaimed the man beside her. Mercer Whitty clasped bony hands, sounding as giddy as the children running around outside. The kids had the excuse of sugar overload. BOOK IT! had arrived with accompaniments more suited for a carnival than a mobile library: a cotton candy machine, buckets of suds and giant bubble wands, and—most astounding—a miniature pony named Lilliput. As if on cue, the little horse neighed. Kids squealed, and words that made Cleo shudder sliced through the din: *Lilliput, no! Don't eat the book!*

"Delightful?" Cleo repeated.

"Thrilling," Mercer declared. He unlocked his thin fingers only to clap and clasp them once again. He beamed at the woman to his left.

Fresh shock shook Cleo. Mercer Whitty, president of

the Catalpa Springs Library Board, was not a man given to thrills. Although only in his early sixties, Mercer seemed ages older, as stiff and serious as an antique portrait. Small and slight, he wore his usual outfit of fastidious pinstripes and a polka-dot bow tie. Something scaled—snake, alligator, or armadillo—had perished to produce his shoes. Cleo eyed him, thinking he resembled an amphibian. A snapping turtle with a beak of a nose, a chin tucked tight to his chest, and a tongue twitching to lash out.

"Simply stunning," Mercer continued, head shaking in apparent awe. "Don't you agree, Cleo?"

The question challenged Cleo's manners. She could hear her dear, departed mother, and generations of southern ladies before her, issuing that most trite but true adage: *If you don't have anything nice to say, shush your mouth.*

"Well . . ." Cleo patted her fluffy white hair, buying some time.

Two pairs of eyes watched her. Mercer's narrowed toward his beak. The other set sparkled with pearly eye shadow and belonged to Mercer's invited guest, Belle Beauchamp, driver and self-proclaimed innovator of the book-lacking BOOK IT! Belle and the Airstream hailed from Claymore, a neighboring town to the west. Their reputations preceded them through the local librarian grapevine.

Belle had recently retired from corporate branding—at the young age of fifty-something—and moved back down from Atlanta to be near her aging parents.

Retirement hadn't suited her, so she'd rebranded herself, creating the title of "outreach innovator" and convincing the Claymore library to hire her. Her first big act was starting up a bookmobile.

Cleo fully understood Belle's issues with retirement. Cleo had tried retirement too. Twice. It hadn't suited her either. She also understood the joy of bookmobiles. Cleo planned to keep driving Words on Wheels for as long as her eyesight and the DMV allowed. She adored the open road and the wind in her hair. Most of all, she loved delivering books to all those who depended on the mobile library.

Belle leaned in expectantly. Her platinum hair shimmered in a sleek, asymmetrical bob. Her perfume smelled of musky lilacs. "Well, what do you think? Isn't BOOK IT! the cutest?"

"It's very . . . uh . . . very bright," Cleo said. "Bright and uncluttered." There. She'd said something nice and hadn't fibbed.

"Aren't you a doll!" Belle slapped Cleo's shoulder. "That's exactly what I'm going for! Streamlined. Fresh. Like you say, I didn't want to clutter it all up with too many books."

"I didn't say—" Cleo protested.

Mercer cut her off. "Yes, take note, Cleo. New. Fresh. *Exciting!* We in Catalpa Springs could learn a thing or two from this marvelous bookmobile. You're an amazing woman, Ms. Beauchamp."

Belle rewarded him with an affectionate arm squeeze and deemed him a honey doll.

Cleo awaited his snap. Mercer loved to mock phrases lacking literal sense. He preyed on common, benign idioms and endearments. *Honey doll* would surely make a sweet target. Cleo waited. Mercer wasn't snapping. *"GLOW!"* in pink light flashed across his gaunt cheeks. Underneath, Cleo could swear that Mercer Whitty really was glowing. The man was blushing!

"Oh, no, no," Mercer stammered. "I'm honored. *We're* honored. Honored you accepted my invitation to join us today, Ms. Beauchamp, and bring such verve to our dull little bookmobile event."

The music covered Cleo's huff. Mercer wouldn't have noticed anyway. Cleo marveled. Could it be? Could cold-blooded Mercer Whitty be smitten? He was laughing—giggling—at something Belle said.

Cleo had seen enough. "This is lovely, but I shouldn't keep you. I need to get back to Words on Wheels."

"Why?" Mercer's grin twisted into a mean smirk. "You don't seem to have many patrons. All the more reason to stay and learn. Look at the crowd Ms. Beauchamp has attracted."

Cleo bit her tongue.

Belle waved a flirty hand. "Y'all are so sweet!" she said. "I'm blushing!"

It was Mercer who was aflame. "You know, Ms. Beauchamp," he said, fingers twining. "The Catalpa Springs

333

Library has a job opening. We're looking for a woman with just your exciting skills."

Cleo had been backing toward the exit. She stopped. "Just a part-time position, nothing *exciting*," Cleo said quickly, although she considered all library work a thrill. "We need someone to fill in hours. Our library is reopening soon. I'll still be head librarian, but I'll be on the road a lot with Words on Wheels. We have another part-time librarian returning, and we recently promoted my assistant, Leanna. She'll become full time when she graduates from college in a few years. She's studying library sciences and technology, and taking extra classes to get done early."

Cleo could gush on. She was proud enough to burst, picturing young Leanna taking over the library helm, the perfect protégé to carry on Cleo's legacy. Leanna had overcome a tough childhood. She'd bounced about in foster care, with only one place she'd always called home: the Catalpa Springs Public Library. In the disco din, Cleo smiled, remembering Leanna as a shy kindergartener, craning her chin up to the circulation desk to request more books. Or the many times she discovered little Leanna rehoming misshelved volumes or stepping in to help patrons. Leanna was a natural librarian, the best kind: she cared about people and books.

Mercer made a *pah* sound. Cleo had heard the same noise emitted from vultures. "She's inexperienced, a girl," Mercer said.

"She might only be twenty-two, but she has loads of library experience and passion, and she's acing all her classes," Cleo countered. She held in further protests, knowing Mercer fed off getting under people's skin. "I'm sure Belle wouldn't be interested in our job," Cleo said. She prayed this was true. She didn't need a librarian who considered books clutter.

Belle, however, did look interested. "I *am* in the market for new opportunities. A place I can stretch my leadership and innovation skills."

"You've come to the right place," Mercer said.

No, you haven't, Cleo thought. Then, however, she reconsidered. If Belle wanted to butter someone up, she'd definitely come to the right man. As board president, Mercer had sway over the other members and the library's budget. He also had buckets of old money and a family foundation through which he dribbled small grants to causes that appealed to him and people he liked. He definitely liked Belle.

"We already have new directions at the library," Cleo said, both to remind Mercer and to dissuade Belle. Cleo embraced new technology and trends. But she also held certain traditions sacred. The reading room was quiet. Books filled the shelves and were handled with respect. "Our plans are well on their way. We'll be brand new and freshly reopened soon."

Cleo's stomach fluttered, thinking of all there was to do. Last spring, a toppled tree had shuttered the library.

A shifty mayor had then almost shelved the institution permanently. However, thanks to a new mayor, an unexpected inheritance, and loads of work, the main library was about to be back in business. The grand reopening was just over three weeks away. Cleo and Leanna planned to throw a big party. The whole town was invited, and Cleo wanted everything just so, from the restored shelves to the technology station Leanna had designed. Cleo took a deep breath. They had it all arranged, a fine, sensible plan.

Cleo continued on. "Our part-time position entails shelving, checking books in and out, and helping patrons. I'll still be in charge of the day-to-day operations of the library and the bookmobile. Leanna will be managing some library-science interns from the college."

Mercer snorted. "How dull."

Belle shrugged slender shoulders covered by a red suede jacket. "That's a pity. I always say, going with the flow doesn't break the mold. I like to break the mold." She winked at Mercer and added, "But then I can be a little naughty."

If Mercer were a puppy, he'd be a puddle of wags and wiggles. "I'll see what I can do," he said breathlessly. "Cleo, with you out of the way driving that bus, it's a perfect time to break the mold. We can change up the old ways in the main building. Yes, yes . . ."

Old ways? Out of the way! Cleo had heard enough. In

tight yet sugary tones, she thanked Belle for the tour and bolted.

* * *

The bouncy dance tune grated on Cleo's ears but made her feet tap. She stood on the top metal step of BOOK IT! The chilly breeze helped clear her head. The familiar view grounded her. Fontaine Park, the leafy heart of her hometown, looked lovely. Early camellias bloomed in ruby and cream petals around pollen-gold prongs. The air smelled of wood smoke and the cinnamon scents of autumn. It was the first week of November, Cleo's favorite time of year, a season to stock up on cookbooks for holiday meals and novels for chilly nights.

Feeling braced by the fresh air and view, Cleo made her way down the steps. BOOK IT! stood on the park's lawn, ruts marking its track and that of the cherry-red pickup that pulled it. Mercer was right about one thing. Belle's bookmobile had attracted a crowd. Kids ran in giddy circles. Adults clustered in chatty groups. The little horse wore a velvet cape and hooved a periodical.

Among the throngs, Cleo saw a familiar figure. Leanna. She spotted another welcome sight too. Books! A side panel of the camper was rolled up, accordion style, revealing two bookshelves.

"What do you think?" Cleo asked when she reached her young protégé. She valued Leanna's take. Leanna was up on the current library tech and trends, if not fashion, which she preferred retro. Today Leanna wore head-to-toe cable knit, from thick mustard tights to a pumpkin sweater dress. A knit band decorated with a crocheted cat face held back her honey-colored hair.

Leanna turned to Cleo, eyes wide behind sparkly cat-eye glasses, her tone set to scandalized. "Do you see this? These books—they're arranged by color! Spine color! And look! Look at this cover! Oh, I can't even . . ."

Cleo selected a book and quickly grasped what Leanna wasn't able to utter. "Someone put on new covers." Inside, the title page revealed a recent bestseller. The teal canvas reminded Cleo of a craft project she'd undertaken with her granddaughter. They'd decorated a kitchen stool with decoupage, using magazine images and pretty bits of cloth. She'd never dismember a perfectly good book.

Leanna tapped her shoe, a shiny Mary-Jane with a silver buckle. "This novel is brand new. So are the others. It's like someone tore off the originals and glued on canvas, for no good reason. Is this legal? Ethical? I bet not. I should ask my professor. And look at the organization. There is none! Mystery, romance, fiction, nonfiction—they're all jumbled together. Not a Dewey decimal in sight! It's not right!"

"The person who designed this bookmobile is new to libraries," Cleo said charitably. "Belle Beauchamp. She's innovating, she says."

Leanna huffed. "*Innovating.* More like endangering.

Did you see the giant bubbles the kids are making? All that sticky cotton candy? And the little horse . . . He's as cute as a speckled puppy, isn't he? But he's eating a magazine! We don't even allow gum onboard our bookmobile."

They both glanced toward Words on Wheels. The refurbished school bus stood up on the street, quiet and legally parked. *Lonely,* Cleo thought.

Cleo patted Leanna's arm. "We should get back to work," she said. "Let's make sure our displays are in order."

Leanna's shoe tapping ended in a stomp. "That's the worst of it. Why's everyone over here? We have our new fall reading list and actual books. Shelf after shelf of *books*! Plus, our bookmobile is just as pretty. Prettier!"

"Absolutely," Cleo said. She thought Words on Wheels was the most beautiful bookmobile in the South, if not beyond, but then she was admittedly biased. A grandson and some of his Boy Scout pals had repurposed the decommissioned school bus. The clever boys had replaced most of the bench seats with handmade bookshelves. They'd lined the floors with squishy, colorful tiles and designed a backseat reading nook and kids' section. The exterior was just as fun, with *"READ!"* painted across the brow, flanked in airbrushed flames. Along each side, cursive script in opalescent emerald paint spelled out "Words on Wheels."

"Our mascot is better too," Leanna said.

Cleo agreed with that as well. Her pretty Persian, Rhett Butler, lounged on the bookmobile's hood, his fluffy orange belly aimed at the November sun.

"You know how folks are," Cleo soothed. "They're attracted to the bright, new, and flashy. Books will always endure."

Leanna exhaled heavily. "You're right, Miss Cleo. I wasn't just fussing about the shelving and covers. It was ugly jealousy, plain and simple. Like my kindergarten teacher used to say, blowing out another's candles will *not* make yours burn any brighter."

"Swamping another's boat won't help yours float," Cleo said.

Leanna grinned. "Be nice if it kills you!"

A shiver shook Cleo. "Let's not go that far."

Last spring had seen more than the library wounded. A patron had been murdered, and Cleo and Leanna had almost joined him in the grave beyond.

When they reached Words on Wheels, Leanna leaned over the hood, tapping her fingernails. Rhett yawned, stretched, and deigned to saunter over for a chin scratch.

"Who would hire a librarian with no experience?" Leanna muttered to Rhett, who purred in response.

"Not us," Cleo said. She wouldn't upset Leanna by revealing Mercer's smitten enthusiasm for Belle. There was no need. Cleo and the full board ultimately made the hiring decisions, and they'd already agreed on the skills they wanted for the extra part-time position.

Leanna rubbed Rhett's ears and gave him a quick kiss on his furry noggin. "Can you two hold down our patron rush?" she joked. "I have a computer delivery coming at the main library soon. Then the painter's stopping by to test more paint colors. It's going to be gorgeous! I can't wait!" She glanced toward the party atmosphere. "I just hope people will come."

"They will," Cleo said firmly. "Our patrons are loyal. They're readers and library lovers. We have absolutely nothing to worry about."

A horn blared over her final words, rumbling low and long, like a foghorn across a watery deep. Rhett's fur bristled. Cleo's scalp prickled. She didn't have to look. She knew the vehicle. She knew who'd be driving it too.

Leanna groaned. "Nothing to worry about? I'm not so sure."

Neither was Cleo.